CURSE

OF INFINITI

The Infiniti Trilogy

One

First printed in the United States of America in November 2020

Cover Design by MiblArt
Editor: Enchanted Inc. Publishing

ISBN 978-1-953139-00-9 (paperback)
ISBN 978-1-953139-01-6 (Ebook)

Published by Via Veritas Vita Press
Website: www.rachelhetrickwrites.com

First Edition
10 9 8 7 6 5 4 3 2 1

CURSE

OF INFINITI

The Infiniti Trilogy

One

Rachel Hetrick

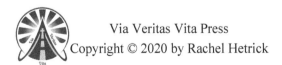

For my parents,
who encouraged me to pursue my dream
of being a published author since
I was a little girl writing strange stories
in all of the journals they bought me.

I love you guys.

SIGN UP FOR MY AUTHOR NEWSLETTER

Enjoy extra scenes, short stories, and other exclusives from this series by subscribing to my newsletter and visiting my website at:

www.rachelhetrickwrites.com

Prologue

ame. Name. What was his name? Her hand shook, the pen wobbling and making her handwriting illegible. Inside her head felt fuzzy, like the skin of a peach, and she found it more and more difficult to focus on the piece of parchment in front of her. Knowing her time was short—she was already beginning to question what she was doing in the tiny cave—she wrote down the sentence she was whispering over and over. She hoped that by clinging to it, the words wouldn't fade away with the rest of her. The letters curved, wavering when she couldn't keep her hand steady.

Name. Name. What was her own name?

Inkblots dropped from the pen as she stared in a daze at the sentence she had just written.

Or had she written it? True, the pen was in her hand, but she couldn't remember forming the words of the sentence.

Her body tingled all over, invisible ants crawling up and down her skin. The depth of her vision kept switching from the far wall to the fair hairs hanging down in front of her face. Her chest was heavy, an anvil weighing her down to the cold, rocky floor. As she collapsed, she pulled the parchment off the rickety table with her, and it fluttered down to land next to her face.

The words danced in and out of focus in the low lighting of the cave, but she mouthed them over and over as her body began to shimmer. Her voice faded away as she did.

He's not who you think he is.

The candlelight continued to burn in the empty cave, the wick flickering briefly when the occupant disappeared, leaving the room vacant once again.

Chapter One

From the first moment of cognition, a heavy mist muddled her mind, and emptiness echoed like the silence that rang in her ears. With her eyes still closed, she opened up her mind to her other senses, inhaling an odor of mildew that left her forehead wrinkling. Her tongue stuck to the roof of her mouth, drawn there by the moisture it lacked. Her lips cracked as she pressed them together. As she thought about the lack of taste in her mouth, her stomach rumbled, vibrating through her core.

Lying on her back, she placed a hand over her abdomen, and the scratchy wool from a blanket tickled her fingers in response. In the stillness, she could feel her pulse beating beneath the blanket. Focusing on the steady rhythm, she inhaled deeply and let it out, feeling her limbs come to awareness in a slow ripple from the epicenter of her torso down to her toes.

Her eyes flitted open, adjusting to the light coming in from a small window with burlap curtains covering it. *Where am I?* Whispers of questions began swirling in the recesses of her mind. She straightened her head from where it had tilted to the side on a thin pillow. The gray wool blanket that covered her from the chest down rustled as she pushed herself up, resting on her elbows.

Not an ounce of familiarity came to her as she took in the small room. Besides the bed she was perched on, there was a chair by the window and a body-length mirror hanging on the wall opposite the single door. A skeleton of a room.

What is this place? Even her thoughts dripped with drowsiness, slurring in her mind. She sat all the way up. Her legs swung over the edge of the bed in one swift motion as she pushed the blanket off. The clothing the blanket revealed caused her muscles to tense. Like the room, they were foreign to her: a pale green dress with a cream apron tied around the front covered her torso and legs down past her knees. Her hand shook as she smoothed the fabric of the apron.

The scuffed floorboards had seen better days, and were rough and cold on her bare feet as she rose from the bed and stepped to the center of the room. Her breathing hitched and her heartbeat fluttered in a rapid tempo as soon as she laid eyes on her reflection.

A young woman with long, wavy blond hair stared back at her, brown eyes wide and growing mistier the longer she gaped into them. The reflection copied her actions as she raised a hand to her head, feeling the shape of her face from the temple down to the jawline in a slow trail. Every inch she touched seemed to place a heavier weight on her chest.

As her fingertips traced down the curve of her neck, she watched her hand stop at a thin silver line—a necklace glimmering in the light. Her fingers caressed the cool metal.

She examined the necklace up close. It was a medallion the size of a small coin. The side that looked up at her had a crest carved into it and at the center was what looked like a dragon with a sword through its heart. The image sent a shiver down to her toes, and she flipped it over to inspect the back. There was something inscribed in minuscule, scrawling lines, but she couldn't decipher what it was. After a minute of staring at it, all she could see were interlacing curves without much of a pattern.

She lifted her chin to look back into the mirror, letting the necklace return to its resting place above the neckline of her dress. Taking a step closer, she stared straight into her own eyes, searching them for answers to the questions that continued to grow louder in her head.

What happened to me? There was no controlling the heat pooling in the corners of her eyes as frustration replaced the numbness she'd felt up to that point. The first droplet traveled down her cheek, and when it stopped momentarily in the corner of her nostril, she watched until another tear followed its trail and moved it farther down her face. It dropped off her chin, and she squeezed her eyes closed.

Emptiness dug sharp claws into the crevices of her mind, refusing to budge as she pulled at it. She raced to recall what had happened before she woke up, but she hit a dark wall in the center of her brain. The paths she tried to follow ended abruptly, and soon her thoughts were dripping in a swirling black mist.

The battle in her mind crippled her.

Her legs buckled, and she hit her knees. Covering her face, the real tears began as her shoulders heaved. Frustration clashed with fear, and despair bit sharply back. Together they mingled in her mind, controlling her as she pushed against her eye sockets until bright shapes danced just behind her lids. Her breaths ripped through her chest, leaving it in tatters.

Name.

She searched and searched, but couldn't find a single sign that revealed her name. *How can I not have a name?*

Moving her hands from her face, she opened her eyes. The room closed in around her—a cage. It squeezed more air out of her than she had to give.

"Who am I?" she whimpered, her voice reverberating off the empty walls and bouncing back to her ears. It too was unfamiliar. "Who am I?" she repeated over and over. The woman in the mirror mouthed the same question with her. Her violent sobs turned to weeping, with hitched breaths and hiccups. But she didn't stop asking the question. *Who am I? Who am I? Who am I?* She didn't notice she was rocking back and forth with her knees to her chest until she saw the other woman doing it in the mirror.

Time ticked away while she moaned. *Why can't I recognize my own face?* She wiped at her eyes, carrying away some of the salty wetness. She stopped rocking. Caught in the hypnotic pull of rediscovering her own features—the now puffy eyes, crooked red nose, flushed cheeks—her breathing leveled out, hitching less and less. Her body stopped shuddering while she sat there, transfixed once again by her mirror image.

The silence returned, pushing down on her as she straightened up. Behind her in the mirror, the door caught her attention. She sniffled and rubbed her nose with the back of her hand. Pressing off the floor, she stood and turned her back on her reflection. The mirror had made the door seem farther away, but it now stood a few feet in front of her.

Another step carried her closer, and she found herself rubbing the back of the necklace with her thumb as she considered whether to turn the handle or not. Making her decision, the floorboard creaked once more as she leaned forward and placed her hand on the worn metal handle. With a quick exhale, she pressed it down and pulled the door open.

Chapter Two

A piece of parchment tacked to the outside of the bedroom door caught her eye. Something was scrawled in long, elegant cursive. The loops in the first word transfixed her, and she traced them with her finger. *Ellayne*, it read, and the breath in her lungs caught. Hope sparked, but she forced the light out, not letting herself attach to the idea that "Ellayne" might be the name she'd forgotten—her name.

She reread the name and continued on. *Ellayne. Had to go in to work. Food is on the counter. Do the dishes for me. I'll be back. B.* The last letter was signed at the bottom of the page, and the young woman wondered whether she was the person the letter was to, or the writer. Or neither.

After reading the letter one more time, she walked through the door into a narrow hallway. Opposite the room she left stood another door, and when she pressed her ear to the wood and heard nothing on the other side, she opened it. Though she struggled to see in the low lighting, a silhouette of a small toilet and a metal tub stood out in the darkness. The strong smell of waste made her shut the door and cover her nose with her hand.

The hallway ended to her left, so she turned the opposite direction and found an identical door next to the one she had exited. The handle squeaked, but did not resist as she peeked inside. Her eyebrows arched before curving inward. It was the mirror image of the room she had woken up in. The window perched on the opposite side of the room, still across from the bed. The same furniture decorated it, except for a trunk that sat at the end of the bed near the door.

She left the mirrored bedroom, closing the door behind her, and walked back into the first bedroom. An identical trunk waited in the same place. In the midst of her breakdown, she hadn't recognized that's what it was. Her hands shook as she knelt down in front of the aged wood, fumbling with the latches. With a click, her heart jumped, and she lifted the lid.

A breath left her in the form of a sigh, one she didn't know she'd been holding. All she saw were threadbare clothes in pale, washed-out colors. The trunk released a musty smell, and after riffling through and finding nothing but dresses and a few tunics, she closed it. No pieces of parchment, no books; nothing but itchy fabric.

Once she relatched the trunk, she left the room. The hallway was short, unfolding into a kitchen and living space. The kitchen consisted of a small stove with a bit of counter space, a few cabinets, and a two-person table accompanied by chairs.

A window stood above the table, and there was another beside a heavy-looking front door. With one hand, she moved the burlap curtains out of her way. Green grass tinged with patches of brown surrounded the front of the house, though a worn path sliced through the sea of weeds. In the distance, a line of trees loomed like an army at attention. The trees wrapped around the clearing as far as she could see from the one window.

The curtain tickled her shoulder, and she stepped back, returning her attention to the kitchen. Remembering the note from the mysterious "B," she inspected the counter for the food mentioned and found a loaf of bread made from a dark grain. There was also a bowl covered with a cloth, and when she lifted it, she smelled herbs and vegetables in the broth. It wasn't hot when she bumped the edge of the bowl with her fingers to test it.

Next to the food was a basin with several plates, bowls, and two pots. According to the note, the dishes she discovered were to be cleaned by "Ellayne," and though she wasn't sure it was her, she made the decision to help. She cleaned them with water in a bucket on the floor near the stove. Something about the action soothed her, though she wasn't sure why she was doing dishes for someone she couldn't remember.

When the dishes were drying on the counter, she sat down in the chair closest to the door and began rubbing the necklace with her thumb. Though her stomach rumbled more since finding the bread and soup, she refrained from eating, fearing it was not hers to enjoy.

Instead, she sat there trying to picture the person or persons who lived in the tiny house she now found herself in. *Who's "B"?* She gazed out the window as her mind wandered. Her initial thought was there might be a relation between herself and the person who wrote the note. If she was Ellayne, it meant someone knew her. And what's more, they said they were coming back. That thought alone kept her from leaving the house and seeking help. Images of wandering through the foreboding forest outside, lost and with no identity, made her shudder, and she planted her feet even more firmly on the dark wood floor beneath her. If "B" was coming back, she was going to be there when they did.

Without warning, her thoughts began down a new path. *How is it I can't remember my mother or father, or whether or not I have siblings?* She sighed, turning the necklace over in her hand to see if time had given her a new perspective on what was written there, but there was no change. Even though she couldn't decipher the writing, she still found comfort in rubbing the medallion between her fingers.

With yet another sigh, she stood and went back to the bedroom, running away from the temptation the food caused her. She sat on the edge of the bed, but moved over to the chair after sitting in silence. Dust rained down on her as she pushed the curtains back. The sun poured into the room and shone proudly from the highest part of the vast, blue sky. Midday, she guessed.

The trees were much closer on this side of the house, and she stared into them. However, the light level under the roof of leaves was low enough that, even in the bright sunlight, she struggled to see anything past the first few rows of trees.

As she studied the edge of the clearing, a noise in the front of the house made her stand up, nearly knocking the chair over in the process. She froze next to the window, every muscle contracting. The front door grated open, and the wood creaked in the kitchen. It closed with a subtle thump. She was no longer alone.

Chapter Three

ootsteps clicked in the hall. She watched the doorway, which she'd accidentally left open. One more agonizing second passed before a woman walked in and faced her.

"Good, you're up," the woman said, placing her hands on her hips, where her inky black hair flowed down in a thick braid. "I need you to go refill the barrel around the back. Then you can start on the laundry."

"You know me," the young woman whispered, taking in a shallow breath. "Who am I? What's my name?" She took a step forward, but hesitated to take any more toward the stranger.

"Oh no." The woman's nose wrinkled as she scrunched it. "Again? Seriously Ellayne?"

"Ellayne? Is that my name?"

The woman tilted her head back like she was interested in the ceiling, except she'd closed her eyes. "Why am I not surprised?" She groaned, rubbing her temple with her fingers.

"Surprised? I don't understand. Is my name Ellayne? Who are you?" Her voice wavered, and she felt her core tighten as she waited for answers. Anticipation raced through her, leaving her limbs trembling.

"I don't have time for this right now," the woman muttered as she ran a hand over her forehead and back into her hair. "Fine." Her lips tightened into a thin line before she continued, "Yes, your name is Ellayne. I'm Blanndynne, and I only have a few minutes before I have to go back to work. I only came back to change and make sure you'd done the chores."

Ellayne felt her head begin to spin, and she stepped back and collapsed onto the chair, placing her hands over her face. "Where am I? What's happened to me? What—"

"Before you drown both of us in your questions, I need you to put on your shoes and come with me because now I apparently have to show you to the river. Again." Blanndynne turned on her heels and walked out before Ellayne could say anything else.

The house creaked as Blanndynne rustled around in the room next to her, but Ellayne didn't move. Instead, she waited for her head to stop spinning. Blanndynne returned in a matter of minutes, her demeanor altered by a new outfit, which was a rather low-cut, dark blue dress that ended right above her knees. Though, the more she thought about it, Ellayne realized it was a tunic, not a dress. It was split up the middle, and leather leggings peeked out, ending with a pair of knee-high black boots at her feet.

"You haven't moved." Blanndynne crossed her arms over her chest. "Hurry up and get your shoes on."

"What's happening? Why can't I remember anything?"

The other woman huffed, "If you get your shoes on now and hurry up, I'll tell you on the way to the river."

"Where are my shoes?"

Blanndynne nodded toward the trunk at the end of the bed before leaving the room. She called down the hallway, "You have one minute before I leave."

Ellayne hopped up from the chair and opened the trunk again, ignoring the musky wave assaulting her nostrils. When she'd fished through it earlier, she'd not noticed the pair of slip-on shoes at the bottom right corner. She closed the trunk and sat on it to put them on.

Blanndynne waited for her outside the house, standing with a basket balanced on her hip. She looked up from examining her nails when Ellayne shut the front door behind her.

"There are two buckets around the back," Blanndynne said, nodding to the left side of the house. "I'll wait."

Nodding, Ellayne followed the unspoken order and walked around to the backside of the small building. *If it means answers*, she started thinking, but stopped when she reached the back of the house. Her eyes widened. An expansive garden grew with all sorts of crops. The soup in the kitchen made more sense, and she regretted not eating it when her stomach grumbled again.

The two metal buckets Blanndynne had mentioned sat in a muddy puddle next to a barrel, which was nearly empty. A few inches of clear liquid collected at the bottom. Ellayne grabbed the buckets and rejoined Blanndynne near the front door.

"Great, let's go," Blanndynne said as soon as Ellayne came around the house. Blanndynne didn't wait for Ellayne to reach where she stood before she turned her back and strode down the worn path.

"Will you tell me what's going on now?" Ellayne asked, trying to conceal the frustration behind the question by raising the pitch of her voice a bit. Even to her own ears it sounded too perky.

Blanndynne waved her hand to the side, blowing off Ellayne's question. "First I want to make sure you know what chores I need done before I return home tomorrow. Okay?" She didn't wait for Ellayne's confirmation before continuing. "I need the laundry done; I specifically laid out the clothing I need washed on my bed. I also need you to—"

"I'm sorry," Ellayne interrupted, clearing her throat, "but I can't think about doing laundry until I get some clarity on why I can't remember anything."

"Look, Ellayne." Blanndynne stopped walking and turned to face her. "I don't have all the answers to your little questions."

"Little?"

They stood near the line of trees, which now towered above Ellayne, much taller than she'd thought from inside the house. The smell of decaying leaves and damp earth filled her nose, and she breathed in deeply, doing what she could to stay calm. Ellayne focused on standing straight, not wanting to show how much she wanted to run back to the safety of the house.

Blanndynne threw her hands up in the air and let them slam down against her sides. "Look." She brushed a piece of hair out of her face. "I shouldn't be so blunt, I know. I suppose I've answered your questions so many times that my patience is gone when it comes to your memory loss. You think it's hard on you? Well, I'm the one who provides for you since you can't hold down a job, what with your memory going every month or so. This amnesia thing comes at the most inconvenient times." She placed a hand on her chest and rolled her eyes, heaving out a sigh.

Despite Blanndynne's brusque manner and the growing heat in Ellayne's stomach, she felt her shoulders slump. "It's happened before?"

"Yes. It seems like it's been constant for years now, and if I had known you were going to lose your memory again today, I would've asked one of the others to cover my shift, but I guess that's not possible now. If we don't keep going to the river, I'm not going to be back to work on time, and I could get in trouble and lose the job that supports the both of us. So would you keep up?"

"Sorry," Ellayne mumbled, following Blanndynne as she started into the forest. The two women were quiet for a few minutes before another question emerged. "Why am I like this?"

Blanndynne shrugged, which Ellayne could barely see because the trees were blocking out a majority of the light.

"There was an attack and you lost your parents. It left you with memory loss, and I suppose your brain brought you somewhere you thought was safe; my front doorstep. I've been taking care of you ever since."

Ellayne's mouth opened in a silent gasp, but it was more from the sudden chill that surrounded her. Instinct told her she should be in a fit of tears. However, there were no faces or memories of her parents to mourn. As a result, numbness occupied the space where the emotions were supposed to be.

She felt no despair over the loss of her family, and no relief at knowing Blanndynne knew her and was looking out for her. Ellayne felt nothing. Emptiness flared its nostrils at her when she tried to probe it for answers or any sort of confirmation that Blanndynne spoke the truth.

"Come on, the river is this way," Blanndynne said from farther ahead. The latter lagged behind with the news of loss she couldn't remember.

Chapter Four

ater trickled into the bucket as Ellayne bent down, testing the water with her hand. She didn't recognize its low temperature until she pulled her hand out and the once chilly air felt warm. Her fingertips were pink after mere seconds in the water.

When both buckets sloshed in her hands, Ellayne stood back up and faced Blanndynne. "All right, now what?"

"If you follow this path"—Blanndynne pointed back in the direction they'd just come from—"you should make it to the clearing."

Her words caused Ellayne's heartbeat to quicken.

"Should? You aren't going to show me the way back?"

"I'm showing you right now, aren't I?" Blanndynne raised a perfectly shaped eyebrow at her. "Besides, it's not that difficult to follow this path through the Black Forest. I do it almost every day. And so do you." She adjusted the basket. "You'll probably see the clearing before you see the house, because the house is hidden by the hill at the angle you'll be entering."

"How do you know that I'll make it back?" Ellayne tossed a hesitant glance in the direction Blanndynne pointed.

"You've always made it back before," Blanndynne said. She noticed Ellayne's posture and stepped over a root to grip her by the shoulders. "You'll be fine. And I promise to answer more questions when I come back tomorrow. But I need to leave now." Ellayne took a deep breath and nodded. Offering a small smile, she thanked Blanndynne and watched her recede in the distance along the river. Light leaked through the scattered branches, but she turned away from it and reentered what Blanndynne had called the Black Forest.

Every step brought her deeper into the trees. Ellayne squinted and tried to recognize any landmarks she might've passed on the way to the river. A shadow resembled one of the uprooted trees Blanndynne had pointed out, so Ellayne continued in the direction she hoped they had come from.

The handles from the buckets cut deep into her hands, weighed down by the cold water from the river. *Why don't I have callouses if I do this as often as Blanndynne says I do?* Ellayne grimaced.

Every once in a while, the water splashed onto her dress or her legs, and she shivered, spilling more. The journey dragged on, and at one point, she took deep breaths to stay calm when she thought she'd made a wrong turn. But soon enough she found the light level changing, getting brighter the farther she went.

The clearing opened up before her, and she blinked in the sunlight. It warmed her, drying the dress as she crossed through the tall grass to the tiny house. Her already sore arms ached even more by the time she heaved the first bucket up and over into the barrel, splashing water all down the front of her dress.

Grunting, she lifted the second bucket up and dumped it before replacing the buckets next to the barrel. The grass and mud squished under her feet as she walked around to the front of the house. Though they lived in the middle of a clearing with no one else seemingly nearby, it still surprised her that Blanndynne didn't feel the need to lock the front door. Not that there was much to steal.

The loaf of bread on the counter called to her in a soft, beckoning voice, and having clarified that it was in fact meant for her, she sat down at the table with the bread and a knife. The soup bubbled on the wood stove. Her stomach leapt with jubilation at the first bite of bread, and she kept herself from giggling when she let out a loud sigh of satisfaction.

She left half the loaf for breakfast the next day, but ate the entire bowl of soup. There was, however, an herb in the broth itself that she was not particularly fond of because it left a soapy taste in her mouth.

While she cleaned the bowl and spoon, she began contemplating Blanndynne. *I should be thankful for her. She's taken care of me with the memory loss. Her indifferent attitude though . . .* Ellayne paused in the middle of washing the bowl. She clenched her jaw.

Ellayne's annoyance continued when she entered Blanndynne's room to gather the laundry she'd laid out. She scrubbed one of the tunics outside in the sun, letting the rays warm her back. She tried to see her situation from Blanndynne's perspective, and as the day wore on, and the more she considered it, the more gratefulness grew inside her. Being the sole provider for the household, keeping track of where Ellayne was, answering the inevitable questions that came with every strike of amnesia . . . *It can't be easy for her.* Ellayne sighed.

Despite her flippant attitude, Blanndynne hadn't given Ellayne any reason not to trust her. Still, a little thought at the back of her mind had her questioning the explanations her caretaker had given her.

By the time she finished all the housework and entered her bedroom, the light was disappearing before her eyes. Placing her shoes by the trunk, she moved some of the clothing around until

18

she found what she was looking for—a simple, long tunic she would use to sleep in. She changed, laying the dress out on the chair as a reminder to wash it with the next round of laundry. However, she didn't particularly desire to wear it again. The dress made her appear sick; the pale green shade caused her skin to lose any color it had.

Peering out the window, she saw the sun sinking behind the scar of trees on the horizon. It would be completely dark soon, and even though she'd only been awake for a few hours, her body ached for rest, if for no other reason than to quiet the rioting thoughts in her mind.

Before she lost all light from the sun, she went back to the kitchen and searched for a candle. She found one in the cabinet, along with matches. It felt like she'd remembered they were there, but of course she hadn't. It was just a lucky guess, a fifty-fifty chance of opening the correct cabinet out of only two.

Upon reentering the bedroom, she lit the candle and placed it on her trunk as far away from the bed as she could. She turned toward the mirror, feeling for the briefest moment as if she wasn't alone.

Her reflection caught her off guard, and she stepped closer to the mirror. This time her cheeks were no longer stained and her nose no longer pink. Her reflection stared back at her, waiting for a motion to copy, but all Ellayne did was stand there.

The tunic hung shapelessly around her, surrounding her in a cream-colored box. She could already see bruises forming just above her knees where the buckets had bumped against her on the way back from the river.

After the third pass up and down the length of her body, she noticed something she'd not seen before. On the inside of her left wrist, just above the palm of her hand, was a narrow, black, diagonal line. It was about three inches long from end to end. She didn't know why she hadn't noticed it earlier, and as she pulled her wrist up to examine it, she saw it was a scar—not ink like she'd originally hoped. The skin around the scar lifted, red around the edges, but pitch-black in the center of the line. When she touched it with the pad of her finger, it didn't hurt at all. In fact, besides the visual difference and the slight disruption to her otherwise smooth skin, it was hardly noticeable.

Ellayne rubbed her finger over the scar, hoping it would rub off somehow. When she lifted her thumb, it was still there, gaping up at her. Her mind traveled back to the Black Forest, and she wondered for a second if something in the trees had scratched her; however, she ruled that out, knowing she would've noticed. *I probably would've dropped a bucket, or both.*

The thin line contributed all the more to the chaos in her head, and it intensified the headache forming around her temples. Ellayne decided to sort out the questions already flooding through her mind without adding any new ones to the list. Putting her arm down, she hid the scar behind her back. Her feet skimmed over the floorboards when she crossed to the bed and sat down. She let out a long sigh before she even realized she was doing it, and a moment of silence later, she blew out the candle and pulled the blanket up over her legs.

The bed was firm and groaned under her as she lay down. Turning onto her side, she faced the wall instead of the window. It didn't take long with her eyes closed for her to drift off to sleep, despite the mind full of unanswered questions and unknowns.

Before she knew it, she was dreaming. A clear image of a flower on the tip of a mountain opened up in front of her. It was an icy lavender shade with delicate petals closed up in a bud. She watched with a smile growing on her lips as the flower unfurled to reveal a brilliant yellow center the moment she got near it. As she walked along a sandy white path, she grinned wider as more flowers similar to it burst from the ground all around her. They grew tall, taller than her, and she ran her hand along the stems, which twirled like ivy, connecting with each other in a weaving pattern. Softer than feathers, the stems bowed under her touch, and she couldn't help but let out an elated laugh. Spinning around, a sea of purple sprouted behind her.

The sky radiated a brilliant blue in all directions, and she turned her face skyward, basking in the sun. The rays shone down and warmed her skin, and as she continued up the path, she could hear the soft rushing of water nearby. A river trickled down the side of the mountaintop, tinkling over smooth river rock and around bends and curves of hard granite. She could see other mountains surrounding the one she was on, but none of the others were covered in the light purple flowers.

As she twirled around and enjoyed the sunlight, she saw a flash of darkness in her peripheral vision. One of the mountains in the distance turned black, and the mountains next to it were also beginning to darken, taking on the same appearance as the first one. For a moment she wondered if a fire had started, but there was no smoke rising on the horizon, and she couldn't see any indication of flames. She stopped moving, and instead focused her attention on the domino effect taking place. The sky above the blackened land also lost its color, fading to a dark gray as clouds rolled in.

Looking around, isolation screamed at her, and she searched for anyone else witnessing the strange sight. As a third mountain fell to the blackness, she turned on her heels and started to run back down the path she'd come up. Whatever was withering the mountains was heading straight for her, and she didn't want to find out what it was.

She hadn't made it halfway down the path before the sky above her was drained of color. The flowers withered away as she ran past them. The petals, now a dark brown, crumbled to the ground, putting off an acidic odor. Her nose burned. The vines and stalks stayed put—giant walls surrounding her on every side. It wasn't until her loose hair got snagged on one, yanking her head back, that she noticed thorns three inches long covering the vines. The light green color transitioned first to a dark green before going to a shade of black that absorbed the light around it.

Her lungs felt as though they were bursting as she struggled to breathe, and she let loose scream after scream. The gnarled vines ripped at her arms and legs, and the walls surrounding her slithered, growing tighter and tighter until they closed in around her, wrapping around her limbs and tearing into her skin. The plants hissed and whispered, sinking deeper and deeper into their victim. Ellayne cried out as the ebony weeds held her. Over her wailing, an unnatural laughter echoed somewhere in the distance.

Chapter Five

Ellayne sat straight up in bed, her hair slicked across her sweaty face. Her chest heaved up and down, and even though she was in Blanndynne's house, it didn't feel safe. Suffocated by the stale air in the bedroom, she ripped off the blanket, stumbled to the window, and tried to open the latch. The sun had long since set, and she couldn't navigate the lock in the dark, even with the light of the three moons in the sky.

Giving up, she ran to the bedroom door and yanked it open, reaching the front door in a few long strides. She didn't bother to shut it as she ran out into the humid night air. And she didn't stop running—not when she passed the first tree, nor when she passed the fiftieth. Only when she could no longer feel the lingering stabs of pain from her nightmare did she come to a stop. When the silent calm of the trees settled around her, Ellayne crumpled and sank onto an exposed root.

The terror from the dream was beginning to fade, but an afterimage clung to her mind with sharp claws. In her panic, she recalled the setting of the dream, seeing the deadly vines in the unmoving trees. With adrenaline filling her mind, she imagined a figure standing in the distance. Had the shadow been the one to laugh? Had she even heard a laugh? The nonexistent vines faded, transforming into the low-hanging branches of the trees; however, the figure in the distance didn't disappear. Hooded, it stared at her through the branches—through the darkness. Ellayne didn't take her eyes off it, waiting for it to shift into a stump or some sort of bent trunk.

It didn't.

Sweat, built up during the nightmare and her sprint through the trees, cooled on her skin. She shivered. Her heartbeat had no time to slow as she stood up, bracing herself against the rough tree bark. The shadow, which was the shape of a person, hadn't moved.

Ellayne took small steps backward while squinting, not taking her eyes off the shape. She tried to see any defining characteristics in the shadow, but the leafy roof impeded the glow from the moons.

The figure stood in the direction she'd come from, blocking her path back to the humble protection the tiny house offered. Ellayne chastised herself for running as far as she had, though she knew her regret didn't change her situation.

The shadow charged her. Ellayne gave up watching and turned to run as fast as she could in the opposite direction. Branches snapped under her bare feet, and the cold night air whipped through her thin tunic. A tiny voice in her head told her to turn around. *If you get lost in this forest, you'll die.* That thought fueled her. *I have to find a way to navigate back to the tiny house without the figure following me.* Her stomach squeezed at the thought of leading a killer psychopath back to Blanndynne. Ellayne couldn't hear the footsteps behind her, but she knew with one glance over her shoulder that the shadow wasn't only following, but gaining on her.

Outrunning it wasn't an option anymore, not with her sides cramping and her lungs crying out for air. She blinked through the wind. *Nowhere to hide.* Trees sprouted out of the darkness and blurred past her on all sides. She avoided running headlong into a few, moving at the last second when one would appear inches from her face. The brush scraped at her legs, stinging her skin and reminding her of the pain from the nightmare. She tried to stay left in an attempt to avoid the thickets, only to be slowed by underbrush dragging at her tunic. The underbrush grew well past to her shoulders. Panic seeped into her bloodstream, stealing the oxygen from her lungs.

As she dangerously cast another look over her shoulder, a new idea formed in her mind. The figure was struggling through the brush just as much as she was, but unlike her, it towered well above it. Sucking in her breath to mentally prepare herself for what she was about to do, she clenched her fists, barred her arms in front of her face and swung right—straight into the wall of brush.

It gripped and tugged at her, tearing her clothes and in some places her skin, but it wasn't as bad as she'd expected. The inky vines in her nightmare had paralyzed her in fear. The brush scratched her, but it didn't have the same effect. Instead, determination seized her, urging her forward.

Ellayne kept her head well below the top of the bushes, and she didn't stop moving forward. Her feet were in the most pain as she stepped on the stumps of the bushes over and over again. At that point, it wouldn't have surprised her if they were torn up and bleeding, but she wasn't going to stop to check. However, after continuing for what seemed like a lifetime, she paused to listen for her pursuer. Silence. It sent relief coursing through her aching muscles, and she shifted to look back through the dark to search for any sign of the shadow.

Nothing.

Ellayne grimaced as she stood all the way up and peered through the darkness in every direction. There was no sign of the figure, not another sound in the forest beside the ones she was making. Her body began to relax bit by bit, but her heart continued to beat at the pace her mind was racing.

She navigated her way back to the part of the forest with less scrub. Ellayne began to wonder if she'd imagined the figure from the start.

It became abundantly clear when she got out of the brush just how difficult getting back to the tiny house was going to be— even without the threat of being pursued by a maniac. Besides the section of brush, the forest blended together in an unending landscape of tall trees. If she'd passed any recognizable landmarks, she hadn't noticed them during the chase.

Several times she thought she found the tree where she'd stopped before seeing the figure, but no. Wrong. Every single time. This section of the Black Forest had not been in Blanndynne's vague description on how to get back to the clearing. Everything felt unfamiliar.

It must've been an hour before Ellayne let the anxiety she was suppressing step into the forefront of her mind. *I'm lost in the middle of a forest I can't remember*. She started muttering out loud about whether she had seen certain trees or not, sometimes walking in circles to make sure she hadn't missed something familiar.

More time passed, and it took a while for her to notice the light level changing. The sun came out far above the roof of leaves. However, to her dismay, it was still dark under the trees. *No wonder this place is called the Black Forest*, she thought. The farther she limped on her tattered feet, the bigger the trees became, until they were at least as thick as four people huddled together—dark giants towering over her.

Exhaustion weighed her down, making each step forward harder than the last. Everything in her body shrieked at her to stop and give up. She didn't listen. Instead, she focused on the small voice in the back of her head telling her she had too many unanswered questions to give up. Her stomach whined that the bread and soup had been so long ago—she ignored it. Her parched throat cried out for relief—she ignored it. Her torn up feet begged for her to sit down and cut them off rather than continue on—yet she ignored them too.

She motivated herself by asking a new question every time she took a step. *Who were my parents?* Step. *Where did they live?* Step. *What were they like?* Step. *How did they die?* Step. *What does it have to do with this amnesia?* Question after question.

Ellayne, though tired, enjoyed the action of putting words to the flow of wordless inquiries in her head. It seemed to her to be progress despite the lack of answers, and she wished she had something to write it all down on. The thought made her let out a small snort. Ellayne was aching, hungry, thirsty, and lost in a maze of trees, yet the thing she desired most in the moment was a pen and several pieces of parchment. The short chuckle turned into a longer, more drawn out laugh until she was bent over, lost in the humor of her strange situation. She knew she had to look insane, cackling to herself in the middle of nowhere with nothing funny around her, but she couldn't stop herself.

Until a branch cracked behind her.

Chapter Six

Ellayne ducked behind the nearest tree, her back scratching against the trunk. *Was I seen? Should I run? Can I run?*

"Ellayne?" Blanndynne's voice filled Ellayne's tired body with relief, and she sagged against the tree. Blanndynne came around the trunk of another tree a few paces away. "Ellayne! What are you doing out here? You should be in the house." She walked to Ellayne's side, lowering the basket she was holding.

"I'm sorry." Ellayne's voice was hoarse from a combination of running, lack of water, and laughing maniacally. "I'm so sorry, Blanndynne. I had a nightmare, and I felt like I couldn't breathe in the house, so I went outside and then—"

"Never mind." Blanndynne had her hands on both of Ellayne's shoulders, and she reached up to brush a hair out of Ellayne's face. "Let's go back to the house and then we can discuss what drove you out of your mind enough to run into the Black Forest."

Ellayne nodded, thankful Blanndynne had cut her off. She would've felt annoyed, except Blanndynne had rescued her moments before she completely lost her sanity. Ellayne decided to hold off on telling her about the figure, still questioning the reality of it. Blanndynne spoke the entire way back; most of it consisted of chiding Ellayne for leaving the house.

Her midnight stroll in the forest had taken her farther than she'd realized, and Blanndynne told her she'd nearly crossed into the kingdom of Cyanthia, where Blanndynne worked at the castle. Blanndynne started talking about her job, but Ellayne's tired mind couldn't spare the energy to pay attention. She nodded every once in a while, forcing her face to react when Blanndynne looked back at her.

By the time the trees began to scatter and they entered the clearing, Ellayne felt like she was sleepwalking. But Blanndynne didn't let her go back to sleep. Instead, she had her wash up in the bathroom—the water in the metal tub bit like a bee sting—and then addressed the more serious wounds on her feet, along with a few on her arms and legs. Ellayne's face came out relatively scratch free, minus one jagged line on her lower left cheek that reached back below her ear.

Blanndynne insisted she eat the rest of the bread, and told Ellayne it would be best if she didn't go to sleep until the sun went down, because otherwise she would be up all night.

Not eager to be attacked by malevolent vines in her nightmares again, nor wanting to vex Blanndynne more than she already had, Ellayne agreed.

Ellayne's body ached from head to toe when she woke up. It had been a long week of hard work around the cabin since her trek through the Black Forest. Part of her thought Blanndynne was trying to passively punish her with never-ending lists of chores.

Though she hadn't had the nightmare again, sleep didn't come easily. She tossed and turned every night, unable to fully get to sleep. Unsatisfied and unrested, she stayed in bed until she couldn't handle it any longer. Ellayne stood up and had to sit right back down because of how sore her feet were. Gritting her teeth, she hobbled over to the mirror. Dark circles slouched beneath her eyes, making her look older. She brushed her fingers through her hair a few times, wincing when they got stuck in knots. When her hair was relatively tangle free, she wove it into a thick braid that hung down past her shoulder blades.

She'd heard Blanndynne up hours earlier. Before the sun had even come out, the floor had creaked in the room next to hers, and before long, Blanndynne was banging around in the kitchen. After many hard days of working out in the garden and doing house chores, Blanndynne had told Ellayne she had to go back to the castle to work. Ellayne was careful not to reveal how relieved she was by that information, not wanting to hurt her friend's feelings by making her feel unwanted. Blanndynne leaving meant she could have a day of rest, and though she was thankful to Blanndynne for everything she'd done for her, she was already beginning to grow weary of what her daily life would look like when her caretaker was home.

The floorboards outside her door groaned, and Ellayne turned to face Blanndynne as she knocked and entered without a welcome. "I wanted to be sure you were up before I left," Blanndynne said, and then to Ellayne's annoyance, she rambled off a list of chores that needed to be completed in the time she was gone. Tilting her chin up, Ellayne kept a grin plastered on her face, nodding as she waited for the list to end.

"When will you be back?"

"I'm not sure. There are diplomats coming in from some northern cities, and though there are only three evenings of events planned, there are often extra festivities until the diplomats leave. My presence is necessary. Honestly, the servants are lost without me. But I'll come back when I can." Blanndynne grasped Ellayne's shoulders like she'd done quite a few times in the last week. "You'll be fine as long as you stay here."

Ellayne stared at a place on the wall behind Blanndynne's shoulder, trying to decide how she felt about being left all alone for at least three whole days. She wasn't sure she liked the idea. Blanndynne may put her to work, but at least she was someone to talk to.

"Ellayne?" Blanndynne said her name again, and it brought Ellayne's focus back.

"Hm?"

"Don't leave the house." Blanndynne stared at her, and it took Ellayne a second to realize she wanted confirmation that Ellayne understood the request.

"Sure," Ellayne said as she nodded. She shrugged her shoulders up to her ears, and Blanndynne let go of her. "I have nowhere to go anyway. Right?"

"Right. I'll see you in a few days." Blanndynne squeezed her and turned to leave, shutting the door behind her before Ellayne could say goodbye.

The front door closed; Ellayne didn't like the way it shook the whole structure of the house. Deciding she'd better start on the chores before she forgot them, she changed into the day clothes she'd laid out the night before: a heather-gray dress that didn't wash out the color of her skin as much as the pastel colors in the other dresses. She also slid her injured feet into the shoes she'd found in the trunk on the first day.

The first thing on the list was washing off the vegetables they'd harvested the day before, and having returned to the river multiple times throughout the week to replenish the water in the barrel, Ellayne had full confidence in navigating that part of the Black Forest. There were still six inches of water left in the barrel when she checked it, but since the next thing on the unending list of chores was washing the laundry, Ellayne decided she'd better start by getting more water from the river.

To save herself two trips, she chose to carry both buckets instead of one—a decision she regretted every time she made it. The bucket handles always cut into her hands. After filling the buckets up in the cold water, she began the fifteen-minute walk back to the house.

Her trip filled the barrel up a third. Satisfied with the water level, she returned to the front of the house to grab the laundry.

Ellayne didn't notice she was humming until she stopped abruptly, her blood running colder than the water in the river. The door she knew she'd closed before she left gaped wide open. A piece of parchment was stuck to the wall beside the open entryway. In large, black letters were the words I FOUND YOU. If that weren't enough to send shivers down her entire body, it was stuck to the wood with the tip of an arrow.

What in the world?

Ripping the note off the door and wiggling the arrow from the wood, Ellayne spun around, half expecting to find someone standing behind her. But she couldn't see anyone through the shade of the trees. Alarm let loose a wave of adrenaline into her veins, and her heartbeat pounded in her ears. The hair on the back of her neck lifted, and the sensation encouraged the feeling she was being watched. But by whom?

Nothing moved—at least not that she could see.

A branch cracked. Her head snapped to the right when the surrounding silence shattered. Once again, she was no longer alone.

Chapter Seven

Ellayne tightened her grip on the arrow, ready to stab anything that moved near her. The arrow was heavier than she expected for something that was built to fly far distances, though she had nothing to compare that observation to, since she lacked memories of any previous encounters with weapons.

A sound like a whistle buzzed through the air, and Ellayne didn't know it was another arrow until it thudded into the door right behind her head. She glanced back and saw the shaft of the arrow wobbling back and forth behind her ear, only then registering her near brush with death.

Ellayne lunged away from the door before a second arrow hit right where her chest had been a moment earlier. Her feet flew beneath her, arms pumping at her sides with the first arrow in one hand and the note in the other. The trees loomed larger as she approached them at full speed, running opposite the direction the arrows had come from.

She navigated her way toward the river in hopes she wouldn't get as lost as the first time. Another arrow hummed by and hit a tree she was running past. The crack of wood made her think to weave in and out of the trees. She hoped whoever was pursuing her was stopping to aim, but she didn't dare check as another arrow pierced a branch to the left.

The sound of water rushing over rocks and around the curves of the land grew louder. For half a second, she allowed herself to be proud of finding the river without the original path Blanndynne had shown her, even if it was a different part of the river. This section, unlike near the house, had a much stronger current, and as a result, a steeper bank led down to the reflective surface. She ran beside the bends in the river along a four-foot embankment.

Caught up in the moment of pride at navigating the Black Forest, an arrow flew past her right ear, causing her to swerve left faster than she intended.

With a shriek, Ellayne lost her footing. She toppled sideways, rolling and sliding down the hill. Dropping the arrow and the note, she clawed at the ground, trying to stop her downward momentum. It didn't slow her in the slightest.

The water swallowed her with a stinging splash, whisking her away with the current. Ellayne kicked her feet, trying to find the surface as the small amount of oxygen in her lungs was depleted. The water chilled her instantly, fogging her brain and making it hard to think. When she broke through the surface coughing, she barely had time for a full breath before the water pulled her back under. It spun her around and thrashed her about until she wasn't sure which way was up.

Ellayne struggled to plant her feet on the bottom, but it was too deep. She felt her hand burst through to the air, and soon afterward her head did too. She surfaced choking on a cold mixture of mist and water. Her lungs burned as she screamed, but she inhaled a mouthful of water when it sucked her down, cutting the cry short. She wasn't sure who she expected to hear her. Besides, the only person she knew to be nearby was the psychopath with the bow and arrow. Still, she cried for help every time she could.

Her head got dizzier and her fight against the current grew weaker with every second. The combination of the bone-chilling water and absence of oxygen coaxed her into submission. She wanted to give in—to let the river take her wherever it wanted.

It seemed easier that way.

Just as she was about to give up and drift into the oncoming blackness, the touch of a strong hand around her wrist shocked her to alertness, yanking her against the speeding current in a swift, painful motion. Her shoulder screeched in pain, and she released whatever air was still in her lungs. The river resisted, trying to steal her away.

Her head broke through the surface.

Another hand grabbed farther up her arm, hoisting her from the strongest part of the undertow. The hands adjusted, gripping her under either arm.

She felt her back bump against another person's chest at the same time she felt the person's leg brush hers under the water. Ellayne's head rested back on the upper torso of her rescuer, staying above the water as she panted and coughed out water. The air was both painful and a relief as she took in all she could. The body shifted below her; she was being dragged through shallow water.

"Can you stand?" Her rescuer's voice was distinctly male, out of breath and spitting out water, but still low-pitched and powerful.

Ellayne hesitated as she lowered her legs and instantly sank her bare feet inches deep into silky sand. Somewhere along the river she'd lost her shoes. The silt squished between her toes, and she nodded.

"Good," the voice said. "Come on then, I'll help you out."

When she turned to face her rescuer, Ellayne faltered. His steady grasp had felt much stronger than what he appeared to be capable of; he had muscles, but he was lean. Her rescuer had dark brown, nearly black hair, which dripped water from curly ringlets around his face. His pointed jawline clenched and unclenched, causing a vein to fade in and out of view on his neck. His black tunic stuck to him like she was sure her dress was to her, and when she looked back up at his face, his heavy eyebrows furrowed down at her.

His hand stretched out toward her, and she took it, not wanting to think about how long she'd been gazing at him before seeing it. He led her to the edge of the river, displacing water as he splashed through. He had a ring on his pointer finger, and when she slipped on a patch of mud, he squeezed her hand and the metal pinched her.

"Watch your step." He dropped her hand when the water was up to their ankles.

Ellayne followed him out of the shallow part of the river, watching him untie a rope that was anchored around his chest. She traced the length of rope up to the edge of the river where it was tied to a horse with another young man atop it. They looked to be about the same age, but the young man on the horse had dark hair made lighter by the sun's kiss. He was also much tanner than the man who'd jumped into the river, and when they got to the horses, the contrast was undeniable.

"Here." The young man on the horse dismounted. Jogging up to Ellayne, he took off his jacket and wrapped it around her shoulders. "You're shaking."

"Of course she is," the pale rescuer said, "that river is colder than your parents." His comment received merely a sneer. The young man guided Ellayne to the horses, where he pulled out a canteen and handed it to her.

To her surprise, it was full of warm, sweet liquid, and she lost herself in the warming sensation spreading from her throat to her outer extremities.

"Hey now," the light-haired one said, "slow down and breathe. We don't need you choking on this, too." His voice possessed a calming effect. "That's it." He took the container from her as she took in a deep breath.

Ellayne's chest ached, and her head pounded from the river's beating, but she still spoke a word of thanks.

"You're more than welcome. What's your name?" the light-haired one asked as he tucked the canteen back into a saddlebag on the horse. Ellayne made sure to stay a couple feet back from the beast, not enjoying the way it was staring at her from the corner of its eye.

"Forget that question," the dark-haired man scoffed, putting on a jacket he must've discarded before jumping in to save her. It was covered in dirt, and he brushed it off once he was wearing it. "What in the world were you doing swimming in the Cylan River, especially in the lower rapids?"

His friend glared at him, but said nothing.

Something about his tone vexed Ellayne. *What makes you think I want to be soaking wet, shivering, and shoeless in the middle of nowhere?* Instead of narrowing her eyes at him like she desired to do, she pasted a plastic smile on her lips as she turned to face him. "I didn't choose to jump in the river just for fun." She put as much sweetness into her voice as she could, hoping it might cover the annoyance she really felt. "A psychopath with a bow and arrow was chasing me through the forest. I lost my balance and fell into the freezing death trap when I was nearly pierced with an arrow. Trust me, that's not how I expected my day to go either."

Chapter Eight

There was a moment of silence, one in which Ellayne worried she'd insulted the men in some way. She half expected them to hop on their horses and ride away, leaving her alone. But to her surprise, the dark-haired man let out a small chuckle, glancing at her through his wet curls. Meanwhile, his companion gaped at her with raised eyebrows.

"You were running from what?"

Ellayne turned away from the man who'd jumped into the river to save her, and instead addressed his friend. "A maniac with a bow and arrow."

"A what?"

"Are you deaf, Kiegan?" The dark-haired man laughed again. "The girl clearly said a bow and arrow," he said, his voice teasing.

When Ellayne cast him a glance, his dark eyes scowled at her. They pierced her and had the opposite effect of his voice. If it had been anyone else besides the presumptuous stranger in front of her, she assumed she would've wilted under the skepticism. However, the way he was acting fired up something in the pit of her stomach, warming her more than the drink from the canteen.

"Ridicule me all you want." She crossed her arms over her chest and stood a bit straighter. "It doesn't make what I said any less true." Talking about her pursuer compelled her to scan the trees on the opposite side of the river. *I don't like being out in the open like this*, she thought, rubbing her hand up and down her arm to ease the chills.

The dark-haired man clenched his jaw again, stepping toward her. He opened his mouth to respond, but Kiegan stepped in front of him and held up his hand.

"We aren't trying to deride you, at least"—he cast a look back at his friend—"I'm not."

The other man sneered at his companion's underhanded comment and huffed, turning his back on the two of them to go to his own horse, which had wandered a little ways away. Ellayne watched him go, trying her best to start a fire on the back of his jacket with only her glare. It wasn't working.

"Don't mind him. He gets grumpy when his hair gets messed up."

Ellayne raised an eyebrow. "Seriously?"

He laughed, grinning at her. "No, I'm just kidding." Kiegan's eyebrows furrowed in an odd way, and she cocked her head at his sudden change. "He's almost always grumpy." His eyes twinkled as he winked at her. "But don't tell him I told you that."

"I have ears, idiot," the dark-haired man said without looking at them, and Ellayne couldn't help but grin as the two bantered back and forth for a moment.

"I'm Kiegan, and the wet, brooding man over there is Kaden." Kiegan jutted his thumb behind him to indicate his friend.

"You'd be brooding too if you had wet socks," Kaden retorted, loud enough for them to hear.

Kiegan grinned down at her. "And just a minute ago, he very rudely interrupted you just as you were going to tell us your name."

She hesitated, unsure whether to tell the truth or not. Something about his smile warmed her more than his jacket, and she spoke honestly. "Ellayne."

"Beautiful name," Kiegan said, and turned his head to look at Kaden. "Do we know any Ellaynes? I know I've heard that name somewhere before, but I can't quite put my finger on where."

"Me neither," Kaden said, "but you're right, I do feel like I've heard it somewhere. And it's Kade, not Kaden. Kaden is what my uncle calls me, and I don't need to be reminded of that talking piece of dung, thanks very much." He walked up and stood next to Kiegan. They were about the same height, and both of them were a head taller than Ellayne.

"Are you injured?" Kiegan asked, inspecting her once over.

"And, more importantly, where are your shoes?" Kade leaned his arm on Kiegan's shoulder, pointing down at her bare feet, which had unfortunately begun to bleed since the bandages and scabs had come off.

How are shoes more important than injuries? She rolled her eyes inwardly. "Not too badly, just a little shaken up I suppose." She gripped the jacket tighter. "And the shoes came off in the river." She stared down at her feet, hating the way they looked, all scratched up and bruised.

"How far do you live from here?" Kiegan asked.

Ellayne looked around, noticing for the first time a small bridge that stretched across the river. It was unfamiliar to her, as was the rest of the terrain. She turned in a full circle.

"Where is 'here' exactly?"

"A couple miles north of Pingbi," Kiegan said.

40

Her eyebrows furrowed and she looked sideways, breaking eye contact with both of them. Raising her hand to her chest, she used her thumb to fiddle with the chain of her necklace.

"You've never heard of Pingbi?" Kade guessed, and he smirked when she nodded. "Living under a rock, are we?"

Ellayne snapped her mouth shut, seconds away from saying something just to spite him. Her temper flared, and she unsuccessfully searched for a memory where she'd let a person fire her up this much. She physically bit her tongue to prevent herself from accidentally blurting out the truth about her amnesia. *I have no reason to tell them. Especially Kade, who seems to get quite a bit of enjoyment out of antagonizing me.*

"Where is Cyanthia in relation to here?" Ellayne asked, her tone was icy. She remembered hearing Blanndynne say the name of the city. It was where she worked. *Maybe if I can find the castle . . .*

"Kade?" Kiegan said it like he expected his friend to respond, and with a sigh, Kade walked over to his horse, the darker of the two, and opened his saddlebag. He fished around in it for a moment before returning to them with a large piece of parchment rolled up in his hand.

It took Ellayne a second to recognize it as a map when he first unfurled it because the detail and color made it appear more like a work of art.

"We're here." Kade pointed to a bend in a blue line, scooped down like a shallow U. There was a little brown slash in the blue line near where he pointed, and Ellayne recognized it as the bridge they were standing next to. Other slashes spread out along the blue line, indicating other bridges. He moved his finger to an area shaded light green. "This is Pingbi, where we're from. A farming town." His finger moved up the blue line to another light green area. "And this is the town of Cyanthia. I assume you meant the town, because we're technically in the kingdom already." It was north of where he'd originally pointed, and

41

Ellayne wondered where the house was on the map, because there was no convenient arrow saying "Blanndynne's house: right here."

Ellayne continued to ogle the land, entranced in the way the world around her was miniaturized on the parchment. The emptiness in her mind caused by her amnesia had her sucking in the information like a sponge.

Names Blanndynne had mentioned over the last week stuck out, particularly The Black Forest, which took up most of the left side of the parchment, sweeping one tendril horizontally across to the right side. At the top of the page, in the largest writing, was the name Phildeterre.

"Phildeterre," she murmured under her breath.

"Yes." Kade drew out the word. "What about it?"

"Nothing." Ellayne shook her head. "It's just that it's huge."

"What do you expect? It's the largest country in the world. This isn't even all of it." Kade stared at her while she continued to devour the map.

The drawings that marked each area mesmerized her. Even the small grain fields that marked The Level Plains were drawn with a very fine pen tip. The person who'd drawn the map spent a lot of time on it, and she envied that person for the ability to get lost in their work the way they so clearly had.

"So where are you headed?" Kiegan asked, leaning over Kade's shoulder and interrupting Ellayne's moment of appreciation for the map.

The question was harder to answer than she wanted it to be. The simple answer that should've slid from her parted lips was Blanndynne's house. It was the obvious answer. But besides the fact that a sociopath with a primed weapon and a desire to end her life—for reasons unknown to her—knew about the house, she also didn't have a huge desire to return to her chores. She'd had a glimpse of the world around her on the map, and there were places she wanted to see before returning to do laundry and work in a garden for the rest of her life. Then again, Blanndynne said her amnesia returned at random points in time, and the idea of traveling with amnesia ran a shiver down to her toes.

"I'm not sure." She wrapped her arms around her chest, squeezing them as a chilly breeze blew past her.

Kade hadn't taken his eyes off her since unrolling the map, and there was a new emotion peeking out from behind his guarded eyes: interest.

"We can help get you wherever you need to go." Kiegan smiled at her and tilted his head toward the horses. "Probably a lot faster than walking barefoot."

"That's okay." Ellayne's hand went back up to the necklace again. "I don't—"

"Where did you get that?" Kade asked, cutting her off. He was halfway through rolling up the map when the sun reflected off the silver medallion around her neck. His hands froze mid twist.

"What?" Ellayne stopped too, the chain tugged away from her neck. "This?" She held out the necklace for him to look at as he stepped closer. "It's just a necklace."

"Kieg," Kade said, ignoring her, "take a look at this." Kade finished rolling up the map and tucked it under his arm.

Kiegan came to his friend's side and examined the necklace in the palm of Ellayne's hand. She held it away from her neck, aware of how close the two men were to her. If they hadn't gone through the trouble to save her life, she would've backed away.

"Is that the crest?" Kiegan asked, and Kade shook his head.

"That's not just the crest of Cyanthia, that's *the* crest."

Ellayne lowered the necklace. "The crest? What's that supposed to mean?"

"Where did you get that?" Kade asked, straightening up and jabbing a finger toward the necklace. "There are only so many of

43

those, and only specific people are allowed to wear them. If you stole that—"

"Kade," Kiegan snapped. "What he means to say," his voice softened as he addressed Ellayne, "is that very few people remain alive who wear that crest. Actually, only one: King Diomedes. There shouldn't be any more of these floating around. People who have these medallions are buried with them when they die, and their bodies are guarded in the royal crypt. So—"

"So unless you went scavenging among those at eternal rest and magically didn't get arrested, a commoner like you shouldn't have a necklace like that," Kade finished, crossing his arms over his chest.

Ellayne looked from the necklace to the two men, then back again. Her amnesia had somehow found an even more intense way to bite her in the rear end again.

Chapter Nine

Well?" Kade asked. "Where did you get the necklace, Ellayne?"

"I—" Ellayne took a step back, but Kade didn't let her back up any farther. His hand reached out faster than she could track, and it latched around her left wrist. Unlike in the river, where the tight grip had been for her preservation, his hand squeezed her as a python would its prey.

Let go of me, she thought, clamping her mouth shut.

"Where?" He pulled her closer, glaring down his nose at her. "Where did you get it?" He said each word through gritted teeth.

"Kade—" Kiegan put a hand on his friend's shoulder, but Kade shrugged it off.

"Answer me."

"I don't know," she answered, her voice cracking. His intense eyes instinctively made her cower down, but the warmth from her core simmered again and she rolled her shoulders back. "I don't know where I got it, and I'd appreciate if you took your hands off of me . . . please."

Ellayne narrowed her eyes at him, and for a second, they were locked in silent combat. Her determined eyes fought the nonverbal battle with his stubborn ones. She wanted to look away, but wasn't willing to give up. In the end, Kade broke the stare-off first, turning his chin to gesture toward her wrist in his hand.

"How did you get that?"

The blackened scar on her wrist glimmered with moisture where the jacket sleeve revealed her arm. She'd forgotten about the scar after the first day, too busy and tired from chores to care, but as she rediscovered the line on her skin, her stomach turned. Unlike before, where the black hue had only outlined the scar, tiny veins carried the darkness under her flesh, fading back to her pale skin tone after about half an inch of inky lines.

Ellayne ripped her wrist from Kade's grip, surprising him as well as Kiegan. She held her wrist gently, running her thumb over the darkened skin. Just like before, she couldn't feel anything other than the pressure from her own finger, but whatever was in the scar had spread without her noticing.

"May I?" Kiegan pushed past Kade, who stepped back and crossed his arms. Holding out his hand, Kiegan waited for Ellayne to place her wrist in it.

"I don't know." Ellayne pulled her arm to her chest, hiding the scar from view. She took a step back. Kiegan didn't approach her, letting her put distance between them. *Can I trust them? They saved me, but they're strangers.* Ellayne glanced from Kiegan to the trees across the river. *Still out in the open. It'd be so easy to shoot me.*

"I promise I won't hurt you." Kiegan's tone sounded dipped in honey. "We won't let anyone hurt you."

"That's a big claim to make, Kieg," Kade said, and Ellayne agreed with him in her head. "We can't promise that," he said to Ellayne.

46

Kiegan ignored Kade, gesturing for Ellayne to let him see her wrist, which she did, albeit hesitantly. "Interesting," Kiegan murmured as he ran his finger over the scar. He flipped her arm over to examine the back where there was no discoloring. "How long have you had this?"

"I'm not sure," Ellayne said, and because she still wasn't sure if she could trust the strangers, she kept talking to distract them from the fact that she kept answering their questions with the same answer. "It didn't look like that a week ago, all spiderwebby and all."

"What did it look like before?"

"A black line on my wrist, definitely a scar, but black instead of pink or white."

Kade tilted his head up to the sky and sighed, walking toward the river. Kiegan didn't look back at him, and instead continued to put pressure on the scar with his thumb until Ellayne winced. "Does it hurt?"

"Only when you push on it extremely hard with your thumb."

"So maybe I won't do that again," he said with a chuckle.

Ellayne nodded, offering a small smile. "Yeah, maybe don't." She rubbed her wrist when he let her go, and tucked her arms in to her chest. "What do you think it is?"

"Honestly?" He shrugged when she nodded. "I'm not sure. It could just be a wound that didn't heal properly, in which case you should go see a healer."

"And if it's not that?"

"Magic," Kade said, his back still turned to them. "It's magic."

"Magic?" Ellayne asked, her brain frantically searching to find any mention of magic from the last few days. She found none.

"Both of you"—Kade spun around and pointed at them—"seem to have a hearing problem today. Yes, magic." He closed the space between them in a matter of steps. "Magic, as in dragons and fairies and sorceresses and spells. Are you seriously so sheltered that you don't know magic exists?"

Ellayne's head buzzed, and it didn't take her long to feel the rest of her body shaking. She barely heard Kiegan chide Kade for his brash words, because she was too busy trying to stay upright.

"How can she be from Cyanthia if she doesn't know about magic? It makes no sense, Kiegan," Kade was saying, waving his hands in the air. "Something doesn't add up. She's hiding something."

"Kade, cool off," Kiegan said, his voice strained. "You're not helping whatever's happening here. And you're clearly freaking her out."

There was a moment of silence, and all Ellayne could hear was ringing in her ears, before she heard Kade grunt. His footsteps crunched on the grass, fading as he stomped away.

"Ellayne." Kiegan placed a hand on her shoulder, and she pivoted to face him.

"Is it true? Magic exists?" She didn't know what she wanted him to say.

"Yes, it does. But more importantly, why is that a surprise to you?" His warm hand reassured her.

Ellayne closed her eyes, questioning how much she should tell him. "I-I don't know if I should. I don't really know you and—"

"You can tell me." Kiegan smiled at her, his face softening when a little dimple showed on either side of his mouth.

"Kiegan, I appreciate you helping me, but I don't know you."

"I understand." He tucked both hands into his trouser pockets. "Is there anything I can do to get you to trust me?"

Ellayne shrugged. "It's just a lot."

"What is?"

Her foot tapped the ground, and she closed her eyes. "There's just a lot I don't understand."

"Like magic?"

"Magic and sinister scars, among other things. I was just chased through the forest by someone trying to shoot me with arrows."

"You don't know who it was?"

Ellayne shook her head. "No idea, and I can't go back to where I came from because that's where he first started chasing me."

"It was a he?"

"Well, I guess it could've been a girl. I never saw the person. Just the arrows."

Kiegan stayed still except for his eyes, which shifted between both of hers for a few seconds. Then they brightened, sparkling in the sun as he stepped toward her and pulled her into a hug. It caught her off guard, and she tensed, unsure how to react. But his warmth spread to her, and when she pulled away, there was a wet spot on his light blue tunic where her eyes had leaked, as well as where her wet dress had come into contact with him.

"It seemed like you needed that," he said, holding her by the shoulders at arm's length. It was more reassuring than when Blanndynne had held her in the same way.

"I think I did," Ellayne said, raising her hand to wipe her cheek. "Thank you."

"Don't worry, Ellayne. We'll help you figure out what's going on, and maybe we can figure out where that necklace came from at the same time," Kiegan said, dropping his hands from her shoulders.

"No," she said, shaking her head so a few strands of wet hair fell in front of her eyes. His forehead creased, and she tried to explain herself. "You don't need to trouble yourselves. You already saved my life, which I'm grateful for, but you really don't need to help. I'm fine, really. I'm fine. I'll just find a place to stay for a while and—"

She knew Kiegan had stopped listening when he cast a glance over his shoulder, all his attention trained on his friend. Kade had walked to the middle of the bridge and was leaning against one of the railings, staring out at the river below him.

"I'll go talk to him."

"About what?"

"Bringing you back to Pingbi with us. Then you can stay there until you figure out what you want to do next."

"Kiegan, you don't have to do—"

"I'll be right back," Kiegan cut her off. He called his friend's name as he jogged over, and Kade looked up, glancing between the two of them.

Something about the possibility of causing an argument between the obviously close friends made her stomach twist. She rubbed a hand up and down her arm and switched her weight from one foot to the other.

Ellayne watched them from the bank, wringing her hands together over and over again. She couldn't quite hear them over the sound of the river, but could see Kade shake his head and begin to walk to the opposite side of the bridge. Kiegan spoke with his hands; he gestured at the river, then toward Ellayne, and finally pointed at Kade. Kade shook his head again as he turned to face Kiegan, but it appeared less emphatic. Whatever it was Kiegan said next caused Kade to run his fingers through his hair, and over the roar of the river, she could see his lips form the word "fine."

They talked for a few minutes more, but eventually Kiegan turned around and began striding back to Ellayne. There was a grin on his face, and he winked at her.

"Who do you want to ride with? The prickly pear or me?"

Ellayne's eyes widened. "He's okay with it?"

"I told you I'd talk to him, didn't I?" Kiegan said, and he clucked his tongue, beckoning his horse over. It towered over her, and she took a tiny step backward. "She won't hurt you. Anya is the gentlest one at my stable." He patted the horse's neck with a firm hand, and dust and hair flew off her in a cloud.

Ellayne didn't step any closer, and Kiegan noticed. He held Anya's reins in one hand and reached out for Ellayne's hand with the other.

"Kiegan, I—"

"Come on," he said, and pulled her toward the horse's neck, and placed her hand on it. The hair that covered the mare's body felt coarse to Ellayne's touch. Anya snorted, but didn't react otherwise. "See, she's a sweetheart."

Ellayne glanced at Kiegan and back at the beast. *Sweetheart? Seriously?* It wasn't trying to kill her—yet.

"Little faster please," Kade said.

Ellayne hadn't even noticed Kade mount the darker one. Kade directed his horse using his heels, adjusting the reins to keep it in a single spot. One of Kade's eyebrows arched higher than the other, and a small grin formed on his lips when he saw Ellayne's face blanch, her eyes widen. The sight of Kade on his horse caused a new worry to enter her head, one which Kiegan answered as if reading her mind.

"How do I—"

"Up you go," Kiegan said, startling her as he grabbed her around the waist with both hands. He lifted her onto the horse like she weighed nothing, hardly letting out a grunt.

Shaking, she wrapped her arms around the horse's neck, leaning forward as far as she could until her body was flush against the beast. Anya started stomping her hooves and tossing her head back.

"Anya, calm down," Kiegan said, trying to grab the reins as the horse danced and stamped out of his reach. "Ellayne, you need to calm down too and loosen up on her neck. You're scaring her."

Before Ellayne could point out that the horse was returning the favor, Anya took off at a full gallop.

Chapter Ten

ind whipped Ellayne in the face as she gripped the horse's neck even tighter to keep from being flung off. She felt Anya's strong muscles moving beneath her with each powerful stride. The sound of her hooves beating the ground filled Ellayne's ears, and she squeezed her eyes shut as the colors of the world swirled past, making her sick. The horse's mane smelled of hay and manure, and it bristled against her face and tickled her nose.

Over the pounding hooves of the animal, she heard another similar sound getting closer, and in a matter of seconds, she heard Kiegan's voice calling her name.

"Ellayne," he said, and Ellayne risked opening her eyes. He was riding next to her on the horse Kade had been on just a minute earlier. "Reach down and grab the reins!" he shouted.

"I c-can't!" Ellayne squeezed Anya more.

When she didn't move from her position, he clenched his jaw. "Fine, we'll do this the hard way."

Kiegan gripped the reins in one hand while holding on to the horn of the saddle with the other. To Ellayne's shock, he swung both legs up and crouched on the top of the saddle, still gripping the horn. His horse kept pace with Anya. Kiegan kept his eyes focused on a point behind her on the saddle, and without hesitation, Kiegan launched himself toward Anya.

Ellayne squeaked as he landed behind her with his stomach first. He was sideways across Anya, but he righted himself, swinging a leg over the saddle. He breathed heavily as he leaned forward, his chest pressing down on her back. Ellayne became aware in an instant that his face was right next to hers as he reached around her to grab the reins. Her stomach flipped, and she wasn't sure what the cause of it was: Kiegan or Anya.

With a firm grip on the leather straps, Kiegan leaned back and spoke gently. "Calm down, Anya. You know me." He continued to pull back as the horse began to trot, slowing down each second he held the reins. "Good girl," he said, and turned his attention to the other horse, which had wandered off. "Curry, come on, you big brute." He clicked his tongue again and the black horse looked up at the mention of his name. "Don't be stubborn, come here." Kiegan directed Anya to the other horse. Leaning over, he grabbed the reins hanging down around Curry's chest.

"Thank you," Ellayne said, choking on the giant ball of pride as she swallowed it.

"Not much of a horse person, are you?" He turned the horses toward the bridge, which looked like a spot in the distance.

Ellayne sat up, gripping the horn with white knuckles. "Pretty sure that was obvious."

Kiegan started talking to the horses, telling Anya what a good girl she was. Ellayne remained silent, focusing instead on the tree line across the river.

There were almost no trees on their side of the river they were on, and when she looked to her left, she felt like she could see miles of open fields. It was clear which side of the river the Level

Plains were on. In the distance she could see fences, which marked different crop fields. Apparently harvest was soon because the plants in the fenced-off fields grew tall, taller than her by the looks of them.

It took them a few minutes to get back to Kade, who leaned against the bridge, arms extended and feet crossed at the ankle like he'd had time to get comfortable. When they got close, he pushed off the railing and sauntered up to them with his hands in his pockets, a grin plastered on his face.

"Well that's two saves in one day, Ellayne," Kade said, his amusement clearer than the water behind him. "Should we be keeping an ongoing list?"

"I promise Anya really is sweet," Kiegan said, handing the dark horse's reins back to Kade.

"It doesn't like hugs, apparently," Ellayne said, flinching as Kiegan slid off the back, momentarily letting go of the reins. She clenched the horn, not daring to hold Anya around the neck like she had before.

"No," Kade said. He patted Curry's neck and faced her. "She just doesn't like you."

Ellayne would've frowned at him, but she was distracted by Kiegan tossing the reins up around Anya's neck toward her.

"I'll take the front," he said, and she scooted as far back as she felt comfortable.

"You're going to have to let go of the horn," Kiegan said. He nodded toward her hands, which ached as she released them from the saddle.

For a second she didn't have anything to hold on to while he was mounting the horse in front of her. Her hands clamped into fists and she fought the urge to cry out as the saddle shifted beneath her. But then Kiegan sat tall in front of her, stable as if he was born on a horse.

"You may want to hold on," Kiegan said over his shoulder, and he waited for her to wrap her arms around his middle, which she did, interlocking her fingers. "Maybe not that tight," he said in a strained voice.

Her cheeks flushed and she loosened her grip.

"Are you ready?"

"Please, let's just go so I can get off."

She heard Kade laugh from behind them as they started trotting toward the fields she'd noticed earlier. A trickle of relief washed over her, despite the mode of transportation, because the river, and more importantly, the trees across the river, were shrinking on the horizon. Whoever the psychopath with the bow and arrow was, they weren't following her—though she still checked over her shoulder every once in a while, just to be sure.

The closer they got to the fields, the taller she realized the crops were. She'd thought they were wheat fields, and maybe a few of them were, but the ones that towered over them, even on horseback, were a plant she didn't have a name for. *Maybe they're magic.*

"So you aren't from Cyanthia?" Kiegan asked, his voice muffled because he was facing forward and her ear was pressed into his back.

"I guess I am. I'm not sure." Ellayne shrugged. "My friend, the one I live with, works in the castle and commutes from our house."

"In the castle? Well, isn't she fancy," Kade snickered. "How do you know this 'friend'? Do you work there too?" he asked, riding Curry up so they were next to each other.

"No." Ellayne's eyelids felt heavy, and the weight of the day's events caused the animosity toward Kade to fizzle out. "And it's none of your business."

He lifted his eyebrows, but backed off.

They traveled along the unpaved road in silence for a bit longer. Though the horses still made Ellayne jumpy, she felt calmed by the constant patter of their hooves against the solid ground. She fought a losing battle to keep her eyes open. Every once in a while she would startle awake when they turned or the horse made an unexpected movement, but her breathing became deeper and she lost track of how long they'd been traveling.

The next time she opened her eyes, the sky was dark and the three moons rose above them.

Chapter Eleven

The town square they entered glowed with lanterns hung on poles along the dirt road, and a few of the houses still had lanterns burning inside, their light spilling through the cracks in the buildings. It was hard to make out in the dark, but the houses seemed to be made of a combination of wooden planks and cobblestone, each bigger than Blanndynne's house, though some not by much. The streets were empty except for a few stragglers, who stared up at the riders as they passed.

Kiegan nodded to a group of people, mostly women, who waved back at him. "Good evening, ladies." The inflections in his voice led Ellayne to believe he was grinning at them.

Ellayne avoided eye contact with everyone they passed. Kade rode up ahead, ignoring the people in the streets.

All the drowsiness Ellayne had felt before evaporated, replaced by the sensation of being somewhere new and foreign. Kiegan must've felt her straighten up, because he glanced over his shoulder at her.

"Welcome to Pingbi," he partially whispered. "Sorry you can't see most of it."

"Not much to look at anyway," Kade said, falling back beside them. When Ellayne looked at him, she saw he was grimacing as they passed by the houses.

Kiegan rolled his eyes and faced forward again, directing Anya toward a house on a corner. Ellayne could see another, much larger, building behind it. A fence wrapped around the property, and she concluded it was a barn or stable.

Her guess was proven right when Kade and Kiegan led the horses to the building in the back, and Kade dismounted.

"I'll help you down." He held up a hand to Ellayne, who hesitated. "Unless you want to try yourself." He raised an eyebrow, wordlessly challenging her to try.

"How do I know you won't let me fall?"

"You'll just have to trust me."

Ellayne bit her lip, but took his hand. She inched her leg around the side of the horse until she slid off the saddle, stumbling back into Kade. His grip on her was once again solid, but he released her within a second of catching her.

Kiegan hopped off Anya and led her into the building where a stall had her name scrawled on it in blocky letters. He patted her and started to take the riding equipment off piece by piece. Curry went into the stall next to Anya's, and they whinnied to their riders, who tossed hay into the feeders on the wall.

Ellayne watched from the other side of the stable, far away from the beasts. She leaned against the wall, trying to focus on anything but the ache in her rear end. The hair on her neck tickled her, and she reached her hand up to move it out of the way, only to leap forward, shrieking when hot breath spread over her skin. She tripped over a bag of oats and fell on her hands and knees, then scrambled away from the wall. Her eyes widened as she flipped around and stared up at yet another horse, which had been nuzzling the back of her head.

Kiegan's head shot up from behind Anya when he heard Ellayne cry out, and there was a hint of a smile in his voice as he checked to see if she was okay. Kade, on the other hand, doubled over in laughter, leaning on Curry to keep himself from collapsing in amusement.

The horse that had tried to chew her head off snorted in a way that made Ellayne think it was sharing in the enjoyment of her humiliation.

"I'm going to wait outside."

Ellayne pushed to her feet and brushed off her knees, wincing. *Embarrassing, absolutely humiliating.* Her cheeks felt hot, and with emotion boiling inside her, she felt like crying—something she had no intention of doing in front of the strangers.

By the time Kade and Kiegan walked out of the stable, the only evidence she'd been crying was her nose, which was still a little pink. However, that could easily be pinned on the dropping temperature.

Kade's ever-present frown was front and center, and his eyes narrowed in on her as soon as he walked out. Ellayne wasn't sure what she'd done to upset him until Kiegan started talking.

"We discussed the sleeping arrangements for tonight. You can stay in Kade's apartment, and he'll stay with me at mine. I have a bit more room, but it comes with a roommate, and Kade lives alone. So we thought—"

"He," Kade interrupted, "he thought."

"I thought," Kiegan corrected, and rolled his eyes, "that you might be more comfortable there."

"No, I wouldn't want to force you out of your own apartment." Ellayne shook her head, though she liked the idea. "There's probably an inn around here, right?"

"Not an open one," Kiegan responded. "Kade doesn't mind, right?" he asked, but received a grunt in return. "It's really no trouble at all."

60

"I mean," Ellayne paused, "I would definitely be more comfortable in a space of my own. But—"

"It's not 'your own,' it's 'my own.' It's my stuff, and you need to keep out of it." Kade crossed his arms and he leaned toward Ellayne. He was a few inches from her, and she could make out a vein that traveled the length of his neck, bulging when he got fired up.

"Seriously? Are you five years old or something?" Her shoulders lifted and she let out a small laugh. "Of course I won't mess with your stuff. What kind of person do you think I am?" She lifted up on her toes, grinning at him with as much positivity as she could muster.

His frown disappeared and he bit his lip. Confusion filled his eyes as he cocked his head to the side. The corner of his mouth twitched, possibly hiding a small grin. He was still staring at her as he shook his head, backing off a few steps.

"Let's go," Kiegan said. "I'm getting cold."

Ellayne still wore his jacket, but he refused to take it back when she offered. They argued for a few seconds as to why the other person should have it, but Kiegan won, claiming she needed it more since the river stole her shoes. It was as if his words reminded her feet that they were freezing, and she shivered.

"I'll follow you two," she said.

"How else would you find my apartment?" Kade retorted, taking off with long strides.

Jerk, Ellayne thought, falling into step beside Kiegan. "Sharing isn't his strong suit, is it?"

He slowed down for her, pointing out parts of the road she'd want to avoid with her bare feet. "Oh, you noticed?"

"It's just a feeling really," she said, her eyes twinkling as she glanced at him sideways. Kiegan's presence, unlike Kade's, settled her in a way that nothing had since she'd first woken up in the tiny house.

"How are you doing?"

Ellayne's laugh came out more as a honk, and it was louder than she meant it to be. Kiegan's eyebrows knitted together as he watched her. "Sorry," she said, choking out the rest of the giggles. "I've just had a long day."

"I guess it was kind of a dumb question." His hands were in his pockets, and he shrugged.

"No," Ellayne said. "No, there's just no easy way to answer that question. It was thoughtful of you to ask. I just—" She sighed, wrapping her arms tighter around herself. "I just don't know how to put into words all the things I'm thinking and feeling."

"Is there any way for me to help?"

Ellayne shook her head. "You and Kade have been kind enough already."

"There's no limit to being kind," he replied, and though she didn't look, she knew he was smiling at her.

Chapter Twelve

Using a small ring with a few rattling keys on it, Kade unlocked the door to a small shop once they caught up to him. There were no windows into the shop, and a small sign above the door gave the only indication as to what the building was. It said *Hand-Drawn Maps*, and was written in handwriting she'd seen before.

"You made the map from earlier," Ellayne said, tracing the letters on the sign with her gaze. It wasn't quite a question as much as a statement.

"No," Kade grunted. He opened the door and a few bells at the top jingled in protest. "I'm *making* the map from earlier."

Ellayne rolled her eyes and stepped in after Kiegan. Kade closed the door behind them. There was a moment of stillness in the darkness. The only sound came from Kade, who made noise as he traveled around the edge of the room. Ellayne stayed completely still, not wanting to bump into something or knock anything over.

Light filled the room as Kade lit a lantern in the corner. It wasn't a large space, though it was bigger than a combination of Blanndynne's and Ellayne's bedrooms by a few feet. An easel leaned against one of the walls, and on it was a half-drawn map. A desk sat in a back corner completely swamped in rolls of parchment. Books all but spilled out of an old, scratched up bookshelf, but nothing captivated Ellayne as much as the wallpaper.

Maps covered every blank space of all four walls, and Phildeterre opened up before her eyes. Pulled by the drawings, Ellayne stepped to the nearest wall as if in a trance. Most of the charts around her showed a closer view of Cyanthia, some emphasizing a view of the streets while others depicted a more natural view of the trees and the types of vegetation growing there.

"Impressive, right?" Kiegan asked. Ellayne had been so consumed by the maps she hadn't even noticed him beside her.

"They're remarkable," Ellayne breathed, following a trail from one bridge all the way to a tiny drawing of a castle on the right side of one of the maps with her finger.

Kade was in the corner of the room riffling through pieces of parchment on a desk. He started talking, and she turned her head to look at him. "They cost more than you can afford, so let me remind you"—he nodded toward her lifted hand—"don't touch anything." He put a rolled-up map on the desk, swung the bag he'd been carrying onto a chair, and nodded toward the back of the room.

Ellayne dropped her hand. With another glance at the castle on the wall, she followed Kade and Kiegan through a curtain at the back of the shop and up a narrow flight of stairs.

The stairs creaked as Ellayne and Kiegan waited for Kade to unlock another door, this one opening up to his apartment above the studio. More maps covered the walls, but not as many as in the shop below. And unlike the maps down in the studio, many maps in his apartment were of a place she hadn't heard of before.

The name was scrawled on different parts of the maps, sometimes a small dot in the middle of the Black Forest, but other times it was written in large lettering at the top of a map. She read the name out loud.

"What's 'the Dark'?" Ellayne asked.

"Not somewhere you'd want to go," Kade said as he placed his keys on a circular table. The room was a combination of his bedroom, kitchen, dining, and living rooms. He'd squished a bed into the opposite corner from the stove, and the table and two chairs were pressed up against another wall for extra seating. At the end of the bed sat a trunk, which Kade opened. It was filled with clothes neatly organized into piles, and he pulled out a clean shirt and some other items, placing them on the bed.

"It's a different realm, so to speak," Kiegan clarified. He sat on one of the chairs across the room.

Ellayne's forehead wrinkled, the words not making sense in her head.

"The Dark is another world. There's no sun, and some of the deadliest creatures you could imagine live there. Only foolish people choose to go there," Kade said, though he wasn't looking at her. He was too busy searching in the trunk for something.

"That's not entirely true," Kiegan said. "When the war on magic first started three generations ago, a lot of people with magic fled to the Dark because it was out of Phildeterre borders. I wouldn't call them fools. They were just trying to find a place where they could escape the persecution they were up against. In the Dark, they could have magic in their veins without worrying if they were going to be arrested and executed."

Ellayne held up her hand. "You just said a lot of things that make no sense."

"Right," he said, shaking his head. "Sorry." Kiegan leaned forward and put his elbows on his knees, running his fingers through his hair. "I'm not even sure what to start with. There's a lot that you probably don't know."

"You could start with magic," she suggested.

"Are you sure you didn't hit your head or something in the river? It's just hard to believe that you don't know about magic. Especially since you said you were from Cyanthia." Kiegan said, tilting his head to the side.

"Well I—"

"There are two kinds of magic," Kade butted in, whipping around to face Ellayne. He closed the trunk and leaned against the wall next to it. "Pure magic is what most people call light magic, and because of the casualties of the war on magic, it's the rarest."

"What war?" Ellayne spoke at the same time as Kiegan.

"Technically there are three kinds of magic," Kiegan said, but Kade shut him down with a single look.

"Pure magic is passed down by bloodlines, and so is the other kind: dark magic. It's also passed down generation to generation, but I've never met someone with dark magic who uses it for good. And—"

"She gets it."

"I don't think she does," Kade scoffed, "because there's no way she could understand the complexities of dark magic unless she's used it or has had it practiced on her."

"How do you know I haven't?" Ellayne said, her voice low. Both sets of eyes landed on her at the same time.

"What did you just say?" Kade asked, stepping forward from the wall.

"I said, how are you so sure I'm not a victim of dark magic?

"I—"

"And wasn't it you who said that this"—she unfolded her arms and pointed to the black scar on her wrist—"was probably from magic?"

"It very well could be."

"How do you know?"

"Because normal scars don't turn black and travel through

66

people's veins. There's a good chance dark magic is involved."

"So you think I did this to myself?"

Kiegan sat up straighter. "Of course he doesn't."

"Maybe I do. Maybe you're trying to take advantage of Kiegan and me."

"Seriously? Is that what you think I'm trying to do?"

"For all I know, yeah." Kade crossed his arms over his chest, sticking his thumbs in his armpits.

Ellayne's stomach heated. "And you know everything?"

"Maybe I do. I definitely know way more than *you*."

"Well if you know so much, why don't you tell me why I woke up in a tiny house in the middle of the Black Forest without an inkling of a memory left in my head. Tell me why every time I search for some indication of who I am, I hit a wall. If you can tell me that, Kade, then maybe I'll believe you know everything."

"I—"

"But here's what I think," she said, cutting Kade off again and succumbing to the surging rise of annoyance. "I think you're being a jerk to someone you don't even know. I think you somehow justify it because you were the one to jump into the river to save me. And I think you're just plain mean."

"Ellayne," Kiegan said, standing up. Ellayne had stepped forward and she and Kade were face-to-face until Kiegan stepped between them.

"No offense, Kiegan," she said, jerking her chin in Kade's direction, "but I'm not finished."

Glancing at Ellayne's defensive stance and at Kade, who was glaring down at her, Kiegan backed off, going back to sit in the chair to watch whatever battle was about to begin.

Kade's face was a stone, except for his nostrils, which flared at her.

"You have no right to treat me like this when I've done nothing to you. I didn't make you jump in the river; you chose to.

I didn't make you bring me here to Pingpi—"

"Pingbi," Kiegan corrected, but neither of them heard.

"You agreed to. I didn't force you to give up your apartment; you could've said no. But you didn't. You have absolutely no reason to speak to me like this. If you want me to leave, fine. Just tell me. Otherwise, back off and stop being so demeaning." Ellayne took a deep breath, feeling her fingers vibrate with energy. She kept her chin raised, matching his narrowed eyes with a glare of her own.

"Kiegan," Kade said, his voice low, "we're leaving."

"In a minute."

"Now."

"I'll meet you down there in a minute." Kiegan lowered his voice and matched his friend's glare. He waited for Kade to leave, which he did, slamming the door on his way out. "Ellayne, why didn't you say you have amnesia?" He turned back to Ellayne, softening his voice.

"Because I don't know you, Kiegan. Why would I willingly tell a stranger something so personal? I shouldn't have said anything, but he riled me up and it just—"

"Came out. I know. But you can trust me."

"I'm sorry, you've been nothing but kind to me. It's just . . ." She sighed. "I can't remember past a week ago." She kept her eyes closed, not wanting to see how he reacted. "I woke up in a house in the forest with a woman who told me who I was. She told me that I suffered from amnesia. I couldn't even remember my own name." Ellayne felt a powerful urge to cry, but she clenched her jaw. *Do not cry in front of him; hold it together.* "That's why I don't know where the necklace or the scar came from. They were both on me when I woke up without my memories. And then some maniac with a bow started chasing me a week later and I have no idea why." She peeked at him when she finished.

"I'm going to help you figure this out." Kiegan stepped toward her, placing a hand on her shoulder. "And when I do, I hope I can get to know you better."

She nodded. "I hope I can get to know me better too."

He chuckled. "Those are for you." He pointed to a small pile of clothes on the bed. "I asked Kade to set them aside when we were at the stable. Figured you might want a change of clothes. There's water in the jug over there, and the toilet is in that room. We'll come back in the morning with breakfast." Kiegan grabbed Kade's keys off the table where he'd tossed them.

"Thank you," she mumbled, watching him leave through the door. *Telling Kade was an accident*, she thought. *But maybe Kiegan might actually help me.* Ellayne sat on the edge of the bed, calming down.

Chapter Thirteen

Ellayne stayed up reading the maps on the wall longer than she'd intended. Kade's attention to detail and the way he drew each little indicator hypnotized her for over an hour; that is, until her heavy eyelids won out. She'd changed into the tunic Kade had left out on the bed, and though it was a little big for her, she imagined it was probably a bit small for him.

After the way he'd treated her, she had half a mind to rifle through his stuff and upturn the apartment. But then she considered Kiegan's kindness and thought better of it. Besides, Kade may not have liked her, but he was allowing her to stay there. *Better than sleeping in the woods where a psychopath with a bow could find me.*

The apartment, along with the studio beneath it, smelled of fresh parchment and the wax used to seal maps in order to waterproof them. But as she crawled under the blanket, the smell of lye from the soap used to clean it overwhelmed her. The mattress was firm, but that didn't stop the exhaustion from lulling her into deep sleep within a matter of minutes.

A scene unfurled in her mind, placing her at the center of a field covered in tall grass. It reached up to her knees, and a light wind lifted her hair off her shoulders. The sky was an expansive sea of blue, brighter in the center where the sun was situated. She turned in a circle, seeing nothing but the same grassy field in every direction. It reminded her of the Level Plains.

The ground began to tremble beneath her, and Ellayne scoured her surroundings for what was causing it, but she couldn't find the source. The tremors grew more intense, and Ellayne struggled to stay upright as the ground bucked. A grinding noise filled her ears, and she pressed her palms against them to keep the screeching from bursting her eardrums. The field in front of her began to sink away, and she saw a giant chasm forming, spreading in her direction. She leapt to the side, tumbling in the grass. The sky changed, but not in any way she'd ever remembered seeing it. On one side of the growing crevice the light blue faded to dark gray, then to pitch-black. However, on the side of the chasm she had leapt to, the sun continued to burn in the middle of the day.

When the shaking began to settle and the grinding of rock against rock ended, Ellayne rose, trembling, to her feet. The mouth of the gorge was at least ten feet across, and she couldn't see where it started or where it ended. Her stomach twisted as she leaned over to try to see the bottom of the chasm, but there was no end in sight.

Too distracted by the split in the earth, she didn't hear anyone behind her. But she felt strong hands push into her back, sending her plunging into the chasm with a scream that failed to leave her lips. As she fell, she looked up to see the ground above her sealing itself back together. And in the second before she was enclosed in the belly of the world, she saw a shadowy figure peering down at her. Then darkness.

The first thing Ellayne sensed when she woke up was that she wasn't alone, and sure enough, when she opened her eyes, Kiegan and Kade stepped into the apartment.

"Sorry," Kiegan said, dumping his jacket on one of the chairs, "did we wake you?" His dimples appeared when he smiled at her.

"Not sure," Ellayne mumbled, rubbing the back of her hand across her face.

Kade opened a small window Ellayne hadn't noticed the night before, and the breeze that filled the room made her shiver. She pulled the blanket up around her waist, sitting cross-legged on the bed.

"Sleep all right?" Kiegan asked.

Ellayne shrugged. "Well enough, I suppose."

"What's that supposed to mean?" Kade raised an eyebrow, sitting near her on the trunk. It was closer than she liked, but he hadn't glared at her yet, so she supposed he might have taken to heart what she'd said the previous night.

"Nightmare," Ellayne muttered as she fidgeted with the blanket in her lap. "Don't want to talk about it."

Kiegan and Kade exchanged looks, and Kade shrugged. "We brought breakfast." He lifted a bag off the ground next to him, and when he pulled out a small bundle wrapped in a tan cloth, the room filled with the smell of yeast and flour.

Ellanye's stomach growled and she grinned. "I think that's the best thing you could've said."

Kiegan chuckled as Kade unwrapped the light brown loaf, ripped off a piece, and handed it to her. The bread was made from a light grain, but Ellayne didn't take time to appreciate the fluffiness as she inhaled that piece and the next two Kade passed her. Kiegan handed her a cup of water from the small kitchen counter.

"We probably should've thought about dinner last night," Kiegan said as he watched her finish a fourth piece of bread.

"Wasn't hungry," Ellayne said, pushing the bite she'd taken into her cheek with her tongue so they had a better chance of understanding her with her mouth full.

"Could've fooled me," Kade said. He sat up straighter. "We should talk about what the plan is for today, besides getting Ellayne a pair of shoes." He turned his head to look at Ellayne. "I want to figure out where that necklace came from and whether it has anything to do with your amnesia."

Ellayne's shoulders slumped and she stared down again, looking at the last little bit of bread in her hands; her appetite disappeared with his words.

"I know a guy who might be able to help. He runs a trade shop on the northwest edge of town, near the Black Forest," Kade added.

"Why not just ask the jeweler here in town?" Kiegan asked, indicating to Ellayne they hadn't discussed it earlier.

"The one next to the butcher?" Kade made a grunt that sort of sounded like a laugh when Kiegan nodded. "The man who runs that shop couldn't tell when I handed him a bunch of fake bracelets I'd found at the market in the Black Forest. I doubt he'd be able to tell a fragment of glass from a diamond."

"You tried to make money off fake jewelry?" Ellayne raised her head and stared straight at Kade, who shrugged.

"That's beside the point. We should go to the shop near the Black Forest. This guy knows real from fake better than anyone else."

"How do you know him?" Ellayne asked.

"Met him when I was mapping out a place. Got him out of some trouble and we've been business partners ever since."

"Business partners?"

"My job has me travel quite often, and my friend is a bit of a collector. When I come across a seemingly rare and interesting item, I bring it to him for a small profit."

"This is the guy you met in—"

"Yes," Kade snapped, cutting Kiegan's question off. "And he's great at what he does."

When Ellayne didn't say anything, Kade exhaled loud enough for them both to hear.

"If we go to him, he might give us some insight into where the necklace came from, which might help us figure out what you've been doing up until a week ago." He watched Kiegan and Ellayne swap glances.

"What if he can't help me?" Ellayne asked. She ran her fingers over the blanket in her lap.

"What if he can?"

Ellayne rubbed her hands from the bridge of her nose to her temples, massaging her eyelids in the process. "Shoes first, magic con man after," she said with a sigh.

"He's not—"

"Shut up."

Chapter Fourteen

Where's Kiegan?" Ellayne asked, stepping out of a pair of leather boots.

Kade nodded toward the front counter. Kiegan leaned over, talking to the woman who'd welcomed them to the store. He had a smirk on his face, and the woman batted her eyes.

The store was mainly for clothing, but the owner had directed Ellayne toward a section near the back that housed a few shelves with shoes on them. It took a while to find her size before she found boots that fit her. *I have no idea how I'm going to pay for these*, she thought as she watched Kiegan.

The woman behind the counter laughed at something Kiegan said, and he grinned at her, shrugging his shoulders playfully. He tilted his head to the side, and the woman leaned forward, whispering something in his ear.

"I don't trust you." Kade's out-of-the-blue statement had her twisting her neck so fast it almost cracked.

"Excuse me?"

"I think you heard me."

"You don't trust me?" Ellayne's eyes widened, but she covered it by narrowing her eyes at him. "Tell me, Mr. Know-it-all, what makes you think I care if you trust me or not?" She kept her voice to a whisper, not wanting to draw the attention of the clerk or Kiegan.

"You care. I can see it in your eyes. You're like Kieg. You want people to like you." He raised an eyebrow. "And I don't."

"You've made that crystal clear, Kade. But you're wrong." She popped her hip out, placing the hand that wasn't holding the boots on her side. "I don't want or need you to like me. I don't even need you to trust me. There's no reason for you to be here right now. Kiegan said he'd help me. No one is telling you to do the same." She stuck her tongue in her cheek. "So tell me this, Kade, why are you here?"

Kade glanced at Kiegan before scowling back at her. "I'm here for Kiegan. And the necklace. You have it for a reason, and I'm guessing it's not a good one. Kiegan and I have been studying the royal family for over five years; that's why he's helping you, if you were wondering. It's not because he cares. And that necklace is why I'm here too. So like it or not, until we find out why you have a necklace that belongs to the royal family, I'm going to be here."

"Well if that's the case"—she ran a finger over her top lip, lifting it into a sneer—"tone down your insufferable attitude, would you?" She stomped toward the front counter before he could respond. *How dare he?* Even though all she wanted to do was sulk, she glued a smile on her face before approaching Kiegan.

"Find a pair?" he asked as she stepped up to the counter next to him.

She raised the boots. "Yes."

"Great." Kiegan winked at her. "You put those on and I'll meet you outside."

"But how do I pay?" *With no money,* she added in her head.

Kiegan waved his hand. "Don't worry about it. I've got it taken care of, don't I?" He turned his wide grin to the woman behind the counter. She bobbed her head.

"All right then." Ellayne smiled at the woman. "Thank you," she said to both of them. "I'll meet you outside." She tapped Kiegan on the shoulder.

"This doesn't seem ominous at all," Ellayne muttered, her face scrunching up. She sat behind Kiegan. They were on horseback again, riding to the merchant Kade had mentioned.

The trees climbed up taller as they entered the outskirts of the Black Forest. It wasn't as dense as the section Blanndynne's house was in, but the height of the trees was still shocking at times. The leaves above them scattered the light from the sun and made indiscriminate patterns on the forest floor. It smelled heavily of damp moss and deteriorating vegetation, which the horses padded over.

"It's a bunch of trees," Kade said in a flat voice from his horse beside them. "How in the world is that 'ominous'?"

The path they were following wasn't much of a path anymore as they wove between the trees. "We're going to a house in the middle of the forest. How could it be anything else? Besides, the last time I was in the Black Forest, someone tried to kill me with a bow. Excuse me for feeling unsafe."

"You're safe with me," Kiegan said, patting one of her arms around his waist with his hand. "What is this guy's name again?" Kiegan asked, ducking as a branch tried to take his eye out.

"Macario."

"Sounds—" Ellayne started, but Kade held up a hand.

"Don't say ominous."

"I was going to say minatory."

"Do I want to know what that means?" Kade looked at her out of the corner of his eye.

"No."

Anya whinnied. Standing in the distance was the shadow of a man between two tree trunks. The figure didn't move as the trio laid eyes on him.

"Now that's ominous," Kiegan whispered as the person started to stride forward.

What if he's the archer? Are we in danger? I should run. Ellayne's chest tightened, and her arms must've too, because Kiegan glanced back at her.

"It's fine, you're fine."

Kade dismounted from Curry. Taking the reins, he walked toward the stranger. The ground crunched beneath his boots, reverberating in the ambience of the forest around them.

Forcing herself to breathe, Ellayne loosened her grip on Kiegan's torso.

"Macario," Kade said with a wide sweep of his arm, "long time no see."

As the man stepped into the fragmented light, his features came into focus, the most notable thing being a large smile stretching all the way across his face. Macario was as tall as Kade, but was about two and a half times heavier, carrying most of the weight around his belly. His tunic opened halfway down his chest, revealing white chest hair that matched his head. Despite his age, he had a full head of hair, which was shaved short on the sides and longer on top.

"Kade Willows," his voice rumbled, and he reached forward to shake Kade's extended hand. "What brings you back to my little shack?"

"Now that, my friend, is a great story." Kade put his hand in his pocket, still holding Curry's reins with the other. "And as you know, any good story deserves a cup of tea. What do you say mate? Care for a listen?"

Macario glanced up at Kiegan and Ellayne, still on Anya. "I suppose this is that friend, Kiegan Greene, you've mentioned several times." He glanced at Kade, who nodded. "But you've never once mentioned such a lovely woman as this."

Ellayne wasn't sure how to react to the compliment; part of her wanted to thank him, but the other part wanted to squirm out of his line of vision. Something about the way he scanned her up and down made her stomach tighten.

"This is Ellayne," Kade said, keeping his eyes on Macario. His voice was thin, his words clipped.

"Well I hope she's part of your story," Macario said, finally peeling his eyes away from Ellayne. "I've left a pot on. Why don't you tie your ponies up and come inside for a bit?"

Kiegan and Ellayne dismounted from Anya and walked through the forest on foot, letting Kade and Macario lead the way.

"He's interesting," Kiegan whispered to Ellayne.

She nodded, not taking her eyes off the man. "Not sure how I feel about him."

"If Kade trusts him, I guess I do too." Kiegan tugged Anya's reins when she started to wander.

Ellayne shrugged. "If he gets me answers, then I'll be happy about it. But I'd appreciate it if he'd keep the staring to a minimum."

"Can't blame the guy," Kiegan said. Realizing what he'd said, he rubbed his hand on the back of his neck. "Sorry, that came out wrong."

Heat burned Ellayne's cheeks, and she looked away. "Can you imagine living in a place like this? Where the sun barely reaches?" *At least Blanndynne's house is in a clearing where the sun shines*, she thought. She didn't like having to squint in the low light.

"Not my first choice in locations," Kiegan said, "but it could be worse."

"How?"

Kiegan's shoulders lifted and dropped. "There could be no sunlight *and* it could be filled with terrifying things that want to kill you."

"You're referring to that dark place, aren't you?"

"It's called the Dark, and yes."

"Have you ever been there?" She cast him a glance through the curtain her hair made.

"No," Kiegan replied, shaking his head, "and I don't want to."

"Kade made it sound pretty awful."

"He would know. He's been there a few times to map it out. He wanted to be the first cartographer to have a cohesive map of the Dark, but he hasn't gone back for a while. I—" Kiegan paused. "Something happened there." He snapped his mouth shut and turned to face her. "You can't let him know I told you. He'll be ticked."

"He seems like a private person."

"He is, and he'll be upset we were talking about him."

"Got it." She nodded. "I won't mention it." *Though if it could make Kade lose the ego . . .* She stopped the thought before it progressed any further.

When Kiegan still looked at her with wide eyes, she placed a hand on his arm. He'd let her use his jacket again that morning, bringing a new one for himself. The one he wore was rough under her touch. Their eyes met in the silence. The sound of a deep belly laugh faded as Macario walked ahead with Kade, and all Ellayne could hear was the wind that lifted her hair from her face.

"We should—"

"Catch up with them," Ellayne finished, removing her hand and placing it in the pocket of the jacket.

"Right."

80

The stillness broke when they resumed walking, making small talk about the scenery around them.

Macario's shop was camouflaged to match the forest around it, made of the same dark wood as the trees. The moss and ivy growing up the sides disguised it even more. Ellayne didn't see it until they were twenty feet away.

"Your friends are slow, Kade," Macario said. He was leaning against the frame of the shop, and Ellayne disliked the way his eyes went straight to her.

Kade had his back to them, but turned around when Macario spoke. "They certainly are. Did you get lost, Kieg?"

"Anya got distracted," Kiegan lied, glancing at Ellayne, who nodded.

"Right." Kade drew out the word and raised an eyebrow when he glanced between the two. "Shall we go inside?"

Chapter Fifteen

here did you get all of this?" Ellayne asked when they entered the shop. Her eyes didn't know where to focus. Piles of items covered multiple tables, some stacks reaching the ceiling. Shelves spread across every wall, some with books, but most were stacked full with items of all sorts and sizes.

"People bring in something for a trade, others just drop their unwanted gems at my doorstep. I get a little bit here, a little there, and over time this place has become the junkyard it is." Macario leaned against a table with a giant jar of what looked to be beetles in it.

Ellayne squirmed, though she wasn't sure if it was because of the bugs or the old man.

"There's a lot here," she said, offering a smile to be polite.

"If you find anything you like, bring it to me, and if you ask nicely, I may even let you have it." He winked at her.

Kiegan cleared his throat, drawing Macario's attention away from Ellayne. *Thank you*, she mouthed to him, and he bobbed his head once.

"It's quite a collection," Kiegan said.

"You could probably name any item and I'd have it somewhere in these piles."

"I don't doubt it."

Ellayne turned her back to them, trying to distract herself with the items in her immediate area. The table nearest her had a small pile of discarded bracelets. As she started looking through them, she noticed different designs; some had large jewels while others were barely as thick as a few strands of hair bound together. A silver bracelet with interlocking bands caught her attention, and as she picked it up, she noticed an inscription carved into one of the thicker bands in a language she didn't understand.

"Quite a lovely bracelet, isn't it?" Macario said from behind her, and she spun around to face him. Apparently, Kiegan hadn't kept his attention very well. He was a short distance from her, and she could smell a mixture of body odor and herbs on him.

"Yes."

He held out his hand, and she handed him the bracelet, but when she tried to return her hand to her side, he caught it. She let out a startled gasp, drawing Kiegan's and Kade's attention. Kiegan moved forward as if he was going to put an end to whatever was going on, but Kade placed a hand on his shoulder, stopping him before he took more than a step.

"It has a bit of a trick, this one," Macario said, unfazed by her resistance to his touch. He slid the bracelet onto Ellayne's wrist, and she froze as he twisted one of the bands. Ellayne's eyes opened wide as one of the bands slithered around her wrist one full time, dancing in between the other bands.

"What did it just do?" Ellayne pulled her hand back, looking down at the bracelet. The inscription started to glow a light red.

"It's a bit of rune magic," Macario answered. "Nothing particularly special, but still a gem." He held his hand back out like before, and Ellayne hesitated before returning her wrist to his outstretched palm. "A few simple twists and—" The inscription flashed green before turning purple.

"What did it just do?" Ellayne's voice echoed from the bracelet, reflecting the same tone she'd used moments earlier.

"Is that me?" she asked, and Macario nodded.

"Captures a few minutes or so of sounds and conversations, which can then be accessed later." He spoke over his own voice coming from the bracelet.

"That's incredible," Kiegan said, stepping closer to them. Kade backed off, smirking from the wall he was leaning on. "How much for it?"

"I'll tell you what," Macario said, glancing from Ellayne to Kiegan. "I'll give it to you free of charge if"—he held up a finger—"this story is as interesting as Kade makes it sound."

"Deal," Kiegan said.

Kade shrugged when Kiegan looked at him. "Works for me."

"All right Kade, let's hear this tale," Macario said, letting Ellayne go once again.

"Well—"

"Have a seat, darling," Macario interrupted, his attention back on Ellayne. She was inspecting the bracelet, but looked up when he spoke to her. Macario nodded toward a chair near her. "I've learned this young man takes a while to tell stories." Macario walked to a counter near the back and picked up a pot of a greenish-brown liquid. Separating it into four cups, he first handed one to Ellayne, Kiegan, and Kade, then finally took one for himself.

"Sorry Kade," he said, sitting down on a stool near the beetles. "Please continue."

"Right, well." Kade took a sip of the tea. "Imagine you were me—"

"Wouldn't that be nice."

Kade didn't hide the grin that snuck up on his face as he kept going. "And you were surveying the land for the map you were working on."

"Hard to imagine, but okay."

Rolling his eyes, Kade continued his story, raising his hand to sweep the imaginary scenery. "And imagine you were near the lower branch of the Cylan River when you thought you heard someone screaming."

"Hey," Macario interrupted again, leaning forward. "Do an old man a favor and stop trying to make me imagine this as if it were me."

"All right." Kade's hand lowered, but with a small shake of his head, he proceeded. "Kiegan and I were at the Cylan River and we heard a scream. I saw someone in the rapids just as they sunk underneath again. Kieg and I rode to the bridge, where I tied a rope to my waist and jumped in."

"Not the smartest thing, but I suppose it's not out of character for you to come to someone's rescue. You came to mine, after all," Macario muttered.

Kade ignored the last comment. "I grabbed her out of the river," Kade said, pointing a finger at Ellayne. "She was shaking and shivering like a wet cat."

Ellayne looked down when Macario stared at her.

"What were you doing in the river? Not the best time for a swim," Macario said.

You don't know me, she thought. However, she bit her tongue and forced a smile on her face.

"As I told them," she said, doing her best to keep her voice even, "I fell in because I was being chased by some nutjob with a bow and arrow. When the psychopath nearly hit my head, I overcorrected and fell into the river. Wasn't intentional."

"Bow and arrow?"

"Bow and arrow," she repeated, asking Kade with her eyes to keep going so Macario would take his attention off her.

"Doesn't stop there," Kade said. "She then decided to take a little joy ride on Kieg's horse after we decided to help her out."

"Help her with what?" Macario glanced between the three, waiting for someone to speak up.

Both Kiegan and Kade nodded at Ellayne, who shifted in the chair. "Well, I—" She wasn't sure how to say what exactly she needed help with. "I needed a place to stay since the person with the bow tracked me down to the house I was living in." She waited for Macario to interrupt her like he had Kade, but he stayed silent. "I wasn't sure where to go, and then Kiegan offered to let me go back to Pingpi with them."

"Pingbi," Kiegan corrected for the second time. "But it's true." He smiled at her, and she returned the favor, tucking a strand of hair behind her ears.

"That's an interesting story, but I was promised a great one."

She'd run out of words to say, but Kade stepped in. "The necklace."

"Necklace?" Macario's voice rose as his posture did. "What's this about a necklace?"

Ellayne took the necklace off, untangling it when it snagged her hair. She passed it to Kiegan, who came to stand next to her, and he passed it to the old trader. Being that much closer to Kiegan relaxed her tense muscles in a way she hadn't expected.

"How did you get this?" Macario asked, examining the necklace up close with his shiny eyes. "This is marked for the royal family."

"Is it real?" Kade asked, leaning closer to Macario.

"Sure is." Macario nodded. "But how did she end up with it?"

"That's what we're trying to figure out," Kiegan said. He and Kade exchanged an extended look. Kiegan shook his head, but Kade didn't listen to the silent command.

"What if it belonged to—" Kade started, but Macario stopped him.

"Don't start all that conspiracy nonsense with me again. It's a figment of your looney imagination, and besides"—he held the necklace back out to Ellayne—"I know who it belongs to."

Ellayne took the necklace, avoiding his hand. "Who?"

"That necklace belonged to the late Queen Evangeline Maudit."

Chapter Sixteen

vangeline Maudit?" Kiegan asked. "Are you serious?" He tossed his arms out to the side, moving one of the lower items in a nearby pile. The odds and ends in the heap began to teeter. Both he and Ellayne lunged for the items to stabilize them before they fell over in an avalanche. "How is that even possible?" he asked after they'd balanced the pile.

"Queen Evangeline should've been buried with it when she died," Kade said, standing up straighter.

Macario nodded. "I'm not arguing with any of that. I'm simply saying that this necklace is real, and it belonged to the late queen." He still sat near the beetles, watching Kiegan steady the pile while Ellayne put a large spoon on the edge of the table. Noticing him staring, Ellayne folded her arms over her chest.

"The question is, how did your pretty little friend here end up with it?" Macario continued, glancing over at Kade.

"Ellayne doesn't know," Kiegan said before Kade could answer. He placed a warm hand on the small of her back, and she released a breath she didn't know she was holding.

Her heart raced, and she remained unsure of how to take the news. *Who is Queen Evangeline?* She was a complete stranger as far as Ellayne knew. Without thinking about it, Ellayne ran her thumb over the crest on the necklace.

"How do you know it was Queen Evangeline's?" Kade asked.

"The inscription on the back."

Ellayne flipped the necklace over and looked at the intricate lines she hadn't been able to decipher before. It still appeared to be a pretty design with no meaning. Kade walked over to Ellayne and leaned in to see the inscription.

"ELS." As soon as he said it, Ellayne was able to find the letters hidden in the design.

"But didn't you say Queen Evangeline's last name was Maudit?" Ellayne asked.

"That was her married name," Macario corrected. "Her maiden name was Shry."

"So the royal line is the Maudit line or the Shry line?"

"Maudit," the older man said, tapping his knees with one hand. "There are many generations of royal Maudits going back for a couple centuries."

"Does that mean the queen came from a different royal line?"

He shook his head. "She didn't come from any royal line. The people loved her, but amongst the other royalty there was a lot more tension. Quite the scandal actually. When they—"

"What does the *L* stand for?" Kiegan interrupted. He leaned over Ellayne's shoulder, peering down at the letters.

"Her middle name," Macario said. "But I can't remember what it is."

Ellayne shook her head. "Why do I have it? And what does it have to do with the person trying to put an arrow through me?"

"I think we'd all like to know the answer to that question." The old man stood up, causing the stool to creak. Macario went to a shelf near the front counter, and after lifting a few flat, round objects, he pulled out a round mirror. "Why don't we take a little peek into the past, hm?"

"But how will we—"

"With magic, of course." Macario held his hand out again, waving his fingers to ask for the necklace back. "We'll look at the past of the necklace."

Ellayne handed it back to him, watching as he cleared off a spot on a table to lay the mirror on. He placed the necklace in the center of the mirror, the chain clinking against the glass surface. Macario pulled a small pen out of his pocket and started to trace a symbol on the edge of the mirror, but no ink came out. Instead, it began to glow with soft, blue light.

"Magic?" Ellayne whispered. "You said he didn't have magic." She looked at Kade, who smirked down at her.

He shook his head. "No, *you* said he was a magic con man, and I was rudely told to shut up before I could correct you. He's not a con man. The magic part was accurate. I told you about pure and dark magic, and this is the third kind that Kiegan mentioned: rune magic."

"The runes are magic, not the person doing them," Macario said, still focused on what he was writing on the mirror. "I have neither pure nor dark magic in these old veins, just a bit of elf blood somewhere on my mother's side. That helps me focus the rune magic."

"Remind me again, what are the three types?" Ellayne asked.

Kiegan answered, "Light or pure magic, dark magic, and rune magic."

Kade crossed his arms over his chest. "Like I said, people are born with light and dark magic, but rune magic is something people study."

"Can anybody do rune magic?"

Macario answered the question, his voice strained as he concentrated on the mirror. "You've got to have some bit of magic in your veins, so if your ancestors were magic beings, meaning they had light or dark magic, or you're from a half-and-half family like me, you probably can do rune magic. Elves are particularly fond of rune magic, but I'm getting off track here. If you take the time to learn it, you can do rune magic." He stood up straighter, tucking the pen back into his pants. "There. It'll take a moment to retrieve the history of the necklace, but we should be able to watch parts of its existence on the mirror."

Kiegan stepped closer, and he motioned for Ellayne and Kade to join him.

"Did you study from someone when you learned?" Kiegan asked.

"Mainly from books," Macario replied. "Albeit banned books, up until the last few years."

"Why were they banned?" Ellayne asked.

Macario raised an eyebrow at her, then looked between Kade and Kiegan. "You're telling me she doesn't know about magic or the war it caused?"

Kade nodded. "She's a bit sheltered. Not big on history. Or culture." He lifted a corner of his mouth and smirked at her.

Ellayne pinched her mouth shut. *I shouldn't have asked that—at least, not here,* she scolded herself.

"Really? Well I suppose nowadays you could ignore magic in Phildeterre. Most of the people are gone anyway." Macario scratched the side of his head. "But I still recommend learning about it. Learning ain't gonna hurt you."

"Of course not," Ellayne said. "That's exactly why I asked. Wouldn't want to be uncultured." She gritted her teeth together with the last few words, narrowing her eyes at Kade. *How dare he make me sound like some sort of brainless fool.* She balled her hands into fists by her sides.

"We've discussed the war on magic in passing, but we didn't go into detail," Kiegan explained, referring to the night before.

"Why don't I try to explain a bit of it?" Macario asked, and he waited for Ellayne to nod before he continued. "About three generations ago, those without magic started a war against those who possessed the gift. Many people were arrested, tried, and executed, and since the purges began in Cyanthia, where most of those with pure magic resided, many pure magic family lines ended. Since Phildeterre is so hard to get out of, what with all the out-of-country transportation laws, people went to the next best place: the Dark. People with magic fled to portals around Phildeterre, but the non-magic side destroyed almost all the portals. The magic folk fled to the Black Forest where the last portal stood, and that's where they fought back. That's the only portal still standing." Macario swallowed hard, his eyes flitting down for a second. "The last portal to the Dark."

"Is it technically another country?" Ellayne asked, picturing the maps in Kade's apartment.

"A different world entirely," Macario said.

"Keep going," Kade said with a grunt.

"People like me, not fully human, also had to escape the persecution, because we were seen as a threat; we can study rune magic. To prevent us from studying runes, the non-magic side raided houses to destroy and confiscate all magic or rune books. Many of those books ended up here at my little shop when magic folk wanted to get them out of their houses, because they were scared of being caught with them. I took the time to read them and that's how I know rune magic."

"You said they used to be banned," Ellayne said. "So they aren't banned anymore? Is the war over?"

Macario frowned again. "Where did you say you were from?"

"I didn't."

"Right." He cocked his head, looking her up and down. "And you don't know what happened five years ago?"

Ellayne glanced over at Kiegan, who stared at the ground. *Thanks for failing to mention any of this on the ride over here,* she thought. She shook her head at Macario.

"Okay." He rubbed his chin with two fingers. "When King Butch and Queen Evangeline were murdered, their son and only heir, Diomedes, became king and ended the war. Magic is slowly coming back to Phildeterre, and we have no reason to fear practicing magic. Well, almost no reason. There are still some extremists on both sides who would prefer the other side were completely eliminated."

"I don't understand that mindset though, never have," Kiegan muttered, crossing his arms. "I have no magic, yet I have no issue living life with those who do."

"Most of those with magic feel the same way about non-magic people. There's no reason to be hateful toward either side, if you ask me," Macario said. "But there are those who think the only way to make up for the war is to take blood for blood. Kill those with no magic just like they killed us."

"That doesn't seem right." Ellayne shifted, goose bumps crawling up her arms.

"That's because it's not," Macario said.

The conversation left her heavy, weighed down with a past she couldn't remember. To her relief, the mirror glowed light blue, spreading from the runes Macario had written.

"History lesson over," the old man said. "Let's have a look to see if we can figure out what that necklace is doing hanging around that neck of yours, shall we?"

Chapter Seventeen

The mirror flashed white and then, to Ellayne's amazement, it showed a clear image of a young man peering at them through the mirror.

"It's perfect," he said, though his voice sounded distorted, almost like he was talking through a long tunnel. "She'll love it, I'm sure."

"Who is that?" Ellayne asked, noticing the way the three men stood up straighter and exchanged looks with each other as soon as the man's image appeared.

"That's the late King Butch," Kade said, "though I don't remember ever seeing him that young."

"She's coming," the king said. "Quick, give it here." It looked like the king picked up the mirror and tucked it into his pants pocket. The mirror was imitating the perspective of the necklace, like the necklace was a person in the room with the king, and they were viewing the scene from its metallic eyes.

The surface of the mirror turned black, and for half a second Ellayne thought it stopped working, until she heard someone with high heels walking closer. Ellayne glanced over her shoulder, expecting to find another person, but there was no such person in the shop with them.

"Your Majesty," a female voice rang out through the mirror.

"Evangeline," the king said. "Please, come sit." The click of high heels got even closer and mixed with King Butch's own footsteps. They stopped and a chair scratched as it slid across the floor.

"Thank you," Evangeline said. "How are you feeling? Healing well I hope?"

Ellayne raised an eyebrow toward Kiegan, who shrugged and nodded toward the mirror. The conversation continued, and he apparently didn't want to miss what was being said.

"Well enough, thank you." The king cleared his throat. "Evangeline, Phildeterre has you to thank for its safety from the sorceress, and I personally have you to thank for my life."

"Butch—"

"Please let me finish, Evie." Rustling noises sounded before he continued. "After Lenora left my son and me, I thought I'd have to go through life alone. But you changed that. I have learned that there's no one I'd rather have fighting by my side than you."

"Butch, I don't come from a royal line."

"The people don't care. They adore you, though not more than I do. Evangeline Lia Shry, would you please marry me and become my queen?"

There was a moment of silence, and someone—probably Evangeline—sniffled. Ellayne looked at Kade only to find him watching her. She wasn't sure how long he had been, but he didn't stop when she noticed him. His eyes continued to bore a hole through her skull until she too nodded at the mirror, asking him to stop.

"I will," Evangeline finally said, and more rustling followed. King Butch took the necklace out of his pocket, and for a moment, the enormous room swam in circles while the necklace twirled around. When it stabilized, Ellayne stepped back from the mirror with a gasp.

"I had it carved with your maiden name, because I know it means a lot to you." King Butch handed the necklace to a young woman—a woman who could've been Ellayne's twin sister.

Kade, Kiegan, and Macario all lifted their heads to stare at her.

"Well that's an interesting development," Macario said, crossing his arms over his chest.

"You look exactly like her," Kiegan breathed, and he shoved his hands into his pockets. He looked down at the mirror and back up at Ellayne.

"Like looking in a mirror." Kade's voice petered off toward the end.

Ellayne reached up to her neck. Finding it bare, she twisted the bracelet around her wrist instead. Her cheeks burned with their eyes on her, and all she could do was look down at the image of the queen.

A light flashed in the mirror and the scene changed. It showed Evangeline's hands. In one she held a lantern, and in the other, a small dagger. From the perspective in the mirror, the necklace must've been around Evangeline's neck. Leaves crunched under her boots and she passed tree after tree, clearly in the Black Forest.

"You're back," an unfamiliar voice crooned from somewhere in the darkness, and Evangeline whipped around, holding the dagger out.

"I am."

A silhouette of a woman appeared a short distance away, flickering in the light from the lantern. "What brings you back here?"

Evangeline lowered the dagger. "I needed a reminder of where I came from—of home."

The mirror flashed white again, and if Ellayne had blinked she would've missed the brief image of a shopfront with a broken "open" sign. The store name said *Barty's Books*, and before the scene changed, Evangeline walked in.

The next flash of light had the mirror in complete darkness again, making the onlookers listen for any indication as to what was going on.

"Are you sure you want to give it away? She'll get her own eventually. She is family after all." King Butch's voice was back, and he sounded nearby.

Evangeline spoke next. "Yes. It seems right to pass it on."

"All right then," King Butch said, a sigh escaping from him. "Let her in." The sound of a door creaking echoed around a large room. The mirror flashed again.

Ellayne stumbled backward, catching herself on a table as the final image came into focus on the mirror, revealing the necklace's last memory. The necklace was no longer around the queen's neck, and instead was across the room from her. The room she was in had a peaked roof and was large enough to hold hundreds of people. However, the person the necklace seemed to focus on was Evangeline, though there was someone standing behind her.

Queen Evangeline had aged since the scene they saw her in last, but that wasn't what made Ellayne scream. The queen lay crumpled on the floor, surrounded by a growing pool of blood coming from a large slash on her neck. No light radiated from her eyes, which were left wide open. A buzzing sound filled the room, and the mirror vibrated. Seconds later, it cracked right down the middle, the shards returning to their natural reflective surface as the spell the runes had on it broke.

"Ellayne." Kiegan went to her side and wrapped an arm around her shoulders. "It's over. That happened five years ago. It's okay."

"There was so much blood," Ellayne said, her voice catching in her throat, and she felt her stomach churning. "So much blood."

"Look at her face. Take her outside," Kade said, "she needs fresh air."

Kiegan didn't argue as he guided Ellayne out the front door. The air was not so fresh as it was moist, clinging to her skin and making her shake more. As soon as they crossed the threshold, Ellayne broke away from Kiegan's arms to bolt to a nearby tree. She heaved and emptied her stomach. The acid and bile burned her throat, but when it was over, she felt her head clear. The image of the late queen dead on the floor still floated in the empty space where her memories should've been, her corpse flickering on the ground everywhere Ellayne looked.

It was like she was trapped in that room with the body, unable to look away from the stain of blood creeping along the floor.

Chapter Eighteen

Ellayne wiped her mouth with the handkerchief Kiegan passed her, then accepted his help to get to her feet. He led her away from the tree she'd retched in front of to another one, where he let her sit down.

"I should've prepared you for that." Kiegan sat down next to her as she pulled her knees up to her chest.

All she could do was nod.

"The court never released the details of the deaths." He leaned his head back against the tree trunk. "I didn't know—"

"I can't talk about this right now," Ellayne said, rubbing her eyes with the palms of her hands. *She was just lying there. Alone.* Ellayne ran her hands to the back of her neck, digging her fingernails into her shoulders. The pain did nothing to draw her mind from the images threatening her over and over again.

"Macario says you can keep the bracelet." Kade's voice made Ellayne look up. He stood in front of them, and beside her, Kiegan rose to his feet.

"Did he say anything else?" Kiegan asked. He offered his hand to Ellayne, and she let him pull her to her feet.

Kade shook his head. "We should go."

"Go where?" Ellayne wrapped her arms around her stomach. It still rumbled—unsteady and unsettled.

"Back to Pingbi." Kade started to turn away, but Ellayne stopped him.

"I forgot my necklace," she said, rubbing her collarbone. Her muscles tensed when she didn't feel the chain.

Kade reached into his pocket and pulled it out. "I grabbed it, but after what we just saw, I think I should hold on to it."

"That belongs to me."

"Oh," Kade raised an eyebrow, "so you're the queen?"

"Well it certainly doesn't belong to you. I don't see *your* long blond hair."

"And I don't see your crown."

Ellayne's lip pulled up on one side. Sneering, she said, "Must've come off with my shoes in the river. Hand it over."

"Or what?"

"Or I'll—"

"Kade." Kiegan stood between them. "Give it to her."

"After what we just saw?"

Kiegan nodded, and after another moment of silence, Kade jerked his hand out, dropping the necklace in Ellayne's outstretched hand. She placed it over her head, enjoying the sense of relief it gave her.

"I'm getting Curry." He turned and stomped off.

"You don't really think you're the queen, do you? How would that be possible? She was dead in the mirror."

Ellayne winced at the mention of the body, all the heat she felt toward Kade dying out with just a few of Kiegan's words. "I don't know what I believe, but I somehow look a lot like her."

"The spitting image, but what does it mean?"

"It means I've got another long list of questions filling my head to the point of a major headache." Rubbing her temple, she

100

fought for focus amidst the pool of questions. *What does the queen have to do with me? Why do I look so much like her? Could I really be* ... She stopped herself, following Kiegan to Anya.

"Ellayne," Kiegan looked back at her from where he sat on Anya, "you haven't said anything since we left Macario's. Are you—"

"Okay?" she finished, spitting out the word. "Far from it, actually."

"We're nearly to Pingbi," Kade said, pulling Curry up so he was riding next to Anya, "then we'll head back to my place to figure out what to do next, and we'll go from there."

The sound of hooves trampling the ground reverberated when no one else spoke. The sun shone past its peak, inching its way toward the horizon. It reached the tree line as they trotted into Pingbi. The town was more alive than the last time they'd arrived, which had been in the dead of the night. People walked in and out of shops, most carrying parcels or bags with the items they'd purchased.

"Hey Greene," a young man called, and Kiegan turned his head toward the voice. "I checked the stable for you earlier, but you must've been out."

"Hi Finn," Kiegan greeted, slowing Anya down. "I've been out all day. Why were you looking for me? Something wrong with Murph?"

"He's limping again," the man said. Finn had sandy blond hair that grew well past his ears. A pair of glasses made his eyes look larger than normal, and freckles danced across the bridge of his nose.

Kiegan tossed a look at Kade, who nodded and dismounted from Curry. The unspoken words didn't take long for Ellayne to understand, and Kiegan returned his focus to Finn. "All right, I'll come take a look." He turned and spoke to Ellayne next. "Sorry, but I have to go check this out. You and Kade can head back to his place and I'll meet you there later."

Ellayne nodded, and took Kade's help getting off Anya, still as ungraceful as before, though she didn't fall backward as hard.

"Was Murph limping this morning?" Kiegan asked, getting down from Anya.

Kade handed Curry's reins to Kiegan and patted his friend on the back. Kiegan walked away with Finn. If Finn responded to Kiegan's question, Ellayne didn't hear it. She was too busy watching the gentle way Kiegan patted Anya on the shoulder.

"If you hadn't noticed," Kade's voice drew Ellayne's attention from the receding silhouettes, "Kieg's got a gift with the beasts."

"I noticed," she said, following Kade as he led the way toward his shop. Just as they were about to turn down one of the smaller streets, a woman crossing in front of them stumbled on a loose stone and dropped her basket of apples.

Instinct kicked in, and Ellayne knelt down to help her pick them up. She had two in one hand and was reaching for another when Kade picked it up before her. *How is it that he acts like a jerk, but comes to the aid of anyone who needs it?* Ellayne raised an eyebrow at him, then picked up one last apple, placing it in the woman's basket.

"Thank you," she said before scurrying off down the road.

"You're welcome," Kade muttered, continuing toward his apartment.

"Kade, stop. I need to say something."

"What? You can't walk and talk at the same time?" He turned to look at her, placing his hands on his hips to mirror her. "Fine."

"Look, I know you don't trust me, but can we please just be civil to each other? I'm tired of—"

"Sure."

102

"Really? Just like that?" Ellayne crossed her arms. *Is he being serious, or . . .*

"Yeah. Can we go now?"

Ellayne shook her head. "No. Why did you agree so quickly?"

He shrugged. "I saw the way you reacted at Macario's. It was all as much a surprise to you as it was to us. Either that, or you're a better liar than I gave you credit for."

"I'm not lying."

"I know. But it doesn't mean I trust you." He nodded toward his building. "I'll try to not be as—"

"Rude?"

"Sure," he rolled his eyes, "if that's what you want to call it."

"If not rude, what would you call it?" She popped her hip out.

"I don't know, but I'll try not to do it as much anymore. Now, can we go?"

His shop had been closed all day. There were a few pieces of parchment tacked onto a board outside the door, which Kade unstuck and brought in with him.

"Letters from your admirers?" Ellayne asked. She closed the door as Kade lit one of the lanterns. He placed the letters on the desk in the corner, chuckling at her question. But as she watched, his face froze and then fell.

"Pass me the knife near you," he said, looking down at a sealed envelope he held in his hand.

Ellayne searched around her for a knife, but she couldn't see what knife he was talking about. "Where?"

He glanced up and pointed toward the wall behind her head. When she turned around, she saw the hilt of a knife sticking out of the woodwork. She wiggled it up and down to get it out, and placed it in Kade's outstretched hand, handle first. His attention was still on the envelope.

"What is—" Her voice got caught as soon as she saw the familiar handwriting.

FOUND YOU AGAIN.

"Ellayne." Kade's voice stayed low. "What is this and why is your name on the envelope?"

Her mouth felt like a desert, and the room spun as she stood still as a statue. "We need to go." She started toward the door, but Kade caught her arm in his hand. "Kade, we have to—"

"Not until you tell me who wrote this."

"Kade—"

"No." He pulled her closer, locking the muscles in his arm so she couldn't move away. His dark eyes stared down at her, but unlike when they first met, he wasn't glaring. He was searching for answers—answers that weren't there.

"I think it's the person who shot arrows at me," Ellayne said, pulling her arm back from his grasp. He let her go and looked down at the letter still crumpled in his other hand. "It's the same handwriting. I don't know how they found me. I'm sorry Kade, I-I don't know what to do."

He took a deep breath and ran his fingers through his hair, a few strands falling above his eyes. "Okay," he said, "here's what's going to happen."

Minutes later, Kade dictated a letter for Ellayne to write for Kiegan while he stuffed a few maps, food, and canteens into two bags. They were up in his apartment, and Ellayne's hand shook as she copied down the words Kade spoke out loud.

"We will meet you there," he said, tucking an extra shirt into his bag.

Ellayne's hand cramped at the pace she was writing, but she shook it out and kept going.

"Sign it K and E, write his name on the back, and then stick it to the front door of my apartment so he can find it."

"How will he get into the shop to get up to your apartment?" Ellayne asked as she wrote the last few letters of Kiegan's name.

"I gave Kieg a key when I first got the place," Kade said, slinging his bag over his shoulder. He held the other bag out to Ellayne. She took it from him and slipped it around her neck so that it rested on her shoulder.

Ellayne stuck the letter to the front door of the apartment, and Kade locked it as she walked down the stairs into the shop.

"You're sure he'll find us? You didn't really give specific directions," she said, recalling the words she'd written down.

"He'll know what I mean by 'the place we became friends.' He wouldn't be my friend if he didn't." He looked at her, watching as she shifted her weight uncomfortably. "Are you ready?"

"Ready as I'll ever be."

Chapter Nineteen

Well we haven't been shot by a mysterious archer, so I suppose that's a good thing," Kade said in response to Ellayne's most recent comment.

"That's the best you've got?" Ellayne pressed. "You're only proving my point further." She breathed heavily, trying to keep up with Kade's long strides, but doing her best to hide it.

Kade shook his head, a small dimple showing near the corner of his mouth. "What do you want from me, Ellayne? So I'm not a rainbow. That doesn't mean everything I say is negative."

Ellayne rolled her eyes. "That's not what I said." She adjusted the strap of the bag so it would stop smacking against her hip every time she took a step. "All I said was that you barely have anything positive to say."

"Well"—he lifted his arms, shrugged, and let them flop back down to his sides—"what do you want me to say?"

"Something positive."

"Like what?"

"I don't know, Kade," she said. "That's why I asked." *Because I'm running for my life from a psychopath with a bow and I need someone to tell me something positive*, she remarked in her mind.

He stayed silent for a moment, and she looked over at him to see his eyebrows furrowed together. Kade opened his mouth, but shut it right after. He repeated the action several times and something about it struck Ellayne as humorous. She snickered.

"You look like a fish out of water," she said when he looked at her with a raised eyebrow.

"What?"

She mimicked him, opening and closing her mouth. Kade shook his head. He was doing the best he could not to grin, but the fake frown eventually vanished, and Kade joined her in laughing.

"Where is this place anyway?" Ellayne asked when she calmed down. The sun had fully set and they were using a lantern to light their way.

"It's near the edge of the Black Forest."

"I realized that when I started seeing these," Ellyane said, nodding toward a tree she was passing.

"Then why'd you ask?"

She scowled at him.

His grin lit up in the glow from the lantern, and she could hear the amusement in his voice. She stayed silent until he continued.

"Kieg and I studied at the same school," he said.

Ellayne tilted her head sideways. "That's great, but what does that have to do with where we're going?"

Kade ignored her. "I kept to myself."

"Not surprising."

"Rude," he snapped, but the dimple in his cheek still showed. "I may be a bit prickly—"

"A bit?"

"But," he emphasized the word as Ellayne covered a giggle with her hand, "I was taught to help others."

Ellayne kept silent, not denying that it was true. *He jumped into the river to help me at the risk of his own life. Macario said Kade helped him. And then there was the woman in the street.* There was no doubt he meant it, what with all the action behind his words.

"No witty comment?" He paused, but continued when she said nothing. "All right then. Most days I would see Kiegan talking with a few of the other students outside school before it started; he was everyone's favorite person. But one morning he was outside alone. I was a little late, so I was going to go straight in, but I saw that he'd been crying—not that he'd want me to tell you that.

"Having been raised the way I was, I forwent going into class and instead asked him what was wrong. He went on about how he'd been given the chance to raise a young horse, but that she'd gotten out of the pasture that morning, and there was no sign of her."

Kade held back a branch for Ellayne, and she thanked him as she walked through. She was imagining Kade and Kiegan as younger boys, trying to picture what they would've looked like. Probably more alike than they did as adults.

"—wasn't very good at it, but I guess that's how you get better."

Ellayne shook her head. "I'm sorry, what weren't you very good at?"

"Cartography," he repeated. "I was interested in it, but hadn't had many opportunities to practice. I was working on my first large-scale map, and if I'm being honest, I wanted an excuse to explore what I was mapping. So I told him I'd help find his horse."

"Anya?"

"Don't ruin my story," he said, pointing his finger in her face and narrowing his eyes, "but yes. It took almost the entire day to find where she'd gone, but we eventually tracked Anya to a place near here, and we became friends after that. He's been like my brother since then. Helped me get over my fear of horses. Kieg's also accompanied me on a lot of my trips for work."

Ellayne grinned. "You"—she jabbed a finger in his direction—"were scared of horses?"

"That's all you got from that? Seriously?"

"I can't believe you were scared of horses."

"You're one to talk, Ms. Jumps-any-time-a-horse-whinnies."

"Maybe I have a good reason for being scared of horses, and I just can't remember it."

"Like what? A horse bit one of your fingers off?" He placed the lantern on the ground and reached toward her, grabbing both wrists before she realized what he was doing. "Nope, you've still got all ten fingers," he said, holding her hands up between them. "So maybe—" His voice cut off when a branch cracked nearby.

The archer's found me, she thought, every muscle tensing to run.

Kade dropped one of her wrists, but slid his other hand down to hers, tugging her through the trees. With the lantern abandoned on the forest floor, Ellayne relied on Kade to see through the darkness, which he did better than she thought he would. Kade navigated over roots and under branches, whispering for her to duck or watch her step as he did.

Ellayne couldn't hear whether or not they were being followed, but as her eyes adjusted to the low light level, she couldn't see anything when she looked back.

"Almost there," Kade whispered, slowing down. "It should be around here somewhere." He dropped her hand, feeling around a tree like all the others. He stuck his hand inside a crack in the bark. Something clicked and a ladder tumbled down from the higher branches.

"There. Up, now," he ordered.

Ellayne tested the ladder first, making sure it would hold her weight. When she looked up, she couldn't see where it ended, but Kade didn't give her time to examine much more before he climbed up behind her.

The ladder twisted with both of them moving on it. Ellayne tried to ignore the jostling. After climbing for a minute, Ellayne reached up, and instead of finding another rung, she reached a wooden plank.

"Where do I go from here?" she asked as she gripped the ladder, not wanting to look down.

"Up and in," Kade replied.

"In where?" Ellayne asked, but she pulled herself up onto the plank. It was a patio of sorts, suspended between two trees. In the center stood a small shack. Ellayne got to her feet, holding up her hands to balance as the wood creaked beneath her. "Is this safe?"

"Of course," Kade grunted as he crested the edge. "Kieg and I made it." He began pulling up the ladder, setting it in a pile on the edge of the patio. Kade attached a small string and hook to the end of it before standing up. He brushed off his trousers and went to the front door, opening it.

Kade had to duck as he went through, but the top of the frame barely brushed Ellayne's head as she followed him. The shack seemed even smaller on the inside, with Kade bending his neck, unable to stand up straight. There was a crate being used as a table with three candles on it. Kade lit one, and the room glowed with a soft orange light, allowing Ellayne to see that, similar to Kade's shop, there were maps on these walls as well. In the corner were a few pillows and a pile of blankets.

"You two built this place?" Ellayne asked, drawn once again to the maps on the walls. They weren't as detailed or elegant as the ones in his shop, and Ellayne guessed it was because these were older maps he'd drawn when he was a young boy.

Kade was placing blankets on the ground, one across the threshold and one against the back wall. The makeshift beds were separated by the crate and the bags they'd placed on the floor. He nodded.

"We found Anya near here drinking water from a stream. We kept coming back, and a few years after we became friends, we brought some wood out here and built this place."

"When was the last time you were here?" she asked, noticing quite a bit of dust on the crate.

"A few years ago," Kade replied, tossing her a pillow, which she caught and hugged to her chest. He ran a hand through his hair. "I got the shop and Kiegan took over the stables. Both of us got too busy to come back."

Ellayne nodded, her chest getting heavy with the weight of his words. *I wonder if I had a best friend like they have each other. Is Blanndynne the closest thing I'll ever have to a friend? I wonder if she's found the house empty, or if the archer's found her. Can he find us here? I wonder if I've ever been in a tree house before now, or if I'll ever have a normal life where I know my past and I'm not being hunted down by some psycho with a bow.* She turned away from him to place the pillow on the blankets toward the back of the tree house.

"What is it?" Kade asked, surprising Ellayne with the softness in his voice. "Something I said upset you, I can tell."

Her hair fell in front of her face as she looked down, and she didn't bother to tuck it behind her ears. "I'm fine."

"No," Kade said, stepping over the bags to stand in front of her. "You don't have to tell me what's upsetting you, but don't lie and say you're fine when you aren't."

She stared at his feet. "It's stupid. It's just—I'm jealous," she muttered, hating the words as they spilled out of her mouth. *Not to mention terrified of being found by the person trying to kill me.*

"Jealous?" Kade tucked his hands into his pockets. "What are you jealous of?"

"It's not important."

"It clearly is."

"Do you always have to argue?"

"Yes. What are you jealous of?"

Ellayne reached up to the necklace, moving it between her thumb and fingers over and over again. "I'm jealous of—" The words caught, and she stopped. "Of your memories." Her shoulders sank and she wrapped her arms around her waist, spinning so she wasn't facing him anymore.

"Ellayne." He placed a hand on her shoulder, turning her around. She wouldn't make eye contact with him on her own, so he lifted her chin up. His gaze bore down on her. "Look at me," he ordered, his voice still quiet, yet commanding. She gave in and peered up at him, which satisfied him enough to keep going. "We are going to figure this out. Someone or something has to know what's going on."

Chapter Twenty

Did you sleep at all?" Ellayne asked Kade, yawning. She hadn't dreamt, and it felt like the moment her head hit the pillow, she was out. Kade, however, was sitting with his back against the wall, staring at a map in his hands. He didn't respond to Ellayne's question. "Kade?"

"What?" He looked over at her. "Did you say something?"

"Yes." She drew out the word, pushing the blankets back. It had been a little cold during the night, but not unbearable. The shack provided quite a bit of protection from the wind outside. "I asked if you slept at all."

Kade shrugged, turning his attention back to the map. "A little." The parchment crinkled in his hands. "Kiegan never showed up, and I'm trying to figure out where he could've gone. If he had the horses, then he should've been here not long after we arrived."

"Maybe he didn't get to your apartment until this morning?" Ellayne offered, sitting cross-legged on the blankets. Her hair was in knots and she did her best to fix it with her fingers. "He could be on his way now."

"I've thought of that," Kade said. "I'm just weighing other options."

"Not a great idea, Mr. Pessimist."

"I didn't ask for your opinion."

There wasn't much light in the tree house, and the candle had gone out in the night. Kade had cracked the door and was using the light from outside to examine the map.

"I'm going to sit on the patio for a while, if that's okay," Ellayne said. She wasn't sure why she was asking him for permission, but he nodded, moving his legs out of the way. She stepped over him and exited the shack. The air was fresher outside, and still held a hint of the chill of the night. Though the leaves that surrounded her provided a lot of shade, it was brighter up near the leafed roof than it was on the forest floor. Ellayne sat down on the edge next to the ladder.

A breeze lifted her hair as she wove it into a long braid. The words Kade had said to her the previous night left her mind whirling. The idea of bringing her troubles into the two men's lives left a bad taste in her mouth, especially with Kiegan not showing up. She thought of the note posted to Kade's door, written in the same handwriting as the one she'd found at Blanndynne's. If the person who wrote that note had found Kiegan—she shuddered.

But then again, the thought that even Kade was determined to help lifted her spirits. She began humming an original tune. She liked the way the notes blended into one another, and she closed her eyes, listening to the sounds of the forest as they accompanied her: the wind rattling the leaves, the birds calling to each other, the sound of hooves trotting over the forest floor.

Ellayne opened her eyes and peered over the edge, making out the shape of a man on a familiar horse with another horse in tow behind them. Kiegan dismounted from Anya and led her to a tree nearby. He tied both Anya's and Curry's reins to a branch before walking toward the tree Ellayne sat in.

"Kade," Ellayne said, backing away from the edge, "he's here." She tapped on the door, and Kade came out.

He placed his hands on his hips around the time the ladder snapped down from the patio. Tension pulled at it, and before long, Kiegan hoisted himself up.

"Did you get lost?" Kade asked, clapping Kiegan on the shoulder as they hugged. "You almost had me worried."

"Did I really?" Kiegan looked from Kade to Ellayne, and she nodded.

"He didn't sleep because his motherly instincts took over."

Kade glared at Ellayne. "Seriously though, Kieg, what took you so long?"

Kiegan nodded toward the house, and Ellayne entered first, followed by the two men. He placed his bag in the pile with Ellayne's and Kade's before sitting on one end of Kade's makeshift bed. Kade sat on the other, and Ellayne plopped down on hers. When they were all comfortable, Kiegan explained what happened.

"The issue with Murphey, that other horse, took a couple hours to sort out because it ended up being a problem with his joint instead of—"

"You don't have to go into detail about the horse," Kade interrupted. "Even if it took you a few hours to fix, you still said you were going to go to my place."

"It was late when I finished, and I figured you'd already headed back to my place, so that's where I went." Kiegan lifted his hands. "Don't be mad, but I didn't check the spare room to see if you were there. I was so exhausted that I went to bed."

"Seriously, mate?"

"I said don't get mad."

"Of course I'm mad," Kade said, and Ellayne saw his jaw tightening. She looked down when he glanced at her, and he jabbed a finger at Kiegan. "Outside. Now."

Ellayne couldn't hear the whispered argument at the bottom of the tree, though she did try. She caught a few words, and none of them made sense without other context, so she gave up and read the maps on the walls. The most detailed one was the innermost part of Cyanthia, and she looked at the way the roads intersected and parted in different directions. The palace was one of the only landmarks besides a few bridges. The castle appeared on the east side of the city, and young Kade had marked it with a simple rectangle and his scrawling handwriting, crude compared to the intricate details on the maps he sold in his shop.

The sight of the castle made Ellayne think of Blanndynne, and guilt replaced her fascination. She'd been so frightened by the rogue archer that leaving a note hadn't even crossed her mind. When her friend eventually returned to the house, she wouldn't know what had happened.

Ellayne knew she needed to return to the tiny house. Blanndynne was the one who had looked after her since the death of her parents, and as far as Ellayne knew, she was the only one who knew anything about her past. *I should tell Kade and Kiegan that I could lose my memories at any moment.* However, for some reason, that wasn't something she was eager to tell either of them.

She jumped when they came back through the door, surprised by how they'd climbed the tree in such a silent manner.

"Sorry, Ellayne," Kiegan said. "I hope you can forgive me."

Ellayne glanced at Kade, who glared at Kiegan. She wanted to ask what had been said, but thought better of it. "Of course, Kiegan. I'm just glad you're all right." She patted his arm, and he caught her hand, covering it with his own.

"Thank you," he murmured, his eyelashes fluttering as he looked down at her.

"Right," Kade muttered. "Now that we have this all"—he waved his hand in the air, motioning to Ellayne and Kiegan— "figured out, I say we decide what our next move is."

Ellayne pulled her hand back, breaking eye contact with Kiegan to stare at the map on the wall. "I have an idea."

Chapter Twenty-One

So, you really think we'll find answers there?" Kiegan asked. The old map of Cyanthia was completely forgotten, replaced by the new one Kade rolled out on the makeshift table.

Ellayne nodded. "We're more likely to find them there than we are here."

"That's true," Kade said. He leaned against the wall beside the crate. "And besides, the necklace is from there."

"So we head for Cyanthia, then?" Kiegan asked.

Ellayne bit her lip as she fidgeted with the chain around her neck. "I'm going to Cyanthia, but don't you two have jobs? I don't—"

"Don't worry about that. Seriously. Stop worrying," Kiegan said, reaching over to place a hand on her arm.

"Saying 'stop worrying' to someone who is worrying is like telling a blind person to read the road signs when they ask for directions," Ellayne said. "It's unhelpful." She glanced down at his touch, making him pull away.

"What he meant to say," Kade interjected before Kiegan could apologize, "is that I run more of a long-term business, which can afford some days off. And there are other people who work with the horses and can cover for him at the stables. There's no need to be concerned with our daily lives. Our focus is on answering the questions behind that necklace."

"And my memory loss," Ellayne added. "And it could be dangerous with the archer and everything."

"You're safer with us than alone." Kiegan's dimple popped out when he smiled at her.

Kade nodded. "I agree. We should go to Cyanthia."

Ellayne stared down at the castle. "If you think you can fend off a psychopath with a deadly weapon, then we'll do it, but at the first sign of a maniac with a bow, you two had better not blame me."

Fifteen minutes later, they were riding toward Cyanthia. The forest whispered around them, the birds quieter on the forest floor than they had been up in the branches. Ellayne gripped Kiegan by the jacket, holding on as Anya navigated the exposed roots. The trees became more and more scattered as they exited the forest, and Ellayne heard water rushing nearby.

"Faster than going by foot, isn't it?" Kiegan said, grinning back at Ellayne as they reached a river.

"I'm glad you got here safely," she said. *And you weren't shot by a bow-wielding psychopath.*

The trees weren't completely gone, but they were few and far between. The river shimmered blue, reflecting the midday sky above it.

"How close to Cyanthia are we?" Ellayne asked Kade. Every time she thought about the castle on the map of the city, her veins vibrated with a spark of something, and she rubbed her arms to make the tingling go away.

"An hour or two of travel by horse to get to the main city near the castle," Kade said, bobbing his head toward the direction they were heading. "We should reach the edge of the city before the sun sets. Technically though, we're already crossing into Cyanthian—"

An arrow zipped by his face. It buzzed past Kiegan and Ellayne too, landing somewhere far behind them. Curry jerked as Kade changed direction, veering left. With a tug of the reins, Kade avoided running Curry into Anya, who reared up. A scream escaped Ellayne's lips as she started to slip off the back of the saddle. Ellayne wrapped her arms around Kiegan's waist even tighter, locking her legs around the horse's midsection by squeezing her thighs together.

"Go!" Kade hollered. He rode Curry away from the river, back toward the Level Plains. Kiegan prodded Anya in the side with the heel of his boot, and she took off in a gallop like Curry. Ellayne didn't release her grip around Kiegan's waist. They bounced up and down as Anya raced beneath them, and though she wasn't as fast as Curry, she didn't struggle either, even with an extra person.

Another arrow shot through the scattered trees, striking a trunk a few feet from where Kade had just been and just ahead of Kiegan and Ellayne.

"Can you tell where the arrows are coming from?" Kiegan asked, and it took a few adrenaline-filled seconds for Ellayne to understand that he was asking her.

The hidden archer let loose another arrow. Ellayne didn't have time to see where it came from because she was too busy crying out in pain as it skimmed across the top part of her back, right below her neck.

"Kade!" Kiegan shouted, his voice cracking.

"We need to get to more cover!" Kade barked back.

Ellayne still gripped Kiegan with her left arm, but with the other she reached back and placed her hand on the wound. Her fingers felt the sticky, warm blood, and she flinched at the sting of her own touch. *How did the archer find me?*

"Hang on, Ellayne," Kiegan said. She tried to tighten her grasp with her left arm, but she was unbalanced. He must've felt her slipping because he let go of the reins with one hand and gripped her arm instead. "I've got you."

She wasn't sure if there were any more arrows shot after the one that hit her. All she could focus on was her heartbeat, which hammered in her chest as well as through the back of her neck, where her hand was clamped firmly.

The sound of the hoofbeats changed for a few moments, a hollow pounding echoed, and Ellayne saw a flash of blue as they crossed a bridge over the river. From the brief glimpse she got of it, the bridge wasn't the same as the one where she'd first met the men, which had been made of a lighter wood. But in her dazed state, she couldn't be sure. It got darker as the branches overhead knitted into a woven rooftop.

Anya breathed heavily, her hooves thundering on the ground behind Curry's. Ellayne felt her body rock back and forth, the only anchor being Kiegan's hand on her arm. Her sight fogged up, and she wasn't sure if it was from tears or light-headedness, both of which had started as soon as the arrow struck her.

"Kiegan," she breathed, "I can't—" She didn't have the words to finish, but he didn't need her to.

"Kade!" Kiegan called. "Slow down."

Curry's gallop transitioned into a canter, and then a trot. Anya followed suit.

"We need to find somewhere to stop for now," Kade said. "Start looking."

The trees were dense, and Kade and Kiegan weaved their horses around them. Light from the sun decreased, and when Ellayne's eyes opened, she had to squint.

"We aren't in Cyanthian territory anymore," Kade said. "We entered the Black Forest Peninsula because I knew the trees would be good cover from the arrows. I—" He saw Ellayne slumped over behind Kiegan. "Ellayne!" He stopped and dismounted from Curry, running over. "Careful," he said as Kiegan pulled Anya to a stop, jostling Ellayne.

Ellayne moaned as Kade slid her off the back of the horse. Wrapping an arm around her waist, he led her to an exposed root.

"I need a lantern," Kade said to Kiegan, who'd finished tying Anya to a branch and was whistling to Curry. Kade pushed Ellayne's braid away from the wound. He told her to lean against the trunk of the tree, her back toward him.

"Here," Kiegan said, and Ellayne saw the area around them light up.

"Hold it here." Kade rustled behind her. "Good. Ellayne, stay still. Understand?"

Her response was another moan. His cold fingers were barely noticeable because she was focused on not wailing as he pulled the ripped jacket and tunic away from her skin. It must've pulled at the cut too, because even the smallest motions sent Ellayne into rasping breaths.

"It's not deep, but it's bleeding. We need to stop—" He paused. "That'll do. Grab a canteen so we can be ready to clean it." Kade pressed something soft against the cut and Ellayne winced, clenching her jaw.

The light changed, fading as Kiegan's footsteps receded and becoming brighter when he came back. Kade worked quickly and quietly, muttering a few commands to Kiegan and reassurances to Ellayne when necessary.

"I've seen worse. Seriously," Kade said when she hissed under her breath at his touch. The moments dragged by, and all she could do was stay as still as possible while he dabbed at the skin around the cut.

"What do we have to use as temporary bandages?" he asked, but there was no response except the rustling of fabric. "I don't think that'll stay on. The cut is at a weird angle," he said.

Kade asked Ellayne to hold the jacket, and it sat in a ball in her lap. The shirt she wore was more torn than what the arrow had done because Kade had needed more room to work. The breeze from the shaded forest puffed its cool breath down her spine. She tried not to shiver.

"It's not bleeding as much anymore," Kiegan pointed out. "Maybe she can just keep the cloth pressed against it until we get to somewhere with bandages. Where's the nearest village?"

"Not sure," Kade responded, his voice and attention distracted by the cut again. "I don't want to risk her losing more blood than she already has."

"I'll be fine," Ellayne mumbled, but neither of them acted like they'd heard her. *What if he finds us again?* "We need to go." Still no response.

"Grab the map with the green border and bring it over here." There was another pause. "You have to unroll it. I've got her blood all over my hands."

Kade muttered under his breath. *What's he saying? Safe haven?* Her attention tottered away, instead focused on the trees in the distance. Besides their sturdy trunks, the only visible object was the wall of blackness that stood behind them, created by the shadows.

As she scanned the line of trees again, something changed. Bright silver eyes watched her from the middle of the featureless dark wall, reflecting in the light of the lantern behind her.

When she blinked, they were gone.

Chapter Twenty-Two

She wasn't sure why she didn't say something about the reflective eyes to Kiegan, or even Kade. Some part of her wasn't sure she'd seen anything, just like the shadowy figure on that first night. *Maybe hallucinating things is part of whatever's wrong with my mind,* she thought. Ellayne told herself she didn't want Kiegan and Kade to be concerned with more than they already were.

"Don't move too quickly," Kiegan said. He supported her arm when she stood up from the root, her body aching from holding still for too long.

"There's a small village that shouldn't be too far away from here." Kade was already untying Curry, having used a wet cloth to wipe his hands as much as he could. He hoisted himself into the saddle. "I'm going to ride ahead to see if I can't get some bandages. Kieg," he looked down at them from where he sat on Curry, "I trust you to start making your way in the same direction I showed you, but take it slow. With any luck, we'll meet up somewhere in the middle when I return from the village."

"Otherwise we'll meet at the village," Kiegan said. "Got it.

Don't push him too hard," he added, nodding toward Curry. "He's had a long day."

"So has she," Kade said, but he tilted his head toward Ellayne instead of Anya. "Keep that in mind." He prodded Curry on the side, leading him off into the darkness.

Ellayne leaned against a tree, holding a piece of cloth against the back of her neck with one hand while the jacket draped over her other arm. Kiegan untied Anya from the branch, and with a little finagling, the two of them managed to get on the horse without causing Ellayne too much pain. The cut still stung, but the initial burst of fire that had originally made her light-headed was gone, leaving a dull ache.

She was beginning to enjoy the silence of the forest when Kiegan interrupted it by speaking.

"The last time I was this far into the Black Forest, I was with Kade doing some research for a map he was constructing for a new client. It was the first and only time I've ever seen magic being used for evil," he said, and Ellayne felt his body give a quiet shake, as though it was trying to rid itself of the memory.

"What do you mean? What did you see?" Ellayne asked, her voice muffled since she was leaning her head on his back.

"Kade and I had been riding for most of the day, and we were trying to find somewhere to stop, but we heard voices shouting in the distance. Kade wanted to make sure everything was all right. Against my better judgement, we went to investigate." He paused, his back muscles expanding as he took a deep breath. "We nearly walked into a full-on fight between a man with dark magic and a woman with pure magic. Thankfully we'd left the horses some distance away, otherwise we definitely would've been heard, or maybe spotted."

Goose bumps raised on Ellayne's skin, and she tightened her grip around Kiegan's waist. His warmth poured into her the closer she got, and with the chills his words gave her, she needed all the heat she could get.

"The only bit of magic I saw the woman do flashed so bright I couldn't watch it directly. But the man's dark magic, it—" He paused. "It leaked out of his fingertips like black smoke. I could hear whispers calling, tempting me to come closer, and I would've, had Kade not grabbed me and shook me out of it. Whatever the spell was the man cast, it drew the woman in against her will. The dark cloud of magic—" He stopped, shaking his head. "I don't know why I'm telling you this. I'm sorry."

Ellayne could feel her head pounding to the beat of her heart, but she needed to know what happened next. "Tell me."

"Are you—"

"No, but say it anyway."

"It killed her," he said, his voice flat. "The smoke entered through her nose. There wasn't anything she could do about it, because his previous spell had paralyzed her. I remember"—his voice cracked—"her eyes were pitch-black. When she collapsed, the dark magic left her body the way it had come and went back to him. He walked off in the opposite direction."

"He just left her lying there?"

Kiegan's silence answered her question.

"Did you two do anything?"

"Kade went to see if he could help as soon as the man left, but she was already gone. He had me stay with her while he rode to the nearest town. Come to mention it, it's probably the one he's going to now. He brought back two people with him, the healer of the village and another man. One was a siren and the other was part fae."

"What are sirens and fae?" One of Ellayne's eyebrows raised.

"Sirens come from the sea, and—"

"Then why was a siren in the middle of the Black Forest?"

"I'm sure he's the one Kade is going to. You can ask him when you meet him." Kiegan readjusted in the saddle. "And as for fae, they're descendants of fairies."

"Can they fly?"

Kiegan shrugged. "I suppose some can. I haven't ever been that close to anyone who was fae, or even part fae."

"Flying would make this go a lot faster."

"Yeah," he snorted, "it would. But I'd choose a horse over flying any day."

"Why? Scared of heights or something?"

"Actually," he rubbed the back of his neck with one hand, "yeah."

Ellayne let out a surprised chuckle. "Sorry, I'm not laughing at you. It's just—" *It seems ridiculous to be scared of heights when things like lunatic archers are out here flinging arrows.* "It's just that you and Kade made a tree house at the top of the forest, and it had to be at least several stories up."

"The tree house was all Kade's idea. I went with it because—"

"He's your best friend."

Kiegan nodded. "He's like my brother."

It seemed Kiegan had said all he'd intended to say, because the journey resumed its normal soundtrack of natural ambiance: branches cracking and wind whistling, birds chittering and insects buzzing.

Ellayne's skin was still covered in goose bumps from Kiegan's story, and she regretted asking to hear the end. She watched the shadows for movement. Despite the desire to wipe it from her memory, her mind tried to imagine the scene Kiegan had described.

Everywhere she looked, she could picture a tall, jet-black figure standing over a crumpled body on the ground. Her mind began to play an even crueler trick on her, and the featureless body on the ground took on an identity—Evangeline Maudit. The late queen's blond hair was soaked in her own crimson blood as it pooled around her. The figure looming over her still had no features, simply a tall shadow.

Even when she closed her eyes, the image followed her.

"Kiegan," she said. Ellayne didn't know what she wanted to say next, just that she needed a distraction.

"Yeah?"

"Tell me more about the end of the war . . . please."

"What about it?"

"Anything."

He tried to turn around to look at her, but he focused instead on not getting knocked in the head by a branch. "Is everything okay?"

"It's fine," she said. "Just curious." The figure loomed in her vision, and she grimaced into Kiegan's back. Her skin tingled, and she shivered, hating how vulnerable she felt on the back of the horse. *Like someone could pull me off without warning.*

He didn't notice. "Well, it ended when King Butch and Queen Evangeline were murdered."

"How did that end the war?"

Kiegan shrugged. "The king's son, Prince Diomedes, became king. He was the first king in three generations who didn't see the destruction of magic as a profitable or beneficial move. King Diomedes removed the ban on magic and even made alliances with some of the leaders from the magic forces northeast of here."

The wind swept across the back of Ellayne's neck and she shivered again, her hand aching from holding the cloth for so long.

Alliances? That sounds dubious, she thought. Once again, her body filled up with energy. The tingling returned, like millions of microscopic ants crawling in her veins.

"How did he change everything so quickly? That seems…"

"Suspicious?" Kiegan finished for her. "Yeah, other people think the same thing. There are different thoughts about it. Some people say he was always on the side of magic. Others say he was forced to end the war by the same forces who had the king and queen killed, and maybe he's still under their thumb today. Those are the two main theories."

"Which one do you believe?"

"Not sure," Kiegan replied, his voice thoughtful as he considered her question.

Ellayne waited for a response, but when she didn't get one, she asked a new question. "What's he like?"

"King Diomedes?" he asked. "Not sure about that either. No one really sees him much, and when he does make a public appearance, he doesn't get close enough to get a good look at. All I really know about him is that he's a bit of a recluse, and that in the attack on the castle that killed the king and queen, he was injured. He lost both his eyes, so he wears a blindfold."

"That's … " She paused, searching for the right word.

"Grotesque?"

"No."

"Horrifying?"

"Harrowing." Her heart went out to the orphan king. *To lose parents I can't remember is sad, but to lose parents I could remember seems entirely worse. I wonder how often he thinks of them.* She couldn't begin to imagine the haunting nightmares King Diomedes had to deal with.

"It's a tragedy," Kiegan said. "What happened to the late king and queen, I mean. I don't remember them all that well since I was raised out in the Level Plains, and I only went into Cyanthia a few times before the war ended. Even with the war though, Cyanthia was a wonderful city. It was full of music and merchants. I remember one entire street full of food stands; the aroma changed depending on what part of the street you stood at."

"That sounds delicious," Ellayne said, trying to picture the streets from the maps she'd seen at Kade's shop.

"It was." She could hear his grin in the breathy way his words came out. "This one time, my parents got upset with me because I left them to go find the roasted turkey legs."

"I'd be mad at you too if you were my child. I'm sure it was crowded."

"You couldn't walk without bumping into someone, but they weren't mad because they lost me. They were mad because I stole my father's coin purse to go buy something they told me I couldn't have."

Ellayne snickered. "That sounds like something Kade would do, not you."

"I had my own little thieving streak. Until I got a real job."

"At the stables?" She felt him nod again. "How old were you when you started working there?"

"Nine or ten."

"That's so young!"

Kiegan shrugged, and she felt his back muscles tighten when he spoke next. "When my family left, the stable owner let me stay there since I already spent so much time with Anya. I worked my way up to where I am today, running the place."

Where did your family go? She couldn't bring herself to ask, and she could feel how the discussion of it made him go rigid, so she changed the subject back to the country and the royal family.

"What was the prince's name?"

"Diomedes."

"What did his father do to deserve being murdered?"

"Compared to his father and grandfather, nothing. But there are a lot of people who resent the Maudit line for all the grief they've caused in the magic community. However, I'm partially convinced that if King Butch hadn't met his end the way he did, he might've ended the war himself one day. He was a great king, but he never got the chance."

"Who attacked the castle?" Ellayne asked. The prickle in her veins intensified to buzzing, and it felt a bit like needles pricking her all over.

"King Diomedes's new officials reported that a group of radical rebels from the magic side of the war infiltrated the castle and committed the crimes."

"Then why did he end the war if the magic folk were the ones to kill his father and mother?" Ellayne asked, and she could hear the clipped way in which she spoke. *Maybe magic is dangerous.*

"Queen Evangeline wasn't his mother, the first queen was. But that's beside the point. And like I said earlier, there are a couple different theories on it."

"What do you think about him? About King Diomedes?"

Kiegan sighed. "That's a good question." He paused for a little while as Anya wandered back and forth through the trees. "On the one hand, I'm glad the war is over, and it's true I have him to thank for that. I've always thought the war was foolishness. Just a way to lose lives." He slumped as he exhaled again. "But Kade and I have a shared suspicion that not everything is what it seems in the castle."

"What do you mean?" Her posture straightened.

"Kade and I seem to remember things differently from most people when it comes to the castle and the royal family."

Ellayne was about to ask another question when she heard the sound of a horse approaching.

"Don't tell Kade that I mentioned our varying thoughts, at least not yet," Kiegan whispered as Curry and Kade rode into view.

Don't worry, you didn't tell me anything anyway. She scrunched up her nose.

Chapter Twenty-Three

He says he'll take a look at you when we get there," Kade said, replacing the cloth with a bandage. He let her hair fall back down over her neck, sending a tickle down her spine.

"This Calder guy, is he human?" Ellayne asked, turning to face him. *Or is he a—*

"Siren, actually." Kade tossed the bloodied cloth into the saddlebag. "Both he and his sister are."

"Oh yeah." Kiegan grinned in the lantern light, handing Ellayne a piece of bread. "I forgot he mentioned a sister." He grabbed a carrot out of his bag and snapped it in half, giving one to each horse. "We met her once, didn't we?"

"Yeah." Kade bobbed his head, but didn't elaborate. "Calder says we can stay with them while we rest and figure out what to do next."

"And you trust him?" Ellayne asked, swallowing the bread with some water from a canteen. "Some guy in the middle of the forest?"

"Short answer?" Kade raised an eyebrow. "Yes. Unless you have a better idea?"

He's challenging me. Ellayne gritted her teeth as she forced a smile. "Just trying to be careful. I have a psychopath after me, remember? You can never be too cautious."

Before long they were entering a small village with a dozen or so buildings, each built either next to or around the trees of the Black Forest. Just like Macario's shop, they were all made out of the dark wood from the trees in the forest. Where lanterns should've hung, instead there were gems that glowed from the writing that covered them, and when Ellayne squinted, she saw it was similar to the style of writing Macario had done on the mirror.

However, the thing Ellayne noticed most was how people stared at them. Unlike when they'd ridden into Pingbi, everyone in this village stopped what they were doing and turned to watch the newcomers pass by.

Every individual wore some sort of dark cloak, most with the hood up and covering their faces. Through the darkness, she made out unnatural features: eyes sparkling vibrant pink, pointy ears peeking through braided hair, scaly skin reflecting light in different directions, and grins revealing extended canines.

Ellayne began to understand that she and her companions were some of the few visitors the village received. She tried not to ogle the villagers, but her eyes kept going to the idiosyncrasies in the people around her.

Up ahead, Kade dismounted from Curry in front of a shop in the middle of the village. A person in a dark teal cloak shook Kade's hand before looking up at Kiegan and Ellayne.

"Hello again." He nodded toward Kiegan and Kade, glancing only once at Ellayne. "You can tie your horses up in the back, and we'll move them into the stable if you end up staying for more than one night. After that, head inside."

He must be around the same age as Kade and Kiegan. Maybe mid to late twenties. Ellayne stared at him. He was about as tall as Kade and Kiegan with broader shoulders. When a female voice came from inside the shop and he turned back to look, Ellayne could see thin, horizontal slits down the side of his neck like the gills of a fish.

"Cal," the female voice said again. "I can't find the bucket and it's leaking again."

The man glanced at Kade and then back at the house. "I'll be inside."

Kade nodded and led Kiegan and Ellayne around the back of the building. There was a trough, and not far off, another horse stood in a pen. Anya and Curry seemed to be having a conversation with it as their owners tied off their reins.

"What is this place?" Ellayne whispered to Kade as she stretched her legs out.

"It's what some magic-bearing people call a safe haven. If you held any ideas of doing ill will to someone with magic, the wards around this village would've deterred you from entering. But since none of us do, we were able to come in," Kade responded.

Oh, so that's what a safe haven is. Ellayne shifted her bag to sit on her hip. *And all of those people in the village must've been brought here or escaped.*

"The people here are—" Ellayne started, but Kade cut her off. She pressed her lips together.

"Magic, in one way or another. Most, if not all, are descended from magical beings. You just met Calder. He owns this healer's shop, and was the one who sold me the bandages. We've met on more than one occasion."

So he and his sister are here for protection? And how in the world do they survive without the sun? I think I'd go mad. Distracted by her thoughts, it took her a second to catch up with Kiegan and Kade, who were heading back around to the front of the shop.

Kade held open the door for Kiegan and Ellayne. The light inside the shop was blinding compared to the darkness of the outside world, and Ellayne squinted while her eyes adjusted. There was no way to tell from the outside how bright it was on the inside because there were no windows, which she saw as she got used to the light level.

"Kade!" A girl appearing quite a few years younger than Kade burst through a curtain that hid a back room. Light violet hair curled down to her shoulders, and she twisted a strand around her finger as she waltzed right up to Kade. "Cal just told me you came back. I wasn't sure if you would or not, but I'm *so* glad you did." She batted her eyes up at him.

"I said I would," Kade said, his face devoid of emotion. He nodded toward Kiegan and Ellayne. "These are my friends I mentioned. This is Ellayne, and I think you've met Kiegan before. Guys, this is Calder's little sister, Dayla."

Ellayne looked her over, noticing the differences first. Her eyes were a striking pale blue, and her hands, which she clasped together in front of her, were covered in iridescent scales. However, despite both Kiegan and Kade mentioning she and her brother were sirens, Ellayne saw no sign of a tail. *What kind of person from the sea doesn't have some sort of tail?*

Dayla was a couple inches shorter than Ellayne, and her face had all the angles Ellayne herself lacked. Most impressive were her cheekbones, which seemed like they could cut glass.

"Right, Kiegan. I remember you," Dayla said, her attention mainly on Kiegan. "I was just getting ready to sing, would you like to come—"

"No, they would not," Calder said from a doorway at the back of the shop. He'd gotten rid of the cloak and stood with his feet firmly planted shoulder width apart, his arms crossed over his chest.

With the distraction Dayla posed, Ellayne hadn't taken in the shop around them. Besides the light, which came from the incandescent writing all over the ceiling, there weren't many items on display. Shelves along one wall held bottles full of colorful liquids, and the opposite wall held a bookshelf with a few books in various conditions. The front counter was made of dark blue sea glass, and in the back of the room near Calder was a desk and on it was a small pot over an open flame in a bowl. The smell of salt mixed with something fishy had assaulted Ellayne's nose when she first walked in, but it had worn off.

"Come on Cal, please?" Something about her singsong voice made Ellayne's hands curl into fists, and she had to force them to loosen up.

As casually as she could, she took a step in front of Kiegan, finding in herself a desire to keep the purple-haired woman away from him. She would've done the same for Kade, but he let Dayla drag him by his hand to the back of the shop with no complaint.

"I'll show you to your room Kade. And you too." She grinned at Kiegan, showing a few pointed teeth.

"All right," Kiegan said, stepping around Ellayne, but Calder held his hand out, stopping Kiegan.

"I'll show you gentlemen to the room you'll be staying in." He grabbed Dayla's wrist and forced her to let go of Kade. "Dayla, show Ellayne to your room."

"Cal—"

"Now."

"You can sleep over there." Dayla pointed to a mattress on the floor of a rather small room. Although, small seemed like the wrong word. *Cramped* was a better way to describe it, because there was so much furniture in it. Besides the mattress on the floor, which turned out to be a few pillows with a blanket over them, there was a full-size bed, a dresser, a full-length mirror, a bookshelf, and a desk. Everything in the room was some shade of blue or green.

"Thank you," Ellayne said.

Dayla shrugged. "I'm going to go make sure the men are finding their accommodations to their liking." Her pale eyes flashed. "You should go talk to my brother. Kade told him you were injured. Knowing Cal, he'll want to take a look at it."

"Where is your brother?"

"Room at the end of the hall," Dayla said, already halfway out the door.

Ellayne stared longingly at the pile of pillows making up the mattress in the corner. Every muscle in her body begged her to lie down and rest for a moment, but she ignored the aches and pains. *Business first, rest later.* She left the room and entered the hallway.

Calder and Dayla's rooms were on the floor directly above the shop. Near Calder's room was a door which led up a narrow staircase to the attic where Kiegan and Kade were staying. Calder's door was shut, but when Ellayne got closer to it, the door opened and the siren walked out.

"Oh, hi. I was just coming to find you. How are you feeling?" he asked, leaning against the doorframe. In the light from the ceiling, which was the same light as down in the shop, Ellayne could see various shades of teal tipped the ends of his short hair.

"Exhausted," she said, offering a small smile. "Dayla said you wanted to see me?"

"Right." He bobbed his head up and down. "Kade said you were injured." He waited for a response.

"Yes." She grabbed her elbows with opposite hands. "On my neck."

"Do you mind if I take a look?" He scratched the back of his neck, then shifted his weight from one foot to the other. "It's just that, well, I'm sort of—"

"A healer," Ellayne said, and he nodded.

"Right, a healer. And I thought, well, maybe you might want . . . but you don't have to . . . I could maybe help?"

Everything he said sounded like a question, and Ellayne couldn't help but widen her smile at his reddening cheeks.

"Of course."

Ellayne let Calder lead her down the stairs to the shop, where he sat her in a chair near the desk at the back of the room. She shivered at his first touch, but relaxed when his warm fingers moved her hair off her neck.

"Your friends did a great job of stopping the bleeding." His fingertips skimmed over the bandages and she winced. "Sorry. I'm going to remove the gauze and clean the injury to prevent it from getting infected. It's not going to feel very good."

"I'll be fi—" Ellayne sucked in air as Calder began pulling at the edges of the bandages. The blood had dried to the padding and pulled at the torn skin. "On second thought, maybe not."

Calder apologized again, but didn't stop. "How long have you been in the Black Forest?"

It was a simple enough question. *How much do I tell him? He seems kind.* Ellayne bit her lip. "We just got in today."

"So you've never been here before?"

"Not that I know of."

"Interesting," he said under his breath.

"What? My answer or my injury?"

"Both." He stepped away and a clang of metal against metal echoed around the room. "How did you say you got injured?"

Ellayne fiddled with the sleeve of her tunic. "I didn't say."

"All right, you don't have to tell me. It would just help with my process to know what caused this." Calder pressed something cold against her neck, and it sent a wave of relief through her.

"Can I ask you a question?"

"Sure."

"What are you and your sister doing in the Black Forest?"

Calder's hand, which had been rubbing a sour-smelling liquid over the injury, froze. "Er, well, um—"

"Sorry, I didn't mean—"

"No, it's just—"

"Really, you don't have to tell me."

"It's a fair enough question." He sighed behind her. "Dayla and I are from up north in the Cyro Coves. It's where we grew up."

I'll have to look for that on one of Kade's maps, Ellayne noted. The skin around where the archer shot her tingled, and whatever Calder put on it filled the room with an acidic aroma.

"Our village, it was, well, it was attacked in a raid. Dayla and I were in school, which was on the outskirts of the cove. I got her out and we escaped onto land. Over the years we came farther inland. We've been here for a little over seven years."

"Is it just the two of you?"

Calder went silent again, and after a rustle of fabric, she heard a sniffle coming from behind her.

"Yeah, it's just the two of us."

They lost people too. Ellayne weighed whether to ask who he'd lost in the raid, but Calder answered the unspoken question.

"My older sister, Mira, and my parents were killed," he spoke in a low voice.

Ellayne turned in the chair and faced him. "I'm sorry Calder. I shouldn't have asked. It wasn't—"

"You're fine." He shrugged, wiping his nose on the back of his hand. "If I came across another siren here, I'd ask what brought them here too."

"Still," Ellayne tilted her head toward the floor, looking up at him through her eyelashes, "I shouldn't have been so nosy. I'm sorry."

He nodded, tossing the old bandage onto a basket of rubbish. "I forgive you." He folded his arms over his chest. "Besides," he shrugged, "it's not so bad here."

"Do you miss the water?"

"There's a watering hole near here where I spend a lot of time when I'm not working. Great place to clear your head." He paused, and his eyes narrowed on the exposed skin of her wrist. "What's that?"

Her instinct was to cover her scar with her right hand, but she held it out for him to see.

"May I?" He asked for permission to examine it, and she nodded.

Calder ran his fingers over the black scar. The veins extended down to her hand and up to her elbow now. *It wasn't like this a few days ago.* Ellayne bit her lip, flickering her gaze from Calder's furrowed eyebrows to the spidery veins traveling up and down her arm.

"Where did you get this?"

"I'm not sure."

"It's spreading." He traced a finger up to the inside of her elbow. "That's rarely a good sign." Calder met her eyes, and then he blinked a few times. "I know I've already asked this, but are you absolutely positive you haven't been here before?"

Ellayne raised her eyebrows. "What? Why?"

He let go of her wrist and walked over to the front desk. Pulling out a piece of parchment, he said, "I can't remember how I got this, but it has very specific instructions of who to show it to. And I'm pretty sure it's for you."

Chapter Twenty-Four

Ellayne's hands shook as she took the paper from Calder. The handwriting was familiar, as was the name on the back. *Ellayne*. She read it over a few times before glancing up at Calder.

"How did you—"

"Like I said, I don't know."

Without saying anything else, Ellayne unfolded the paper.

"Seek behind watery curtains," she read aloud. On the bottom were the instructions Calder mentioned, which told him to only show the letter to a girl named Ellayne with a scar on her left wrist.

"What's this supposed to mean? How did this end up here?" Ellayne asked. *Why is it in my handwriting?* To her memory, she'd only seen her own handwriting once, but when she thought back to the letter she'd written to Kiegan, she couldn't help but think it was similar.

"I'm not sure, but I think you're the right person." Calder washed his hands with a wet rag, tossing it back into a bucket after he finished. He put his hands on his hips. "Where did you get that scar?"

"I'm not sure," Ellayne said, her attention still focused on the letter. *How did I leave a letter to myself? And why?*

"—could show you—"

"What?" She looked up from the parchment. "Sorry, I was distracted."

"Of course." He smiled. "I was just offering to show you the watering hole if you wanted to wash up. You don't have to worry about this. It's probably just some—" He reached to take the parchment back, but she stepped away from him.

"Can I keep it for a little longer? It's..." she searched for the right word—*terrifying, disturbing, frightening*—"intriguing."

"Oh, um, sure. I guess." He pulled his hand back and ran it through his hair.

"But getting clean sounds wonderful," she said, straightening up. "How about I go tell Kiegan and Kade first, and meet you down here?"

"All right," he said with a nod. "I'll wait here."

She slipped past him and climbed one set of stairs, then the steep and narrow staircase to the attic. The door was shut. However, the closer she got to it, the more she could hear a screeching sound, like a fork scraping against glass. Her hand hesitated on the handle, and she decided to knock first.

As soon as the first knock rang out, the screeching sound stopped. Not a few seconds later, Kiegan opened the door with a smile on his face, but the smile didn't reach his eyes, which were droopy.

"I'm sorry, were you sleeping?" Ellayne asked, glancing behind him into the room.

Kade rubbed his eyes with the palms of his hands. Sitting next to him was Dayla. Her posture was slouched, and she leaned back against the headboard of one of the cots while she inspected her nail beds.

"No," Kade replied, standing up. He rubbed the back of his neck, cracking it from one side to the other. With a raised eyebrow, he cast one glance at Dayla, who winked at him. "What's up?"

Kiegan stepped out of the way, letting Kade talk to Ellayne while taking Kade's place on the bed next to Dayla.

"I'm going to go wash up at some nearby watering hole, and I figured I should let you know." She shifted with all three sets of eyes on her. *And Calder gave me a letter addressed to me in my handwriting and I'm freaking out.*

"Do you want one of us to go with you?" Kade asked, nodding back toward Kiegan. "Do you know how to get there?"

"No." Ellayne shook her head. "Calder said he would show me."

Kade raised an eyebrow. "All right, enjoy yourself."

"Thanks," Ellayne mumbled, and she heard the door close behind her as she made her way down the staircase. She stopped in Dayla's room and grabbed a clean, borrowed tunic out of the bag Kade had loaned her. With nimble fingers, she also tucked the letter with her handwriting into the front pouch of the bag. *I'll deal with you later*, she thought as she left the room.

The steps creaked as she walked down them. Calder was pouring a lime-green liquid into tiny vials when she entered the shop from the back. He looked up mid pour and nearly missed the opening in the vial he was filling. Scrambling to readjust his angle, he managed to avoid a spill.

"Well that could've been messy. Are you ready?" He placed the beaker of liquid on the desk, but it was on the edge of a notebook.

"Calder—" Ellayne couldn't get the words out fast enough.

It tipped over.

Calder jumped and scrambled to pick it up. He righted the beaker and mopped up the liquid, then wiped his hands off on a rag. There were a few splotches of green on his shirt, and he used the rag to try to dab them off, but ended up smearing them instead. He rolled his eyes, a dopey grin on his face.

"As I was saying before I made a mess, are you ready?"

Ellayne nodded. "I'm always ready to get clean."

"By the looks of it, I should join you." His eyes flicked down to his ruined shirt, but then his cheeks went pink. "Not that I want to see, I mean, I wouldn't want to intrude. And of course you want to bathe alone. I just, because it spilled—"

She held up her hand, putting an end to his rambling. "Let's go, Calder," she snorted.

The watering hole was much bigger than Ellayne expected, fit with a waterfall backed up against a wall of rock. The water thundered down into a pool at least thirty yards in diameter, and tapered off into a river due to a dam that looked man-made.

"It's not too deep, unless you get too close to the falls. Just be careful where you step because it can be slippery, and there's a pretty powerful undertow," Calder said over the pounding of the water.

"You're going back, right?" Ellayne asked, hoping his answer was yes. She didn't feel comfortable washing in front of him, even though she only planned on partially undressing anyway.

"Yes." His hands went to his hips. "I like to keep an eye on the shop, and my sister."

"Right," Ellayne said. "Thanks again."

"No problem. Think you can find your way back on your own?"

Ellayne nodded.

"All right," he said, "then happy bathing." He turned halfway around, but faced her again, sticking out his finger. "That sounded weird."

She pinched her lips together. "It sure did."

"I'm going to go now."

"I'd appreciate that."

When his figure receded back into the darkness, Ellayne prepared to get into the watering hole. Stones with glowing runes lit the area, and when she peered down into the glassy water, she saw rocks on the bottom of the pool also lit up. With the waterfall churning the water and rippling the surface, it blurred all the light together so the water itself looked like it was glowing.

She took off her shoes and socks, and dipped her big toe in to test the temperature. It was warm. Ellayne wasn't sure how it was possible, but she wasn't going to question it too much. *The stones probably have some sort of heating runes on them.* She grinned. *Maybe there are some good things to magic.*

No one else was around when Ellayne pulled off the jacket first, followed by her tunic. She expected to wince when the skin near the cut on her neck was stretched or jostled, but whatever Calder had put on the injury had made it numb.

"I've got to remember to thank him for that," she muttered aloud as she laid the tattered shirt over a branch alongside her trousers, and placed the clean tunic on top. The breeze hadn't bothered her a few seconds earlier, but now it bit at any exposed skin. She hobbled over the stick-strewn forest floor to the water's edge.

Warm relief spread up her legs and to her torso the deeper into the pool she went. The water enveloped her, causing a sigh to escape her lips. It only went midway up her torso, so she stayed on her knees to keep herself submerged in the warmth the water offered. Holding her breath, she slipped under the surface. The silence that followed relaxed every muscle in her body even further. More importantly, it numbed the buzz in her mind she hadn't even been aware of until that moment. For the few seconds she was under the water, she could hide from the reality of her situation. No memory loss, no archer trying to kill her, no mysterious necklace that once belonged to the late queen of a kingdom she barely knew; there was only the current of water that cradled her ever so gently in its embrace.

She longed to stay in that peace, but her lungs burned for air, so when she couldn't stand it anymore, she stood up. The chaos in her mind returned in the same moment the ambient noise of the waterfall and the Black Forest did. Ellayne didn't go back under, not because she didn't want to, but because there was a nagging thought in the back of her head whispering she wouldn't get the same effect as the first time. So she went about washing her hair, running her fingers through it in the water.

She felt at ease, so much so that she wasn't sure how long she'd been at the watering hole. Not wanting Kiegan or Kade to worry—though she had a sneaking suspicion that with Dayla around, they hadn't thought about her once—she reluctantly wrapped her arms around herself and got out of the water. The air raised goosebumps on every inch of bare skin, and she put on the tunic and pants as fast as she could manage. Even then, her wet hair kept her damp and shivering.

Ellayne had just finished twisting her hair to get the excess water out when something carved into a nearby tree caught her eye. Her name was written in delicate script, and underneath it was one word—waterfall. *The letter*. She stepped closer. *I wrote this, too.* She ran her fingers over the words. They weren't new; in fact, they were a bit faded. With her hand still on the tree, she turned, her eyes traveling up the length of the waterfall. *But why? The note said seek behind watery curtains, so maybe . . .*

From where she stood, a bit of land was visible that went around the right side of the waterfall. She glanced once more at the writing on the tree, and made up her mind.

She put her socks and shoes on first before walking toward the waterfall. An overgrown path led uphill along the cliffside; she wasn't the first person to approach it. However, when she got about ten feet from the wall, the ratty path ended in a huge grove of thistles. There was no way around it, and since she was standing on a ledge almost halfway up the height of the cliff, the only other direction was toward the waterfall itself, which was spitting water at her. The wind mixed with the spray, causing her to shiver even more than she had before.

I don't know why I thought I'd find something, she thought as she turned toward the enormous, never-ending liquid curtain. The light from the pool below lit up the waterfall, and she took a step toward the edge.

The ledge extended near her foot right before her eyes. She leapt back, her eyes widening as the rock that had appeared receded into the side of the overhang. Taking a smaller step forward, Ellayne gasped as once again, a rock path about four feet wide extended out from where she stood. With two more steps, she stood completely on the new path, and every time she took a step forward, the rock extended another few feet in front of her.

Her heart dropped into her stomach when she turned around and the path was gone except for about four feet behind her. She stood on a floating piece of rock over twenty feet in the air. Not only that, she was standing right in front of the thundering waterfall.

The path in front of her turned sharply, and instead of taking her parallel, it prepared to take her straight into the center of the pounding water. With another step forward, Ellayne watched as a split ripped the waterfall in half all the way to the top.

Ellayne stepped forward. Without another glance back, she walked through the waterfall.

Chapter Twenty-Five

The curtain of water closed behind her as soon as she was a few paces in. Not a drop had landed on her when she stepped through. Upon her entrance, a candle on a small, unstable looking table lit by itself, casting a flickering orange light over everything inside.

"Have I been here before?" she mumbled, running her hand along the wall.

The cave itself was about thirty feet by thirty feet, and a bar counter ran along the back wall. Empty bottles, some broken, were scattered over the dusty surface. There were two more dilapidated tables toward the right side of the room with chairs resting upside down on them. Scraps of parchment littered the floor as well as the surface of the table next to her, and when she picked one up off the floor, she froze. The handwriting was all the same, every word written in the same neat hand: hers.

The note she held said, *He's not who you think he is.* She picked up another note on the table, which read, *Ellayne, my name is Ellayne.* Another one only had her name written over and over and over again, each copy becoming sloppier than the one before it.

Ellayne sat down in the chair next to the table, her eyes skimming over the words on the parchment fragments.

Nobody knows me, I don't know me.

The blackness spreads with time.

She didn't want to believe she had been the one who wrote the notes strewn around the cave. Her hand shook as she reached for a pen on the ground. The ink bled onto the page when she tested it on a corner of parchment. The only way to confirm her handwriting was to write her name and compare it to the others. She froze, the pen hovering centimeters from the page. The chills that ran through her body told her not to write her name, but she did it anyway.

Wetness spread over her cheeks.

The curve of the *E* and the loops in each *l* were the same as the ones written many times before. Placing the pen back on the table, she covered her face with her hands and bawled. *The words are all mine. How could I have been here before, yet not remember any of it? What happened to me?* Her shoulders shook. She'd hoped her memory loss wasn't something that had happened before, that maybe Blanndynne had been lying. But the writing in front of her confirmed her friend had spoken the truth.

Not only had she been in the cave once before, but by the looks of the notes, she'd been there many different times. She tried to take a deep breath to calm down, but she hiccupped in the middle and started crying again. The weight of hopelessness bearing down on her washed away the moment of peace under the warm water outside. She wiped her eyes with the sleeve of the jacket, and picked up one of the papers from the bottom of the pile on the table. It was a longer note, and Ellayne rubbed a finger over her bottom lip as she read.

Ellayne, I don't know how far gone you are when you are reading this, but I hope you got here early this time. The sooner we get here, the clearer our heads are. It's me, I mean you. We are cursed. I don't know what curse, and as far as I can remember, which as you know, isn't much, we've never found what curse we are under or who cursed us. But there have to be answers. Don't spend all of your time in this cave; go find out what happened to us and fix this. We have limited time, but I can only hope you found the Pub Under the Falls faster than I did.

From what I've gathered this go-round, the curse wipes our memory and the memory of everyone who we come into contact with. We forget who we are and they do too. I met a man named Calder who has a sister named Dayla in a nearby village. I thought it was the first time I had met him because he didn't seem to know me. He was the one who showed me the waterfall. But when I found this place, I saw that I had written his name a few times before. We've met so many people and we can't remember them, or them us.

Another thing; the scar on your arm, it's a warning. The blacker your arm gets, the less time you have before you get reset. The dark veins have spread well past my shoulder now, and it's moving faster; I only have a few hours before it reaches my heart and I get reset. I've tried to mark the trees around this place so that you can find it better, and I gave a note to the healer, Calder, in case you show up.

I considered trying to find my way back to the house with Blanndynne to leave a note there, but I don't think I could find it. We seem to wake up there every time, like we are anchored there in some way. I'm not sure how she remembers us, but she's mentioned many times in these papers. So many.

If you have more time than me, you need to leave this place in search of answers, but if you don't have time—if you're already forgetting who you are, write down what you know. Anything that comes to mind. I've found so much in these papers. It's all we have. Help me, help us. Fix this.

Ellayne clutched the letter in her hand, her eyes skimming over the words again and again. The word "cursed" stood out to her every time, staring back at her with the malevolence of a person rather than a simple word. As soon as she finished reading it again, she pulled up the sleeve on the jacket and her tunic. The paper was right—the blackness was spreading farther and farther from the scar, and it was nearly to the crease of her elbow. *How long do I have?* Her heart raced faster.

She scanned a few more papers, some written in clearer states of mind than others. She didn't know what she was looking for. Most of the information written in the scraps of parchment was in the longer letter she still held in one hand. There wasn't any way to tell how many times she'd been there, and many of the notes were repetitive.

Out of the corner of her eye, she saw a word that had not been in the letter, one that made her blood run cold. *There is an archer after me, but I can't remember why. I haven't gotten a good look at him, although I suppose it could be a woman. A very tall, menacing woman in a cloak with wicked aim.*

Ellayne flipped the paper over to see if the narrative continued, but it didn't. The mention of the archer reminded her of her companions back in the village. Kade and Kiegan would be helpful in sorting through the information she'd found. *But,* she reached up to rub her necklace with her thumb, *what if this curse hurts them? Or the archer finds them? Maybe I shouldn't.* She stared down at the writing. Hundreds of scraps of parchment covered the table and the floor. *There's so much here.* She sighed. *I need help. I trust Kiegan, even Kade, to sort these notes out.*

Standing up, Ellayne decided to take the longer letter with her for no other reason than to provide some evidence of what she'd found. As she approached the drop-off of the cave near the waterfall, the rock path appeared in front of her. The curtain of water split down the center and she passed under it, looking up at the water magically dispersing around her. When the path curved toward the cliffside, the waterfall closed behind her, covering any sign of the cave behind it.

Her ripped tunic forgotten by the edge of the watering hole, Ellayne ran as fast as she could back in the direction of the village. She had no trouble finding it, and as soon as the lights came into view, she slowed down so she wouldn't seem as out of place as she felt. The door to Calder's shop rang as she opened it. She expected it to be empty like it had been when they first arrived, but there were three customers talking to Calder around the desk. One of the men—there were two—was short and had a wolflike snout that took up a majority of his face, though his eyes were distinctly human. The second man, twice as tall as the other, was scratching one of his two fangs with the edge of his pinky nail. The woman was covered in scales, and when she turned to look at Ellayne, her eyes closed vertically instead of horizontally.

Controlling her facial expressions, Ellayne gave a small smile and nodded toward them. Calder grinned and tilted his head toward the back of the shop. She took his cue to go, and scurried through the door and up the stairs to their living quarters. By the time she got to the top of the stairs that led to the attic, she was out of breath, her heartbeat thudding in her ears. Reaching for the doorknob, she twisted it, realizing too late that she should've knocked.

It was becoming clearer to Ellayne why Calder needed to keep an eye on his sister.

Chapter Twenty-Six

The screeching noise was back, and it was coming from Dayla. The siren sat reclining on the bed, singing a song that to Ellayne sounded like a bird being scrubbed on a washboard with the laundry. But not to her two companions. Kade sat near the end of the bed, his fingers rubbing small circles on Dayla's dainty feet. Kiegan sat at the head of the bed, and he brushed her hair out in long strokes with an emerald comb.

Ellayne's entrance made no difference as Dayla continued to screech her song. Kade and Kiegan both had their eyes closed, and their hands moved to the same repetitive rhythm. Neither of them opened their eyes when Ellayne walked in, and for a moment Ellayne wasn't sure what to do. The tingling sensation under her skin returned, and she gripped her hands into fists, the paper with the letter crumpling as she did so.

Dayla made eye contact with her, and a sly grin pulled at the sides of her mouth as she sang the next note.

"Kiegan?" Ellayne said, her voice shaking a bit. "Kiegan, can you hear me?" She watched for any sign of movement from Kiegan, but there was no reaction.

Dayla shook her head, raising her eyebrow. She stopped singing. "They can't hear you. They only respond to me, because they love me."

"Love you? They hardly know you. What in the world are you talking about?" Ellayne asked, stepping closer to the bed. She called out Kiegan's name again, but even with the awful song finished, Kiegan wouldn't respond.

"They won't listen to you. They wanted desperately to be loved, and I was happy to fulfill that desire. Now they do what I say." Dayla snapped her fingers, and both Kiegan and Kade stopped what they were doing and straightened up where they sat.

Dayla stood up from the bed, and the two men followed her action. She flipped her hair over her shoulder and popped her hip out to the side.

"For example," she continued, "Kiegan, take this." She pulled a small knife with a gem-covered hilt from her belt. Kiegan opened his droopy eyes and stepped forward.

"Kiegan, stop," Ellayne said, her voice cracking.

"Kiegan, love, show Ellayne how much you love me. You'd bleed for me, right?" No sooner had she spoken than Kiegan dragged the blade over the palm of his hand, not wincing at all.

Ellayne drew in a ragged breath. "Stop this. Why are you doing this? Stop!" *She's insane.* Ellayne clutched one hand around her torso.

"Why should I?" She ran a finger down Kiegan's arm, all the way to the palm of his hand, which still faced upward, pooling with blood. "I was given this power, so why shouldn't I use it?"

"Because you're hurting them."

"So?" Dayla shook her finger at Ellayne. "Besides, that's not true. I didn't cut him. Kiegan cut himself, didn't you, darling?"

Kiegan nodded his head, his eyes closed again.

"You told him to!" Ellayne shrieked. "That's not him."

"Of course it is." Dayla let out a shrill laugh. "Why don't we have another demonstration?"

"No."

Dayla grinned. "Kaden, do you love me?" She let out a breathy gasp when he nodded. "Then kiss me."

Kade stepped toward the siren. His arms wrapped around her waist, but as he bent down to obey her, Ellayne felt heat inside her veins.

"Kade, stop." The firmness in her voice surprised Ellayne, and her eyes widened as Kade froze.

It took a second, but his eyes fluttered open, and when he saw what he'd been about to do, he pushed Dayla away and stumbled backward.

"How did I…" he mumbled, falling onto the bed. He rubbed his head with both hands, massaging his temples.

"How did you do that?" Dayla demanded, her glare narrowing on Ellayne. "Never mind," she said, shaking out her hair, "I can fix this." She opened her mouth again, but before she could start singing, Ellayne leapt across the room and rammed her shoulder into the siren's rib cage, tackling her to the ground.

They hit hard, rolling across the floor toward the wall. Dayla ended up on top of Ellayne, pinning her to the ground. In less than a second, the nails at the end of Dayla's fingertips extended, turning into talons. Ellayne had no time to protect her face as Dayla brought her hand down, slashing at Ellayne's skin. Her cheek burned like fire, but she didn't give Dayla a second chance to strike. Ellayne bucked her hips, causing Dayla to topple over. Ellayne squirmed out from under her and stood up, lifting a hand to cup her bleeding face. She blinked back involuntary tears. Dayla was on her feet too, and she charged Ellayne, slamming her against the wall. Ellayne wheezed when Dayla brought her taloned hands up and squeezed her throat. She was shorter than Ellayne, but her grip was steel.

"Enough," Calder's voice boomed from the doorway. "Dayla, enough."

Ellayne coughed, bending over with her hands on her knees as Dayla backed away. The air burned as it went through her bruised throat. "Thank you," she rasped to Calder.

He gripped Dayla by the upper arm. "Fix this." He pointed toward Kiegan.

Dayla made a noise that was like a hiss, but Calder tightened his grip on her arm. "Fine. Kiegan, I release you."

The second she said it, Kiegan dropped the knife and gripped his bleeding palm in a fist, clutching it to his chest. He too stumbled back, landing on the bed next to Kade, who stared at his best friend like he was a stranger.

"Your room," Calder growled at his sister. "Now."

Dayla yanked her arm from Calder's grasp and stomped down the stairs. Her brother's posture loosened and his shoulders slumped once she left. He crossed the floor to Ellayne in a few steps.

"Are you all right?" he asked. He clicked his tongue as he examined the scratches Dayla had left. "Let me try to—"

"What did she do to them?" Ellayne interrupted, pointing to Kade and Kiegan. They looked around like they were lost.

Calder shook his head. "How much do you know about sirens?"

"Nothing really, besides the fact that sirens come from the sea," Ellayne said, looking back up at him.

"A siren's song has the power to bend the mind of any man—or, for male sirens like me, woman—who hears it," Calder said, sounding like he was reading a passage from a book. "Dayla hasn't come of age yet, so she hasn't gained the ability to resist the power singing gives all sirens."

"But you have?" Ellayne asked.

He chuckled, scratching behind his ear. "Yes. I can control the power of the song, and one day Dayla will too. But I think I'll let you sleep up here tonight." He cast a glance at Kade and Kiegan. "They should be back to normal in about ten minutes, but you should keep an eye on them." Calder made quick eye contact with her, then stared down at the floor. "I . . . um, well . . . I'm sorry this happened." He looked up at her through his thick eyelashes. "I should've known she'd sneak up here."

Ellayne wasn't sure how to respond, so she stayed silent.

"This probably doesn't give a good first impression, huh?" he said, sticking his hands in the pockets of his trousers.

First impression? I've met you before. His words reminded her why she'd returned from the cave, and her eyes found the discarded letter on the floor behind him. It wasn't Calder's fault his sister had put Kiegan and Kade in a trance, but she still hesitated to share her findings with him.

"Thank you for letting us stay here," she said, straightening up. "I appreciate your kindness. If you don't mind, I'd like to make sure my friends are all right."

"Of course." He nodded and backed out of the room, inches from stepping on the paper. "I'll leave some medicine and bandages on the steps out here for when you need them. And I'll grab your belongings from Dayla's room."

She said thank you and waited for him to close the door before she picked up the letter. It was crinkled, but other than that it was fine. Ellayne knelt on the floor in front of Kade and Kiegan. Kiegan held his bloody fist to his chest, but since his initial reaction to being released from Dayla's spell, he hadn't shown any signs of pain.

Kade looked down at her, taking in her face. "What happened?" he finally asked, his voice drained of the pride it normally carried. "Last I remember, Dayla came up to tell us something after Calder showed us to this room. Did she—" His eyes widened. "She sang, didn't she?"

Ellayne bit her lip, nodding her head once. "Calder said she can't control herself or something like that. I don't completely understand it."

"What happened to your face?"

She put a hand up to it, smearing blood with the tips of her fingers. "Dayla was going to try to put you in her trance again, so I," Ellayne paused, a grin making her cheek sting, "I may have tackled her."

"You *may* have?" Kade asked, his eyebrows rising in bewilderment. He stared at her for a second, and buried his face in his hands. The ring on his pointer finger reflected in the light. "You're surprising." His hands muffled his words and laughter, but when he sat up and ran a hand through his hair, his smile faded. "Are you all right?"

Ellayne nodded toward Kiegan, who was still staring at the opposite wall. "She had him slice his hand open."

"She what?" Kade turned toward Kiegan and pulled his friend's hand toward him. Kiegan's shirt was stained red in the middle, making it look like he'd been stabbed.

"I'll see if Calder left the bandages on the stairs." Ellayne stood up, placing the piece of parchment on a crate nearby, and opened the door. Sure enough, there was a small box with medical supplies tucked into it sitting next to her messenger bag. She carried the box to the bed and sat on the other side of Kiegan, placing the box behind him so both she and Kade could reach it.

"Why is he still like this? I mean, I know it takes a while for someone's head to clear after being under a siren song, but..." Kade shook his head as he dabbed at Kiegan's hand with a sterilized wipe. "Didn't we come out of her spell at the same time?"

"No."

"What?"

Ellayne handed him a piece of cotton and gauze to wrap around Kiegan's hand. "She told you to—" Ellayne stopped, thinking about what to say next. "She gave you a command, and you didn't listen. You broke the spell yourself. You don't remember?"

"The victim has no memory of being under the spell. And the victim breaking the spell? Yeah, not possible," Kade said. "Sirens' spells can only be broken by the siren who cast them or when the siren dies. Their magic makes the victim fall in love with them in a superficial way, and that's why the victim listens to whatever they command. You can't just break a siren's spell."

"I don't know then. Maybe it's because she's not of age yet." Ellayne shrugged. "All I know is that when I told you to stop, you did. It surprised her, too. She didn't seem to think it was possible for you to break it either."

"You told me to stop?" He raised an eyebrow, pausing mid-wrap to look at her. "Stop what?"

Ellayne avoided his eyes by staring down at the medical supply box. "Stop listening to her, I suppose." He narrowed his eyes at her, but he didn't push any further. She changed the subject. "How did you learn to take care of injuries?" She nodded toward Kiegan's hand.

Kade shrugged. "I've traveled plenty, and some of the places I've been to aren't the safest. I learned as I went."

Kiegan groaned between them.

"What happened?" Kiegan's voice was rough. "And why does my hand feel like someone cut it?"

"Because someone did," Ellayne answered. "You did."

"I-I did what?"

Kade let go of Kiegan's bandaged hand so he could inspect it himself. Standing up, Kade went to kneel in front of Ellayne, surprising her. "Your turn." He grabbed a new cloth and began to dab at Ellayne's cheek.

She barely breathed, but winced every time the cloth caught on a piece of torn skin. Just like when he'd fixed her neck earlier that day, he was gentle with every touch. Ellayne didn't look at him, and instead distracted herself with Kiegan, though that didn't mean it didn't sting.

"Dayla sang a song that put the two of you in a trance, and while you were out of it, she told you to cut your hand with a knife." Ellayne gasped when a liquid Kade put on her cheek burned. *I wish Calder was doing this.* She grimaced at Kade's touch.

"Why did she—"

"Because she's nuts."

"But why—"

"It's not a 'why' kind of question, Kiegan," Ellayne cut him off again. "Her brother said she can't control herself when she sings. While we're here, Calder promised to keep her away."

Kiegan scoffed. "We should leave now, find somewhere else to stay."

Kade placed an adhesive bandage across the gashes on Ellayne's cheek. They were uncomfortable and hindered her ability to move her face, but she didn't complain.

"We can't yet," Ellayne countered. "Not until I show you what I found."

Chapter Twenty-Seven

Why didn't you tell us?" Kiegan asked, pacing the floor.

"I barely know you." Ellayne rubbed her temple. "And besides, I'm telling you now, and I already apologized."

"You should've said something." He rubbed the back of his neck.

"Like what?" Kade asked, sitting on the cot. "Hey guys, I'm going to lose my memory again. Just so you know." He shook his head. "I get why she didn't tell us. There's nothing we could do about it."

"I just—" Kiegan stopped and folded his arms over his chest. "I just thought you trusted us."

Ellayne stood up and crossed the room to him. "I do, Kiegan, but also we only met a few days ago." She looked up into his eyes. "But I trust you. It's why I came back to tell you. I need your help." She glanced at Kade. "Both of your help, to figure out what's going on."

A moment of silence followed as Kiegan stared down at her. *Please,* she begged in her mind, *I need your help.*

"Of course I'll help you." Kiegan placed his warm hand on her arm, pulling her into a hug. Her muscles relaxed, and she sighed.

"Thank you, Kiegan," she said into his chest.

"If you were wondering," Kade's voice was muffled by Kiegan's arms around her, "I'll help too."

"This just looks like a waterfall," Kiegan said over the pounding thunder. He tucked his hands in his jacket pockets. "A nice one, but still. I don't see a cave behind it."

"I don't know why it's not working," Ellayne muttered to herself. She stood in the same place she had when the rock had extended before. However, this time the ledge didn't change.

"Did you do something to make it work last time?" Kade asked, searching the surroundings. "Maybe you accidentally triggered something."

"There's no secret button," Ellayne snapped. "All I did was step close to the edge and it made a path for me."

"What do you mean 'it' made a path?" Kade crossed his arms.

Ellayne cast him a sideways look. "I don't know, magic?"

"Maybe it has to be one person at a time," Kiegan suggested.

"Fine," she said, "you two go stand over there."

The two men stepped back, and their eyes widened as they stared at the area behind her. She heard the terrain shifting, and a grin pulled at the adhesives on her cheek as she stepped backward, not even needing to turn around to know that the ground had formed a path like before.

Taking another few steps backward, she saw the path that connected her to the mainland disappear, and she was once again standing on a floating chunk of rock.

"That is—"

"—incredible," Kiegan finished Kade's statement. "I want to go next." He stepped up to the edge of the cliff, but no rock came out like it had for her. In fact, the closer he got to the edge, the more of her little piece of land disappeared. *What? No, no, no.* She took another step back, convinced she was going to tumble into the dangerous waters below.

"Kiegan," Kade barked, noticing before his friend did. Kade pulled him back by the jacket, and Ellayne's piece of land reappeared.

"Maybe I should get farther away," she said, moving more toward the center of the waterfall. "Now try, but maybe a bit slower this time."

"Are you sure?" Kade asked, his eyes covering the distance from her to the swirling, wet vortex below.

She nodded. "Slowly."

Kade stepped forward this time instead of Kiegan, and with his eyes locked on her platform, he shuffled toward the edge. No path appeared; however, Ellayne's section of rock didn't disappear like seconds earlier.

"Why isn't it working?" Ellayne crossed her arms over her chest and huffed.

"It is working," Kiegan said, stepping up next to Kade when he saw Ellayne was safe in the middle of the air. "It's just not working for us."

"But why?" she asked.

Kade mimicked her, crossing his arms over his chest. He stared down, but she couldn't tell if he was looking at the ledge or the water below it. "I'm not sure. But that letter you showed us called it the Pub Under the Falls. We might be able to look into that in some books somewhere."

"What do we do now though? You two don't seem able to come through the waterfall, but all of my past notes are in there."

"Bring them out to us like you did the first one, and we might be able to make some sense of it," Kade responded, and Kiegan nodded next to him.

"We'll wait here."

Ellayne turned to the waterfall, which split in half. She passed through, and like before, it closed behind her.

Several hours later, Ellayne struggled to keep her eyes focused on her handwriting. Kade had already gone to sleep on a cot in the attic, and Kiegan was close to drooling on one of the pieces of parchment where he sat on his cot. Ellayne lay on her stomach on the floor, piles of handwritten letters displayed in an arch around her. When she hadn't been exhausted, she'd placed the notes in piles with key terms; "curse," "scar," "archer," and quite a few names that repeated, including their hosts, Calder and Dayla.

But as time wore on, Ellayne found it increasingly difficult to focus on the words. She twisted the bracelet she'd gotten at Macario's around and around her wrist, then switched to fiddling with the necklace again. After what seemed like the longest day of her life, Ellayne cradled her face in the crook of her elbow and fell asleep on the floor.

She wasn't aware she was dreaming because it was pitch-black in the dream, similar to the nothingness of dreamless sleep. But the fact she was aware of the darkness helped her to understand her dream state. There was nothing to see, but she could hear the clicking of footsteps echo in a hallway near her. She could smell a woman's perfume, light and airy as flowers in spring. A young girl's laughter echoed down the same hallway, followed by the low rumble of a man's chuckle and a woman's soft giggles.

Ellayne wasn't sure where the hallway was, but she wanted to be with those people who were laughing, not in the pitch-black room. It was lonely in there, and as she wandered around in the dark, she found the room was quite small. A few paces carried her from one wall to the other. It was a box, one she was locked in with no door and no way out. Her fist ached as she banged on the wall, but no sound came from the action. When she tried to call to the laughing voices, no voice came from her mouth.

All she could do was listen to the voices as they continued to laugh without her. After a while, the sound of more footsteps marching down the hallway covered up the laughter. The organized group passed by whatever room she was in. A shrill scream cut through every other sound, but it ended, forced to finish before it completed. The smell of flowers altered too, twisting into the sharp notes of copper—heavy and overpowering. Another shout erupted, but was once again cut short.

The footsteps resumed. This time they marched in her direction, and when she thought they couldn't get any louder, they stopped. With the clink of a key in a lock, a door appeared and the room filled with so much light that Ellayne had to close her eyes. But before she did, she saw the silhouette of a man and two other figures behind him.

An arm reached out and grabbed her wrist. She screamed.

Chapter Twenty-Eight

Ellayne," Kiegan's voice shushed her, "calm down. It's just me." He let go of her wrist and backed away on his knees.

"What were you thinking?" she spat at him, scrambling to her knees.

"Well I wasn't expecting you to freak out." He rubbed his temple with his injured hand. "That's for sure."

She tucked her hair behind her ears. "What else were you expecting by waking up someone in the middle of a nightmare?"

His eyes softened. "You were having a nightmare?"

"That wasn't completely evident?" Ellayne's cheeks felt warm, and she looked down at her hands. "How loud was I?"

"Kade's still out," Kiegan nodded toward the shape of Kade in the cot against the wall, "so not loud enough."

Leaning against the wall, Ellayne swung her feet out so they were in front. Kiegan crawled over and sat next to her.

"Sorry."

"I wasn't looking for an apology," he said, fidgeting with the bandage on his hand. "I wanted to make sure you were okay."

"I can't remember a time when I was okay."

"That's depressing."

"You're telling me," she sighed, leaning her head back against the wall. She closed her eyes. "These nightmares are going to kill me."

Kiegan nodded. "I'm still here if you want to talk about them."

Ellayne's chest puffed out as she sighed, and she leaned her head on his shoulder. "Thank you, but I really don't want to relive it. It was bad enough the first time."

They sat still for a while listening to the way the wood in the building creaked. *I wonder if I've been up in this attic before.* The thought made her chest tighten. She looked up at the small window between the two cots. It was pitch-black, which wasn't a surprise since the window faced the woods instead of the village.

"Kiegan?"

"Hm?" He turned his head to look down at her.

"Can I ask you a question?"

"Sure."

"You don't have to answer it if you don't want to, but," she paused, "are there any memories you wish you could forget?" His shoulder became a rock under her cheek.

"Why are you asking?" He leaned away from her and furrowed his eyebrows. A wrinkle formed between them.

"Well, I—" She stared down at her hands. "I just need a distraction, and I guess I thought—"

"Everyone has memories they wish they could forget."

Ellayne shook her head. "I don't."

"Right, well, I do." He sighed. "But I'm not sure I want to say it."

"Then don't. I shouldn't have asked." Ellayne moved to stand up, but he caught her wrist, pulling her back to him.

"But if it's important to you, then I'll tell you." His eyes softened as he nodded to her. Kiegan let out a big sigh. "The truth is . . ." He rubbed his eyes with his fingers, pinching his nose at the bridge. "The truth is, my family left me in Pingbi."

"Left you? As in abandoned?"

He let out a long, low breath. "Yes. I came home from the stable one day, and both my parents and two younger siblings were gone. Packed bags and empty house. I found a note." He held his arm out.

Ellayne hadn't paid attention to the thick leather cuff around his wrist until he undid the clasp, sliding it off. Inside the bracelet was a tiny pocket, from which he pulled a piece of parchment. The yellowed edges crinkled in her hands when he gave it to her to unfold.

"Do you want me to read it out loud?" she asked, staring down at the faded ink.

He shook his head. "I know what it says."

Ellayne watched him, biting the corner of her lip. "Are you sure you want me to read this? I don't have to if you—"

"Go on." He gestured to the paper. "I'll wait."

Kiegan, you were never ours to begin with. We are taking our family to start a new life. We suggest you start your own too. It went on to explain what they'd left him, which wasn't much.

"Kiegan, I'm so—"

"Don't." He took the note, slipping it back into the cuff. "I don't need sympathy. This happened years ago. I'm fine. I did what they suggested, and I'm happy."

"What did they mean by you weren't theirs?" Ellayne asked, watching him fasten the cuff around his wrist again.

"I was adopted and never knew it until then." He rubbed his thumb along the inside of his hand. "And it doesn't matter. The stable manager took me in, and I couldn't have had a better upbringing. I don't need to know where they went. They chose a

168

new life without me, and I don't need to keep them in mine by thinking about them."

Ellayne placed a hand on his arm, and he met her gaze. "Thank you for telling me."

Kiegan shrugged and put on a forced smile. He placed his hand on top of hers.

"You've shared with me, even if it was delayed."

"I'm sorry."

Kiegan patted her hand. "You've already apologized. I've forgiven you, and now I have a question for you." He leaned against the wall, and she curled up to him again.

"All right."

"Are you scared?"

"Of what?" she asked.

"Scared of losing your memories again?"

"Oh, that." She bit the skin on her lower lip. "Scared, maybe. But I'm more anxious than anything. It's awful that I have to forget, but now I know this curse affects other people's memories; that somehow seems worse."

She could feel his steady breathing, but he was silent for a while. For a moment, she wondered if he'd fallen asleep, but he spoke again.

"You're strong, Ellayne. I admire that about you." He angled his head, and she could feel him looking down at her.

"I wish you were right, Kiegan. I really do," she said, but it came out as a yawn. "I'm not strong. Just desperate for answers."

"Whatever it is," he said, pausing to yawn, "I think it makes you wonderful."

His words hung in the air until he was asleep, his head leaning on hers. Ellayne, however, kept playing the last sentence he said over and over in her head with a smile on her lips.

Kade was up before the two of them, and he glanced over the paper he was reading. "Morning you two." He raised an eyebrow at Kiegan. "Sleep well?"

Kiegan pushed himself up so he wasn't slouching, and Ellayne groaned as she stretched her neck. Whatever Calder had put on it the day before made the injury heal faster than she thought possible, but it still ached when she sat up.

"If I'd known the floor was so comfortable, I would've joined you down there." Kade looked back down at the paper. "But by your moaning, I'd say I made the better decision to sleep on a mattress."

"Find anything yet?" Kiegan asked, using the wall to stand up. He gingerly stepped over Ellayne's piles of parchment on the floor.

Kade shook his head. "Not much in the way of new stuff, but I did find this one." He held up the paper he was currently reading. "It talks about the necklace."

"I have a few of those over here," Ellayne said, nodding to one of the piles, "but they only say what we already know. Less even, because I don't know if I've ever confirmed that the necklace belonged to the late queen."

"It wasn't the paper that told me something," Kade said, placing it on the floor, "it was something I remembered from our time at Macario's."

Ellayne twisted the bracelet around her wrist. "What did you remember?"

"When he placed the necklace on the mirror, we all saw the king give it to the queen, but do you remember the next thing it showed us?"

Kiegan nodded. "The queen wanted to give it away, and then she died."

The way he said it was so nonchalant. *She was murdered. She didn't die of natural causes.* Ellayne's stomach squirmed, but she nodded in agreement.

"You're right, kind of," Kade said. "She came to the Black Forest first, remember?" He motioned for them to come over to his cot, and when Ellayne did, she saw a map of the Black Forest rolled out. "There was a bookstore in the memory, and I don't remember the name of it, but I recognized that it was in the Black Forest."

He pointed down to the map, and Ellayne followed his finger around to several different points.

"What are those?" she asked.

"They're all the bookshops in the Black Forest, and I bet one of them is the one from the necklace's memory."

"Right, because necklaces apparently have some sort of awareness," Kiegan said under his breath, but he grinned at Kade when his friend glared at him. "That's a lot of ground to cover."

"And I'm not sure how much time I have before I lose my memory again." Ellayne rubbed her hand over the scar under her tunic sleeve.

Kade nodded. "I know, so I've narrowed it down to these three." He pointed to three located in the main forest farther north. "From what Kiegan and I have studied, the late queen was probably from somewhere in this area, so it's more likely that she was returning to one of these places."

"Why should we go to that bookstore anyway? What do you expect to find there that we can't find at any other bookstore? Or even in Cyanthia?" Ellayne pushed.

Kade shrugged. "I think the necklace only showed important moments. Think about it; it showed the king giving it to the future queen, then her returning home, passing it on, and then the late queen's death. Why would it show the bookstore unless it was an important part of its history?"

"Maybe it was trying to tell us to read more," Kiegan muttered.

"Or maybe we might learn something by going to that bookstore," Kade said, tapping on the map.

"Maybe," Ellayne said, rolling the necklace between her thumb and pointer finger.

Kiegan watched her, but his eyes were unfocused, like he was staring right through her. "How long will it take us to get there?" he asked.

"Barring any more interference from our mystery archer, we can reach the first one in a few hours."

Ellayne felt the urge to shrink back when they turned to her. "Okay," she mumbled, "but I want to put all these papers back in the cave in case we don't figure this out in time, and I want some time to write what we've figured out so far to leave here in case I don't have time to come back." *And in case I forget everything and everyone forgets me.*

Kade nodded. "I think that's a good idea."

"I'll go ask Calder for some paper," Kiegan said, already walking to the door.

"And something to write with," Ellayne called after him.

About an hour and a half later, Ellayne placed the notes back in the waterfall, now organized into stacks of papers that seemed to go together with the same topics. She left the long letter she'd written in the center of the table. There was no way of knowing whether she'd come back to the cave or not, but she wanted to give herself a fighting chance should the worst happen.

When she left the waterfall, they went back to the shop to grab their belongings, which they had packed beforehand.

Dayla had been instructed to stay in her room, but she cracked her door open when Ellayne came down from the attic; Kade and Kiegan were already waiting for her in the shop.

"You're leaving?"

Ellayne stopped in her tracks, having not spoken to Dayla since their scuffle. "Yes." She repositioned the bag on her shoulder, holding the strap at the front with both fists.

"Are Kiegan and Kade leaving too? Or is it just you?"

172

"All of us." Ellayne forced a smile. "Thank you for having us." She tilted her chin up, and turned before Dayla could get another word out.

They said goodbye to Calder in the shop, and Ellayne gave the original note back to him.

"Hold on to this," she said, placing it in his hand.

"It's not yours?"

"It is, and I need you to keep it here." She patted his hand, ignoring the confused look on his face. "Thank you Calder, for everything."

"Of course." He rubbed the back of his head, and his gills shifted in the light. "Come back anytime. But that doesn't mean I want you to get hurt. I hope that didn't—I mean, I don't want—I hope you, well, you should be careful."

"We will." Ellayne grinned up at him. She waved goodbye over her shoulder as she followed Kiegan and Kade out of the shop.

They got the horses from the stables, and Kiegan gave Ellayne a leg up onto Anya. As they left the safe haven behind and continued farther into the Black Forest, they were unaware of the silver pair of eyes watching them from the trees.

Chapter Twenty-Nine

Well this doesn't look like a bookstore." Kiegan kicked a singed piece of wood out of the way with his foot. "More like a pile of rubble."

The town they'd ridden into was in shambles. No buildings were undamaged, and Ellayne felt a wave of cold cover her as they made their way to where Kade remembered the bookshop to be.

"It was standing last time I was here." Kade dismounted from Curry and joined Kiegan near the rubble. "This has to be it."

"Only bookstore within a day's travel," a woman with sleek green hair said as she stepped down from a tree.

Ellayne jumped back, grasping Kiegan's arm. He winced at her grip, and she muttered an apology for digging her nails into his skin.

Kade held up his lantern. The woman's long green hair was woven into ropes. They hung down well past her hips and flowed as she stepped away from the tree. *How did I not see her?* Ellayne glanced from her to the tree, and realized her skin was about the same shade as the bark.

"I am Elowen," the woman said, cocking her head to look at each of them individually. "What brings you here?"

"We're looking for a bookstore," Kade answered. "I've been here before and I'm pretty sure it didn't look like this. How recent was the raid?"

"A week ago," the woman responded, running her hand up and down the tree. Ellayne squinted, not believing her eyes when the bark of the tree peeled back to reveal large gashes in the wood. "The forest is still healing."

"And the people?" Ellayne asked.

"You see the state of the village." Elowen gestured around. "I'm the only one left."

Ellayne skimmed the rubble and destruction around her. The only buildings left standing were skeletons of what they'd once been. *What did they do to this place?*

"Where did they go?" Ellayne turned her attention back to Elowen.

"Those who survived scattered, probably in search of other safe havens."

"This was a safe haven?" Kiegan asked.

"Yes," Kade answered. "One of the bigger ones, actually."

"That's why we were attacked. Someone gave away the location, and the raiders came with ward-breaking magic. Tore the place down in a matter of hours."

"Calder mentioned an influx of people coming to his village when I went to get you bandages," Kade told Ellayne. "I bet it was people from here."

Worry made Ellayne's forehead crease. "Does that mean Calder's village is in danger now?"

Kade didn't respond, and instead faced Elowen. "Is there anything we can do to help you before we leave? We need to keep going to find a different bookstore."

"No." Elowen stroked the trunk of the tree. "I am simply staying here until the forest heals. Then I will move on."

"Move on where?" Ellayne asked.

"Wherever the trees call me." Elowen grinned. "I wish you luck in finding your destination, and safe passage on your journey."

Ellayne smiled. "Thank you—Elowen, did you say it was?"

"Yes. It was a pleasure meeting you." Elowen leaned against the tree, and before Ellayne realized what was happening, the woman slipped into it, disappearing completely.

"This last one has to be it," Kade said from Curry.

"Especially since the last two weren't," Kiegan muttered back to Ellayne so Kade wouldn't hear.

Over the last two days, they'd traveled north, and after stopping in the raided village on the first day, they stayed the night in a nearby village at a small inn. Before Ellayne got to enjoy having her own room, the men woke her up to start again the next day.

They crossed a river, leaving the Black Forest Peninsula, and found the second bookstore was closed, and it shared no similarities to what any of the trio remembered seeing in the mirror.

"I hope you're right," Ellayne said, rubbing her wrist. After reading the notes from the cave, she was keeping a much closer watch on the blackness spreading up her arm and down to her fingers. "I—"

"I know," Kade said. "We're almost to the edge of the village." He pointed up to a few trees that leaned over and created an arch. "This gateway leads to it. If I remember correctly, we'll have to present ourselves. Then when we—"

"Who are you?" a scratchy female voice asked from the trees.

Ellayne leaned around Kiegan to try to get a better view of the person who'd spoken, but she couldn't see anyone. Nothing in the darkness moved in front of them, and the silence that followed had Ellayne questioning whether she'd imagined the voice completely.

"Kade Willows," Kade replied, his voice booming louder than Ellayne had ever heard before. His posture changed. He sat straighter, his chest puffing out with confidence, not with the casual pride he normally carried.

"The others, who are they?"

"Kiegan Greene," Kiegan said in front of her.

Ellayne felt her throat close up, her name getting caught. Instead of speaking, she coughed, and both Kade and Kiegan turned around to look at her. "Ellayne," she sputtered after catching her breath.

"Last name?"

"I don't know."

"What is your business here?" the voice spat back.

"All we want to do is see the bookstore in your village. I've been here once before," Kade said when the woman didn't say anything else. They waited, listening to the wind move the branches above them.

More silence followed, and Anya pawed at the ground with her front hoof. Kade went back to narrowing his eyes at the darkness surrounding them, but Kiegan looked back at Ellayne and gave her a reassuring smile.

"Pass through," came the reply.

With a shrug back at Kiegan and Ellayne, Kade directed Curry forward in the direction of the archway. Kiegan followed with Anya, and try as she might, Ellayne couldn't see who had spoken to them.

"What was that about?" Ellayne whispered to Kiegan.

"My best guess? They're protecting themselves from raids."

"What about wards?"

"Never hurts to be extra cautious." He shrugged.

After they passed through, a path began to form, marked by glowing stones, which were scattered at first, but formed an organized pattern the farther they went. Ellayne reached up and rubbed the necklace under her thumb, her heart beginning to beat faster the closer they got to the village.

They passed a building constructed between two trees, but it appeared to be abandoned with the windows all boarded up. Another structure they passed had a front door that hung crooked by one set of rusty hinges. However, the farther into the town they got, the better shape the buildings were in.

Similar to Calder's village, the people had strange features, and they stopped to stare at the newcomers amidst whatever they were doing. One woman with bright blue hair froze while carrying a basket of green fruit, which caused one of the fruits to roll off the top and fall to the ground. She didn't notice. Another boy, no more than six years old, dropped the book he had under his arm, the pages splaying out underneath the weight of the cover.

"They apparently don't have many visitors," Kiegan whispered to Ellayne. She nodded, using the curtain of her hair to avoid direct eye contact with the villagers.

"Is it her?" a woman with thin, silvery hair said to the man next to her. He didn't respond. His eyes stayed transfixed on Ellayne, who looked the other direction, pressing her non-injured cheek into Kiegan's back.

"Impossible," someone else said.

"What are they talking about?" Ellayne asked, lowering her voice. "Are they talking about me?"

"Well they aren't talking about me," Kiegan said, his shoulders rising and falling as he laughed at his own joke.

Ellayne ignored him.

"Where is the bookshop?" Kade asked a group of people, but nobody answered his question. Instead, they all talked to each other in hushed voices. Kade huffed, but kept going at a slow pace so he could read all the shop signs.

"Maybe you should ask—" Ellayne started, but stopped when her sight landed on a sign with familiar markings. Kade pulled back on Curry's reins, coming to a stop in front of the bookstore labelled *Barty's Books*.

A light flickered and faded in the stained glass window, through which Ellayne could see stacks and stacks of books. Kiegan helped her off the horse, and as soon as her feet hit the ground, she reached up and felt the necklace. The metal, made warm by its place on her chest, didn't soothe her as much as it normally did, and she could hear her heart pounding in her ears.

"This certainly looks like the one from the mirror," Kade said. "Right?"

Ellayne nodded, unable to form a verbal response. *We're really here.* Up until that point, she'd had the ability to write off what she saw in the mirror as fiction, simply the illusions of magic messing with her mind. But standing in front of the bookshop, she no longer possessed that ability.

"It's real," she breathed to herself. To the others she said, "What are we looking for in here again?"

"Anything that might give us a clue to your history or how you ended up with the necklace," Kade replied, looping Curry's reins around the branch of a nearby tree. "Or any mention of the Pub Under the Falls. Or the curse."

"We don't know what curse it is though."

"Doesn't mean we can't look," he said, leading the way to the front door.

She held her breath as Kade opened the shop door. A little bell at the top of the frame rang, alerting the store owner to their presence.

"Hello," said the woman sitting behind the back counter. "How can I—" As soon as her eyes landed on Ellayne, she froze. "Evie?"

Her voice. Ellayne's eyes widened. *It's the same as in the mirror.*

"No," Kade corrected. "This is Ellayne. I'm Kade, and this is Kiegan."

The woman had dark hair speckled with long strands of gray all wrapped into a tall bun on the top of her head. She wore a pair of square glasses pushed back to the bridge of her nose, and her eyes appeared unnaturally large behind them.

"I'm sorry," she said as she stood up from the stool she'd been perched on. "You look like someone who used to be very close to me." She held out her hand to Kade, but every few seconds her birdlike eyes would shift over to Ellayne. "My name is Linetta. What can I do for you?"

"Well," Ellayne started, but Kiegan cut her off.

"You can start by telling us how you knew the late queen." He shook her hand when she held it out to him.

His comment made the woman twitch her head to the side, as if she could only listen out of one ear, but she righted herself and smiled. "You mean Evie?"

"Queen Evangeline." Kade nodded. "How did you know her?"

"Why don't you follow me," Linetta crooned, holding her hand out to Ellayne, who took it. She was surprised by the older woman's strong grip. "I have some questions of my own."

Chapter Thirty

They followed Linetta to the back of the bookstore, which held more books. The entire shop was filled floor to ceiling with stacks upon stacks; bookshelves lined every wall and made three aisles down the center of the store. Every nook and cranny of the bookshelves were stuffed with books; old and new, tall and short, thick and thin. Where the bookshelves ran out of space, crates lined the floor, overflowing with more written words. There were books stacked vertically in piles taller than Ellayne, which wobbled as she walked past them. Linetta assured them they were all organized, but Ellayne had trouble understanding what *Glass Blowing for Beginners* and *Magnificent Homes in Phildeterre* had in common.

"Do you know of a place called the Pub Under the Falls?" Kade asked as they followed her.

Linetta shook her head. "No, I'm afraid not. But I have a book here about famous pubs in Phildeterre. That might have some information on it." She paused near the back of the shop, bending down to grab a book off a lower shelf. "Here, start with this and let me know if you need something else."

Kade took the books she handed him and followed her as she led them to the apartment above the shop.

"I wasn't expecting visitors, so please excuse the mess." Linetta cleared a few plates off a table when they walked by, placing them in a washbasin in the kitchen. "Please, have a seat." She gestured toward a couch, pulling a chair from the dining table to sit on for herself.

Ellayne sat next to Kiegan, and Kade perched on the arm of the couch. "Thank you for inviting us in."

"If you were wondering, I don't typically invite customers up to my apartment," Linetta said, smoothing out the fabric of her skirt. "But I saw your necklace, my dear, and I wanted to ask how you came to possess it?"

Ellayne reached up, feeling the medallion. "Not many people have noticed it," she said, raising an eyebrow. *Why did you?* Ellayne tried to find any similarities between the few glimpses she'd had of the late queen and the woman in front of her. They were night and day. Evangeline stood tall and elegant while this woman was short and stout. *But the way she talks, that's like Evangeline.*

"I've seen it before. Do you know to whom it first belonged?" Linetta asked.

"Queen Evangeline." Ellayne felt the engraved initials on the back.

"That's correct. Tell me," she folded her hands in her lap, "why do you have it? It should be buried with her."

Ellayne glanced at Kiegan for help. *I don't know what to tell her*, she tried to pass her thoughts to him.

"We aren't sure. You said you knew the late queen," Kiegan reminded the older woman, who nodded.

"I can show you her room if you'd like."

"What?" Kade asked, straightening up. "She lived here?"

182

Linetta pointed down a hallway. "She did. Would you like to see her room?"

The three exchanged glances and cohesively nodded at Linetta. She took them to a crowded bedroom which, apart from the cot in the corner and a little wardrobe near a window, seemed more like a storage room for books than an area for someone to sleep in. The walls had once been painted a bright yellow, but the paint was peeling off, and places near the ceiling were stained a dark brown from what was probably water damage.

"So you mean to tell me this was where Queen Evangeline grew up?" Kade asked again. "This was actually her room?"

"This was her room, yes," Linetta said, moving a box of leather-bound books from the cot to the floor. "Please," she motioned toward the bed, "sit."

Instead of sitting on the cot, Ellayne choose to sit on the small chair by the desk. It creaked when she first sat down, but remained quiet after she got comfortable. Kade and Kiegan sat on the bed while Linetta chose to sit on the box she'd moved.

"How did you know Queen Evangeline?" Kade asked again, spreading his legs out sideways and leaning forward on his elbows. He wasn't as drawn to the books as Ellayne thought he would be, and instead he stared at Linetta.

"You look like her, you know? Before she became queen." Linetta stared at Ellayne from across the room. "You could be her sister, if I didn't already know she didn't have any."

"I've heard," Ellayne said, resisting the urge to reach for the necklace, and instead rotating the bracelet around her wrist. "How did you know her?"

"It's a bit of a long story, but our father—"

" 'Our father'? As in, yours and Evangeline's?" Kade responded, sitting up straighter. "But you just said she didn't have—"

183

"Any sisters." Linetta nodded. "Not by blood, but we were sisters by marriage. Stepsisters. My father married her mother when her father died."

"You're the late queen's sister?" Kiegan asked, his eyes widening as he too understood the importance of what she'd said. "Why don't you live at the castle?"

Linetta's lips tightened, but relaxed when she sighed. "Evangeline was not fond of my father, her stepfather. I don't blame her. He was a . . ." She paused. "He was a difficult man to get along with. When her mother died a few years after marrying my father, Evie left home. I would've too, but circumstances held me here. When she became queen, she wanted to start new, which meant not bringing her past with her to the castle."

Kiegan's forehead creased, but he didn't ask any further questions. Ellayne spoke up, and both men turned their heads to look at her. Her cheeks warmed when all attention was on her, but she spoke clearly and deliberately anyway.

"Why are you sharing all of this with us so willingly? This seems like"—she searched for the right word, biting her lower lip—"private information. I don't see why—"

"It is private, but you look like her and you have her necklace." Linetta nodded toward the chain around Ellayne's neck.

"That's all? We could be dangerous."

"Are you?"

"Well, no, but—"

"I'm not stupid. I know you had to get past the wards and guards. You don't mean anyone any harm. I'm about as good at reading people as I am at reading books." Linetta smiled, and whatever had been putting Ellayne on edge melted away with that smile. "I remember when she came back to the bookstore after becoming queen. She wore the necklace. She stood regal as a queen; sat straight, like you." Her words made Ellayne aware of her posture, and she tried to slouch a bit without Linetta noticing. The old woman smiled once more and let out a small chuckle, but kept going without saying anything about it. "If she'd been lucky enough to have children, a daughter, you'd be her."

"But she didn't," Ellayne said. "Right?"

"Right." Linetta nodded. "And it's a shame too, because she would've been a wonderful mother. She was older than me by a few years, and when my father would get angry, she was a safe haven to turn to. She had grace and grit. Evie knew how to take care of herself and those around her; I've never met a wiser woman than her. When my father died, she came back to be with me, and to make sure I was doing all right. At that point, she promised to visit more often because he was gone. And she did. We spent many hours together laughing at her old journals and crying over the scars my father left on both of us. She became one of my best friends."

"Do you know anything about how she died?" Kade asked, rubbing his thumb along the line of his chin as he thought aloud. "We aren't sure how Ellayne came to possess the necklace, and we were hoping to find some answers here. Finding you is, well, better luck than we expected."

Linetta shook her head. "I found out about Evie's death when everyone else here did, a day after it happened." Linetta's hand darted up to her cheek, wiped away the wetness, and went back down to her lap in the blink of an eye.

"Do you still have her journals?" Kade asked, his eyes scanning the room.

The older woman shifted, tucking a piece of hair behind her ear. "I do." She sniffled and placed her hand on the box of books she sat on. Ellayne watched her stroke one of the leather-bound books. The men didn't notice.

"Can we take a look at them?"

Looking up at Ellayne, Linetta locked eyes with her.

"All right."

Chapter Thirty-One

This is from when she was eight years old," Kiegan said, flipping through the pages of one of the leather-bound journals. "I can't believe she was writing this much when she was that young. I hated writing when I was a kid."

"You still do, idiot," Kade muttered with a grin on his face. He wasn't looking at Kiegan, so he didn't see his best friend stick his tongue out in his direction. "This one is from when she was sixteen, but it's almost entirely about a guy she liked." He scrunched up his nose. "Maybe not the most useful to us."

Ellayne stayed silent, wrapped up in the words of a stranger. Reading the late queen's journals felt invasive, but the guilt gnawing in her stomach faded away as the pages of Evangeline's journal sucked her in.

Emmalee came by the shop today. She snuck me a bit of cake when my stepfather wasn't looking. The mark of a true friend. I hid it away to share with Linny later. If Jonathan found out, all of us girls would be in trouble. But thankfully, he was sleeping from his night out.

I heard from Violetta next door that another magic person was put to death in Cyanthia yesterday. It's atrocious, the things King Valryn is doing to these poor people just to "keep up morale." The only morale he's keeping up is his own.

Surprisingly, Emmalee doesn't seem as upset about it as I thought she would be. I mean, she's always ranting about how wrong this war is and how "you can't blame someone for the magic that came from their ancestors." But today she told me to be thankful it was only one person. I suppose she's right. It could've easily been the hundreds of people living around us. Then again, they haven't killed that many people in one execution since the first days of King Kylian. What a nightmare that must've been.

I couldn't sleep last night because I kept thinking of the Split of Phildeterre. Someone brought in a new book on the Split, and I spent most of yesterday reading it. There wasn't that much I hadn't already learned. However, the images stuck around in my mind long after I put the book on my desk and blew out the candle. I couldn't help but picture the families in the pages. But worse yet, I saw them with the faces of people I know who have magic, kneeling before the soldiers of the past, mothers trying to block their children from seeing the arrows coming. So much blood. Even now my mind is clouded with the voices I never heard; shouts for help and screaming children. It isn't right. It never has been.

Ellayne put the journal down, tears blurring her vision. Mixed in with all the thoughts Evangeline poured into the journals was the memory of the queen dead on the floor. Ellayne couldn't escape it. No matter what she read from the journals, it was always there, nagging her, reminding her that the words she read were those of a dead person.

"Hey," Kiegan said, and Ellayne looked up to see him staring at her. "Let's take a break, okay? We've been here all day, and my eyes are starting to hurt." His voice was soft.

"He's right," Kade agreed, marking his place in the journal he was reading by flipping it over on the bed. "We should get some food and rest our eyes for a bit."

"Maybe Linetta can help us find a place to stay for the night."

"We should ask," Kade said in agreement.

Ellayne glanced down at the words again, and they called to her, asking her to keep reading them. "I would rather—"

"They'll still be here when you get back," Kiegan assured her, and he stood up, stretching his arms above his head. "But for now," he yawned, "let's get some food."

"Can I help you clear the table?" Ellayne asked Linetta, who rose from her seat. She'd made them dinner, consisting of soup from poultry—Ellayne hadn't asked what kind—and root vegetables that Linetta said grew best in the Black Forest.

"That would be lovely." Linetta smiled at her as she took the leftover soup to the counter.

"While you do that, Kieg and I are going to take the horses to the stable," Kade said, pushing his chair in. "You said it was down the main street and to the right?"

"Yes," Linetta said, "you can't miss it."

"Is there an inn around here?" Kiegan asked, covering his mouth at the end as he yawned. "I'm going to be ready to sleep soon."

The older woman shook her head. "The innkeeper died a few weeks ago."

Ellayne's eyebrows furrowed. "What happened?"

"Natural death." Linetta waved her hand. "He was older than dirt. I'm surprised he didn't go sooner. Nonetheless," she put her hands on her hips, "you're welcome to stay here."

"We don't want to be a bother," Ellayne argued.

"Nonsense, I insist. Ellayne, you can have Evie's room. Unfortunately for you two," she turned to Kade and Kiegan, "my other guest room is currently filled with books to the ceiling. You're welcome to share my room, though."

"Where would you sleep?" Kade asked, leaning on the back of the chair.

Linetta gestured toward the couch. "Right there."

"Absolutely not." Kade shook his head. "Kiegan and I will sleep out here." He glanced at Kiegan, who nodded. "He'll sleep on the couch, I'll take the floor."

"But—" Linetta started.

"You've been so kind, and I'll not be the person who kicks you out of your own bed. Come on, Kieg." Kade motioned toward the door that led to the shop. He grinned at Linetta. "We'll be back soon."

As soon as the door shut, Linetta scurried back to the kitchen and pointed to a spot on the counter for Ellayne to place the dirty dishes.

"Where'd you find such fine gentlemen?" Linetta asked, a wide smile still on her face.

"They found me, actually." Ellayne explained how they'd pulled her out of the river, leaving out the part about the archer. *The archer. I wonder if they're still tracking me.* Ellayne shuddered, and Linetta noticed.

"Is everything all right? Are you cold?"

"Just remembering the water," Ellayne lied, taking the clean, wet plate Linetta handed her to dry with a rag. "It was freezing."

"It certainly is, especially up north here near the Cyro Sea."

"Now that you mention it, I guess it does feel colder up here." Ellayne pressed her lips together, remembering the chilly winds that had increased as they'd made their way to Linetta's village. "Is it always cold?"

"Not always, but most of the year. It should be getting warmer within the next weeks. We're approaching summer."

"You said you moved here when your father married Evangeline's mother. Where did you live before, if you don't mind me asking?"

"My father and I lived west of here, near the border of the country. We lived on the coast and my father was in charge of imports in and out of Phildeterre at one of the harbors. When the monarchs of Phildeterre made changes to the importing and exporting laws, my father decided to move inland. Took me with him."

"What was it like on the coast?"

"Wonderful, actually. I got to see the sun and be near the sea. My mother always thought there must've been some sort of siren in our family line, because I've always loved the water."

"Are there?"

"Hm?"

"Any sirens in your family line?" Ellayne said, stacking another plate on the counter.

"My mother was never able to prove it, so I doubt it."

"I met some sirens a few days ago. The guy was nice, his sister was"—Ellayne searched for an appropriate word for Dayla—"complicated."

"Loyal friends if you treat them right." Linetta turned her head to grin at Ellayne. "Can be tricky if you get on their bad side though."

Ellayne lifted her hand to her cheek, feeling the scratches. *That's for sure.*

The two of them finished washing the dishes, and Ellayne let questions come up about Linetta's bookstore, her favorite authors, and other things that distracted her from the heavier questions forever circling in her head. Talking with the older woman put Ellayne at ease like she hadn't been before. Kiegan made her feel safe, and even Kade's determination for answers gave her a fragment of hope. But sitting at the clean table with

Linetta, listening to the older woman laugh over the smallest memories, filled her with peace.

Ellayne struggled to get to sleep in the queen's cot, not because it wasn't comfortable—it was surprisingly so—but because the temptation to keep reading the journals across the room pulled at her. Reading the struggles and successes of Evangeline's daily life distracted Ellayne from her own obstacles. It was a relief from the burden on her tired shoulders.

When Ellayne woke up early the next day, though it could've been late—in the Black Forest it was hard to tell—she tiptoed into the living room and saw Kiegan stretched out on the couch with both his feet and one arm hanging off the edge. *These men could sleep through an earthquake.* She grinned, watching him breathe deeply. Kade, however, wasn't sleeping on the pile of blankets, and was nowhere in the small living room.

Spurred by curiosity, Ellayne crept through the room, toward the door that led down to the shop. When she shut the door behind her, she breathed out and walked down the stairs, hoping the creaking wood wouldn't wake Kiegan.

She heard whispers before she saw Linetta and Kade sitting at a table in the back of the shop. The older woman held a mug of steaming liquid, and there was one on the table in front of Kade too. They didn't notice her, and Ellayne stood as quiet as she could behind a stack of books, listening to them speak in hushed voices.

"—when she left, right?" Kade's low voice vibrated through the air.

"Yes, though she wasn't sure which side it came from. Neither of her parents ever told her."

"She wrote that it scared her, but I don't see why, unless it was—"

"It wasn't," Linetta interrupted before he could finish. "It wasn't like that."

Kade stayed silent, and for a moment all Ellayne could hear was Linetta sipping from her mug.

Finally Kade spoke again. "Did her husband know?"

"I'm not sure she ever told him. How could she?"

"Right, I get it. I just wonder how she could keep it a secret from him for so long. It seems like she would've slipped up at some point."

"I told you she was the wisest woman I ever knew, and I wasn't lying. She had a way with people. Nearly everyone loved or at least respected her, and those who didn't couldn't bring up anything to judge her by. She lived as blamelessly as she could."

"But—"

"I'm not saying she was perfect," Linetta corrected. "She had a temper and could be as stubborn as an ox, but if she saw that she was hurting someone, she was usually selfless enough to admit her mistake and rectify it in turn. She was meant to be queen."

Kade remained quiet, so Linetta continued.

"I know it's impossible, but I see Evie in your friend, Ellayne. Women like her are meant for great things."

"I don't disagree," Kade said, "which is why I want to help her figure out what's going on."

Ellayne's eyes widened, not because Linetta had compared her to the late queen, but because Kade had told Linetta about the amnesia. Anger replaced the pleasant warmth of being appreciated, and the heat intermixed with tingling throughout her body.

Without thinking about it, Ellayne sprinted out of the store and ran down the street. She barely heard the bells ringing as Kade ran out after her, calling her name. He hollered for her to slow down, but she didn't. She pumped her arms at her sides and pushed faster when she heard his footsteps keeping pace with hers.

"Ellayne, stop. Why are you running?"

She passed a building with a red door, and the only thing surrounding her now were the tall trees of the Black Forest. Her muscles begged her to stop, and with one last push, she did. Ellayne pressed her hand against the trunk of a nearby tree and leaned into it, inhaling the chilled air with deep breaths.

"What was that all about?" Kade hissed at her as he jogged to the tree she was using to support herself. "Why did you run all the way out here? It's not safe to—"

"Because you told Linetta about me, about my memory loss," Ellayne snapped, turning to face him. The lack of glowing stones made it hard to see his face, but she could at least make out his eyebrows furrowing together.

"I—"

"That wasn't your secret to tell, Kade." She jabbed a finger in his chest, and he took a step back. "I'm the one who can't remember a thing about the past, so I get to choose who I tell and don't tell. That is mine, and I can't believe you took that choice away from me. How dare you think that—"

"I didn't."

Ellayne faltered, her mouth forming words that never made it out. She lowered her finger. "What?"

"I didn't tell Linetta you have no memories." His voice was even, not betraying any emotions he may have been feeling.

"But you said . . ." Ellayne stopped, trying to remember what had made her think he'd betrayed her trust. "You said you wanted to figure out what was going on with me."

Kade put his hands in his pockets, his shoulders rising a bit. "I do, but that doesn't mean I went around blabbing about your amnesia to everyone. It just means I want to help you figure out where the necklace came from, which Linetta already knew about. I didn't tell her about the curse. But of course I want to help figure out who did it and why."

"Why?"

"Yes, why they cursed you."

"No." She shook her head. "*Why* do you want to help me?"

"Oh." He shrugged. "Honestly?"

"Yes."

Kade leaned his shoulder against the tree. "I think something big has been covered up at the castle, and I think you're the key to figuring it out."

Chapter Thirty-Two

Two days later, Ellayne sat in the desk chair in Evangeline's room, a chair which she had become quite familiar with in the last few days.

"Did you move the journal I was reading yesterday?" Kade asked when he and Kiegan came into the room. "I placed it here." He pointed to the desk. He moved the other books and items around, scattering papers and journals everywhere.

"I didn't touch it," Ellayne said, "but there are plenty more where that one came from."

Instead of choosing another journal, Kade sighed and flopped down on the bed. He flipped through the book Linetta had given him when they first arrived. It wasn't long before he found an excerpt about the Pub Under the Falls.

"It looks like it was a bar before the war ended," Kade summarized.

"An exclusive one, apparently," Kiegan said. "You know, since Ellayne was the only one of us who could get in."

"Jealous, Kieg?" Kade raised an eyebrow.

"Definitely. You're not?"

"Maybe." Kade shrugged. "It doesn't say much else besides the fact that it was shut down before King Diomedes inherited the throne. Apparently it wasn't widely known."

Ellayne nodded. "But then, how did I find it?"

"Add that question to the list," Kade remarked, tossing the book onto a pile of journals he'd already skimmed through.

They were working their way through the journals, taking breaks every so often to recap anything new they'd learned.

The woman, Emmalee, whom Evangeline had mentioned in the first journal Ellayne read, seemed to be a key player in most of the journals, starting from when Evangeline was eight years old. The journals written when Evangeline was between the ages of eight to twenty years old were more consistent, written almost every day. They took up most of the journals. The topics varied for the most part, often discussing the cruelties of her stepfather, Jonathan, or the dreariness of village life. In a particularly entertaining entry, Ellayne found herself giggling as she read Evangeline's detailed account of the blacksmith's apprentice attempting to teach Evangeline how to use a sword, and nearly losing his left ear because of his generosity.

These were the journals they'd been reading since they'd arrived.

However, there were about thirteen other journals that weren't in the original crate. Linetta brought the new journals to them on the second day when she found them in her own bedroom.

"I forgot about these," she'd said, placing the stack on the desk.

The new journals were written from the time she was twenty-one to thirty-four years old, and were spotty and less consistent, missing large chunks of time. Kade found the first entry from when Evangeline had moved out of the village.

However, Ellayne found out later that he'd refrained from telling Kiegan and her about it until he'd read it twice. When asked why he hadn't said anything right away, he gave an excuse, insisting that he knew they would get to it eventually.

That was the journal entry Ellayne now read.

I've had it. I can't live here anymore, not with that monster in charge. I wanted to stay a little longer for Linny, and for my father's store, but I can't. If I have to stay one more week, I'm going to explode. Every time I'm near him I feel like my veins are alight with fire. I turn twenty-one next week, and I'm leaving on that day. I don't know where I'm going, but at this point, I don't care if I have to sleep on the forest floor and scavenge for food for the rest of my life. It'll be better than living under the same roof as Jonathan Dipthy.

The passage ended there, and the next one picked up several months later. Kade told her that she needed to keep reading the next few entries because they were important, though he wouldn't explain why. He simply said she needed to read it for herself.

Emmalee looked lovely in her dress. I don't think I've ever seen her smile so much in one day. The ceremony was short; only long enough to say their vows and promise to love each other forever. Then they were off to celebrate their new life together. I was so proud to stand by her side, even though it's been a bit unsteady between us since my powers started showing.

I've managed to get a bit of a handle on the outbursts, but it takes a lot of concentration. I need to keep practicing if I want to go to the coronation of the next king. I heard from some of the old ladies here that he's younger than his predecessors, but I can't decide if that's a good or bad thing. Part of me wants to believe that something good will come out of this next king, but the other part of me fears now more than ever. Now that my magic has revealed itself, my own head is on the line.

Ellayne's eyes widened. "She had magic?"

Kiegan looked up from the journal he was reading, his eyebrows raised. "What?"

"Evangeline," Ellayne repeated, "she had magic?"

Kade nodded. "I had a sneaking suspicion. How else would she have done the things she did? She defeated the evil sorceress all by herself. How could she have done that if she didn't have magic?"

Ellayne made a mental note to ask about the evil sorceress detail at a later time when she wasn't fuming. "You knew she had magic and didn't bother mentioning it to either of us? Kade! Why would you keep that to yourself? That's important information."

He shrugged. "I asked Linetta about it because I had a hunch that she had magic. But it was the day you ran out into the forest. I would've told you, but I forgot when you went barreling out into the wilderness alone."

"You ran out into the forest?" Kiegan asked. "Where was I?"

"Don't put this on me." Ellayne ignored Kiegan's question entirely, narrowing her eyes at Kade. "It was your choice to keep this a secret. Why didn't you say anything?" Ellayne marked the spot in the journal with her finger and closed the book. "That's one of the most important things we've found yet." Her voice raised in pitch. "You should've said something."

"It wasn't my secret to tell," he replied, his tone smooth, mocking. "It was Queen Evangeline's."

"You're infuriating, you know that, right? Of all the things to keep quiet, you decide to leave out the part where the queen of Phildeterre had magic? You're ridiculous!"

Kiegan glanced from Ellayne to Kade, both locked in a staring contest. "When did you go out into the forest?" he asked again.

"When you were asleep on the couch the first morning here," Ellayne said, breaking her eye contact with Kade. She ignored the prickling beneath the surface of her skin, instead focusing on the spine of the journal. Evangeline had written her initials, ELS, on the faded leather, matching the letters found on the necklace.

"And neither of you told me?" Kiegan's voice rose.

"It wasn't a big deal, Kieg, seriously." Kade leaned against the wall on the cot, and a smirk crept across his face. "Ellayne got upset over something she thought she heard me say, and then went charging into the Black Forest. I caught up with her, we talked through it, made up with hugs and kisses, and that's the end of it."

"Well I'm glad you two have gotten so friendly with each other." Kiegan shut the journal he'd been reading. "But hey, maybe next time you decide to take a little trip together in the Black Forest, think about inviting me." He stood up and stormed out of the room. Ellayne could hear him go all the way down the stairs into the shop. The front bell rang faintly as he left.

"Great," Kade huffed, "now his panties are in a bunch, too." He crossed his arms over his chest.

"First of all, I can't believe you just said the word 'panties.' " Ellayne refrained from grinning, reminding herself that she was upset with him. "Secondly, you could've told him about the forest more like a friend and less like an emotionless jerk."

"Well now, tell me how you really feel, why don't you?"

Ellayne closed her eyes, grinding her teeth together as she thought through what to say next. "I think—"

"You think I'm some sort of inhuman monster with no rudimentary empathy for others, and that I selfishly go about life looking for the best way to spit on everyone else's good days. Right? You think I kick puppies and drown kittens in my spare time? Or maybe that I have some deep desire to bring a raining cloud over the head of every person I meet?"

"I think you should go talk to him," Ellayne said as soon as he paused. *Kiegan's family ran off and left him, and that's what I did.* Her hands relaxed from the fists they'd been in. She kept her eyes closed. "You're his best friend. Go."

She heard him release all the air he must've been keeping locked in his lungs, and with a simple "All right," he left her alone in Evangeline's room.

With no men in the room to distract her, Ellayne opened up the journal and began skimming through once more.

I was sure one of the soldiers saw me sneak into the festivities of the coronation, but if he did, he didn't alert anyone. Maybe it's because so many people are in Cyanthia right now to celebrate. I don't know anyone who can say with an honest heart that they wished King Valryn had lived a longer life. I think we are all ready for a change, but I just hope it's one for the betterment of all magic folk. Myself included, of course.

The rumors were true. King Butch looks much younger than everyone expected, and though I don't typically sympathize with the people persecuting me, I honestly feel a bit bad for him. The wife they found for him is, well, let's call her mouselike. It seems like a butterfly might give her a heart attack. And I know it's a bit rude of me to say, but she has mean eyes.

I suppose it doesn't matter what she looks like, though. As long as she can produce an heir, she's done her part. I wonder if either of them feel trapped. How funny that when I lived in the

200

village with Jonathan, I felt like a caged animal. I assume that's what it would feel like to live in that castle; bound by stone walls and kept prisoner in your own home. Though, if you've been bred in captivity, I suppose it can't seem that bad because you don't know what you're missing.

Ellayne continued to read about the coronation and all the different food Evangeline tried while she celebrated with the rest of Phildeterre. She could picture the food carts and merchants taking advantage of the influx of foot traffic. Her mouth watered at the details of the roasted duck dripping in butter and the tart juice from the slices of pomelo Evangeline mentioned.

And then the coronation was over and the next passage brought her to a time several months later.

Emmalee's daughter, Hazel, is the most precious baby I've ever laid eyes on. I cannot believe that Emmalee is now a mother. What a glorious title to have. And the fact that she wanted me there when she gave birth; what an honor. That little girl will be loved all her life.

She has her mother's nose and her father's eyes. Emmalee was so strong during labor, and her husband stayed near her the whole time. I think even the midwives were impressed at how well she pushed through the pain.

Of course, it all makes me hope that I'll get to marry and have children someday, but then again . . . I don't want to risk passing on my magic to a child and having that precious life taken from me because of the war. Thinking through it now, I don't think I could ever bring myself to have children, not in a world as broken as ours.

But maybe Hazel will live in a different world. Maybe the new king will bring a new era. Maybe Hazel will have children who can live alongside people like me without fearing the heavy losses that those before her have felt. Maybe.

Chapter Thirty-Three

Ellayne, wrapped up in Evangeline's journal, didn't hear the thunder of footsteps up the stairs or through the living room until they were right outside the door to the bedroom. She looked up, her eyes widening when she saw Kade and Kiegan burst through the door.

"Grab your bag," Kiegan ordered, his voice tenser than normal. "We're leaving now."

"What's—"

"The village is being raided by anti-magic rebels," Kade responded, shoving some of the journals into his bag. "We need to leave."

"None of us have magic," Ellayne said, jumping to her feet.

"Won't matter to the raiders," Kiegan said.

Kade agreed. "They have more of a 'maim now, ask questions later' type of mindset. Hurry."

Kade's left cheek was swollen, but Ellayne didn't have time to ask about it. Instead, she grabbed the bag, which lay by the foot of the bed, and put the journal she'd been reading as well as two others in. There wasn't time to consider that she was possibly stealing the late queen's journals.

She was reaching for another one when Linetta came running down the hallway. Her hair was not in the neat bun, and instead flew up around the sides of her head. "Grab the journals and come with me." She turned and went back down the hallway. "They have the village surrounded and are already breaking down doors and attempting to burn down buildings."

"Won't that set the whole forest on fire?" Ellayne asked.

All four of them sprinted down the stairs. As they got closer to the shop, shouts and screams echoed from outside.

"You would think, yes," Linetta replied, "but this part of the forest is enchanted with special runes to prevent such events. After the fire on the western half of the peninsula many years ago, they started putting up fire-repelling wards."

"Can't wards be broken?" Ellayne asked. *Like in Elowen's village.*

"It'd take extremely powerful magic to take down the anti-fire wards," Linetta replied, "but the buildings aren't protected by it, only the trees and surrounding vegetation."

Instead of taking them to the front door, which Ellayne could see was locked with a giant chain, Linetta led them to the back door, which was about as narrow as Ellayne's shoulders. The two men had to turn sideways to exit.

"How will we get out if they have the area surrounded?" Ellayne asked, much quieter now they were outside. The crash of glass breaking sounded from a building nearby, and a sharp, high scream rang out. Something cut it short.

"There's a tunnel that leads near the river," Linetta replied in an equally hushed voice. "Evangeline showed me, and I'm one of the only people who knows about it in town, so there shouldn't be anyone else heading there."

"Is it big enough for horses?" Kiegan asked, and Ellayne could tell where he was going with the question. Anya and Curry were in the stables still.

"I'm afraid not."

Kiegan grabbed Kade by the upper arm, yanking him back after hearing Linetta's answer. With his eyes wide he said, "I'm not leaving Anya here."

Kade clenched his jaw. "We don't have time for this, Kiegan. We'll come back for—"

"No." Kiegan released Kade like his arm was on fire. "I'm not leaving her here." He took a couple steps backward. "I'm sorry, Ellayne." Before Kade could stop him, Kiegan ran around the side of the house and disappeared into the smoky chaos on the main road.

"Kiegan, no, don't—" Ellayne hollered, but Kade wrapped his hand around her mouth, silencing her cry.

"Don't draw attention," he whispered in her ear.

Ellayne elbowed him in the ribs, forcing him to let go. "Don't touch me," she hissed. "How can you—"

Kade's eyes widened when something behind her caught his attention, and he shoved her to the side.

Ellayne hit the ground hard on her hip, yelping as pain radiated up and down her side. Kade landed next to her, but jumped to his feet faster than her. When she looked at where she'd just been standing, she saw a large man yanking an axe with a long handle out of the soil. On the tip of the axe sat a spear, and it dripped with blood. *My blood? No.* She searched for pain anywhere other than her hip and found none. *Kade?* She focused on Kade, who drew attention away from Ellayne by circling around the large man. *No, he's fine, and Linetta is too.* The older woman ran over and helped Ellayne to her feet.

"Are you all right?" Linetta whispered, pulling Ellayne away from the two men as soon as she stood up.

"Fine, but whose blood?" Ellayne knew the question didn't make sense, yet Linetta still understood her.

She pointed to a body several feet away. "My neighbor's."

Ellayne didn't have time to react to the body because the raider, who wore a scarf that covered the lower half of his face, swung at Kade, jamming his strange axe into a tree an inch above Kade's head. Kade dove out of the way, taking an extra second to get to his feet.

It didn't take long for the raider to get his weapon unstuck, and he swung it back toward Kade again. *I have to do something.* Ellayne's mind raced, and her hands shook. She turned in a full circle, searching for something she could use to get the man off Kade. They were about the same height, but the raider was at least twice Kade's weight. An idea began to form in Ellayne's mind, and she pulled Linetta to the nearest building.

"Stay here," she whispered, "and hold this." Ellayne handed the bag on her shoulder to Linetta, running toward the raider before the old woman could stop her.

With a jump, Ellayne wrapped her arms around the large man's neck, gripping his torso with her legs. He stumbled forward, catching himself on a tree trunk. Knowing she didn't have much time, Ellayne yanked at the scarf around his lower face, moving it down so that it was only around his neck.

"Get off!" the man hollered in a deep voice. He spun around and slammed Ellayne against the tree trunk. In a desperate attempt to get her off, he dropped his axe and tried to reach her with his arms, which were too short.

Even with the wind knocked out of her, Ellayne pulled the scarf tighter, using all the muscles in her arms to close his windpipe. *A little longer.* She counted to ten, pausing when he slammed her against the tree again. Her head ached from hitting the tree trunk, but she didn't stop until the man dropped to his knees. She straddled him before he could crush her legs underneath his body. He face-planted into the dirt. Ellayne knelt on his back, still clutching the scarf for an extra few seconds before letting go.

"You're nuts," Kade said, pulling her to her feet.

205

"You're welcome," she said, shaking as adrenaline cycled through her.

Linetta handed Ellayne the bag, brushing a twig out of Ellayne's hair as she did so. Ellayne clutched the bag at her side, still expecting to see Kade chase after Kiegan, but instead, Kade turned back to Linetta.

"Take us to the tunnel."

A few of the buildings they crept behind were on fire, and Ellayne blinked her eyes over and over to try to stop the smoke from burning. Blurry vision was the last thing she wanted. The screams from the villagers continued to ring out sporadically, making Ellayne jump anytime they were nearby.

People dressed in cloaks ran through the space between the buildings into the Black Forest around them, trying to escape the attackers. The raider's damage devastated the area and people around them, but they had yet to run into another one.

A man ran past Ellayne, covering his bleeding face with one hand and dragging a little girl with his other. A woman with green skin and raven hair gripped her arm, which was bent at a strange angle, and stumbled past Ellayne.

They'd made it five buildings away from the bookstore when Ellayne, who was behind Linetta and Kade, felt a hand grasp her wrist, yanking her back. Opening her mouth, her scream never came out as another hand covered the lower half of her face. With her one free hand, she tried to pull the hand on her mouth away to scream, but it wouldn't budge.

The attacker dragged her in the opposite direction. His grasp on her wrist was entirely on the bracelet, and with a little twisting, she slipped her hand out of the bracelet and his grasp. In the same second, Ellayne swung her fist back low, hoping to hit him between the legs. She missed and hit his thigh, but with the second blow, she hit her target, and he let go of her mouth, stumbling backward.

Ellayne didn't get a good look at him when she punched him in the face, because he wore a scarf over his nose and mouth, like the first raider, and the hood from his cloak covered the upper half. However, she did feel the impact of the hit on all her knuckles. She yelped, and the man grunted, tripping over a root.

"Ellayne," Kade grabbed her wrist, dodging her other fist as it swung near his face, "are you all right? Come on." He took one look at the man on the ground before pulling Ellayne away.

When she looked over her shoulder at the man who'd grabbed her, she saw a bow over his shoulder alongside a quiver of familiar arrows. The dark cloak camouflaged him as he disappeared and was gone.

"Did he hurt you?" Linetta asked by the doorway to a cellar.

"No." Ellayne shook her head. "Just startled me."

Kade let out a surprising chuckle. "He got more than he bargained for."

"What do you mean?" Linetta asked.

"I got away," Ellayne cut in before Kade could waste more time. "I'm fine, but we need to leave."

"Right. The tunnel is through here, and I'm going to close it up after you go. I should've given this to you earlier, I'm sorry. Take it." Linetta held a sheathed dagger out to Kade. "I hope you won't have to use it, and if you do, that you know how."

"I don't," Kade said, weighing the dagger in his hand, "but I don't have to tell that to the person I'm using it on."

"You're not coming with us?" Ellayne asked, ignoring the knife completely. "Where will you go?"

"Back to the shop." Linetta smiled and pulled her into a quick hug. "I'll keep out of sight there until this all blows over. It's not the first time. We will rebuild and continue on."

"But—"

"I'll be fine." Linetta opened the cellar door and Ellayne saw a staircase open up before her. "You need to leave before someone sees you escape through here. You don't want someone chasing you through these tunnels. I'll keep an eye out for Kiegan, and if I find him, I'll send him in the direction I'm sending you." She gripped Ellayne's hand. "I hope we meet again."

"Thank you," Kade said, shaking her hand as he passed her. He entered the stairs first, disappearing into the black hole.

Ellayne was about to follow him, but Linetta tugged on her hand.

"Here." She placed a small, cold object in Ellayne's open palm. "This should help light your way." Linetta stepped forward and pulled Ellayne into a hug. She smelled like books, and her hair tickled Ellayne's nose. Linetta backed up, tucking a piece of Ellayne's hair behind her ear, her hand lingering on her cheek.

When Ellayne opened her hand, a small stone with what she'd come to recognize as the light rune carved into it glowed in the dark. It lit up Linetta's face just as her expression fell. Her eyes widened and her mouth opened. An orange light flickered in the reflection of her glasses, and Ellayne turned to see what paralyzed her friend. The bookstore, with all of the pages as fuel, erupted into flames.

"No," Linetta breathed, and without another word, she shoved Ellayne toward the cellar and ran toward the bookshop.

"Linetta!"

"Ellayne, no." Kade reappeared at the mouth of the stairway, and he pulled Ellayne back as she was about to run after the older woman.

"Let go!" Ellayne fought against Kade as he pulled her toward the dark tunnel, but he was stronger by far. He wrapped his arm around her waist and lifted her off her feet.

The last thing she saw before Kade shut the cellar door was Linetta's silhouette as she ran toward the bookstore engulfed by the flames.

Chapter Thirty-Four

G et off me." Ellayne shoved away from Kade in the dim light. The stone from Linetta had tumbled down the stairs when Kade grabbed her, and she pushed past him to go pick it up. "How could you just leave them?"

"Let's go."

"We can't just leave them here, Kade."

Kade stayed silent, passing her on the stairs, which led down a steep incline. His footsteps echoed in the tunnel. The noises of the outside world and the chaos up above had instantly quieted the moment the heavy door shut. Ellayne's steps caught up with his.

"Kiegan is your best friend. How can you just walk away from him when he could be in danger? And Linetta—"

"Linetta made me promise that I'd get you out safely." Kade spun around, and with him on a lower step, they were the same height, eye to eye. "And Kiegan made his choice. He's a big boy. He can take care of himself."

"But you'll go running after me when I run into the Black Forest? How does that make any sense? I don't get you."

"No one said you had to," he snapped, turning back around. He continued walking down the stairs, but he didn't get far before her words halted him in his tracks.

"You aren't worried something might happen to Kiegan?"

"Of course I am, Ellayne. I'm not heartless." He leaned against the wall, which was made of compacted dirt. The air, thick with moisture, intermixed with overwhelming earthy scents.

"Then why are you leaving him behind?"

"Because of you."

Ellayne's feet cemented to the tunnel floor, the weight of his words bearing down on her like a boulder. "Excuse me?" *This is exactly what I didn't want to happen.* Her chest tightened. *I didn't want to get between their friendship, and now . . .*

Kade sighed and pushed his hair away from his face. "Kiegan is my best friend, yes. And yes, I'm worried something has already happened to him. But I made a promise to Linetta to make sure nothing happened to you. She saw something in you, something I don't understand, but I can't deny is there. A promise is a promise."

"What did she see?"

He waited a moment before answering.

"Power." Kade hadn't been looking at her until that moment. "I see it every time you speak; every time you move; every time you even take a breath. It's there, a whisper of what's really inside you. Something you don't seem to see yourself."

"You're wrong." Ellayne shook her head, and all the anger she felt about leaving Kiegan and Linetta turned to guilt. It was because of her that Kade had abandoned them. It was all her fault. "What you see is false. It's not real." She leaned on the wall across from him. Their feet met in the middle, toe to toe. "The only thing in me is fear."

As soon as the word left her mouth, her chest compressed, and an old ache, which had worn on her since she'd first woken up in the tiny house, rubbed her raw once more.

"It's fear of my past, fear of my future, and fear that I'm doing all of this in vain, and someday soon, the darkness spreading over my arm is going to leak into my memories and erase those too. Then I'll be back to the beginning again, forgetting my identity and everyone I've come to care for."

"Even if what you're saying is true, which it's not," he added, "you wouldn't start back at the beginning. Kieg and I would come looking for you. And you have your notes in the cave."

"You obviously weren't reading very carefully when we found the Pub Under the Falls. Everyone else forgets me, too. This curse doesn't just hurt me."

"You're right," Kade said. In an instant he stood up straight, his eyebrows furrowing one second and rising into his hairline the next. "Everyone forgets. Everyone forgets!"

Ellayne pushed away from the wall, unsure of how to react to Kade's outburst. "Why are you making that into a good thing?"

"It's not a good thing, but hear me out. In all your papers, who is the one person who always remembers you?"

"Blanndynne," she answered, trying to process what he was trying to get at. "But why—"

"If everyone else can't remember you, why is she the only exception? Have you thought of that? She must know something. Maybe she's the one who cursed you in the first place, and that's why she remembers." Kade had one hand on the strap of the messenger bag, and the other he waved in the air as he spoke, using it to emphasize his words.

"That's a good question," Ellayne said, "but we can't just go accusing her of cursing me."

"Why not?"

Ellayne let out a sarcastic snort. "Well first off, I don't remember how to get back to the house."

"Not a problem, I'm a cartographer, remember? I make maps for a living. What else you got?"

"Secondly," she continued, "if, for some legitimate, non-evil reason, she's the only one who can remember me, and she's taken care of me out of the kindness of her heart, I wouldn't want her to stop because I accused her of a wicked crime. Wandering around without my memories is bad enough without completely lacking an identity. Don't forget that she's the one who told me my name. Without her, I wouldn't even have that."

Kade shrugged. "So we bring it up with less accusing language. I can do that."

"Can you though?"

"I can." The grin that had slipped onto his face disappeared, and his normal granite expression replaced it. "And I will. Come on." He nodded toward the dark tunnel ahead of them. "The sooner we get out of here, the sooner we can get back, see the sun, and hopefully get some answers."

The tunnel went on for what seemed like hours. After the stairs ended, the terrain stayed flat, continuing for many miles. Every once in a while, Ellayne thought she heard a small creature scurry somewhere in the darkness surrounding them, but she never saw any other animals besides a few spiders that made their homes in the crevices of the walls. They stopped twice, eating the few rations they had left in their bags and drinking the last of their canteens.

"Is yours empty?" Kade asked, nodding to Ellayne's canteen. She nodded, and he grunted. "Mine too."

"How much farther do you think it is?"

Kade used the rune stone to look at one of his maps. "I can't be sure, because the only description Linetta gave was that the tunnel led near the river. The Cylan River in the Black Forest runs from here"—he pointed to a blue line near the top of the map—"to here." He pointed to the same blue line at the bottom.

"It even forks off in two directions here and here. I have no idea which part of the river we're going to."

"Can you tell which direction we're walking?"

He shook his head. "I'm not a compass, and the tunnel isn't exactly straight. It's twisted back and forth too many times for me to keep track of which direction we're going."

"So we keep walking?"

"We keep walking."

Ellayne's feet ached from the heels all the way up to where her pinkie toe jammed into the side of the shoe, slamming the nail into her toe with every step. Her shoulder was sore from carrying the bag, made heavier by the three journals she'd grabbed. The bag pulled at the cut on the back of her neck too, and at one point, she was afraid the scab had ripped off. Worried she would bleed on yet more clothes, she had Kade check. It hadn't reopened, but it was red and angry.

"I'll take your bag for a while," he offered, but she shook her head. "Suit yourself."

Most of their walk was in silence, but every once in a while they struck up a conversation.

It was Kade's turn to start. "When we figure out what your curse is and how to break it, what will you do? After, I mean."

"*If* we solve all of this, and that's a huge 'if,' " she shrugged, "I honestly don't know."

"Now who's the negative one? Hm?"

"Not negative, just realistic. We don't even know the name of the curse, so how are we supposed to break it?"

Kade paused for a second, catching Ellayne off guard. She stopped before she ran into his back. When he turned around, she saw a glint of something in his eye, but it was gone before she could recognize what emotion it was.

213

"Don't get upset, but I might know the name of it." He waited to see her reaction, but she left her face blank.

"What?"

"Evangeline mentioned a curse," he said, and when she raised an eyebrow at him, he pointed toward her bag. "I was reading one of the journals from when she was around twenty-five years old. King Butch had ordered a raid on a few villages in the Black Forest in order to find the magic folk who were rumored to live there. Emmalee, Evangeline's best friend, lived in one of those villages with her husband and her daughter."

"What happened? Did Emmalee—"

"Emmalee was visiting Evangeline in a different village when the raid occurred, but the soldiers killed her husband and her daughter, Hazel."

Ellayne's face fell, and she slid down the wall until she was sitting down. "Oh, poor Emmalee. She must've been devastated."

"Heartbroken is a better way to put it." Kade sat down across from her. "There must've been someone in her family who had dark magic, because when she got the news, dark magic exploded out of her. Pure magic comes for most individuals at the age of twenty-one, but people with dark magic in their blood may never know they have magic until their heart is broken for the first time.

"Evangeline said she'd never seen anyone completely succumb to their power that quickly before. Dark magic, like pure magic, takes a few months, if not a year, to come to full power. But Evangeline said that within a few minutes, Emmalee had reached the average person's amount of dark magic at full power, and it continued to grow after that."

"So Evangeline had pure magic, and Emmalee had dark magic?" Ellayne asked.

Kade nodded. "And the journal I was reading yesterday— the one that wasn't on the desk this morning—was from two years later. Emmalee ended her friendship with Evangeline as soon as her powers manifested. You see, pure magic and dark magic have a natural repulsion to each other."

"Where did she go?"

"I'm not sure," Kade said. "I didn't get far enough into the journal to find out. That's why I wanted to know what had happened to it this morning. It was one of the journals Linetta found in her room, and she gave it to me yesterday before she found the other ones. Evangeline wrote that she'd been hearing rumors of a sorceress who had been collecting volunteers for an army to overthrow the king of Phildeterre and bring magic back to the land. She thought it was Emmalee, so she started to track her."

When Ellayne didn't say anything, Kade rolled his eyes. "Of course, you probably don't know about the evil sorceress and how Evangeline became queen?"

"You assume correctly. I would've asked earlier when you mentioned her, but I was distracted by how mad I was at you for keeping Evangeline's magic a secret. It seems I should be mad at you again, but—"

"You'll let it slide."

Ellayne raised an eyebrow, but remained silent.

Kade took it as a hint to explain, so he continued. "King Butch faced a new leader in the magic community, an evil sorceress who was said to be more powerful than her predecessors. She even tricked the first queen, Lenora, into deserting her son, Diomedes, and husband, King Butch. The sorceress got the queen to join her on the side of magic."

"You think the sorceress was Emmalee."

He held up a finger. "I don't 'think' Emmalee was the evil sorceress, I know she was. Evangeline became queen because when King Butch fell into the thick of the war, wifeless and desperate, Evangeline showed up saying she knew how to stop her. How would she know how to stop a powerful stranger? Even with magic, which she would've needed to hide from her future magic-hating husband, it would be nearly impossible to stop a stranger with dark magic as powerful as the evil sorceress. She'd have better luck if she knew who the evil sorceress was, because she used to be best friends with her."

"You make a fair point." Ellayne crossed her legs and put her head in her hands. "But how does this help us with my curse?"

"Evangeline wrote a few years later that Emmalee wanted revenge on King Butch for killing her husband and Hazel. It took her a while, but she heard that a curse might be involved, so she started to do research on all the curses she could."

"You're the worst at giving timely information. Why didn't you say something earlier? This was all really important stuff that you kept from us—from me."

"I don't like presenting unfinished ideas." His posture got worse as his shoulders slumped. "But, I'm sorry."

"Did you bring the journal with you?" Ellayne asked, all but ignoring his apology.

Kade shook his head, his hair falling in front of his eyes. "No. I read it on a piece of parchment shoved into the same journal as the one that went missing."

Sighing, Ellayne rubbed her pointer finger in small circles on her temple. "Then what good is it if we don't have it?"

"I remember the name of the curse, or at least I think I do." His eyebrows furrowed. "The Curse of Infiniti, or the Infiniti Curse. Something like that."

"That's great!" Ellayne beamed at him. "Now we can look that up in other books."

"I grabbed this." He reached into his bag and pulled out a book titled *Curses, Hexes, and Spells for Your Exes*.

"Great start, but King Butch wasn't exactly an ex-lover of Emmalee's, unless that's part of the story you left out."

He snorted, and confidence seeped back into his face. "Not quite. And I haven't really read any of it, but it might give us some insight into what kind of curse we're dealing with and how it might be broken."

Ellayne tucked a strand of hair behind her ear and flicked her eyes between Kade and the book. "So you're basically assigning us more work?"

"No one said breaking curses was easy."

"Peachy."

Chapter Thirty-Five

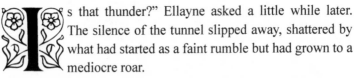s that thunder?" Ellayne asked a little while later. The silence of the tunnel slipped away, shattered by what had started as a faint rumble but had grown to a mediocre roar.

"It's too consistent to be thunder." Kade held the stone up to shine what light he could ahead of them. "But it might be the water from the river up above."

It hadn't taken Ellayne long to notice the ground tilting upward, though not at as steep an incline as the one that led them down into the tunnel. It was the subtle burning of her calves that told her they were no longer walking on a flat surface.

"We must be right under it if that's the case." Ellayne had to raise her voice, the noise had gotten so loud.

"I think we might be crossing under it!" Kade shouted back, and he waved for her to follow him. "Watch your step. It's a little slick." He pointed to the ground. Ellayne could see the compact dirt under their feet was reflective with moisture.

She placed her hand on the wall to balance herself, but it came away muddy. "How has this tunnel not collapsed with this much water in the structure?"

"Magic."

"The problem is, Kade, I can't tell if you're kidding or serious."

"Neither," he replied. "I'm guessing."

Ellayne groaned when she took a step and a puddle of water enveloped her entire foot. Kade looked back to see why she'd stopped, and barked out a quick laugh when he saw her wringing out her sock.

"Jerk," she spat, which made him laugh again.

"At least I'm dry." He winked at her, his dimple creasing at the corner of his mouth. Kade crossed his arms and smirked while she put the cold, damp sock back on and slipped her foot into the soggy shoe.

She slapped him on the arm as she stomped past. "That's for laughing."

His next laugh was halfway out when he stopped and pointed. "I see light up ahead."

Ellayne squinted, and she could see what he was talking about. What seemed like another half mile away shone a small white light. They kept walking, but it wasn't as far away as she thought. Instead, it was a circle of light coming from the ceiling where there was a door similar to the one they'd come in through hours earlier. However, this one had light runes carved into small stones in the wood of the hatch door. Connected to the wall stood a ladder leading up to the door.

"Should we open it?" Ellayne asked, looking past it where the tunnel continued in darkness.

Kade had one hand gripping the ladder, and his foot propped up on the first rung. "Would you rather stay down here in the dark for the rest of your life?"

"Me first." She pushed his hand away from the ladder and scurried up as fast as her sore legs would carry her. When she got to the top, she raised a hand and pushed all her weight into the door, but it wouldn't budge.

"Would you like some help?" Kade asked, his voice dripping in fake sweetness.

Pride destroyed, Ellayne lowered herself down the rungs, after which Kade climbed up. It took two shoves of his shoulder, but on the second one, the door flew open, slamming into the ground.

"You just lacked a little elbow grease," he said with a grin as he looked back down at her.

"And you lack humility," she said under her breath.

Fresh air swept in when Kade opened the door, and it washed over Ellayne, giving her new energy as she hoisted herself back up the ladder. Kade offered his hand to help her up, but she ignored it. She used her arms to push herself out of the dark hole.

"So, Mr. Map Man," Ellayne brushed off her dirty hands while she looked around at the ever familiar view of Black Forest trees, "where are we now?"

Kade's back muscles flexed, framed by his jacket, as he shut the hatch to the tunnel. "We're in—"

"If the next words out of your mouth are 'the Black Forest,' I'm going to open that hatch back up and shove you down it."

He raised an eyebrow. "As much as I'd like to see you try, I was going to say that we're in the western part of the Black Forest Peninsula."

"How can you tell? The only thing I see is more of these stupid trees." Ellayne let out an exasperated sigh and pointed at one nearby.

Kade closed his eyes and shook his head, grinning. "These 'stupid trees' have protected hundreds of thousands of lives from the unfair persecution of those without magic. And these 'stupid trees' in particular happen to be different than the ones that grow in the eastern part of the peninsula."

Ellayne placed her hands on her hips. "Go on."

"This type of 'stupid tree' is—"

"I get it," Ellayne cut in. "I'm sorry for calling your precious trees stupid. What makes these ones so obviously different?"

"These ones are infested with a type of beetle that gives off a sweet smell when it dies." He sniffed the air, and waited until it was clear Ellayne had too. "It's very obvious when you've come into contact with it before."

After he said it, Ellayne could tell what he meant. The scent was so potent, she wasn't sure how she hadn't noticed it as soon as the hatch opened. The air tasted like sugar combined with decaying leaves.

"Why don't the beetles infest all of the Black Forest? Why is it just the western part?"

"It's something about the trees that grow over here." Kade shrugged. "They're newer than the ones on the other side. Remember that fire Linetta mentioned? It was a long time ago, but most of these trees are younger."

"They look the same to me," she mumbled. Her posture dropped at the mention of Linetta. "How is Kiegan going to find us? I mean, if he—"

"We'll leave him a note."

"Where? All of these trees look the same, and there's no promises that he'll find it."

"So we leave him multiple notes all over the woods as we go. Unless you have a better idea?" He was fishing in his bag for a map, and when he found the one he was looking for, he unrolled it and began to study the markings.

"We can leave him a few notes here," Ellayne said, "but then I think we should wait for him in the nearest town. We need more supplies, and—"

"You're the one who keeps pointing to the scar on your wrist to remind us how little time we have. And you want to use

221

more of that precious time waiting for Kiegan?" He stared at her over the top of the map.

Instead of arguing back, Ellayne locked eyes with him and stared back. She crossed her arms over her chest, popping out her hip. Her lips tightened, and she rolled them inward. It didn't take long before Kade made a grunting noise and looked back down at the map in his hands.

"The nearest town is probably several hours south of us. We can wait one day while we read through the journals a bit more, but then we have to move on. We can stop in Calder's village again and maybe spend another day there to wait for Kiegan."

"I'm sure Dayla will love that." Ellayne reached up to touch the scratch marks on her cheek, which had scabbed over and were starting to heal. "She might even try to balance out the beauty marks she gave me."

"We don't have much of a choice." His voice sounded strained, and she noticed his shoulders were tensed. Instead of making him more annoyed, she didn't argue.

"Let's leave a few notes and start going then."

Chapter Thirty-Six

I miss Anya more than I ever thought I could miss a horse. Ellayne glared at the forest floor, keeping Kade's heels at the top part of her vision. She wasn't looking for branches near her face after tripping multiple times. *If my toenails don't fall off at the end of this, it'll be a miracle.*

By the time they made it to the nearest village, the arches of her feet were aching. Blisters had formed and broken open in several different hot spots. Even though she was hungry, she couldn't stay awake long enough for Kade to return to the inn they were staying at. She was fast asleep when Kade knocked. When she didn't answer the door, he opened it enough to see her sleeping, and silently left some bread and her refilled canteen on the chair by the door.

Ellayne woke up even more sore than she'd been the first week when she worked out in the garden doing chores for Blanndynne. Each little movement sent shooting pains through all her muscles.

Finding the food, Ellayne mentally thanked Kade for leaving it and letting her sleep. She hadn't bothered to pay attention to where the innkeeper said Kade's room was, and instead of getting herself lost in the maze of door-lined hallways, she decided it was better to stay where she was and wait for Kade to come to her.

And he did.

A few minutes after she finished the loaf of bread, footsteps echoed in the hall, and a soft knock on the wooden door caused her to look up from the journal she held in her hands.

"Can I come in?"

"I don't know," she replied, "can you?" She closed the journal and tucked it back into her bag.

The first thing he did when he walked in was roll his eyes at her. "I see you found the bread." He nodded toward the crumbs on her shirt.

"I did, and I hope you weren't expecting me to share." She wiped off the crumbs. "Thank you for that, and for not waking me up."

"I don't think I could've if I tried." He sat on the chair. "For half a second I thought you'd died, but then I heard you snore."

Ellayne's mouth opened, and she crossed her arms. "I do not snore."

His dimple appeared as he shook his head. "You sure do. Loud enough to wake the dead, I'd wager."

"Liar." She examined his face as he continued to smile at her. The part of his left cheek that had been swollen the day before was now a dark violet shade, the bruise more prominent than when she'd last seen him. "Did one of the raiders hit you yesterday?"

When he gave her a confused look, she pointed to her cheek. The confusion faded back to amusement, and he let out a low chuckle. "No, Kieg was kind enough to give me this." He pointed to his cheek. "He apologized right afterward, though," he said when he saw Ellayne's expression.

"Kiegan hit you? Why?"

Kade shook his head. "He wasn't in the best mood when you sent me after him."

"I'm so sorry," she said. "I didn't know—"

"You don't need to apologize. You didn't punch me in the face"—his eyes twinkled—"yet. But when that time inevitably arrives, I'll count this as your apology, prepaid."

Ellayne wanted to press further, but Kade changed the subject.

"When we get back to Calder's village, you should make a copy of what we've learned from the journals and put it in the Pub Under the Falls so you can be one step closer to figuring all of this out if we don't succeed this time."

"I can't tell if that was optimistic or pessimistic."

"It was realistic."

Kiegan didn't show up that day, and sticking to Kade's predetermined plan, they left a few more notes for him around, as well as with the innkeeper, before taking off the next day for Calder's village. Ellayne's feet had no time to heal in between the long days of walking, and she and Kade moved slower than they wanted.

With the roof of trees taking away the outside light, Ellayne found it difficult to determine what time of day it was. However, Kade took no issue with this, answering her questions with little more to go off of than the slight changes in the light level and, as he called it, a gut feeling.

"I don't understand how people can live here," she mumbled, lifting her foot over a root. "I haven't seen the sky in days. It's always dark and hard to see. And—"

"Many people didn't have a choice, remember? It was either move to the Black Forest, or worse, the Dark, or be killed for possessing something they never had the choice in possessing."

Kade's words reminded her of what Kiegan had said about Kade's past experiences with the Dark.

"Kade," she said after a moment of thinking her question through, "can I ask you something personal?"

"Maybe."

"Why do you hate the Dark so much?"

Kade, who had been walking a bit in front of her, stopped mid-step. His shoulders tensed, and he gripped the messenger bag in both hands before turning around. Ellayne held the rock with the light runes to guide her steps, and she used the glow to illuminate his features. He narrowed his eyes at her, but then turned his head sideways, looking away into the forest.

"Because I found answers I didn't want when I was in the Dark."

"Answers? To what questions?"

His nostrils flared, and Ellayne had no doubt she'd hit a soft spot in his steely exterior. "I was raised by my uncle; a lousy excuse for a man. My mother abandoned me when I was born and my father was never in the picture, so I got left with a man who had no issues leaving a three-year-old on the curb to swindle people out of their money in the streets of Cyanthia."

"Kade, I—"

"And when I asked to go to school like the rest of the kids my age, he got so angry that he left me with a broken rib, a busted lip, and a black eye. Why? Because I was his main source of income, and when I left, he'd have to actually get off his lazy bum and work. So I ran away. Ended up going from Cyanthia to Pingbi, where I lived in an alley behind a shop until a woman named Olinda took me in. She's the one who taught me to take care of others, because she took care of me."

It explains so much. Ellayne tucked a piece of hair behind her ear, feeling the warmth of his stare on her face. Her cheeks heated up as she continued to listen.

Kade shifted his weight to his other leg, crossing his arms over his chest. "As a young boy, I wanted to know how in the world I'd ended up with such a scumbag for an uncle. Well, I stopped asking that when I was in the Dark. I met a man with magic, dark magic. I should've known better. He told me he could feel the questions of my past, and if I was willing to pay the price, he'd answer them for me. He didn't tell me that the price would be any peace of mind I had left."

"What do you mean?"

"He told me that the man who claimed to be my uncle wasn't related to me at all. And when he was about to tell me who my parents were and, better yet, where they were, he keeled over and died at my feet."

Ellayne's lips parted with a gasp. "Are you—"

"I can barely go one night without seeing the body." His posture sagged. "I may as well have killed the guy myself. And what's unnerving is that I'm more perturbed over the fact that I have even more questions now than I am about the man who died in front of me."

For the first time since she'd met him, there was a new emotion flickering in his dark eyes. He squeezed them shut and scrunched his eyebrows together. *He has no family, like me,* Ellayne thought, watching him fight against his trembling lip. Before he could stop her, she closed the space between them and wrapped her arms around his torso. He stumbled backward a few steps when her body collided with his, but regained his balance. Unsure of what to do with his arms, he held them out sideways. She waited a few seconds before letting go.

Stepping back, she offered a small smile. "Thank you for telling me."

Chapter Thirty-Seven

omething isn't making sense to me." Ellayne placed her finger in the journal she was reading. A chilly breeze blew in from the single window in Calder's attic, and Ellayne pulled the blanket up to her chin.

"What?"

"Queen Evangeline had magic."

"Yeah. So?" Kade stretched his shoulders, yawning as he asked the question.

"Why didn't she use her magic to save herself and her husband? Linetta thought so highly of her, but the person she described wouldn't just sit back and give up. She would fight for the ones she loved. "

Kade shrugged, lacing his fingers together behind his head. His biceps bulged under the tight sleeves of his tunic, distracting her for more than a second.

"King Butch and the entire Maudit line were against magic. They were the ones who started the Split of Phildeterre in the first place. She could've gotten into huge trouble if she exposed herself. Better not to risk it," he said.

"But she would've at least been alive. I mean, I would try to save my husband if I had the means to do so." *And if I had a husband*, she added in her mind.

"Maybe she couldn't use it."

"What would stop her from using her magic, especially in such a dire situation?"

Kade bit his lip, thinking in silence for a moment. "A spell." He held up his pointer finger and his eyes widened. "I know of a few metals that dampen the effects of magic. Maybe she didn't use it because she couldn't physically."

"I guess." Ellayne weighed his words in her head. *Maybe she did fight, and we just didn't see it in the memory.* She added that explanation to Kade's, tucking them into the recess of her mind.

"Why do you ask?"

"It's just been bothering me that in the last memory of the necklace, it was across the room from the queen."

"You think someone else was there when she died?"

"It's just a thought." She watched his reaction.

He scratched his chin. "Something to keep in mind, I suppose."

"You're sure you can't stay another day?" Calder asked, leaning against the doorframe of his shop. Dayla glared at Ellayne from behind Calder inside the building. Despite her annoyance at Ellayne, Dayla had apologized to Kade for putting him under her siren spell during their last visit. It had been a heavily supervised apology.

"We're sure," Kade responded. His bag swung side to side on his shoulder as he put it on, filled with fresh supplies.

Ellayne nodded. "Thank you again for letting us stay with you while we waited for Kiegan."

"If I see him, I'll let him know that you two passed through," Calder said. Reaching around, he pulled a small piece of parchment from his pocket. "And I'll make sure to give him this."

"Thanks." Kade shook Calder's hand, and then nodded to Dayla, who sulked behind her brother.

"Be safe out there," Calder said, and he waved as Kade and Ellayne headed toward the entrance of the village.

With half a day of walking gone, Ellayne began to notice the trees thinning out after they crossed a bridge. She vaguely remembered crossing it while riding Anya after the archer grazed her with the arrow. However, the memories were tinged with fuzziness.

"We're getting close to the edge of the Black Forest, aren't we?" she asked, breathing out each word in between short wheezes.

"We should be out within the hour." Kade did a much better job of hiding how out of breath he was. She hated that he'd barely broken a sweat during most of their time traveling, and the only difficulty she'd seen him have was on the second full day of walking when he groaned getting up from the ground after a snack break.

"Lovely," she said, dodging another branch threatening to take her head off.

When the first ray of sunlight hit her skin, Ellayne couldn't stop a grin from stretching across her face. Warmth spread through her, filling up the cold emptiness she hadn't noticed the forest created in her. The sky shone radiant with sunlight; it was as bright as she could remember it ever being.

"Wow," she breathed, closing her eyes as the light covered her skin.

"Always a relief to get out." Kade stopped too, watching her take in the sun. "And we've ended up farther east than I thought we would. We can either stop in Pingbi first, or we can head straight to the bridge where we told Kieg we'd meet him in the notes."

"We should go to the bridge," she said as she opened her eyes. "We don't want to make him wait any longer than we have to."

"Good point. Besides," he glanced at her left hand, which was almost completely blackened by the curse, "by the looks of it, we're running short on time."

She wasn't sure why, but something about the way his stare lasted longer than a second caused her cheeks to flush, and she shoved the hand into the pocket of the jacket so it was no longer visible.

"Right," she muttered, "let's go."

They heard the Cylan River—the sound of it rushing past the rocks—before they could see it.

"We must be near the rapids. My guess is we're near where you fell in, because you wouldn't have lasted much longer farther up the river," Kade said, walking past another tree. The trees were few and far between now, but there was quite a bit of brush, and Ellayne could see another wall of trees in the distance.

"But I was running through the forest," Ellayne said, glancing around. "We've pretty much left the forest now. How can—"

Kade interrupted her by pointing to the line of trees she'd just looked at. They were getting closer as they walked. "You were on that side of the river. We're on the side of the Level Plains."

"Oh." She kicked a stubborn bush out of the way. "Then how soon will we be able to see the bridge?"

"Once we get to the river, we might be able to see it, but it's still a pretty good distance away. And the river bends here." He gestured to where they could finally see the river opening up before them.

He was right. The river was whitecapped because of the rapids, and as they walked beside it, Ellayne questioned how she'd made it out without drowning or breaking a limb. The answer to her question walked beside her, bringing back memories of that day.

"You were lucky," he said, nudging her with his shoulder. She didn't dare nudge back—he was walking on the edge closer to the river.

"Yeah," she snorted, "lucky you had no qualms about getting your hair wet."

"It was a surprise swim."

"For you and me both."

"But I don't regret it."

Ellayne stopped, and he paused too, squinting down at her because of the sun. His dark eyes flickered all over, taking in her face and focusing in on her eyes. The grin on his face was lopsided, and the dimple in his cheek caught her attention. *Has he ever smiled at me like this?* The dimple drew her focus to land on his lips as he spoke.

"I'd do it again," his voice lowered, "but that's not an invitation to jump in, if you were thinking about it."

"I wasn't."

"That's reassuring."

"Mm-hmm."

Another moment of silence. They stood face-to-face. Some new emotion pulled at her stomach, but she ignored it. Shaking her head, she aimed her thumb toward the direction they'd been walking.

"Shall we?" she asked, nodding her head toward the nonexistent path.

He looked her over once more, and bobbed his head.

"We shall."

The trees were thick on the opposite side of the river, but completely gone on the side they were walking on. This meant Ellayne had a clear view of what was ahead. With her sight locked on the horizon, she finally saw a small sliver hovering over the water in the distance.

"I think I see it," Ellayne said.

"I think you're right."

"Always am." She grinned when he snorted. As she squinted at the bridge, she saw a brown shape moving around, and behind it was a black one of similar size. "Kade, I think he's there." Her pace quickened, and before she knew it, her tired limbs revitalized, propelling her toward the bridge.

Kade hollered after her once, but she could hear him running behind her, so she didn't look back. As she got closer, the two shapes shifted, looking more and more like horses. The brown one, Anya, looked up when she heard Ellayne coming and gave a short whinny. A figure of a man lying in the grass not too far away sat up. Getting to his feet, he looked first at the horses, and then peered in the same direction as Anya.

"Kiegan!" Ellayne shouted, a smile stretching across her face. She pumped her arms at her sides as she closed the last couple feet between them, barreling into his open arms.

He embraced her as he stumbled back a few feet. Kiegan laughed, squishing her in a hug. "It's about time you showed up," he said into her hair. "I've been waiting in this spot for the last two days." Kiegan let go, looking at her from head to toe. "You're all right?"

Kade caught up. "We're exhausted from walking almost the entire length of the Black Forest, but other than that, no trouble." He hugged Kiegan, patting him firmly on the back.

"Makes you wish you'd gone back for these two, doesn't it?" Kiegan nodded toward the horses.

"I'm sorry we left them, Kieg."

Ellayne nodded in agreement. "I've never wanted to travel by horseback so much in my life."

"It's taken us nearly five days to get back here. Did you say you've been here for two days straight?" Kade asked.

Kiegan shook his head. "It took me a few days to get here, and I've been here during the day and back at Pingbi at night. I didn't want to miss you guys, but I also didn't want to be mauled by a wild animal in my sleep."

"How did you get out of Linetta's village?" Ellayne readjusted her bag, which had swiveled around to her back during her sprint to the bridge.

"Linetta helped me." He scratched the back of his head. "I owe her my life and the lives of Anya and Curry."

"How—"

"She caused a distraction at one of the gates to the village in order to make a gap for me to pass through."

"But the last I saw, she went running to the bookstore, which had caught on fire," Ellayne said, glancing at Kade for confirmation. He nodded.

"All I know is I was preparing Anya and Curry to leave the stables when two raiders came in. They didn't really have weapons, though one of them had a large spear he must've made from one of the tree branches. I was cornered in the stall with Anya when Linetta came in from behind and clocked one over the head with the heaviest book I think I've ever seen. I managed to take the other guy down when he was distracted. When I offered to get her out of the village she refused, and instead pulled the attention away from one of the gates. I'm not sure what she did, but she told me to wait a few minutes and then make a break for it when I saw the raiders standing guard at the gate leave. Sure enough, they did."

"Did Linetta—"

"Ellayne," Kiegan's voice lowered, and he reached for her hands, "I don't know. But we have to hope she's all right."

She was distracted by his warm hands, and when her blackened one came into her line of sight, she pushed down the roiling sadness threatening to spill onto her face.

"We need to keep going," she said, pulling her hands out of his and tucking them into her pockets. "I'm running out of time."

Chapter Thirty-Eight

So we're just going to wander around until we accidentally stumble through the front door of the house?" Kiegan asked. He was once again sitting in front of Ellayne on Anya, and Kade was leading the way on Curry. Ellayne's feet swung on either side of the horse, thankful to have a break.

After being deep in the Black Forest, Ellayne recognized a light difference. The section of forest they entered when they crossed the bridge was not as dense, and she appreciated the rays of light that managed to pass through the branches. It seemed so much lighter than the first time.

"I'm not sure where it is," she responded, "so yes."

"I've been in the area we just passed through before, so we probably need to head a bit farther west," Kade said, redirecting Curry a few degrees to the left. "You said your friend mentioned it was near the border of Cyanthia, right?"

"Close enough for her to work in the castle and yet live in the house." She nodded. "I hope she's okay."

Kiegan glanced over his shoulder at her. "Why wouldn't she be?"

"Well," Ellayne sighed, "I don't know. I left in such a hurry. She would've found the arrow the archer shot into the doorframe, and I know he ended up chasing me, but what if he went back for her?"

"You sound like me," Kade said. "Stop." He and Curry rode next to them, and she raised an eyebrow at him.

"What do you—"

"You're the one who pointed out that I'm always negative. Apparently I've passed that on to you, and I'd appreciate it if you'd stop copying me."

"What—"

"Don't steal my 'thing.'" He winked at her, and she smiled despite the concern she had for Blanndynne.

"The trees are clearing up there," Kiegan interrupted. "Do you mind riding ahead to see if it's worth checking out?" he asked Kade.

Ellayne could see how prominent the tendons were on the sides of his neck, making her think Kiegan was clenching his jaw.

"Can do," Kade replied. He nudged Curry in the side with the heel of his boot, spurring his horse on.

When he was out of earshot, Kiegan cleared his throat. "Ellayne," he murmured, "before he comes back, I need to tell you something."

She shifted on the back of the saddle, unsure of how to respond. "You can tell me anything, Kiegan. What's up?"

"When we got separated at the village, I had time to think, and . . . I have feelings for you."

"What kind of feelings?" Her arms trembled at the same time her mind raced. *Feelings? Good feelings or bad feelings? Did I do something wrong? Am I—*

"When I wasn't sure if you'd gotten out or not, I couldn't stand myself for leaving you. In the time we've been together, you've become more important to me than I ever thought a person could be."

"Kiegan, that's really sweet of you—"

"I'm not finished," he interrupted. "I think you're the most beautiful woman I've ever met, and I . . . I think I'm falling in love with you."

Ellayne's mouth opened, but no words came out. Her heart pounded faster than she wanted it to, and chaos existed where the giddiness of being desired and the unfortunate timing clashed. *I care for you too, but why are you saying this now, of all times? I could lose my memories tomorrow. Kiegan, I trust you, and I love being with you. But—I can't say it. Not with the curse. Why couldn't you wait until I was free?* Her stomach rolled at the thought of hurting him, but she couldn't bring herself to say the words back.

When she didn't say anything, Kiegan tried to look around at her, but she buried her face in his back.

"I'm sorry," he murmured, and Ellayne could feel him deflating in her arms. "I shouldn't have said anything."

"Please don't apologize," Ellayne said, her voice muffled from the jacket. "Thank you for saying it. It means so much, and I feel so close to you. It's just that—"

The sound of hooves on the ground marked Kade's return. "I found it!"

Ellayne straightened up, forcing the mess of emotions from their prominent place on her face. "The house?"

"No, the last surviving unicorn." Kade rolled his eyes. "Yes, the house. It's up ahead, come on."

"We'll follow you," Kiegan said, and Ellayne thought she could hear monotony in his voice that hadn't been there before.

Despite the fact that she was holding on to him, Ellayne could feel the new distance between her and Kiegan. Part of her brain screamed at her, telling her she should've said she had feelings for him too. There was nothing particularly that turned her off of him, and she often found her thoughts lingering around him on more than one account; the way his kindness and personality lit up a conversation, the way he made her feel safe during unnerving times, or even the way he showed his concern for her by waking her up from her nightmare when they were in Calder's attic.

But another voice in her head had Ellayne staring through the curtain of her hair at her blackened arm. With the threat of the curse breathing down her neck, the timing couldn't have been worse. His confession filled her with excitement that buzzed through her, followed by a sobering wave of reality; if she didn't find a way to break the curse, she wouldn't remember him, nor would he have any recollection of her.

"Ellayne?" Kade said her name a second time, pulling her attention to the outside world. "Is this it or not? Because I don't see a lot of other tiny houses in the middle of open fields in the Black Forest."

They'd come to the edge of a line of trees that opened out into a clearing with a small house in the distance. Blanndynne's house.

"This is it," she said, and letting go of Kiegan with one arm, she reached up and rubbed the necklace with the back of her thumb.

"I haven't seen you do that in a while," Kade said, nodding in her direction.

"Do what?"

"Mess with your necklace," he said, "or the bracelet."

Ellayne dropped her hand to her wrist instinctively, but the bracelet wasn't there. "I lost it. The bracelet, I mean."

"When?" Kiegan asked. "The last time I saw you, you had it."

She did her best to ignore the way Kiegan's voice made her stomach twist.

Her mind rolled back to the moment in the village when she'd lost the bracelet. "I was caught by someone when we were

239

escaping, and he grabbed my wrist. But he only had a grip on the bracelet. When I pulled my wrist out of his hand, he must've still had the bracelet."

"Where were you in all of this?" Kiegan's voice was sharp as he directed his attention to Kade. "How did you let that happen to her?"

"Don't be so quick to accuse when you were the one who up and left us. You weren't there for her either," Kade said.

"I wouldn't have let her be attacked!"

"You did by not being there."

"Enough," Ellayne snapped. "I won't be the reason you two start bickering. I'm fine and the bracelet is gone. That's the end of it. Either talk this out like adults or stop talking. I'm on a bit of a tight schedule."

The intense staring contest Kiegan had engaged Kade in ended when Kade glanced at Ellayne.

He nodded. "I'm sorry. He's right, Ellayne. I should've noticed that you weren't behind me. I'm sorry I realized too late that you were in trouble. And Kieg," he shifted his eyes back to his friend, "I'm sorry for snapping at you. I was angry when you left, but that's not a good enough reason to hold this over your head forever."

Kiegan shifted on Anya, adjusting his position. "Yeah, well, let's just go to the house."

Kade hesitated, and Ellayne had a sneaking suspicion that he wanted to say more, or at least expected his friend to say more, but he didn't make a big deal out of it as he followed behind them on Curry.

Chapter Thirty-Nine

Blanndynne?" Ellayne knocked on the door a second time, but there was no answer. The arrow was no longer stuck in the wood, but there was a nick where it had once been lodged.

"I don't see anyone inside," Kade said from the window near the front door.

"Here," Kiegan said, stepping forward. Ellayne moved out of his way as he rattled the doorknob. It hitched once, but twisted in his hand. Unlocked like she'd left it. The door creaked open, and after a glance back at Ellayne, he walked in.

"Blanndynne?" Ellayne called when she followed him.

"No one's here," Kiegan said, having popped his head into the three other rooms. He placed his hands on his hips. "Does it look the same as when you left?"

Ellayne nodded and crossed her arms over her chest. "It's the exact same."

Kade stepped over the threshold and looked between the two of them. "No sign of anyone being here for a couple days at least. The water in the barrel outside has gone stale and the garden seems to have been a buffet for some of the wildlife."

"Do you think—"

"If she works at the castle, that's probably where she is." Kade cut off Ellayne's question before it had time to leave her lips. "Besides that, there's better food at the castle." He nodded toward a loaf of bread on the counter that was entirely covered in spots of green, black, and white mold.

"So what now?" Kiegan asked, leaning against the wall near the entrance to Blanndynne's room.

Ellayne crossed to the door of the room she'd woken up in. "I'm not sure," she said as she opened the door. The sight of the room brought back the first memories she could recall. Her body shook, and she contained it as best she could. "Can you two give me a moment alone?"

"Sure."

"Of course."

When they'd left and closed the front door behind them, she made her way into the bedroom and collapsed on her knees in front of the mirror. In more than one way, she was staring at the same girl she hadn't recognized when she first woke up nearly a month earlier. Her nose was tinged pink and her hair was a blond mess. But there were differences, too. The scratch marks on her cheek from her tussle with Dayla were the most obvious.

But the subtlest change was the biggest: her eyes. They were still brown, but as she looked with clearer eyes than she had the first day, she could see golden flecks she didn't remember being there originally. And she was sure those speckles held memories; memories of the last few weeks albeit, but still memories.

Instead of falling apart into tears as she had the first day, she steeled her jaw and clasped her hands into fists.

"As long as I have these memories, I'm not giving up," she whispered to the mirror. Her skin prickled and the hair on the back of her neck lifted, making her question if Kade or Kiegan were watching her, but she didn't see either of them.

Near the floor, a mark on the bottom left corner of the frame surrounding the mirror caught her attention. She was about to examine it closer when she heard Kiegan calling her.

"Ellayne," Kiegan's voice rang from outside, and with a glance at what looked like symbols, she left the room.

Kiegan met her at the front door, and without another word, he pointed toward the tree line. She squinted toward the setting sun, and the figure of a woman moving along the trees.

"Blanndynne!" Ellayne called, and she took off before Kiegan or Kade could stop her. With her sore limbs pumping, she made it to the trees and embraced her dark-haired friend. "Blanndynne, I was so worried."

"Ellayne? Is it really you?" Blanndynne appeared too stunned to hug Ellayne back. "You've been gone for so long, I thought something had happened. I found the house empty and you weren't at the river—"

"There's so much to tell you," Ellayne said, stepping back and grasping Blanndynne by her hands. "And I want you to meet my friends."

As soon as she mentioned them, Kade and Kiegan appeared, the latter out of breath from chasing Ellayne. Kade moved his hand from the dagger at his side when Ellayne gave a subtle shake of her head. He'd worn it around his belt since Linetta had given it to him, but hadn't had much reason to use it.

"Blanndynne, this is Kiegan." Ellayne nodded toward him. "And this is Kade."

Both men nodded at the mention of their names, and Kiegan stepped forward. "It's nice to meet you, Blanndynne." He held out his hand, and after a curious tilt of her head, Blanndynne placed her smaller one in his.

"For me as well." She stood up straighter after she took her hand out of Kiegan's. "I'm afraid I haven't been back in a while, so I can't offer you anything to eat or drink, but why don't we go inside and you can share with me where you've been all this time."

A little while later, Ellayne and Blanndynne sat in the two chairs in the house, while Kiegan and Kade leaned against opposite walls.

"I can't believe you're cursed," Blanndynne said. She reached across the small table and held Ellayne's hand, the one that was now completely black. "And if what you say is true, how is it that I remember you?"

"That's what we wanted to ask you," Kade said. It was the first time he'd spoken in a while, even though Ellayne had seen him fidget multiple times, as if he was fighting to stay quiet. He *had* promised to be nice.

"What are you accusing me of?" Blanndynne's voice chilled, and she pulled her hand away from Ellayne's.

"We aren't accusing you of anything," Ellayne said, reaching for her hand. "We're still looking for more information on the curse, and since you're a bit of an anomaly, we thought you might have more answers for us."

Blanndynne looked from Kade to Ellayne, and raised an eyebrow at Kiegan, who shrugged.

"If you couldn't tell, I didn't know she was cursed," Blanndynne said, returning her gaze back to Kade, "and I don't remember ever seeing her hand in this state." She lifted Ellayne's hand to get a closer look.

"You agree that it's from dark magic, though?" Ellayne asked.

Her friend nodded. "From what I know, it's definitely from dark magic. Have you tried looking up more information on the curse itself?"

"Tried," Kade nodded, "and we found out the name of it, but we still don't know how to break it."

Kiegan raised his eyebrow, and Ellayne remembered they hadn't filled him in on what they'd found out about Evangeline, Emmalee, and the Curse of Infiniti.

"It wasn't much," she said. "Do you know where we could find out more?"

Blanndynne glanced up from her hand. "There may be a place you could do some more research, but I'm not sure if you'll be allowed." The corner of her mouth curled up in a smile.

"Where?" Kade asked, stepping forward from the wall.

"The king has a large library with many of the books that were banned during the war, but it's not open to the public." Blanndynne leaned back, crossing one leg over the other.

"How would we get in?" Ellayne pulled her hand back into her lap.

"Into the castle?" Kiegan snorted. "No way are we breaking into a castle."

"You couldn't break into it if you wanted to. It's heavily guarded," Blanndynne corrected, "but because of my position, I happen to have access to the castle, and I might be able to ask for a hearing with King Diomedes."

Something was rising in Ellayne, and she couldn't help but smile. "Would you really do that?"

"Of course." Blanndynne returned her smile. "I'm happy to help such a dear friend." She reached forward and patted Ellayne's knee.

Dear friend? Ellayne forced her face not to react, telling her eyebrow not to rise, nor her eyes to narrow. *She's never called me a friend. Not that I can remember, at least. I suppose I've called her my friend, though . . . I'll take the help.* She grinned back at Blanndynne. *If it's going to help me break this curse, I'll do anything.*

Chapter Forty

Blanndynne took Ellayne's spot behind Kiegan. Since Blanndynne mentioned how horses also made her nervous, Ellayne suggested she ride with Kiegan because he was the horse whisperer. That left Ellayne riding behind Kade. She felt her jaw muscles tighten every once in a while when she saw Blanndynne gripping Kiegan around the waist. The same emotions she'd felt when Dayla had captivated Kiegan returned, and Ellayne forced herself to focus on the journey instead.

It took half an hour to reach the castle by horse. They avoided the main part of the town because they came in from the east, and the busy part of town was on the west. There were one or two shops closing as they approached the wall surrounding the castle, but nobody seemed to notice them.

Blanndynne assured Kiegan multiple times that the horses would be safe in the royal stables, and he finally agreed to enter the castle with the others. Blanndynne led the way, nodding to two guards at the side entrance. She informed Ellayne when their group passed through the side gate that the servants and guards used that entrance, while the important officials entered through the extravagant main gate.

"This isn't extravagant?" Kiegan asked, lifting his chin to take in all the carvings on the stone walls.

"Not compared to the main entrance," Blanndynne replied as she pulled open a heavy wooden door. "If this impresses you, then the formal entry would render you speechless."

"Where's the library?" Kade asked after peeking his head through one of the doorways. "These all look like servants' quarters."

"That's because they are." She strode ahead, and though the men had no issue keeping up, Ellayne kept falling behind.

Blanndynne continued up a narrow staircase, and Ellayne's eyes widened when they came to a hallway with a two-story ceiling. There was a balcony up above, and Ellayne could see another hallway on the upper floor leading in the opposite direction. Humongous windows let in what was left of the light from the setting sun, and orange beams fell on ornate tapestries along the wall.

"This is—" Ellayne started.

"Incredible," Kade finished for her.

"Follow me, please." Blanndynne hadn't stopped like the other three, and they quickened their pace to catch up. "Wait in here while I go see if the king will hear your request. I can't make any promises, and it is rather late. But I will go seek an audience with him."

She opened a door to a room the size of Blanndynne's house. It had a few couches and reclining chairs. There was a short table in the middle of the room with a bowl of nuts and a few glasses upside down.

"I'll have someone bring in something to drink," Blanndynne said, and she shut the door behind her.

Kade and Ellayne were in the middle of explaining to Kiegan what they'd found in Evangeline's journals when a young servant girl came in with a pot of hot tea. They thanked her and waited for her to leave before continuing their conversation.

"So Emmalee went dark. How is that possible?" Kiegan asked, his head in his hands. It muffled his voice.

"Someone in her family had dark magic," Kade said. He was sprawled out on one of the chairs, lying sideways across the armrests. His feet dangled above the floor.

"I know that." Kiegan picked his head up, glaring at Kade through his hair. "I'm not as much of an idiot as you think I am."

"I don't actually think you're—"

"Yes you do." He stood up, placing one hand in his pocket while jabbing the other in Kade's direction. "You call me an idiot all the time!"

"I'm only joking."

"It's a lousy joke. You belittle everything I do, and you talk to me like I'm a child. I'm tired of it." He stomped toward the door, but as he was about to open it, Blanndynne came in.

"I hope you weren't planning to leave," she said, nodding toward Kiegan, who shoved both hands in his pockets and shook his head. "Good, because the king has agreed to see you."

Ellayne stood up from the lounge chair, and before she could stop it, a tiny thought crept into her mind. *That was easy*.

"Really? That's amazing!" She rushed across the room and embraced Blanndynne in a hug. "When can we see him?"

Blanndynne stiffened, but didn't pull away. "Now," she replied. "He's waiting for you in the throne room."

"Well we should go then," Ellayne said, nodding for Kade and Kiegan to follow.

"Don't want to keep the king waiting," Kade muttered, earning himself a glare from both the women and Kiegan.

The hallway Blanndynne led them down was lined with torches, and Ellayne noticed a servant boy lighting them as they walked past. The sun passed behind the horizon, and the last of the light was leaving the sky as they turned down a hallway that led away from the giant windows.

"I'm sure you are aware of the king's . . . idiosyncrasy, and it's best if you don't comment about it."

"You mean the fact that he's blind?" Kade asked.

She scrunched her nose up at him. "Yes. And it would be wise not to speak of it so blatantly."

"Noted."

"Anything else we should be prepared for?" Ellayne asked, rubbing her thumb over the back of the necklace.

"There's always more, but no time for it now." Blanndynne stopped at a set of doors four feet taller than the top of Kade's head. Two guards stood at attention, each with a longsword at their side. "I'll be out here if you need me. But do me a favor and don't need me. I don't want my kindness in bringing you here to be the reason I lose my job."

Ellayne's hands shook, and she felt buzzing beneath her skin. "You're not coming in with us?"

"No," she replied, giving a slight nod to the guards.

Before Ellayne could beg her to change her mind and join them, the guard pushed open the throne room doors and ushered them in.

"Ladies first," Kade whispered, pushing Ellayne gently on the back. She stumbled as her feet tried to remember how to function. "You can do this," he said more quietly.

Ellayne thought the hallway had tall ceilings, but it was nothing compared to the vaulted ceiling of the throne room. Her eyes trailed up the walls, where curtains hung, looping and twisting in elegant streams of silky, maroon fabric. Above her were many purple dots, which she recognized as flowers, painted over the entirety of the ceiling in a swirling vine-like design.

Straight ahead of them was a raised platform with a wide set of stairs leading up to it. On it sat two ornate chairs, the one on the left much larger than the one on the right. They were empty, and something about that sight caused her to shiver. The cushions on the thrones were made of similar fabric to that of the curtains, but the frame of the chairs was made of silver metal. From her vantage point, she couldn't discern the pattern of the metal, but it looked organic, repeating similar shapes to the vines on the ceiling.

"It's breathtaking, is it not?" A man spoke from a shadow near the back of the room. "I've kept it the same as when my parents had it redesigned."

The first thing she saw of the king of Phildeterre was the black strip of silk tied over his eyes. His hair was as dark as the scarf, and upon first glance the fabric disappeared into his hair. On top of his head sat a crown littered with jewels. It was made from a dark gray metal, which reflected the light of the torches as much as the diamonds. He wore all black, from his velvet shirt down to his leather boots. A silver chain similar to Ellayne's hung around his neck, the end of it hidden somewhere in his tunic. He wore black gloves on both hands, so the only skin showing on his entire person was around his neck and face. His skin was pale; more pale than Kade's.

"It's beautiful," Ellayne said when Kiegan nudged her. "Truly gorgeous, Your Majesty." She curtsied, her cheeks warming when she looked back to see Kiegan grinning at her and Kade raising an eyebrow.

"Please introduce yourselves." King Diomedes stepped closer to them and clasped his hands behind his back. "I've been told that you need access to my private library, but I need to know who you are first."

"Of course, Your Majesty. I'm Ellayne." She paused. "I'm afraid I don't know my last name. Sorry, Your Majesty."

His eyebrows rose, wrinkling the scarf covering his eyes, and his mouth curled into a small grin. He nodded, waiting for Kade and Kiegan to introduce themselves.

"Kade Willows."

"My name is Kiegan Greene, Your Majesty." Kiegan bowed, and shot Kade a glare when he didn't. Kade motioned to his own eyes, and nodded his head toward the king.

"A pleasure," King Diomedes said, and turned his head in Kade's direction. "And for future reference, Willows, I may be blind, but I have excellent hearing. You may bow down to your king now."

Kade's eyes widened, and clenching his jaw, he too bowed down. "My apologies, Your Majesty."

"Now that that's settled, why don't you tell me what's going on?"

Chapter Forty-One

King Diomedes strode back and forth across the room as Ellayne explained how much they'd learned about the curse; Kade and Kiegan pitched in every once in a while when she missed something. He didn't interrupt her once, and without being able to read into his eyes, Ellayne was left to guess what his reaction was.

"The Curse of Infiniti, hmm? So that is why you have come here? To do research? Sounds like a tedious thing to do considering your limited time, but of course I will oblige. You may use my library, though I am not promising you will find anything in there."

"Thank you, your Majesty." Ellayne curtsied again, and there was a small grin on her face.

"But of course you must begin tomorrow, as it is late now." King Diomedes paused right in front of them, and had there not been a scarf covering his eyes, Ellayne would've sworn he was staring straight at her. "I will show you to your room Ellayne, and two of the servants will show your companions."

At his words, the giant doors swung open. Blanndynne and

another servant walked in and stopped behind Ellayne, Kade, and Kiegan. Ellayne had the sneaking suspicion they'd been eavesdropping on the whole conversation, which explained how they knew when to come in.

"You're letting us stay here?" Kiegan asked, unable to keep his voice from rising in pitch.

"Of course," King Diomedes replied, turning his head toward Kiegan. "I wouldn't send my subjects out at a time like this. Not when there's been an increase of raids from both magic-favoring and non-magic groups."

"Thank you for your generosity, Your Majesty," Ellayne said.

King Diomedes nodded. "Come with me, Ellayne." He strode past them, and Blanndynne and her comrade bowed when he walked between them.

Glancing at Kiegan and Kade, Ellayne followed the king after receiving a nod from her friends.

The blind king had no issue navigating the corridors. With his hands clasped behind his back, he turned corners and walked up stairs with ease. Ellayne scurried behind him, often falling behind his long stride.

He led her through a wide passageway into a lengthy hall full of portraits. Ellayne took in the faces on the wall as fast as she could while still keeping up with the king.

"These people," she said, "they're past rulers?"

"Yes, all the way back to the start of Cyanthia as a kingdom to the merging of all five kingdoms of Phildeterre into a country united under one king."

Two faces stood out in the next to last portrait, faces she'd seen before. King Butch sat in an ornate chair next to Queen Evangeline, and there was a young boy with black hair standing to the left of the late king.

"The little boy in this portrait," Ellayne said, "this is you, correct?"

"It is."

"You were adorable, Your Majesty." She grinned, catching up with the king, who was waiting by the exit. "May I ask you a question, Your Majesty?"

"Perhaps," his voice drawled.

"What was it like growing up in the castle?"

"Isolating," King Diomedes answered without hesitation. "It is a life of isolation."

"Oh, I'm sorry. I shouldn't have . . ." Ellayne's words tapered off, and she felt her cheeks heat up. *It's probably more isolating without his parents. I should've kept my mouth closed.* She mentally kicked herself.

However, King Diomedes did not rebuke her for her curiosity, and instead led her down another corridor.

"I hope this room will be to your liking," the king said when he stopped in front of a tall door. "It's one of a kind."

When he pushed it open and stepped back, Ellayne's mouth fell open. The space was enormous. The walls were painted a pale yellow, lit up at the moment by a few well-placed candles around the room. A glass double door opened up onto a balcony, through which Ellayne could see the third moon rising above the forested horizon. Against the center of the left wall stood a four-poster bed with purple silk curtains tied to the posts with yellow ribbons.

A writing desk sat near a window with a small bookshelf hanging on the wall above it. On the opposite wall from the bed was a six-door wardrobe, and Ellayne could only begin to imagine what lovely dresses once hung in it.

"Whose room is this?" Ellayne asked, venturing in a bit farther.

"It belonged to someone who isn't missing it."

She didn't push for more answers. Instead, she walked over to the window and peered out. "We're quite high up," she said, looking at the guards on the ground, who appeared like small ants wandering around.

"This is the floor the royal family would typically reside on."

Ellayne whipped around. "What?"

"I believe you understood me correctly." His mouth curled upward. "It seemed like you needed a good bed so as to be well-rested for the day of research tomorrow. Am I mistaken?"

She shook her head after a moment, and was surprised to see him nod right after.

"Good. Then I will leave you to your evening routine."

"Thank you, Your Majesty." She didn't straighten up from her curtsy until he had shut the door.

The silence of the room hit her first. After King Diomedes's footsteps faded away down the stone hallway, emptiness rang in Ellayne's ears. Since the moment she'd entered the castle, there was an energy rippling through her, and now that she was alone, it overwhelmed her. The only part of her body not vibrating with the sensation was the black portion of her left arm.

She ran her fingers over the scar, examining the blackened skin. Despite the appearance, it still did not cause her any pain. It spread faster now than it had in the beginning. When she removed her tunic, she saw her skin in a nearby mirror. The darkness radiated through her entire hand, and was creeping up her left shoulder, inching toward her neck. According to her papers from the pub, it would head toward her heart next. Then it would be over. *I'll lose everything. My memories, my friends, and any chance at moving forward.*

The heaviness of reality compelled her to sigh. *Time is slipping, and I can't stop it. Just like water through my fingers.*

The bed enveloped her as she lay down, pulling the fluffy comforter up to her chin. As she drifted off to sleep, she contemplated what little time she had left.

Ellayne opened her eyes to see a room full of faces she didn't recognize—hundreds of thousands of people staring at her with blank expressions. They stood shoulder to shoulder; men and women, young and old, human and not. She herself stood on a platform above all of them. The echo of people went far into the distance until she could no longer discern individual faces.

She walked to the edge of the platform to look down. No stairs. No way down. It was a steep drop-off to the first row of people. Ellayne backed up, not wanting to risk falling over the edge.

As she was about to open her mouth to say something, she saw another platform rise from the ground a fair distance away from hers. On it stood a figure shrouded in darkness, as if there was a dark cloud hovering around it. It made the figure appear blurry around the edges, and she couldn't see any distinguishing features. That is, until it turned to look at her. She didn't know how she could tell it was staring at her, but where there might have been eyes, there were two round black holes darker than the rest of the shadows.

Movement in the crowd drew Ellayne's attention away, and she saw a few people in the first couple rows look up to her and place their right fist above their heart in a salute. The rows behind them copied, though still only half of the crowd. A wave passed through the multitude as some of the people saluted Ellayne; one row started as soon as the row in front finished.

Ellayne found two faces she recognized. Kiegan and Kade stood shoulder to shoulder about twenty rows back. Both stared up at her, but only Kade saluted when it came time. Kiegan's stance didn't change.

A rumble like thunder emanated from the dark figure on the platform across from her, and she focused her attention on what she assumed were its hands. Black mist leaked out and poured down onto the first row. The smoke slithered at the feet of the people, who didn't react. But when it came to the first person saluting her, an older man with pointed ears sticking out underneath his white hair, the mist crawled up his legs and around his torso, completely engulfing him.

When the mist cleared, the man was gone. Others who were saluting like him disappeared before her eyes. She wasn't sure what was happening, but when the first ten rows lost half of the people, her heart rate quickened. The mist snaked closer to Kiegan and Kade.

"Run!" she hollered, but no one blinked. "Kade, go! Get out of here!" Her toes curled over the edge of the platform, any concern for falling over the edge forgotten.

A woman with long fangs in front of Kiegan disappeared, and Ellayne could only watch as Kade's body disappeared behind a wall of dark mist.

"No!" Ellayne screamed. When the smoke dissipated, he was gone.

"Time's up," a voice said behind her, but when she turned around, there was no one there.

Chapter Forty-Two

She woke up mid scream. The moment she opened her eyes, she thought she saw two reflective silver ones staring at her near the door, but when she blinked a few times, they were gone.

"Ellayne, calm down," a male voice said behind her. "You're going to wake the entire castle if you keep—ouch!"

Ellayne's fist made contact with something hard, and she felt a large hand grab her wrist before she could swing again.

"Who are you?" she spat, yanking her hand back from the man's grip.

"It's me," Kade said. "And thanks to you, I think I'm going to have a bruised sternum." He rubbed his chest with his hand, rustling the fabric of his tunic.

"Kade," she whispered, her mind pulling her into the nightmare again for half a second. *He's okay.* She shook her head to remove the last afterimages of the dream. "What is with you and Kiegan waking me up? If you want to avoid more bruises, I'd suggest not doing that." She pushed into a sitting position, wrapping the blanket around herself. "What are you even doing in here? How did you find me?"

"I may or may not have been taking a midnight stroll when I heard what sounded like a damsel in distress. Being the knight in shining armor that I am, I came to check on you." His voice lilted, and she pictured him raising an eyebrow.

"I'm not a damsel in distress." Ellayne narrowed her eyes at him. "I'm a woman with a curse. There's a difference."

"Not when you're screaming bloody murder in the middle of the night."

"Where's Kiegan?"

"I don't know." Kade ran his fingers through his tangled hair. "They took us to separate rooms. He was still pretty peeved at me."

And at me. She squirmed. *I need to talk to him sooner rather than later.* Ellayne reached over to the other side of the bed where she'd haphazardly tossed her tunic, and she pulled it on over her undershirt.

"Light the candle, will you?" she said, throwing the covers back.

"Why?"

"Because I asked."

"Well, all right then," Kade grunted as he stood up. He knocked something over, but eventually the room flickered with yellow light.

Ellayne's first instinct when the room lit up was to check the area near the door where she'd seen the silver eyes, but she found nothing there.

"Um," Kade muttered, "have you checked in a mirror lately?"

"Excuse me?"

He pointed to his neck and tilted his chin toward her. "I don't remember it being this bad when I last saw you."

Rushing to the mirror, Ellayne's heartbeat quickened; the blackness crawled up her neck near her collarbone. It had spread all the way across her shoulder and was making its way down her chest.

"At this rate, I'm going to forget everything by the end of the day," Ellayne said, her fingers trailing along her collarbone. Kade watched her in the mirror, standing a few feet behind her.

"Don't be so negative."

"I'm cursed, Kade. I'm allowed to be a little pessimistic once in a while. Especially when I'm about to lose everything for the billionth time."

"You don't know the timing of this thing."

"And neither do you." She spun around, her hands balling into fists. "None of us know anything. But at the end of this, you and Kiegan will go back to your lives while I have to start all over again. At the end of the day, I'm the one who's cursed. Not you, and not Kiegan." Ellayne thought back to the nightmare, and she rebelled against the fact people other than herself were going to lose their memories of her as well.

She closed the space between them and placed both hands on his chest. Pushing him back a step, she continued, this time with hot tears in her eyes, "I'm the one who's going to forget who I am." She shoved him again. "I'm the one who loses in the end." *I'm going to lose everything.*

When she tried to push him back once more, he surprised her by grabbing both of her wrists and pulling her into his chest.

"You're wrong, Ellayne. Totally wrong." He glared down at her. "We all lose if we don't break this curse." His face softened when she stopped trying to pull away. "You lose your memories. But Kieg and I, we lose you. And trust me, that's painful. You've brought more meaning to our lives, to my life, than I ever would have thought possible that day when we found you in the rapids. And while you're still here, I will search for an answer to this curse. I promise you."

260

Ellayne sagged under the weight of his words, and when Kade let go of her wrists, he wrapped his arms around her, pulling her into a hug.

"I'm not giving up on you, and I need you to not give up either," he said into her hair.

She couldn't stop the sobs, and Kade didn't try to stop her. Her tears soaked the front of his shirt. Eventually, the rhythm of his heartbeat calmed her down. He held her for a long time, waiting until she was left hiccupping.

"You should get back to bed," he said, pulling away. He held her elbows gently in his hands. "If nothing else, for beauty sleep."

Ellayne smacked him on the arm, sniffling as she grinned. "Speak for yourself. At least I don't look like a rat made a nest in my hair."

"You're right." He winked, putting his hands back in his pockets. "Yours is more like a bird's nest."

"Get out." She pushed him toward the door, but pulled on his arm before they reached it. "Thanks, Kade."

"Anytime." He fake bowed and slipped out the door into the quiet hallway.

A few hours later, after a maid came in with a breakfast tray of fruit, bread, and cheese, Ellayne reunited with Kiegan and Kade in a hallway two floors down.

"How'd you sleep?" Kiegan asked, a pillow seam still imprinted into the side of his face.

"Not as well as you, I'd wager," she said, avoiding Kade's eyes, which she could feel boring a hole into her.

Kiegan rubbed the palm of his hand against his cheek and shrugged. "I don't think I've ever slept in such a comfortable bed before."

261

"I'm pleased it was to your liking." King Diomedes stepped out from around another hallway, crossing to them. "If you're ready to begin your research, follow me to the library." He walked between the three of them without brushing so much as a sleeve.

They fell in step behind him. Ellayne did her best to keep track of the hallways they turned down, but she gave up after a few minutes of walking. Eventually they stopped in front of a door, which King Diomedes opened for them.

"If I remember correctly, the books on magic are at the back of the room on the shelf on the left." He let Kade and Kiegan go in, but held out his hand to stop Ellayne. "I was hoping for a word."

"Of course, Your Majesty."

King Diomedes let the door shut, and Ellayne rubbed her hands over her upper arms, the wave of isolation causing her to shiver.

"I would like to invite you to have lunch with me in a few hours." He stood with his gloved hands clasped behind his back. "How does that sound?"

"It would be an honor." Ellayne curtsied. "I'll tell the others—"

"The invitation is only for you, I'm afraid." He offered a small smile, the fabric around his eyes crinkling.

"Oh, well," she bit her lip, "of course I'll join you for lunch. How could I refuse?"

"Perfect. I'll send someone to fetch you when it's time. Happy reading." He turned on his heels without another word and wandered back down the hallway they'd come from.

"What was that about?" Kiegan asked when she closed the library door. He had three books stacked in his arms, and Kade was placing another one on top.

"The king just invited me to have lunch with him." She watched Kiegan's face fall, but he recovered before Kade could notice.

Kade was on a stepladder reaching up for another book when he said, "He's not what I was expecting. King Diomedes, I mean." He stacked two more books in Kiegan's arms, and Ellayne walked over to pull one off the top.

"He's been through a lot," Ellayne said, turning the book titled *So You've Accidentally Cursed Your Best Friend* over in her hand.

"So have you." Kade stepped down. "And you're not a creepy hermit in a castle."

"Thanks," she grimaced. "I think."

"I'd be careful what you say about him." Kiegan dropped the stack of books on a large oval table with a thump. "Anything spoken against the king or the royal family could be counted as treason."

Kade shrugged, flipping open one of the books. "Well in that case, with all the things we've discussed in the past, you and I have been breaking that law for a while."

"What do you mean?" Ellayne asked, looking from Kade to Kiegan.

"It's nothing," Kade said, tossing the book onto a chair, apparently deciding it wasn't worth his time.

"We should tell her. She has a right to know, especially now that we're here." Kiegan crossed his arms over his chest. "Besides," he cast his eyes sideways, "I may have already told her."

"You what?" Kade's head whipped around and he glared at Kiegan.

"I told her we think there may be something suspicious going on here."

263

"So did I, but I never gave her any details." Kade threw his arms up and stomped toward the window. He extended his arm and pointed outside. "You might as well shout for them to come arrest us if you're so emphatic about discussing private conversations with every pretty girl you meet."

Ellayne's cheeks warmed as she ran his sentence through her mind again. *Pretty? He thinks I'm pretty?* She pinched her leg to focus on what Kiegan was saying.

"Ellayne has proven she's trustworthy, so why are you so upset about this? It's not like she's shared it with anybody else. And you just admitted to talking to her about it."

"I told her that I thought something wasn't right here and that she might be a part of it, but that was it." Kade shoved his hands in his pockets, clenching his jaw as he stared out the window. "I didn't want her to be in danger. But now she can get in trouble just by proximity. When she didn't know, she was safe." There was a moment of silence before he sighed, his shoulders deflating. "Fine, both of us have shared our theory about some sort of royal subterfuge. But did he tell you about the cover-up we think happened here?"

Ellayne glanced at Kiegan and shook her head.

"Well then, why don't we just dig ourselves a mass grave and give you the details, shall we?"

Chapter Forty-Three

nother heir? How is that possible?" Ellayne's stomach twisted in reaction to what Kiegan had said. "Why is that not widely known? Why didn't Linetta mention it? Or Macario? Or Calder and Dayla? Or anybody?"

"We don't know the exact reason why, but we're the only ones we've found who remember things happening differently than everyone else," Kade said.

"And when either of us mention it, people shut us down," Kiegan replied. "Like when Kade mentioned it at Macario's shop. Macario told Kade he was nuts. And you know what? Maybe we are."

"I'm not insane. I'm not." Kade gripped the back of a chair until his knuckles turned white. "I remember there being another child."

"But no one else seems to. Linetta even said Evangeline didn't have any children. She's her sister for goodness' sake; she would know. And the first queen only had King Diomedes. If there was another heir, shouldn't that—"

"Ellayne, you need to be quieter," Kiegan said, his voice

dropping. He held his hand out to shush her. "This isn't something we want to get in trouble for."

Kade grunted. "This is a mistake."

"Why would we get in trouble for talking about some imaginary royal child?" Ellayne asked.

"Anyone who opposes the royal family commits treason, and by saying what we just said—that there was some sort of cover-up with the royal family—we could get ourselves thrown in prison, or worse."

Ellayne lowered her voice when she spoke next. "How is it possible for something like that to go unnoticed? You can't just remove a person from ever existing, can you?"

"Not that I know of." Kiegan sighed. "We can't be sure. We're the only people who remember that the other child ever existed, but we stopped checking with others a long time ago. It's not good for either of our businesses."

"Neither is leaving your business for three weeks to help a stranger figure out why she's cursed," Ellayne said, popping her hip out.

"The point is," Kade didn't take the bait to argue with her, "we need to be careful about how we talk and act around here. If there are cover-ups, then there have to be measures set in place for people looking to uncover the truth. Understand?"

Ellayne didn't respond to his question. "Girl or boy?" Her question was barely audible.

Kiegan sighed, rubbing the back of his neck. "I don't remember, and neither does Kade. We remember that the child existed, but there are no manuscripts or books or anything with any mention of another heir to the throne. A few days after the chaos at the castle in Cyanthia, when news traveled about what had happened and that Diomedes had taken the throne, I remember thinking I'd gone mental. Everyone was talking about the late king and queen, but no one said anything about the other heir, and when I asked, only vacant stares and furrowed eyebrows greeted me. After a day or two, I began to believe them, that I'd made it all up. I mean, I couldn't even remember the gender."

"But you remembered, too?" Ellayne looked at Kade, who nodded.

"He remembers that the heir existed," Kiegan spoke for him, "but just like me, he can't really remember any details either. When he asked me about it, I was so relieved. We've been trying to figure out what happened in this castle for the past couple years, but we've never found any evidence that another heir actually existed. Neither of us can remember seeing the child, and to the rest of the world, we're looney."

"Is that why you wanted to help me?" Ellayne asked. "Because the necklace belonged to the royal family?"

Kade and Kiegan exchanged a look. They nodded.

"At first we thought you could be the heir we remembered," Kiegan said, "but then the necklace ended up being Evangeline's."

"The necklace is what initially made me want to help," Kade admitted, "but it's kind of faded to the background since learning about your curse. Which is what we should be discussing instead of all this conspiracy nonsense that could end up getting us thrown in whatever dungeon this place has."

Ellayne was quiet, not meeting either of their eyes. "Thanks for being honest with me."

"I guess now we're all on the same page. Let's get to work since we're all going to pay for it if we don't." Kade's comment was more directed toward Kiegan, who was still watching Ellayne closely. Kade walked over to the table, grabbed a book from the stack, and went to sit in the window seat without another word.

Instead of copying Kade, Kiegan walked up to Ellayne.

267

"Can I speak to you for a minute?" He glanced at Kade. "Alone?"

"Sure."

The door closed behind them, and Kiegan nodded down the passageway. "Want to go for a walk?"

"Lead the way." Ellayne strode beside him, her mind twirling with too many thoughts. *What if they're right and there was an heir? Will I ever find out? How much time do I have left? Is there enough time to break the curse? Why did Kiegan want to talk to me? It probably has to do with what he said in the Black Forest; that he loves me.* Her heartbeat quickened as she waited for him to speak.

"I wanted to ask you something," he said, and he shoved his hands into his pockets. "But now—now I'm not so sure."

"I'm sorry, Kiegan." Ellayne couldn't stop the words from tumbling out. "I didn't mean to hurt you after what you said yesterday. I care so much for you. You and Kade are my closest friends. I trust you, and if I had more time, maybe—" She paused. "It's just terrible timing. With my curse about to happen again—"

"What's going on between you and Kade? Is it because of him?"

"What?" Ellayne's eyebrows rose. "No! Of course not. I just said it's because of my curse."

"Blanndynne thought you two were—"

"Blanndynne wasn't with us for those three weeks. She didn't see the fights between us that you had to step between." Ellayne paused and placed her hand on his arm, stopping him. "She didn't see the way you fought to help me, and how Kade grudgingly agreed. You were the one who made me feel safe and warm."

"Then why don't you love me?" He tensed, and his arm flexed beneath her touch.

Ellayne opened her mouth to answer, but no words came out.

"It's because of him."

"It's not." She tugged on his arm when he tried to walk away. "Maybe—" She bit her lip. "Maybe I could feel the same way for you as you do for me, but I can't know until my curse is broken. If I say it now, I may forget you, and you me, by the end of the day. Kiegan, I do care for you, and if things were different, then maybe—"

"Then let's go make things different." He placed his hand on hers, and a new sort of fire lit his dark eyes.

"What?"

"If you're so concerned about your curse getting in the way of your feelings for me, then let's go end this thing." He brought her hand up to his lips and kissed it. "Then we'll have all the time in the world."

"Thank you, Kiegan." Ellayne's cheeks warmed.

Ellayne's mind was weary by the time a servant came to escort her to lunch with the king. It grew tired of jumping from idea to idea: curse, Kiegan, conspiracy, Kade, curse, questions, questions, questions.

When she left the room, Kade still sat in the window seat and Kiegan had a book propped up on the table in front of him, and he was either concentrating hard on one page or taking a nap; she couldn't tell, but she guessed the latter.

"The king takes his lunch in his office most days, but today he has requested to have it in the royal family's parlor," the servant explained as she walked in front of Ellayne.

"All right."

"Do you have any food allergies?"

"Not that I know of."

"I'll let the cook know." The servant stopped at one of the many doors in the hallway. "He's waiting for you inside."

Ellayne inhaled before opening the door and entering. The room was filled with light from three large arched windows against the opposite wall. A table was set in the middle of the room, and though it had room for at least six chairs—four in the middle and one on either end—only two places were set.

On the right side of the room were two couches and two large chairs near an unlit fireplace. Ellayne was taken aback by how cozy it felt, and she attributed the feeling to the ornate rug covering a majority of the floor in the sitting area.

"Hello, Ellayne," King Diomedes said, stepping out from behind the door she'd opened. His sudden presence in the otherwise empty room set Ellayne's heart racing for a few seconds, and she took a bit too long to respond. "Did I frighten you?"

"Of course not, Your Majesty," she lied as she curtsied. "I was just taking in another one of your beautiful rooms."

"Please," he waved his arm toward the table, "have a seat."

She complied, choosing the seat facing the windows. The table settings were made of gold, and she marveled at her reflection in the shiny plates. "Thank you for inviting me to have lunch with you. It's an honor, Your Majesty."

"I'm glad you think so." He stood at his chair, placing both hands on the back of it. "But I'm afraid my reasoning behind the invitation may be a bit, well, selfish."

Ellayne tilted her head. "How so?"

"I have a few questions for you, and I wanted to pose them without the input of your companions."

"Questions?" Ellayne instinctively reached for her necklace, feeling her muscles relax as soon as her thumb rubbed over the royal crest. "What sort of questions?"

"Some might call them prying questions."

"I'll answer them if I'm able, Your Majesty."

"Perfect." He pulled out the chair, which screeched on the floor, and sat down across from her. King Diomedes had a faint line of a grin across his face. "You must forgive me, as I'm afraid I might be a bit blunt. I prefer to be straightforward so my intentions are not confused. My first question is about your parents. Who are they? Where do they reside?"

Her chest tightened. "Well, I-I can't remember them." *How embarrassing. He must think I'm so pathetic*

"Is that because of your curse?"

"Yes, but your servant Blanndynne told me a bit about them."

"Did she now?"

"She did, but I suppose she never gave any specifics."

"What a shame." His words said one thing, but his grin said another. "What were their names?"

"I don't know." Ellayne bit her lip, wondering how that question had slipped her mind in the time she'd spent with Blanndynne. "But I'm sure Blanndynne knows. I'll ask her."

"Do you know what happened to them?"

"Blanndynne said they were killed."

"Do you know when?"

"No." Ellayne bit the inside of her cheek. "I can't remember past about a month ago."

"That's quite some time." King Diomedes took a sip from his cup, and she copied his gesture. "What did you know of the country of Phildeterre?"

"Nothing. My friends told me everything. About the end of the war, and the day you—" She choked on her words when she considered what she was about to say. *The day you became the blind, orphan king.*

"A day we all remember."

271

"Not all of us," she mumbled.

"Come again?"

Ellayne tucked a stray hair behind her ear. "I don't remember that day because of my curse."

"Which leads me to my next question. You have no idea who cursed you? Because I'm sure that information might be useful in your situation."

"I'm sure it would be, but no. I only know that whoever cursed me must've had dark magic, and from what I've been reading, powerful magic at that."

King Diomedes crossed his hands, resting his chin on top of them. "What have you found about the curse in my library so far?"

"Nothing much, but Kade and Kiegan are still looking. I'm thankful for a break, though."

"Not much for reading?"

"No, I love reading." Ellayne sat up straighter. "I was just a bit tired this morning, so it was difficult to concentrate on the information."

It was his turn to tilt his head. "Didn't sleep well?"

"I—" She hesitated. *Well, my friend confessed his love for me and got upset when I didn't return it, and my curse is coming faster than I thought, but I'm nowhere near breaking it, among many other things.* Though she wanted to be honest, she decided against it. "I slept well enough to have a nightmare."

"What was it about?"

"Nothing." She felt her cheeks flush. The idea of sharing her dreams made her shrink back against the chair. "But the nightmare wasn't as startling as when I woke up. I thought I saw, well, I thought I saw a pair of eyes."

His ears perked up, and he lifted his head off his hands. "Eyes?"

"It sounds ridiculous, but yes. I hallucinated a pair of eyes staring at me when I woke up."

"What color eyes, if you don't mind?"

"Silver," she said, "and it's not the first time I've seen them." *Getting that off my chest felt better than I thought it would. Maybe I should tell Kiegan and Kade.* But King Diomedes's reaction had her second-guessing the notion.

He frowned, but didn't say anything else on the subject. "Well, we should start eating so that you can get back to your research. Your story is certainly a riveting one, Ellayne."

Chapter Forty-Four

ith her stomach full, Ellayne walked back to the library with a servant to guide her. There was a platter of half-eaten food on the table, at which Kade sat alone. She looked around the room, but Kiegan wasn't there.

"How was lunch with the king of Phildeterre?" Kade asked, popping a grape in his mouth.

"Strange and delicious," Ellayne said as she sat down across from him.

"Strange?" he asked, dipping his chin down; he still wasn't looking at her. "What, did they serve toes of a giant? I hear it's a delicacy in some of the countries up north."

Ellayne raised an eyebrow. "No. He asked me a lot of questions."

"How was that strange?" Kade asked, not looking up from the book on the table in front of him. "Seems like a normal thing to do when having lunch with a stranger. Especially a stranger as unique as you."

"It just was," she said as she reached for a book she hadn't searched through yet. "Where's Kiegan?"

"He got tired of reading and decided to take a walk. He should be back soon."

"Did you two talk? About earlier, I mean." *Or about the fact that he thinks there's something going on between us? Is there something between us? You seem different.* Ellayne finished an entire conversation with the Kade in her head before the real Kade responded.

He fidgeted in his seat. "Sort of. He didn't hit me this time, so I guess that's an improvement. He's been kind of upset with me recently; he has some crazy theories about things going on behind his back. I assured him he has nothing to be concerned about, but he's paranoid."

She wasn't sure how to react to what he was saying, so she changed the subject. "Find anything?"

"Actually, I might have." He sat up straighter, and when he finally met her eyes, his were twinkling. "I was reading through this old book of curses, and I found something. Care to listen?"

She nodded, a smile creeping up on her face. "Please share."

He opened the book to a page marked with a folded corner.

"You shouldn't do that to books."

"What? Read them?"

"Fold the corners," Ellayne replied, crossing her legs under the table. "You're damaging the book."

"Seriously? I'm trying to help you break your curse and you're lecturing me on the proper upkeep of books?"

Ellayne shrugged. "I suppose it's a pet peeve of mine." *I have absolutely no idea where it comes from, though.*

He stared at her with his mouth agape, the book splayed open in his hands. After several empty seconds, he shook his head. "Your priorities are a mess, Ellayne."

"What were you going to read out of this book you've now defaced? Hmm?"

His white teeth flashed as a wide smile crossed his face. He began reading.

"*Most curses need to be linked to their intended target before being enacted so as to prevent the curse from being placed on random innocents, and if the link is created using the fresh blood of the intended target, a scar may form at the location where the blood is harvested.*"

"First of all, I hate that they used the word 'harvested,' " Ellayne said, shuddering. "And secondly, I guess that's what this is, then." She held up the arm with the scar.

Kade nodded. "My guess is that whoever cursed you cut your forearm to get your blood so they could tie you to the curse."

"I'm almost glad I can't remember that."

"There's more though," he said, flicking his sight off Ellayne's blackened arm and back down to the book, where he continued to read. "*The scars almost never go away unless the curse is broken. Often the scars are used in breaking the curse.*"

Ellayne sat up straighter. "Did you just say breaking the curse? That's great news! What do I have to do? Cut my arm off? Because I will." She spoke faster, her voice rising in pitch.

"Calm down there." Kade chuckled. "As far as I can tell, we don't need to remove any limbs at this point. But I'm glad to see you're all in after last night."

"This is the first hint we've found to breaking the curse." She stood up, unable to sit still anymore. "How could I not be excited? This is amazing, Kade! What else does it say? How do I break my curse?"

"Nothing specifically. It just mentions that curses can often be broken by tracing and reversing the steps the person went through to curse them, but that doesn't always work. Especially if the person who cursed them was powerful enough to place a fail-safe lock on the curse."

"A fail-safe lock? What's that?" The energy she felt from the good news buzzed around her, and she forced herself to calm down so she could listen to Kade's next words.

Kade flipped to another dog-eared page. "I wasn't sure either, so I looked it up in the index." He read straight from the book, "*A fail-safe lock on a curse prevents the cursed person from enacting the curse backward to break it. Often, a fail-safe lock leaves the power of breaking the curse in the hands of the person who set the curse. Creating a fail-safe lock, however, is a very difficult thing to do, and most people with dark magic do not possess enough power to set up the lock before the curse is placed.*"

"No," Ellayne moaned. The gravity of the text hit harder than the exhilaration had. "So I not only have to find out who cursed me, I have to make them reverse the curse as well. I don't have enough time for that."

"You don't know that there's a fail-safe lock on your curse. Don't jump to the worst conclusion."

"Why shouldn't I? I'm cursed, for goodness' sake! Name one good thing that's come out of this."

"Kieg and I met you."

"And if I don't figure out how to break this, that won't matter."

"It still happened, even if we won't remember." Kade put the book aside and stood up. "This is still good news, Ellayne," he said as he stepped in front of her.

She crossed her arms, grabbing her elbows in her hands. "For a second," she whispered, "I thought I could end this thing."

"I think you still can." Kade raised his hands to her arms, his touch gentle.

The words hung in the air around her, making it hard to breathe. Ellayne wasn't aware of how close they were standing. That is, until one of his hands rose from her arm and lifted a strand of hair that had fallen in front of her face, brushing it back behind her ear. His hand lingered there, a soft feather touch that left her cheek tingling long after it left.

What are you doing? Why does my stomach do this twisty thing when you're this close? Is there something here? Is Kiegan right? Ellayne stared up at his face, seeing in the bags under his tired eyes a different man than the one who first saved her in the river. At some point, he'd lowered one of his many walls—walls he'd put up to keep her out.

"I knew it."

The moment shattered into a thousand pieces, and Ellayne leapt away from Kade at the sound of Kiegan's shaky voice. He stood in the doorway, the doorknob still in his tightening fist.

"Kiegan," she started, stepping forward, but he shook his head.

"Have it your way," Kiegan spat. His nostrils flared as he spun on his heels and left, slamming the door.

Chapter Forty-Five

The echo of the slammed door reverberated, and it left Ellayne glancing from Kade to the spot where Kiegan had stood.

"I've got to go talk to him." Ellayne stepped back from Kade. "I have to explain everything to him."

She was surprised when he grabbed her hand. "You don't have time, Ellayne. We still have to figure out who cursed you, and then—"

"I have to see him, Kade. I'll never forgive myself if I don't." She pulled her hand out of his.

Kade's posture straightened, and he clenched and unclenched his jaw. "You won't have to worry about forgiving yourself if you don't break your curse. A second ago you were talking about forgetting—forgetting about this. About him. About me. You need to break your curse first. Then you can worry about Kiegan."

"No, Kade." Ellayne shook her head. "You don't understand. He loves me. He told me, and he thinks there's something between you and me. If I don't go now to explain, he'll never forgive me, and he may never forgive you."

"He's not going to remember if—"

"I'm not going to argue with you. I'll be back." She turned her back on him and ran out of the library.

She looked left, then right, and tried to listen for any sound that might tell her what route to take. A crash resounded from somewhere on her left, and she jogged in that direction.

Unsure of how much Kiegan had heard and seen, her mind and heart raced faster than her legs could carry her. *Let me explain,* she begged the imaginary Kiegan in her head. *It's not what you think.* The surrounding walls confused her as she attempted to hear Kiegan's footsteps. She jumped when she heard the faint sound of glass shattering somewhere in the corridor ahead of her.

It was when she stopped to breathe and listen that she heard it; someone was in a room near her. *Please be him.* She tucked a piece of hair behind her ears.

"Kiegan?" She tapped her knuckles on two doors, both of which led to empty bedrooms, before finding one that was locked. "Please let me in. I need to talk to you."

The lock clicked and the door flung open. Kiegan's height had never intimidated her before, but with his eyes narrowed on her, she took a step back subconsciously.

"I'm done with you."

"Kiegan, listen." Ellayne opened her mouth to keep talking, but he shook his head.

"No, you listen." He gritted his teeth. "You lied to my face. You told me there was nothing going on between you and Kade. You and . . . and my . . . my best friend. But you lied. I knew it. You never loved me."

"You don't understand." Ellayne wished her voice didn't sound so weak compared to his. "There isn't anything going on between Kade and me. I was upset because—"

Kiegan held up his hands like he'd given up. The fast movement caused Ellayne to flinch.

"You were in his arms, Ellayne! He was touching your face." He balled up his hands. "I was an idiot! After those days we spent separated after the raid, I couldn't think of anything but you. How I'd left you. How you could be dead. I hated myself for it. But I was probably the last thing on your mind."

"That's not true."

"You were too busy cozying up to Kade. With me gone, you had plenty of time to forget me." His hand snaked forward and latched around her wrist. "You probably don't even need your curse to forget about me."

"Please, Kiegan." Ellayne's stomach clenched, and the blood drained from her face. His grip on her wrist hurt, and she tried to pull away.

"No." The response sliced through the silence in the hallway. "You two deserve each other, sneaking around. I bet you would've kept me on the line. You would've never told me." He shoved her wrist back like she was on fire.

"There's nothing to te—"

"Stop lying!" he shouted, and she shrank back.

Hot tears boiled up behind Ellayne's eyes. *Don't start crying, don't start crying. Please.* She begged the wetness to dry up, but it didn't.

"Don't you dare start crying," he warned, pointing a finger at her. "You did this to yourself. I won't be strung along by you anymore."

"Kiegan—"

"I'm done"—his voice cracked—"I'm done getting hurt by you. Take your problems and get away from me. I'm done trying to help you with something that's impossible to fix."

Ellayne choked. The words she wanted to say got caught up in the noise in her head, and all she could do was mutter, "I'm sorry."

"The idea of forgetting you used to give me nightmares because I cared. I cared about you, Ellayne. But now," he shook his head, letting out a low, deep chuckle as he crossed his arms over his chest. "I'll sleep just fine tonight. I can't wait until your curse happens again. Then I'll forget all about you and the hurt you've caused me—all the time I wasted the last three weeks. Then I can move on with my life."

"You don't mean that," Ellayne said, clutching her hand into a fist and placing it over her heart. "Please—"

"No, I mean every word of it. I *want* to forget you, Ellayne." With that, he slammed the door in her face.

Everything around Ellayne blurred, and she wasn't sure whether it was from the tears that wouldn't stop leaking from her eyes, or whether the curse was finally taking effect. All she knew was that when she found her way back to her bedroom, she couldn't stop the tears from coming in full force.

Ellayne collapsed on the bed, burying her face in the pillows. Her body quivered, her hands shaking as she wiped her cheeks over and over again. There was too much to process and no time left to do it. She sat up and pulled her tunic away from her skin, seeing the black tendrils had spread an inch or two from her heart.

Time's up, the voice had said in her nightmare. It was right. She was out of time. Not only that, she was going to leave behind bridges she'd burned between herself and Kiegan. *I should've told him I loved him*, she thought. But a voice in the back of her head told her that was a lie.

And Kade. He'd been so disappointed in her when she left him in the library. All he wanted to do was help. She'd done this to herself. *Kade and Kiegan are the closest thing I had to family, and I ruined those relationships just like I ruined my best opportunity to get my memories, to be whole again.*

Ellayne wrapped her arms around her stomach, wishing she could melt into the mattress and disappear amongst the feathers. *I should've never agreed to go with them. I should've kept them out of this so that they wouldn't get hurt. How many others have I hurt before them? And I can't even remember their names or what I did. I can't apologize. Other people are hurting because of this curse—this curse that I'll never be able to end. I'll just keep going in loops until I—*

"Ellayne," Kade's voice reverberated through the door. "Ellayne, I need to talk to you." His voice was quiet, but sounded urgent. He opened the door without an invitation, and before he had time to steady himself after closing the door, Ellayne barreled into his arms.

"I'm sorry. I'm so, so sorry. I messed up," she said into his chest. "He hates me. Kiegan hates me. And you hate me, and I've failed, and—"

"Hey, calm down." He pulled back and held her at arm's length. "What do you mean I hate you? I don't hate you. And why would Kiegan hate you?"

"Because . . ." She sniffled and wiped her cheeks with the back of her hand, wincing as she pulled on the healing scratches from her tussle with the siren. "Kiegan told me he loved me and I couldn't say it back to him because of the curse and bad timing. Then he saw us together and—"

Kade dropped her arms and ran a hand through his hair, his ring shining in the light. "Ellayne, stop. If he loves you, then he doesn't hate you. And we can explain that he didn't see anything. We both know there's nothing between us. "

Do we both know that? Ellayne's stomach tensed. *Why did you saying that hurt me?*

"And even if there was, there's no time."

"Right," she said, "but he doesn't understand that, and he told me he wants to forget me, and—"

"Stop," he interrupted her as she began to hyperventilate. "You'll figure this out. But we've got bigger fish to fry, Ellayne. Your time is almost up." He placed his hands on his hips.

Her shoulders sagged. "There's no time."

"I disagree," he said, and led her to the bed, where they sat down on the edge. Kade craned his head sideways to look at her, and he pulled out one of Evangeline's journals. "I think I found something. And it's big."

Chapter Forty-Six

I sn't that one you've already read though? I recognize it from when we were at Calder's. How have you found something in it now that you didn't before?" Ellayne's gaze dropped to the ground. "Besides, there's no time to find new information anyway, unless it's the name of the person who cursed me. Even then . . ." Her words petered out.

He was half listening as he flipped to a page toward the end of the journal. His eyes scanned over the words, and she watched him while she waited for a response. His eyes flickered back to something he'd read, and his eyebrows creased. Blinking a few times, he passed the book back to her, planting his finger in the middle of the page.

"Read from here." He looked over her shoulder.

Ellayne rubbed the remaining wetness from her eyes and read Evangeline's words out loud. "*Butch and I have been married for three years, and not a day goes by when I don't think of Emmalee. I destroyed so much. I'm thankful for the peace it seems to have created, at least for a little while. But I'm not sure—*"

"That's enough." Kade's sudden touch on her arm made her jump. "Come with me. I need to check one more thing before I can tell you my theory."

"Where are we going?" Ellayne whispered, obeying Kade's last request, which was to stay as quiet as possible. "If we aren't supposed to be here, then why are we?"

"You're allowed to be up here," he said, nodding to a hallway they'd left. It was the hallway that led to the room she was staying in. "But I don't think I'm supposed to be."

"Then we should go back to the library," Ellayne replied. She tugged her hand out of his grasp, and he stopped to look at her. "We don't want to fall out of the king's good graces just as I'm about to completely forget who I am."

"There's something you need to see, and it's just down this hallway. Please." He held out his hand to her again, and with a quick roll of her eyes, she took it.

"Fine."

She let him lead her down a narrow corridor and they turned into the portrait hall King Diomedes had led her through the night before. The taller ceilings and wide space had the same effect on her, and she paused in the doorway, eyeing the walls lined with portraits of past rulers.

"Why are we here?" Ellayne asked, dropping Kade's hand as she closed her arms over her chest. "What do these old portraits have to do with breaking my curse?"

Kade watched as she moved from portrait to portrait, studying the faces of the past royals who'd wandered the same hallways. He stayed quiet as she walked the full length of one wall and started down the other, spending a few seconds in front of each portrait. When she had looked at the people posed in every frame, she came across the last one, which was a portrait of King Diomedes sitting by himself on the king's throne. His scarf covered his eyes, and the artist who had painted him had done a remarkable job of bouncing light off the silk.

Kade stood in front of the next to last one, the portrait of King Butch, Queen Evangeline, and little Prince Diomedes.

"It's the king," Ellayne said, stepping closer toward it to get a better look. She compared the little boy to the man in the portrait next to it. "He's so young. There's King Butch and Queen Evangeline. She really was beautiful."

"That's all you see? Butch, Evangeline, and Diomedes?" Kade stepped behind her and she could feel his breath making the hairs around her neck flicker in the slight breeze. "You only see three people?"

"Yes," Ellayne said, still squinting at the painting. "Why? How many do you see?"

"Four," he said instantly. "Butch, Evangeline, Diomedes, and a small blond girl sitting on her father's lap, right there." He pointed to the king's empty knee.

"What?" Ellayne whipped around and stared up at him. "You're making that up. There's no little girl in that portrait."

Kade wasn't looking at the portrait, but instead stared down at her with his dark eyes. "I'm not lying, Ellayne. When I look at this portrait, I see four people, and that little girl looks an awful lot like you. She has your eyes, your hair, and—"

"She's not real, Kade. That heir nonsense isn't real, and—"

"Ellayne, this isn't the first time I've seen something other people can't."

She faltered. "What? What do you mean this isn't the first time?"

"The reason we're here in this hall is because you read different words in the journal than what I see. In the section you read just a few minutes ago, I saw something different. It's why I hesitated to tell you what I found about the curse at Linetta's; I had to be sure I was seeing what everyone else was seeing because . . . because I don't always see the same things."

Kade pulled the journal from his jacket pocket and flipped to the page they'd examined.

"Just listen. I'll read to you what I see."

"Kade, don't—"

"*Butch and I have been married for three years, and not a day goes by when I don't think of Emmalee. I destroyed so much. I'm thankful for the peace it seems to have created. It means we can raise our baby girl in a world not ransacked by war and violence. Butch says she looks so much like me, but I see his heart and soul in her eyes. My little princess.*"

He closed the journal, staring at her through the fringe of hair in front of his eyes. Ellayne felt her body shaking. Her legs didn't feel as steady as they had moments before. She leaned back against the wall underneath the portrait of the royal family.

"You're making it up," she whispered. "You're lying."

"Ellayne." He stepped toward her. "I think you're the heir, this"—he held up the journal—"this forgotten princess."

"I can't be." Ellayne's voice was hushed. "It's just a fairy tale you've made up for some ludicrous reason."

"Why would I? I'm a mapmaker, not a storyteller."

"I don't know why," Ellayne snapped, and she stood up straighter. "But you did, because this is too ridiculous to be true."

"Is it though?"

"Yes."

"But think about it—"

"Thanks to you, I can't *stop* thinking about it. And it's insane." She stepped around him and paced up and down the hall. "What you're insinuating is madness."

"Ellayne, listen to me. If a princess really existed, then there would be another heir to the throne. That's what Kieg and I have thought all along." He tucked the journal back into his jacket and stood there, watching her walk back and forth.

"Oh, great." She threw her hands up in frustration. "Now you want me running an entire kingdom? You really are mental."

"That's not what I'm saying." He walked straight up to her and gripped her arms, preventing her from pacing anymore. "Would you please just listen?"

When she didn't say anything else, he kept going. "If there was another heir, she would only take the throne if her parents and brother died, or," he loosened his grip on her, but didn't let go of her arms, "if the prince was disinherited. Then she would be the rightful heir to the throne."

"What are you getting at?"

"What happened to the king and queen?"

"Why are you—"

"They were killed, and Diomedes took the throne. But what if he had no right to take the throne? What if he'd done something to get disowned? Then when his parents died, the throne would've gone to the princess, his sister. Unless no one remembered she even existed."

"Then he would be king," she murmured, her damp eyes drying as they widened. "But would that mean King Diomedes cursed me?"

"I think so, or someone he knows." He lowered his voice, taking a step nearer to her. "It makes sense."

He place a hand on her arm, stilling the tremble spreading through her body.

A princess. Could I really be part of the royal family? The longer they stood like that, the easier it was to acknowledge his theory might be right. And it was about time she did something about it.

Chapter Forty-Seven

The king is busy. I'm afraid you can't go in there right now. His Majesty is speaking with someone," the guard in front of the throne room said as he stepped in front of Ellayne. The other guard blocked Kade as well.

"This is urgent," Ellayne said, her mind racing as she tried to think of a way past them. "I have to talk to the king now."

"You'll have to wait."

"It can't wait," Kade retorted, sizing up the guard in front of him. "We promise we'll be brief, if you just let us—"

"Ellayne, Kade. I'm glad I ran into you." Blanndynne came out the throne room doors. "I'm sure the king would be happy to speak with you now. In fact, I do believe he's been searching for you. Gentlemen." She nodded to the guards, who stepped to either side of the doors, and started down the corridor. "And in case you're wondering," she said, flicking her hair over her shoulder as she glanced back, "your friend, Kiegan, has decided to forgo his time with you. He asked me to tell you not to go looking for him."

"What?" Ellayne asked. "Where is he? Why did he ask you to—"

"He's resting." Blanndynne faced her. "He has a serious case of a broken heart. I believe you had something to do with that, didn't you?" She clicked her tongue, shaking her head once.

"I—" Ellayne's voice caught in her throat.

"Never mind." Blanndynne dismissed her with a wave. "His issues are none of your concern anymore. I'm seeing to him. The king is waiting; you'd better go." She pivoted and strode the rest of the way down the hallway.

What did I do? He hates me; Kiegan hates me. I need to talk to him again. Try to apologize again. I should have—

Kade's hand on Ellayne's shoulder was reassuring.

"Curse first, Kiegan second," he murmured.

"I hope you're right." Ellayne bit her lip.

"I'm always right."

The guards opened the doors for them, and Kade and Ellayne walked into the throne room.

"You are right on time," King Diomedes said from the throne. He stood up and strolled down the stairs toward them.

Ellayne's muscles tightened as the giant doors closed behind them, leaving just Kade, Ellayne, and the king of Phildeterre alone in the throne room.

"What do you mean by that?" Ellayne asked, then tacked on, "Your Majesty." She curtsied low, which sparked a new thought in her head. *Maybe I am the princess. Where else would I have learned how to greet royalty, except in a castle?*

"I sent a few servants to find you in the library, but they returned saying you were not there. A little birdy told me you two possibly made some major breakthroughs, and possibly broke the law multiple times in doing so."

Ellayne's heart pounded in her chest, but she fought for composure. "That's ridiculous. Why would we—"

"Who said that?" Kade asked.

"Let's drop the charade, shall we?"

"What?" Ellayne's voice rose in pitch.

"I know who you are, and I'm very aware that you know who I am. So why don't you tell me what you think you know."

"I don't need to tell you anything," Ellayne said, crossing her arms. She stuck her chin out, and breathing in all the courage she could, she said, "Why don't you tell me something, hmm? Your Majesty." She exaggerated his title as a fire began in her stomach. *If he's the reason I can't remember anything, then he's the one who ruined my life.*

"Sure." King Diomedes spread his arms wide. "I'm an open book, here for your reading pleasure. I seem to remember you said you liked reading."

"Who am I to you?" Ellayne squared her shoulders. Instead of wanting to shrivel up so no one could see her, she stood taller and scowled at the king as she waited for his response. Her fists tightened, but with a deep breath, she loosened them, leaning forward on her toes.

He gave a short laugh that bounced around the enormous room, ringing in her ears.

"That's the easiest question of them all." The silkiness of his voice raised goose bumps all over Ellayne, and the tingling sensation returned.

A flash of cold air swept over her—through her. Ellayne's knees buckled, and she collapsed to the ground. She could hear by the exclamation next to her that Kade was in a similar position. Both of them knelt facing the king, who casually pointed his hand in their direction. Ellayne tried to stand back up, unsure of what had brought her to the ground so suddenly, only to find she no longer had control over her body. She was frozen to the ground, unable to even curl her toes in her boots.

"You, my dear, are Ellayne Maudit, daughter of King Butch Maudit and his second wife, Queen Evangeline Maudit. Of course, that also makes you my half sister, the princess. But you already knew that, didn't you?"

Ellayne didn't know whether her heart wanted to leap for joy at the thought of learning her identity, or crumble into pieces when the burden of the title landed on her a millisecond after.

"You had me cursed."

"Actually, I cursed you myself." The sneer on his face pulled at the corners of the silk scarf.

"Why not kill me?"

"I wanted to see you suffer. It was the same thing that happened to me as soon as you were born. Who cares about the firstborn when there's a new baby to adore? It was a perfect punishment."

"For what?" Ellayne's voice carried through the vast throne room. "Being born?"

"Yes," he hissed.

She clenched her teeth. "And Blanndynne—"

"Was standing by my side when I cursed you five years ago. She agreed to keep an eye on you."

"But she didn't know about the curse."

Kade grunted beside her. "She was lying, Ellayne," he said.

"Your friend is right. The beauty of the Curse of Infiniti is that the only people who know it has been placed are the ones, besides the victim, who are present in the room when it happens. Blanndynne was there, so she remembers. Simple as that."

"She's actually the queen or something, isn't she?" Ellayne said, her mouth dry.

"No. She's the head of my council; she can be very persuasive. When she's here, she keeps an eye on you back at that wretched little house using mirrors. They're like little windows if you rune them up the right way."

Ellayne remembered the markings on the mirror she'd found upon returning to the house. She'd been interrupted before her mind had time to register that they were runes. *So she does work at the castle. She told me some sort of tiny truth.*

"She has magic?"

"Of course." King Diomedes shrugged. "She's very powerful."

All the talk about Blanndynne brought another name to her mind. "Kiegan," she murmured, not meaning to speak out loud.

"Oh, she's taking good care of your friend. You did quite a number on him, didn't you? I didn't know my little sister was as heartless as you turned out to be."

"You're the heartless one." Ellayne gritted her teeth, unable to react in any other way due to the binding spell King Diomedes had placed on her.

"I don't disagree. At least I can admit it." King Diomedes shrugged his shoulders, still pointing his hand in their direction. "But let's move on. I do believe you are running out of time."

Chapter Forty-Eight

"I am truly impressed, dear sister, that you've gotten this far." King Diomedes wrapped a piece of Ellayne's hair around his finger. She wished she could move; every piece of her desired to crawl away from his touch. Her brother's voice was dipped in feigned surprise. "Sincerely, I'm shocked. You've nearly figured it out all on your own."

"What?" Ellayne spat. "That you cursed me because, for some reason, I would've inherited the throne, not you?"

"No, you've figured that out once before." He walked around to face her, the fabric that covered his eyes rippling when he pulled his mouth into a wide grin. "This isn't the first time you've visited me here, though it is the first time you've brought friends." He nodded toward Kade, frozen on his knees beside her.

So I've gotten this far only to fail before. And now I've dragged Kiegan and Kade into this. What will he do to them after the curse takes me? Ellayne forced the useless questions out of her mind.

"Then what do you mean? What have I figured out myself?"

"Nearly." He stood up straighter. "I did say nearly."

"Nearly," she growled.

He continued to walk in circles around her. "You've nearly figured out what really happened five years ago."

"Well, if I've *nearly* figured it out, why don't you fill the blanks in for me?"

"Nothing would make me happier." King Diomedes's face contorted. "But I'll spare you the lengthy, depressing backstory and give you the short one instead. My mother saw the benefit of magic and deserted our simpleminded father in pursuit of greater things. I simply followed in her footsteps. What's a mama's boy to do?"

Not what you've done. She glared at him, wishing she could light him on fire with her eyes.

"So I sought the thing that would anger our father the most: dark magic. And I couldn't let it go to waste, not while our father and his tyrannical new girlfriend-turned-stepmother continued to destroy any kind of magic they could get their hands on. It was wrong, what they were doing. Magic is power, and power is what runs this world. Our family has destroyed too much of what is good in this world."

"I doubt you even know what good is."

He continued on as if he hadn't heard her. "But my actions led to me being disinherited and disowned. No shocker there. Father was—how do I put this—horrified? No, scandalized at the thought that his heir would stand against him and the utter destruction of magic. My disinheritance meant that the delightful throne over there would be left to my equally as simpleminded sister. Couldn't let that happen, now could I? Not when your parents successfully brainwashed you into being one of their magic-hating drones." He pinched her cheek, and every muscle in her neck ached to reach over and bite him.

I don't hate magic. At least, I don't remember hating magic. Ellayne clenched her jaw, glaring up at him. "So you killed your parents and took the throne."

"Not exactly." He fiddled with the chain around his neck. "I killed Evangeline, yes. I had to in order to enact your curse." His blunt confession brought back images of the woman she now understood to be her mother, dead in almost the exact spot she was kneeling.

"But as for our father, I wanted to give him a front row seat to the way I run his kingdom now that I'm in charge. It's safe to say I keep him close to my heart."

"You don't have a heart."

"It's a figure of speech," he drawled, pulling the chain around his neck out from his tunic. "Nevertheless, he's here if you'd like to see him."

Next to the pendant with the royal emblem matching her own hung a small mirror, which he held in front of her face. Her reflection glared back at her, but another face appeared, frantic and banging on an invisible barrier. She didn't recognize him at first because he was older than the version she'd seen in the mirror at Macario's shop and in the portrait hall upstairs, but there was no doubt in her mind it was King Butch. Her father's eyes widened, and his tiny reflection mouthed words to her, but no sound came from the magic trap.

"How dare you—" Her mouth froze like the rest of her body.

"I don't need an earful from you, little sister. In fact, you're about out of time. Any moment now you should begin to forget any of this ever happened. On and on it'll go, throughout infinity. And once I die, there'll be no way to break the curse ever again."

Ellayne pushed against the magic binding her mouth shut. "I . . . won't . . . stop."

"Well, aren't you a strong little fighter," he mocked. "Men more powerful than you have never broken free from this nifty spell. Tell me, how did you speak just then?"

297

She felt the spell dissipate from her mouth, and let out a breath from working so hard against it. "Don't know." Ellayne felt winded. "Why do you care?"

"When you sell your humanity for this much power, you've got to question when something can stand against it." He tucked the chain with their father back down his tunic, and raised his hands to the black silk spread over his eyes. "Of course, it came at a fair price."

Because of his binding spell, Ellayne couldn't physically react when he removed the strip of fabric covering his face. Where his eyes should've been were two black holes, which seemed to suck in the light around them. Her most recent nightmare made so much more sense. He was the dark figure with the black holes for eyes. *Somehow, my mind remembers him.* The fabric fluttered down to the floor; the creature in front of Ellayne transfixed her. King Diomedes, the man she was related to by blood, pulled the gloves off each hand, dropping them to the floor as well. His hands, like her left one, were completely black, humming with dark magic. His fingers, however, ended in short talons.

"You're a monster."

"Funny." He crouched in front of her and scratched one of his talons along the side of her neck. It left her skin chilled. "Your mother said that before I slight her throat when I first cursed you," his sneer returned.

King Diomedes stood back up, straightening his crown, which had gone crooked somewhere along the way. "You came to the right place," he spread his arms out wide, "which was the first step to breaking this nasty curse. And you have me here, which I'd say is probably the most important part."

"You think too highly of yourself."

"That may be true," he tilted his head, "but if I weren't here, then I couldn't say the four little words that would set you free."

"And what would those be?"

"Ellayne, I release you," he said, and for a second, Ellayne felt a light surge within her, but the darkness of the Curse of Infiniti stomped it out just as fast. "I can tell by your reaction that you thought I'd actually free you. You are as naive as I remember. Certainly not suitable to run a kingdom."

Though her posture didn't change thanks to the dark magic holding her still, she could feel herself sinking inwardly. There wasn't a chance she would get him to say those words again. Not when she was already out of time. Her brain felt fuzzy, and it continued to bubble up from the depths. She searched for something easy she could remember, like the name of the horse that had brought her there. But she came back empty. *Was it Anna, Annie, Amelia?*

Other details began to fade as King Diomedes continued to explain the freedom she was getting further away from. *Focus on his words, focus on breaking the curse,* she urged her mind. *Hold on a little longer.*

"You see, words are nothing without actions." He reached into his belt and pulled out a dagger made of metal as black as the holes where his eyes were supposed to be. "When I set the curse, my action was to break your heart, similar to what happens to those with dark magic. So I killed your mother, though," he shrugged, "I would've done that anyway. She was almost as useless as her offspring." He swung the dagger side to side as he talked, continuing to use his hands to express himself. "If I were ever out of my mind enough to free you, I would have to perform an action that proved my word. Curses like the Curse of Infiniti require blood. Are you listening? You seem to be slipping faster than I thought you would."

Ellayne's eyes struggled to focus on King Diomedes as her head buzzed with an ever increasing number of questions. Memories evaporated one after another, and she felt like she was hallucinating as she saw a silver pair of eyes come out of the shadows near one of the curtains. But they weren't floating eyes like she'd seen a few times before; this time they were connected to a tall man around the same age as her brother.

King Diomedes didn't sense him, which was why Ellayne thought she was imagining him. But he looked too real to be a creation from her fading mind. Beneath a black cloak, the stranger wore a dark brown vest over an emerald-green tunic. A strap attached to a quiver of arrows hung diagonally across his chest, and a bow hung over his shoulder.

And he held a woven, metal bracelet.

When he noticed her watching him, he raised one long finger to his lips and shook his head. She wasn't sure why she couldn't hear his footsteps on the floor until she lowered her eyes and looked at his leather boots. Glowing runes scrawled up and down them.

"I'm listening," she said, her voice sounding foreign to her own ears. Ellayne knew she needed to pay attention to what the man with no eyes was saying—*my brother, he's my brother*—but she couldn't remember why. And she couldn't remember who the man kneeling next to her was. *Why can't I move?*

"Then listen closely to this." He leaned down and placed his mouth right next to her ear, "As long as I live, I will never, ever set you free."

"Set me free?" she squeaked. "From what?" *Brother, he's my brother. There's a curse. Break the curse. Break the curse.*

"I suppose that's my cue," the man with the bow and arrow said, and his voice caused the king to whirl around.

"Ovair? How did you get in here? Never mind." The man with the crown—*my brother, the curse, break the curse*—stood up straighter, pressing his hands down the front of his tunic to smooth it. There was a vein standing out on his neck, and she could hear the way he clenched his teeth as he spoke. "I told you five years ago what would happen if you showed your face in here again."

"I'm showing my face, but," the man's voice lilted, "because of your bad life decisions, you can't see it. I'm just as handsome as ever, if you were wondering. I've aged well." He dodged a blast of dark magic the king aimed at him. In return, the stranger shot an arrow from his bow, which the king diverted off course with a flick of his taloned hand.

Each time the king heaved magic at the nimble stranger, Ellayne could feel the magic holding her get lighter, until she collapsed on her hands and knees. *Why am I on the floor? Where am I?* The man next to her fell to the ground at the same time. He scrambled over to her, and helped her to her feet, holding her by the shoulders.

"Are you okay, Ellayne?" He had big, dark eyes and thick eyebrows that creased in the middle as he frowned at her.

"Ellayne," she said, testing the name on her lips, "that's familiar. Who are you?"

"Great," he muttered.

"That's a funny name," she said, giggling. However, it cut short when a streak of dark magic struck the ceiling over their heads. *The curse,* her mind screamed, *break the curse.* The man holding her up covered her head with his arms as rubble fell down.

"Kid!" the man with the bow and arrow shouted.

The man named "Great" turned his head.

"Catch!" Something sparkled silver as it tumbled through the air. The man in front of her caught it with his free hand.

"What am I—"

"Twice to the right," the archer said, leaping off the throne in time to avoid another blast. "And be ready to help her."

She staggered as the man let go of her, fiddling with the bracelet in his hand. The item flashed green and purple, and she tilted her head as voices came out of it.

"That may be true, but if I weren't here then I couldn't say the four little words that would set you free." It was a male voice, one she recognized as belonging to the man with the crown—*brother, curse, break*—who whirled around to face them.

"Stop this!" he demanded.

The man with the silver bracelet shoved her against the wall, just out of the way of a blast of darkness, which hurtled through the air toward her.

"Take this," the man said, and he pressed the handle of a knife into her hand.

"And what would those be?" She recognized her own voice from the bracelet.

"What am I supposed to do?" she asked, her voice wavering. She felt light-headed, yet heavy, like every bone in her body was made of iron.

"Free yourself," he said, and he shoved her in the direction of the man with the crown. The man pushed her in time to dodge another blast of dark magic, but he tripped over a piece of rubble. He landed on his hands and knees several feet away.

She stumbled over the floor, and with her hand gripping the knife, she faced the man with the crown. *Brother*. Her feet felt heavy as she tripped toward him. *Curse*. She fell forward into the man with the crown, spearing the knife into his side before she lost grip of it. Something scraped her own wrist. She cried out in surprise, not sure whether it was her blood or the man with the crown's all over her arm. *Break*.

"Ellayne, I release you."

Chapter Forty-Nine

Heat and luminescence burst around Ellayne, blinding her as she stumbled back from Diomedes. It took her a second to comprehend that light was radiating off of her, shrouding her from head to toe. Squinting, she stared down at her hands. A yellow glow replaced the darkness she had grown so used to. Her left wrist was covered in blood, but the light pumping just under her skin lit it up from underneath, tinging the dark liquid pink.

But it wasn't the blood that drew her eye. The scar radiating the curse through her body was gone, as was the haze that had clouded her mind moments before.

"Diomedes." Her hands shook, so she balled them into fists, repeating herself. "Diomedes." Ellayne's shoulders straightened, as did her entire posture. Ellayne Maudit looked her half brother straight in the face.

"Well, that's unfortunate." Her half brother brought his hand to his side, and pulled it away stained crimson. He stuck his arm straight out, palm down toward the ground, and the black dagger he'd dropped when she'd tumbled into him shot up into his grasp. "How is it that my naive little sister managed to break in five years a curse that was supposed to span throughout eternity?"

"You killed my mother." Ellayne shocked herself when her voice didn't crack.

"I mean," he began scraping the blood off his blackened hands with the edge of the dagger, ignoring her completely. "If the person who told me about the curse was alive, I'd kill her myself for giving me false information on a curse that was supposed to torture you forever."

The black holes where the king's eyes used to be stared straight into her. And just like that, she was back in the throne room five years earlier, bound to the throne with thorny vines, staring into the same face of the monster who stood before her now. Her eyes widened. A memory. One she'd been prohibited from accessing for five years.

"I remember."

"Of course you do," he scoffed. "That's because the traitor decided he wanted to die." Diomedes continued to face her, but he stuck his arm out and pointed a taloned finger at the archer.

"Correction, I don't want to die," the man near Kade said, holding up a long finger. "I simply wanted to keep my word."

"Rest assured, I'll keep my promise to you as well, but it's going to have to wait a moment as I now have to fix this." The air around Diomedes's empty hand darkened, pulsating in a small cloud that rippled with energy.

"Armannii Ovair." Ellayne spoke the name, remembering his face from the images that raced through her mind. "Why are you here? To help him finish me?"

At the mention of his name, the man straightened up from where he'd been helping Kade to his feet. "Did you miss the fact that I just helped you break the curse?"

"You were here when he cursed me." Ellayne gritted her teeth, glaring at the man. *Elf,* she remembered. *Diomedes's best friend.* "You restrained my father while Diomedes cursed me—while he killed my mother." Her nose wrinkled as she glared at Armannii.

"You don't know the full story," the elf replied, brushing dust off his shoulder. "I—"

"And you never will," Diomedes interrupted. "Because now that the curse is over, I need to deal with you."

Ellayne pushed through the confusion filling her mind and focused on what the king was doing. He held the dagger out in front of him with one hand, the flat edge of the blade facing her, and he held out the other hand flat so the dark mist surrounding his palm was also facing her.

"Deal with me? What do you mean?" Ellayne held both of her glowing hands in front of her. Most of the light surrounding her had faded, but there was still some source of light pulsing beneath her skin, filling her with an unnatural heat; it was the opposite of what pulsed beneath her brother's.

"I'm going to temporarily put you out of sight and out of mind while I decide how to repair the damage you have caused me, what with the Curse of Infiniti failing." He raised his hand a bit higher, and Ellayne took a step backward.

"Damage?" she asked, her hands still out in front of her like they would somehow stop whatever he threw at her.

"Your memories are returning, are they not?" He didn't wait for a response. "Which means people all over Phildeterre are remembering there was a princess. Not only that, they are beginning to wonder why they completely forgot about her. I'll find a way to fix the fallout you've created. But I can't have you ruining it by being here." He stepped forward, and the dark mist encircling his hand enlarged three times in size.

Ellayne heard Kade call her name, but she didn't see anything after watching her brother's hand release the dark orb of magic in her direction. *Please save me.* She didn't know who she was asking for help when she threw her hands up, but she hoped for protection from whatever he'd shot at her.

Another brilliant light flashed, causing her to close her eyes. Heat flooded through her, concentrating in her hands. A high-pitched noise rang in her ears, and she vibrated with energy like she'd never felt before. *Am I going to die? Is this what it feels like to leave this world? What's happening?*

An image flashed across her mind: her mother's body collapsing in front of her moments after Diomedes had sliced her throat. *So much blood. I can't do this again, not another curse. Is it a curse?* She pictured the thorns slicing through her skin, binding her to the throne. *I need help!* she screamed in her mind.

Silence.

The heat faded, and soon her body stopped buzzing, leaving only the slightest of tingles in her fingers.

"What just—" She opened her eyes and the words caught in her throat. Spinning in a full circle, she searched the throne room for any sight of Diomedes, but found none.

Her brother had vanished.

"Where did he go?" Kade asked, stepping away from Armannii and toward Ellayne. He seemed to forget his question as soon as he got near her, his eyes running over her from head to feet. "You're glowing, Ellayne."

"Where's Diomedes?" Ellayne asked, ignoring his comment on the light emanating from her. She narrowed her eyes at Armannii, who stood past Kade's shoulder. "What happened to him?"

"Not sure, Princess." The archer shrugged. "But I'd say we better not look a gift horse in the mouth. We need to get out. Now."

"You shot me!" Ellayne bent down and picked up the knife Kade had given her before she broke the curse. She pointed it at Armannii. "You've been hunting me for the past five years. You're his best friend!"

"Needed to get you to the pub." Armannii winked at her. "Been doing that since you first found it. It was a good place to keep your information, because Diomedes can't get in there with the light magic protection. Besides," he gestured to her with his bow, "breaking the curse healed you anyway."

He was right. She felt nothing out of the ordinary when she reached back and felt where he'd skimmed her with an arrow. There was no pain when she peeled off the adhesive bandages from her cheek. Her injuries had been healed when her curse broke.

"As for being his friend," Armannii shook his head, "that's no longer the case. If you hadn't noticed, he was trying to kill me just as much as you. Maybe more so. I have no idea where he went, but we need to leave."

"I don't trust you. And besides, we aren't leaving without Kiegan." But when she glanced at Kade, his shoulders slumped and he ran a hand through his dark hair, causing white dust and bits of rubble to come out in a puff. She lowered the knife as Kade opened his mouth.

"He's right," Kade muttered in a quiet voice. "We need to go now while the king is gone. If he comes back, he'll—"

"Kill you where you stand," Armannii interrupted. "Or at least that's what he'll do to me."

Images of the last moments before her brother had cursed her flickered through her mind, but she pushed them away, unable to concentrate on sorting the onslaught of memories while she tried to make decisions. "But Kiegan—" Her mind raced back to Kiegan's confession of his past. *His family abandoned him, we can't—*

"We'll come back for him," Kade said, and he reached forward to grab her hand. "I won't stop until we do. I promise. We need to go now, though."

"I hear footsteps." Armannii's voice drew her attention back to the situation.

307

Ellayne shook her head. "I don't."

"You don't have the sensitive hearing of an elf. No offense, Princess." He lifted his brown hair to reveal pointed ears.

Princess. The word sounded strange. *Princess Ellayne.* She tested the words in her mind. However, she didn't have time to fully process before Armannii cut in.

"Now can we go before your brother comes back to end me for even setting foot in his castle again? Let alone breaking a curse he spent ages putting together."

She clenched her teeth, but nodded.

"What's the best way out?" Kade followed her to the heavy doors. "And aren't there supposed to be guards out here waiting for the king's signal? Why didn't they come in?"

The archer shook his head. "I took care of them before I made my grand entrance." He wiggled his eyebrows, but got no reaction from his audience. "There are secret passages all over this palace. There's one down a hallway to our right. We just have to make it there before the guards are all over us."

"Simple enough," Kade grumbled. "I don't even have a weapon."

"Can you even use one?" Armannii asked, raising an eyebrow.

Kade stiffened. "I could figure it out."

The elf's neck muscles tightened, and a small grin curved up on his lips. "Weapons aren't something you just 'figure out,' kid."

"Here." Ellayne handed the knife back to Kade. "You can use this if it comes down to it." She turned her attention to Armannii. When she looked at him, even though he looked older than her memory of him, she could still see him standing in the throne room the day her brother cursed her. "Now stop the banter and get us out of here."

"As you wish, Princess."

Chapter Fifty

I can never remember which one it is," Armannii said. His bow was nestled over his shoulder as he pushed against bricks on one of the inner walls. Seconds earlier he'd told Kade and Ellayne to keep an eye on the hallways, but Ellayne watched him struggle instead.

He was there; he was there and he did nothing. He helped Dio. She crossed her arms over her chest. Gritting her teeth, she stood behind him, glaring at the back of his head. After several seconds of staring, she finally let out a frustrated sigh and pushed past him. Reaching out her hand, she pushed down on a brick right in front of where the elf stood.

The moment her hand made contact with the stone, the bricks to their right rearranged, revealing a door-like opening.

"So your memories are back." Armannii shot her a grin. "Either that, or luck."

"They're back. Get in," she said, tightening her lips. His smile faltered for a second, but he passed through the arch and headed down the winding stairs.

"You first," Kade said, motioning toward her with his hand.

But she shook her head. "I'll go last and seal it up after I pass through."

Kade nodded, and she followed him through the wall. As soon as they were past the edge of the stone, she laid her hand on a different brick on the other side. The wall resealed itself, and she ushered Kade forward and down the stairs.

"Where does this lead?" Kade asked.

Ellayne pulled the stone with the light rune carved into it out of her right sock, where she'd placed it that morning. It lit up at her touch, though she was still lightly glowing from whatever had happened in the throne room.

"It should lead to the servants' quarters, the place we came in," she explained when he looked at her with a confused expression plastered on his face. "And we can get to the stable from there." She held the stone out to see the steps in front of her.

"And after that?"

"We'll get Curry and get away from here." *Leaving Kiegan in a castle with my deadly brother and the woman who manipulated me for the past five years.* She clenched her hands into fists.

Kade stopped and turned to face her on a lower step. "Curry can't carry the three of us."

"Kiegan's not here. It's just you and me. What do you mean three of us?"

Kade nodded his head toward the dark stairs. "The other guy; Armannii, I think you called him? What about him?"

Ellayne huffed and pushed past him. "Don't worry for a second about him. He's not our problem."

"Then who is he?" Kade jogged down a few steps until he was right behind her again.

Her nose wrinkled as she pictured Armannii and her brother standing next to Blanndynne in the throne room. Blanndynne had subdued her mother, Armannii had subdued her father—both of

310

her parents, kneeling in helpless submission. "He's a criminal and a murderer."

"Not a murderer, Princess." Armannii reached the bottom and leaned against the wall, waiting for them. He was picking at something under his nails when they caught up.

"May as well be," she snapped as she passed him and opened the exit to the passageway.

"Haven't killed a soul," Armannii continued as he followed her out.

"But I get the feeling you're no saint," Kade said. He stood next to Ellayne, facing Armannii with his arms crossed.

"I'd classify myself as a tragically handsome elf with the passion of a young fairy and the wisdom of the oldest dragon." He held out his hands and shrugged, raising an eyebrow. "But no," he said with a wink. "I'm no saint."

Ellayne felt her blood boil. "If you think for a second that I—"

Armannii held up a finger. "You'll have your chance to scold me, or maybe consider thanking me for helping to break your curse, but we need to get out of the castle first."

Her fists shook and heat boiled in her stomach. The dim light beneath her hands grew brighter, and everyone stared at her.

"What—"

"Light magic," Armannii said. "It's why you can get into the pub."

"I don't have magic," she said, peering down at her glowing palms. "I can't—"

Kade placed a hand on her shoulder. "Your mother did."

She never told me. Ellayne took a deep breath and nodded once. "I'll deal with this later. This way."

"The stables will probably be clear, but we need to be careful," Armannii whispered as they left through the empty servants'

entrance. "Because the curse is broken, people will recognize you now."

"Isn't that a good thing?" Kade asked, keeping his voice low. "She's the princess, after all. Shouldn't people be overjoyed that she's back?"

"It's hard to tell how people will react, and that's the danger. There's definitely a better chance that the people Diomedes let stay ali—" He paused and rethought what he was going to say. "The people Diomedes let stay here are more likely to be loyal to him with or without the curse."

Ellayne glared at him as they crouched behind one of the manicured bushes. "Then why aren't you running his guards or something?"

"I told you, not friends anymore. Not even acquaintances. Besides, I did the head guard thing way before I met your brother." Armannii shrugged. "It turned into a big debacle. Not really my style."

"It looks empty," Kade said, breaking the staring contest going on behind him. "I think we can just go in."

"I'll stay out here," Armannii said, placing his hands on his hips. "I'll keep a look out."

"I don't trust you." Ellayne crossed her arms.

"You've mentioned that once or twice." He pressed his lips together, still smiling.

Ellayne wanted to reach out and punch the grin off his face. "How do we know this isn't a trap?"

"Because the stable was your idea, Princess. Besides, you heard your brother. He wants me dead more than you. Also, you see my eyes. Are they gold? I didn't think so. You remember the deal—*silver eyes means no lies; a sparkle of gold, is truth yet to be told.*"

"Stop quoting children's rhymes to me," Ellayne snapped. "I've read the books. I know how you work."

"Then you know I'm telling the truth."

Kade grunted. "Come on, Ellayne. Let's get Curry and go."

Ellayne narrowed her eyes at Armannii's silver ones before brushing past him. She stomped into the stable behind Kade. It didn't take him long to find Curry and get the horse ready to go. Like the first time Ellayne met Anya, Curry acted up; he stomped the ground and backed away from her. It took Kade several minutes to calm his horse down.

"I read somewhere that horses and some other animals can be biased for or against types of magic," Kade said as he brushed his hand down Curry's mane. "I wonder if that's why Curry is acting this way."

"Don't know," Ellayne said, her nose scrunching up from the smell of manure surrounding them. "But I hope he calms down, because I'm not getting on him if he's going to do that." She pointed as the horse reared up again.

Once Kade was up on Curry, he offered his hand to help Ellayne up, but she got up on her own, clutching Kade's jacket to keep her balance.

"It seems you remember how to ride a horse," Kade remarked as they left the stable. One of the other horses, possibly Anya, whinnied as they exited.

"I do, but they still make me nervous," Ellayne muttered. "But now I know why. I fell off one of these when I was six and broke my arm. Told you there was a reason." She tried to smile because she could recall her memories, but her mind was too distracted to let her. She squinted in the darkness to find the elf. "Let's get out of here before Armannii notices."

"Are you sure?"

"Yes. Let's go." She checked over her shoulder as the stables disappeared behind them. "And speed up a bit. I want to put some distance between us and this place."

They were at a quick canter and leaving the castle walls in the distance when Ellayne looked over to her left and nearly screamed. Running next to them at the same speed as Curry was Armannii.

"I get that you don't like me, but leaving me there, that was harsh, even for you, Princess." He smirked at her.

Ellayne leaned over and saw the runes on his boots glowing as he ran next to them. He wasn't even panting.

"Speed runes." He wiggled his eyebrows. "They come in handy when chasing people through the woods. Especially people on horseback."

Kade glanced over every few seconds, as surprised at the elf's appearance as Ellayne. "Where are we headed?"

"We should go somewhere Diomedes won't look," Armannii said.

"I was asking Ellayne."

"The Black Forest," she responded. "We'll figure out what to do from there."

"I have an idea," Armannii said in a melodic, singsong voice.

"I don't want to hear it."

"I think you do." He grinned, and Ellayne's eyebrows nearly rose up off her forehead as he dug a necklace chain out of his pocket. Attached to it was the royal family crest, and a small mirror. "Lifted this off Diomedes when we were fighting. I do believe it's time we put a new king on the throne, or maybe," his eyes sparkled in the night, "an old one."

Epilogue

A young man and a woman with long raven hair stood in front of the bedroom on the second floor of the palace in Cyanthia. A few maids scurried about trying to mend the broken furniture and buff the scorch marks off the floor. The glass in the window had shattered upon the first outburst of magic, and the desk in the corner had taken the second blow, followed by the bed upon the third. Glass, feathers, and scraps of parchment littered the floor, which one of the maids focused on sweeping.

"Is it always this way?" the man asked, turning his head to stare down at the woman beside him. His voice was devoid of emotion, yet his hands were balled into fists by his sides. Black mist swirled off them every once in a while.

She shook her head and smirked. "Dark magic often comes with outbursts in the beginning, yes." She didn't look up at him, and instead grinned at the damage in the room. "But it's rarely this explosive. You've got a lot of power, and therefore a lot of training to do."

"But you'll help me, right?"

"Of course I will, Kiegan. We're going to need all your power, as well as mine, if we're going to get our king back."

"In that case, let's get started."

* * *

Turn the Page for a SNEAK PEEK

At Book 2 in the Infiniti Trilogy

Chapter One

Something happened to him," Ellayne said as she continued to wear a path on the hardwood floor of Calder's healing shop. She'd been pacing on and off for several hours. "Right? Why else would he not be back by now?"

Calder sat behind the front counter where he was measuring out the ingredients for another attempt at a healing potion—one he had messed up earlier that morning. There was still an air of rotten eggs and dead mice wafting about the shop, for which Calder had profusely apologized when Ellayne had come down from the attic with her nose pinched between her fingers.

"I mean," she continued, "Kade left a few days ago, and the village isn't that far by horseback, especially for someone who can read a map as well as he can. What if—"

"Don't." Calder didn't look up from his beaker when he cut her off. His almond-shaped eyes remained crossed, focused on what was in front of him.

"But what if something happened to him? And with Kiegan gone—"

"Don't finish that sentence." Calder dumped the rest of the murky brown liquid into his beaker and finally glanced up at her as he swirled the mixture. "Stop with the what-ifs, Ellayne."

"If something happened to him, to either of them—"

"You can't do anything now to undo what may or may not have been done, so why ask the what-if question in the first place? The only thing hypothetical questions do is stress you out. Not to mention me."

"That's what I mean!" Ellayne flung her arms out and slammed them down against her sides. She placed her hands on her hips. "I *can't* do anything. I'm stuck here with no way of knowing if he's in trouble. How am I supposed to know if my friend needs help if I'm locked in here?"

"You're exaggerating." Calder sighed and stood up, continually moving the beaker around in small circles. "You aren't locked in here."

"Of course I was exaggerating."

"It wouldn't be very good for my shop if I locked the doors during business hours," he said with a grin. Lifting himself up to sit on the sea glass countertop, he patted the space next to him.

She rolled her eyes but sat down next to him anyway. Turning her head to look at him, she noticed that the teal on the tips of his black hair had faded, leaving behind a pastel greenish-yellow. The slits in his neck—his gills—peeked out from behind the high collar of his tunic. Besides a bit of iridescence to his skin, his gills were the only thing that marked him as a siren.

Ellayne dropped her gaze to the item wrapped around her left wrist: a bracelet with interlocking strands of silver. She traced her finger along one of the lines, following its path around

319

her skin. "I just want to know if he's okay, you know?" She watched him with her peripheral vision.

Calder bit his bottom lip and nodded. "I understand your worry for him, and I know you're hoping he brings good news. And, even though you weren't talking about him, I'm sure Armannii is okay too."

Ellayne's posture straightened. "I couldn't care less what happens to that elf," she said. "As long as I get the information, I don't care if he's the one to give it to me, or if I hear it from someone else. In fact, part of me hopes he doesn't come back. Good riddance."

Calder snorted, shaking his head. "You don't seriously mean that."

She gave a vigorous nod. "I certainly do."

"The Ellayne I know would never turn her back on someone who's doing what he can to help."

"Which Ellayne do you know? Because yours sounds naive and honestly pretty dim if she's going to believe that criminal. The only one he's trying to help is himself."

"Hey now, I've met many versions of you over the past five years, and you've always cared about how people were treated." He cocked his head to the side. "So what changed?"

Ellayne shrugged. "He shot me in the neck with an arrow." She ignored Calder's snort. "Then I got my memories back. Now everything has changed."

Calder leaned over and nudged her with his shoulder. "Come on, not *everything* changed."

"Yes it has."

"Now you're just being plain negative. Look at me—I haven't changed. I'm still here, and I've been here every time you've shown up."

His words made Ellayne stare at the door, as if she could somehow see the village outside through the dark, solid wood frame. There were no windows in the shop. A few display cases and shelves offered healing potions, bandages, and other assorted medications. It was the only healing shop in the village and the only one in the immediate vicinity of the Black Forest.

"You're right." She glanced down and craned her neck to look at him. "You really haven't changed. You always welcomed me in, no matter the state of my curse. You were always eager to help."

"It's my job." He leaned back and grabbed a small cylinder of light blue powder, tipping its entire contents into his beaker. The liquid flashed yellow before shifting into a deep orange. Both of them watched the reaction occur, silent for a few moments.

"Much better than last time." He grinned.

Ellayne leapt off the counter when the door to the healing shop flung open but didn't quite make it behind the curtain at the back before the person entered. *Please don't recognize me,* Ellayne thought, facing the back so whoever had entered couldn't see her face.

"Calm down," Dayla's voice rang out as soon as the door closed. "It's just me."

Sighing a breath of relief, Ellayne turned around. "I'm sorry, Dayla," Ellayne said to Calder's little sister. "I thought you were—"

"Someone else. Yeah"—she rolled her eyes—"I know the deal." Dayla was a few years younger than Calder, which left her closer to Ellayne's twenty-two years. Even though Dayla was shorter than Ellayne, her height didn't stop her from bumping Ellayne with her shoulder when she plodded by, making Ellayne take a step back.

321

"Dayla," Calder said to his sister, lowering his voice. "Apologize."

"Excuse me?" Dayla spun around and placed her hands on her hips. "Why should I apologize? She was standing in my way."

Calder narrowed his eyes at her. "She deserves respect."

"Why? Because she's a princess?"

"And our friend." He glanced from Ellayne to Dayla. "So we will treat her with—"

"Respect." Dayla rolled her eyes again. "I got that." She turned to Ellayne. "I'm sorry I bumped into you, Your Highness." She dipped into a low curtsy.

Sarcasm, but I'll take it. Ellayne raised her chin, nodding to her. "I accept your apology. Thank you."

"Whatever," Dayla muttered, flipping her pink hair over her shoulder. She left the room through the back entrance, which led to their apartment above the shop.

"I'm really sorry about her," Calder said when Ellayne went back to the counter to sit next to him. "She'll grow up eventually."

"This is all part of siren adolescence?"

Calder shrugged. "She's worse than most of the girls I went to school with, but yeah, kind of. Not that siren girls aren't nice; I just mean, well, sometimes they can be . . . I mean, it's not their fault that they—"

"Cal" —Ellayne poked his arm—"you're rambling."

"Right." He rubbed the back of his neck.

"Will it be obvious when she reaches adulthood?"

"That's a good question. I'd like to think it will be; however, it isn't a huge change for most sirens. Probably will be for her though. She's got a lot of growing up to do. The difference between an adolescent siren and an adult siren is the balance of control over the siren song. An adult has full control over the power rather than the power having control and wreaking havoc on an adolescent siren's emotions. The switch can be sudden, too. When I reached adulthood, I . . ." He paused, grinned, and shook his head. "Never mind. What were you saying before she came in?"

"I was—"

"*Right*, you were telling me how wonderful and amazing I am." He snorted, putting the bubbling beaker on the counter to his right. "You know, 'cause I helped you every time you wound up back here."

"Uh-huh." She couldn't help but smile. "And every time you forgot me."

"It wasn't my fault. It was *your* curse."

She shrugged. "Mine in that I was the victim, but yeah. It's weird to think I wasn't the only one who had memories stolen."

"It was a surprise to me too. I dropped and broke my favorite beaker the moment all the memories came rushing back. I remember Dayla came sprinting into the front of the shop with half of her hair dyed, and we just stared at each other. It didn't take long for us to realize what had happened."

"I'd shared quite a bit of my theories, hadn't I?" Ellayne tucked a strand of hair, which had fallen out of her braid, behind her ear.

Something she'd said made Calder's crooked grin leave his face. "The amount of times you came in here with that curse spread all the way up your arm . . . and I could never do anything about it." He ran his thumb along his neck, the skin wrinkling near his gills.

"You tried though" —she placed a hand on his knee— "and I can never thank you enough for that."

323

"I should've tried harder. There's only ever been one other time I've felt so . . . so useless." He sighed. There was a long pause before he continued again. "You weren't the only one to share personal information. I told you things that I've never even told my sister."

"Some things are easier to say to strangers."

"I said so much." He rubbed the back of his neck. "I messed up back then too—with the Coves and the raid, the day my parents and older sister died. It's been nine years, almost to the day, and I still regret the choices I made."

"Calder," she said, placing a hand on his back and rubbing it in small circles, "you can't blame yourself. You saved Dayla by getting out and bringing her here. There was nothing else you could've done to save your parents or Mira. Cal, you were only sixteen."

He closed his eyes. "I could've warned them. I should have. I was the fastest swimmer in my class. I should've swum home from school to tell them the raid had started. Then maybe—"

"Then maybe you would have died too. What would Dayla have done without you?"

"If I could've helped," he said, shaking his head, "maybe they would be here too. Mira might still be alive. And maybe Dayla wouldn't resent me as much. Dayla always liked Mi more than me. They had this bond that I—"

"Cal, stop. You're torturing yourself," Ellayne said, glancing at the staircase when she heard a floorboard creak. "What were you just telling me?" She turned her full attention back to her friend. "I shouldn't use what-ifs, right? Well, I say you can't use 'mights' or 'maybes.' " His shoulders dipped, and his posture slumped. *Whatever I'm saying isn't helping.* Her eyebrows furrowed. "Do you remember the time you tried to help me get rid of the curse by making me drink that disgusting

324

potion?" She let her voice rise, filling it with feigned excitement in a desperate attempt to lift his spirits.

"What?"

"That potion for curing withered appendages that you thought might work to stop the curse. Do you remember it?"

"Which one?" He lifted his head higher, and a bit of sparkle returned to his eyes. "The potion with frog urine, or the one with fish blood?"

"You made me drink fish blood?" Ellayne's voice went up several octaves. She smacked him on the shoulder. "Why don't I remember that?"

Calder ducked his chin down, a smile returning as he bit his lower lip. "I think during that reset, I sang to you."

"You sang to me?" Her eyebrows lifted. "As in, *sang* sang to me?"

When he nodded, she smacked him again. The last time she could remember hearing a siren sing, it had been his little sister, Dayla, and had ended in a catfight between the two women.

"Hey now, no need for violence," he said with a laugh. "It was for your own good."

"How is putting me under your siren spell 'for my own good'?" She deepened her voice to mimic him.

"You wouldn't have liked the potion if I'd given it to you straight, so I sang to you and told you to drink it. When I pulled you out of the spell, you had no recollection of how disgusting it was. Really, you should thank me." He shrugged.

"Sure"—she was still grinning—"and were there any other times you sang to me that I don't happen to remember now?"

Calder's cheeks tinged pink, and his interest in the beaker increased. He tilted it back and forth, watching the viscous orange gel spill along the inside of the glass.

"Calder," she said in a warning tone. "When did you sing to me again?"

"Well . . ." He looked up at the ceiling, his eyes following the runes lighting up the room. "There may have been another reset where I may or may not have sung to you."

Ellayne squinted her eyes at him, unable to keep the smile off her lips. "You tell me what you made me do right now, or I'll—"

"As long as you promise not to freak out, I'll tell you."

"And why would I freak out?"

"It just seems like something you might do."

"Calder . . ."

"Okay, fine." He took a deep breath. "I may have asked you to kiss me on the cheek, but I promise that was it." The confession came out in a rush, and his cheeks deepened to a dark shade of crimson. "It was only a peck, and then I let you out of the spell. It was a lapse in judgment. It's just that you're really pretty, and you've always been so nice to me. But that doesn't mean I'm justifying it. I just . . . I'm really sorry, Ellayne, and I know I shouldn't have done it, and now I know who you are, and it makes it even more embarrassing and potentially more of a crime against the royal family, which I didn't mean to commit, but I promise it wasn't a big deal, and—"

Ellayne clicked her tongue, shaking her head from side to side. "Calder, Calder, Calder." She placed her hand on his shoulder, and he tensed. "If that's all you wanted, you should've just asked." Ellayne leaned over and pecked him right in the middle of his rosy cheek. When he let out the breath he'd been holding, she patted him on the back.

At that moment, she heard voices near the door getting louder as people approached. Calder's eyes widened, and he motioned for her to move. Ellayne vaulted off the counter and raced to the back of the shop, closing the curtain behind her at the same time the bells above the shop door chimed.

"Hey, Barry, how's the wife today?"

Dodging customers to avoid being seen doesn't get any easier after the seventieth time, Ellayne thought. She let out a deep breath, grinning as she tiptoed up the stairs to the apartment.

SIGN UP FOR MY AUTHOR NEWSLETTER

Enjoy extra scenes, short stories, and other exclusives from this series by subscribing to my newsletter and visiting my website at:

www.rachelhetrickwrites.com

Acknowledgments

I fully believe that I was created by the Creator to create, and I give God all credit for my writing. He is my inspiration and my motivation, and my biggest prayer is that He is glorified through this novel. My hope and my life are found in Christ.

Next, I want to thank my parents, Marc and Beth, and my sister, Becca, for the encouragement to continue pursuing publishing even when I didn't think it was possible. They are my main cheerleaders and my biggest fans. And while I'm mentioning family, I'm also thankful for my lap warmer and furry writing buddy, Syra. She was with me when I made the decision to publish earlier this year (while still living on the other side of the world.) I love you guys.

My editor, Natalia Leigh, with Enchanted Ink Publishing was a joy to work with, and made me look and sound a LOT smarter than I actually am. Not only is she an inspiration to me (I originally found her on YouTube), but she is also a fellow Colorado resident, and therefore cooler than any other editor. Thank you Natalia!

Of course, my story would be filled to the brim with plot holes and weak characters if I didn't send it through two rounds of amazing beta readers. They were wonderful at pointing out what was working in the story and helping me spot the things that needed to be improved (and they were very patient when I asked them to speak on the phone in more detail, sometimes for multiple hours). Thank you so much to Marc H. Hetrick, Elizabeth Hetrick, Rebecca Gilliam, Heather Cross, Cydney Knight-Pinneo, Emily Littleton, Sarah Orr, Sydney Fowler, and Micah Emmalee Fowler. Thank you all so much!

On top of that, a special shout out to Heather and Cydney who read it again as proofreaders. My mom also proofread it AND suffered with me as I tried to format a book for the first time. You guys are awesome!

I also want to thank Mary and the designers at MiblArt for creating such a beautiful cover and for being patient with me. You guys were such a pleasure to work with.

But a book is nothing without someone to read it, and that's where YOU, the reader, comes in. Thank you so much for reading my brain baby. It has been stirring around in my head for almost nine years now, and I'm so blessed and grateful to get to share it with you. I hope you enjoyed it, and if you did, please consider sharing it, writing a review, or telling your neighbor. I appreciate and love you all so much more than you know!

About the Author

Rachel Hetrick is a Colorado native, who graduated from the University of Colorado Colorado Springs with a Bachelor of Arts degree in English Literature and a Creative Writing minor in 2017. A year after she graduated, she moved to the opposite side of the world and taught English in Asia for a year and a half. However, when the world went nuts at the beginning of 2020, the pandemic led to the closing of her school. It was then she decided it was time to fulfill her childhood dream of becoming a published author. With the inspiration of many incredible authors on Youtube, Rachel grew as a writer, editor, and now publisher. She has since moved back to Colorado and lives with her Siamese cat, Syra (who kicked Feline Infectious Peritonitis, FIP, in the rear end). She looks forward to hearing from her readers!

YOU CAN CONNECT WITH RACHEL THROUGH:

WEBSITE: www.rachelhetrickwrites.com
INSTAGRAM: @rachel_hetrick_writes

CPSIA information can be obtained
at www.ICGtesting.com
Printed in the USA
LVHW041704131120
671369LV00003B/127